Winter's Promise

Winter's Promise

by Janene Wolsey Baadsgaard

spring creek
BOOK COMPANY

Provo, Utah

ISBN 13: 978-1-932898-38-5
ISBN 10: 1-932898-38-7
e. 1

Published by:
Spring Creek Book Company
P.O. Box 50355
Provo, Utah 84605-0355

www.springcreekbooks.com

Cover design © Spring Creek Book Company
Cover design by Nicole Cunningham

Printed in the United States of America
10 9 8 7 6 5 4 3 2 1
Printed on acid-free paper

Library of Congress Control Number: 2005930811

DEDICATION

for
Daniel Webster Jones
and
Harriet Emily Colton

my great, great grandparents

and all pioneers
for their legacy
of courage,
faith and love

PART I

CHAPTER ONE

On a sweltering hot August afternoon when most Missourians had congregated under the welcome shade of oaks or elms, Margaret Jones clutched her sweaty palms around Deborah's arm and panted, "Where's Wiley!?"

"Don't worry, you're doin' fine," Deborah said, trying to reassure her mistress. "Breathe in, deep, slow."

A veteran of dozens of births, Deborah knew this baby was not waiting for his father to arrive. When another pain ripped through her body, Margaret's face turned scarlet as she gripped the quilts then lunged forward filling the house with her scream. Then she fell back exhausted onto the pillows.

"I can't do it! Something's wrong! It never hurt like this before!" Margaret gushed in a panic when the pain subsided.

"Almost over now," Deborah coaxed when another surging pain hit and she caught sight of the baby. "That's it. Don't hold back. Push! Push! Push through the pain. Hold it. Hold it. Just a little more. Yes! Yes!"

Margaret screamed through clenched teeth. Deborah reached out and gently supported the tiny head, then eased both shoulders through. Margaret slowly exhaled, then groaned as Deborah heaved a huge sigh of relief. When she heard the baby cry, Margaret opened her eyes and managed a tired smile. Her child was alive. She watched as Deborah quickly cut and tied off the cord, then placed the naked wailing baby on her chest. Instinctively Deborah pressed down firmly on Margaret's swollen abdomen to help slow the bleeding.

"Done fine," Deborah said as she continued applying pressure. "Mighty fine lookin' boy."

The heavy bleeding had Deborah worried but she saw no reason to frighten Margaret. She worked aptly with her sensitive palms. Margaret focused on her first son, who was sprawled across her breast kicking and bawling.

"There, there," Margaret whispered as she reached out for her baby. She placed her trembling fingers under the child's tiny arms then gently lifted her newborn. A sudden stream caught her in the eye.

"It's a boy all right," Margaret said, blinking to regain her focus.

Deborah propped Margaret's head with feather pillows and handed her mistress a clean woven cloth to wrap the baby in.

"Best nurse the child," Deborah said. "Helps slow bleedin'."

Margaret moved slowly and painfully to sit upright and bring the newborn to her breast. The baby's screaming and kicking abruptly stopped and turned into quiet suckling sounds. Suddenly the door to the bedroom burst open and in raced Wiley, red faced and panting.

"We have a son," Margaret whispered looking up, her eyebrows arching in obvious delight.

Wiley's anxious face softened into an animated smile as he threw his coat on an empty chair and hurried to the foot of the bed. Margaret took the contented babe from her breast and held him out for her husband to inspect.

"Daniel Webster Jones, you took your time getting here," Wiley said as he took the child in his arms. "After making me wait through four sisters, you came so fast I missed the whole thing."

The baby opened and closed his puffy eyes trying to get used to the bright light streaming in behind his father through the opened door.

"Give me that child. Missus needs you. Take these," Deborah said thrusting a stack of clean bed linens into Wiley's arms. "Push here until the bleedin' slows. Then change the beddin'. Now, give me that fine youngin'."

Wiley carefully followed Deborah's instructions. He'd relied on her able care of his family ever since he married her favorite charge. Margaret had refused to leave Deborah behind when they moved to the Missouri frontier. Wiley was glad, for Deborah had become far much more important to the welfare of his family than either set of grandparents.

Wiley gently changed the blood-soaked bedding beneath his wife, and then sat carefully on the side of their bed looking into her tired eyes.

"A son," Margaret said taking her husband's hand. "Finally got your son."

Wiley stroked his wife's sweaty brow until Margaret drifted into a much needed sleep. Then he quietly slipped from the room, closed the door behind him and stepped quickly out onto the front porch.

"Eliza Jane! Angeline! Frances! Susan!" Wiley called to the four young girls who came running and stumbling toward the cabin from the barn. "You have a brother!"

"Is Mama all right?" Eliza Jane gushed in a panic. "I heard her screaming. Deborah made us promise to stay in the barn until you called. What took you so long?"

"Mama's fine and so is your new brother Daniel," Wiley answered. "Come on inside now. But keep quiet so your Mama can rest."

Wiley found Deborah cleaning off his new son near the wash basin and gently rubbing his back. When she was through, Deborah carefully rewrapped the baby then handed him back to Wiley.

"Can I hold him?" all four sisters asked in a quadruple chorus.

"Oldest to youngest," Wiley said gently handing the baby to each daughter one at a time. After each girl took a turn in the rocking chair, Wiley reached for his son. "Now he's all mine."

Wiley glanced into the bedroom and made sure Margaret was still sleeping before he found an extra blanket for the baby and walked toward the front door.

"Where you takin' that child?" Deborah asked in a huff. Wiley didn't answer. He knew Deborah could give him a hard time just for the fun of it. "Don't be lettin' him catch a chill, you hear." Wiley smiled and kept walking. "Oh, go on," Deborah finished, knowing Wiley would have his way this time, as always.

"If Margaret wakes up," Wiley said turning back at the doorway, "tell her I'll be right back. She'll be needing supper."

As Wiley walked from their log house toward the river, he saw the setting sun sinking low into the western horizon. He took a deep breath of the clean country air. As far as his eyes could see, gently sloping hills and valleys rolled outward like a sea of grass. The mellow earthy scent of late summer harvest filled his senses. Wiley relished this rich land, his land, the fighting and wrestling for a homestead carved from the wilderness by his own sweat, hard work and vision. Something about holding his firstborn son made Wiley feel younger and stronger, as if his real life was just beginning. He could envision his future stretching out before him like the rolling hills to the distant horizon. The child stirred, then settled comfortably into a restful sleep in his strong arms.

As Wiley approached the small meandering river near their home, he listened to the whispering trees wash against the amber sky. Cottonwoods, maples, honey locusts, and black walnuts followed the river bank turning into a lush and welcoming retreat. Once inside the canopy and solitude of trees, Wiley heard the hum of insects fill the air with a pulsating resonance. His muscular, sunburned body walked slowly and reverently as if searching for a pew inside a cathedral. Wiley listened closely to the sudden cry of birds and watched the ground squirrels scurry through the underbrush, then climb up the tall slender trunks.

After Wiley located his favorite private enclosure of shrubs and sapling trees near the river, he ducked down and stepped inside. Gently cradling his newborn son near the bend of his neck, Wiley knelt carefully on the forest floor. Then he looked up through the overhanging branches and felt the warm shafts of sunrays on his face. His newborn son stirred inside the blanket. Wiley cupped his broad, callused hands behind his new son's tiny body then brought him forward so he could get a good look at him.

"Hello there," Wiley said as his newborn tried to open his eyes and look up at his father bathed in a halo of light. "I'm so glad you're here."

Though Wiley sometimes wondered about bringing Margaret and the girls out to the wild, untamed American frontier, he had no doubts about a bright future here for his new son. Though the pioneering life was vastly different from the easy ways Margaret had grown accustomed to in Georgia with slaves on her father's plantation, Wiley relished owning his own virgin land and carving out a different sort of life for his family. The American wilderness had made a man of him and would make a man out of his son. Wiley unfastened his shirt and placed his tiny newborn in the cradle the fabric formed next to his bare skin. He felt Daniel's tiny warm body molding comfortably next to his own in the warm cocoon. Wiley interlocked his callused fingers under the tiny bundle to support Daniel's weight.

"Thank you for my son," Wiley quietly whispered as he bowed his head.

Daniel was sleeping peacefully tucked inside his father's shirt when Wiley returned home from the woods. When he opened the door to his rough hewn log home, Deborah glanced up at Wiley, then down at his bulging shirt. She smiled then shook her head. Rhythmically stirring stew in a cast iron pot hanging above the rock fireplace, Deborah returned to singing. Wiley noticed his daughters setting dishes on the wood table he recalled making with lumber left over from the cabin. White embers in the fire flickered and the house smelled like Deborah's famous rabbit stew.

"Best set a place for Brother Gilbert," Deborah instructed turning to the girls. "I 'spect he'll be nosin' around the place like always."

"Not today. Please not today," Wiley said rolling his eyes and shaking his head.

"Man needs his own wife and chil'len. Leave you folks alone," Deborah chided.

"I can't abide the arrogant old bore, even if he is Margaret's brother," Wiley said. "He thinks he's going to save us by forcing us listen to his fire and brimstone preachin' in that stuffy old hall he calls a church."

"Got no soul," Deborah said slopping the stew into wooden bowls with a metal ladle. "Man of God oughta have a soul."

"I hear you two," Margaret scolded from the opened bedroom door.

Wiley and Deborah looked at each other wide-eyed, then silently held their fingers over their mouths before they burst into laughter.

"Bring that baby here to me," Margaret called from the bedroom after their joint outburst, "before you two corrupt him."

❧

"Gonna spoil that child rotten. Aren't you worried about his soul?" Deborah bellowed as Wiley swept stocky four-year-old Daniel from the hard earthen floor and boosted him up on his shoulders. "How come you never makes him go to church? Why you take that child in those dark lonesome woods?"

"The woods aren't dark, Deborah. They're full of light," Wiley answered affectionately. "Brother Gilbert has his way of finding God. I have mine. I don't see you hurrying off to church."

"Most white folks don't want the likes of me around when they's worshippen'. Besides, I got my own religion. But you got the boy to think of. What goin' become of 'im?"

"Margaret takes the girls out of respect for her brother. Can't abide the man. Won't have any son of mine sitting through his pompous prayers and hell-bent ranting and railing," Wiley answered, patting Daniel's chubby legs.

"Sight better than raisin' a wild child," Deborah chortled as she wiped her wet hands on her calico skirt and walked toward Wiley and Daniel.

Deborah was as soft and ample bodied as she was warm witted. Wiley knew his fragile wife would never have survived frontier life without the help of her best friend and childhood Mammy. Daniel squirmed atop his father's shoulders. Wiley raised one eyebrow and grinned, showing all his front teeth. He knew Deborah couldn't abide Reverend Gilbert Marshall any better than he could.

"Know what time Brother Gilbert is expected today?" Wiley asked.

"Why yes sir, I do. Missus makes me promise I won't tell the likes of you, 'cause she knows you just plans to miss him like always if I tell."

"Now Deborah, I've noticed how you get pretty busy yourself when Gilbert comes. Always making sudden excuses to leave the room. If you don't tell me, I'll make you sit and listen to every word he has to say today right along with me."

"Don't do that to your favorite old Mammy," Deborah answered as she reached upward toward Daniel's face.

"I'm afraid I'd do even that torturous thing," Wiley answered.

"You's always wesslin' it outa me. He's comin' tonight for supper, and if you tell the Missus I tol' you, we'll both be in a whale of trouble," Deborah answered.

"Thank you, Deborah. You can have my permission to make yourself scarce when he arrives," Wiley answered.

Daniel giggled as Deborah reached up and took his dirt smudged face in her large loving palms that smelled of bread dough and onions. She kissed Daniel and said, "You beautiful child. God done shining His mighty love on this home with the likes of you." Daniel wrapped his chubby arms around Deborah's moist neck and kissed her on the check. Deborah melted like butter left in the sun. "Child's a gift," Deborah said.

Daniel and Wiley stooped low as they walked through the front door headed toward the river. Though he knew the way himself, Daniel preferred his father's broad shoulders. Wiley held tight to his young son's dangling legs wrapped tightly around his neck. Daniel's curly yellow hair blew around his red, chapped face in the gentle wind. His eyes matched the color of the sky. Keeping one hand on his father's shoulder, Danny pointed to everything that caught his attention and asked his father one question after another, not waiting for an answer.

"Why's the sky blue?" Daniel asked. Wiley was always slow to answer questions. Daniel couldn't wait. "Why can't we fly like birds do? Then I could go ta heaven. E'iza says my dog went ta heaven when he died. Where's heaven?"

"Hmmm," Wiley answered trying hard to decide where to start with his answers.

When father and son reached the woods Daniel sensed the restful peace and quieted. After begging to be put down, he took his father's rough hand and tried to keep up with his long even strides. After Wiley located his favorite enclosure, he guided Daniel inside, then knelt on the soft fern-covered forest floor. Daniel sat cross-legged directly across from his father, glancing up at the azure sky.

"I don't know why the sky's blue," Wiley answered. Do know the sky comes all the way to the ground. The sky's all around us. We can't see it when we're in it. Just looks blue when it's far away.

"But I can't see the sky down here," Daniel answered crunching his face.

"Can't see the wind either," Wiley answered, "but we can feel it."

"Sure do wish I could fly," Daniel added, changing the subject as quickly as a new thought flew through his mind.

"Guess we're too heavy," Wiley answered. "No wings. But if you believe something's possible, it is. They call it imagination, and you have barrels of it, Danny."

"Want my dog back from heaven," Daniel said scratching his head.

"Most people say heaven's up there far away past the blue sky," Wiley answered. "But I believe heaven's all around us."

"Around us?" Daniel asked.

"Only we can't see it when we're in it . . . like the sky," Wiley answered. "But we can feel it, like the wind. Have to believe first. Sometimes if you hold very still and listen, you can feel it."

Danny wrinkled his sunburned freckled nose, obviously unsatisfied. He plopped backward onto the soft moss and looked up at the huge expanse of sky overhead.

"If heaven's right here, why can't I see it?" Daniel asked again, waving his arms in front of his face.

"Maybe we aren't supposed to see heaven just yet. But if we believe it's all around us, like the sky, maybe then we can learn to feel it like the wind."

Wiley stretched out beside Daniel and crossed his hands behind his head. Father and son listened in silence to the quiet swaying of boughs, rustling of trembling leaves in the gentle breeze, bright songs of woodland birds perched high in the tree tops and the steady humming murmur of insects.

"I can feel it," Daniel whispered quietly after a long moment of silence.

"What, son? The wind?" Wiley asked.

"No," Daniel answered, "heaven."

Wiley smiled long and deep. He reached over and swept Daniel's shining golden hair from his forehead with the palm of his work-worn hand. "Me too," he answered. "I feel it too, right here when I'm with you. I love you son."

"Love you, too." Daniel answered.

Later, Wiley carefully planned his return from the woods that afternoon just in time to position Daniel on his lap in a chair by the hearth. He quickly opened the Bible and mustered up a look of quiet contemplation when he heard Margaret returning from her Sunday meetings.

"You ain't foolin' the Missus and you knows it," Deborah chuckled when she heard the horses and buggy pulling up in front of the house.

Wiley tightened the curve in his brow as the girls raced into the room.

"Oh, Papa," Eliza Jane said after she ran up next to him, "it was even worse than usual today. His prayer lasted so long half the folks went to sleep. Uncle Gilbert said amen *five* times. Finally slammed his Bible on the pulpit and shouted it."

"Now Eliza Jane, don't talk that way about your uncle," Margaret said as she came into the room. "He's just trying to put a little of the fear of God into us, and Lord knows some of us need that." She glanced up into Wiley's eyes. "And every single one of you better mind your manners when he comes to visit today."

"How come Papa and Daniel never has to listen to him?" Sarah questioned as her mother shooed her off to change her clothes in the loft with a boost on the behind.

"Shhh!" Wiley whispered.

After the girls climbed the ladder to the loft so they could change their Sunday dresses, Margaret whispered quietly into Wiley's ear, "It wasn't five, it was seven. When he brought down his Bible and shouted 'Amen!' somebody screamed. Rest of us laughed so hard, thought Gilbert was going to tan all our hides."

Wiley laughed out loud. Margaret hushed him, then kissed him affectionately.

"I suppose Wiley's been sitting here studying the word of God every minute we've been gone," Margaret said turning to Deborah. "Correct?"

Deborah chuckled as she left through the front door to take care of the horses.

CHAPTER TWO

Glancing outside from the opened front door of her cabin, Margaret relished the emerald newness of life on their farm in springtime. Wild flowers bloomed in profusion, dipping and swelling like a sea of dappled grass in the wind. She watched Wiley's muscular forearms straining over the leather straps of the plow at the crest of the hill. Twelve-year-old Daniel was chin high to his father and still growing like a weed. Shoeless, he followed in his father's shadow with a long pole and a bag of seed. They worked together in gentle symmetry. After Wiley turned the earth with a horse and plow, Daniel drove a long stick into the soft soil then carefully dropped in a seed or two. Covering the rich black earth over the seed with his bare toe, Daniel then flattened the mound with his other foot.

Daniel and his father worked together in the fields from sunup to sundown as Margaret, Deborah and the girls milked, churned, spun, sewed, washed and cooked. After the family's mid-day meal, Margaret made sure her children spent time on matters she considered equally necessary. She often worried about the rough upbringing her children were receiving on the frontier without a formal education. Margaret insisted each of her children receive their proper schooling, even if she had to do it herself.

"No child of mine will grow up ignorant or unrefined," Margaret often said with pride. "Just because we're poor farmers, doesn't mean we have to smell, act or think like uneducated waifs. We're cultured and well-bred land owners—gentlemen farmers."

Margaret insisted Wiley bring several heavy trunks filled with her favorite books when they moved out to Missouri years earlier. Her beloved

Bible and classic volumes of literature had become her lifeline to the more refined and privileged way of living she'd known as a child growing up on a plantation. Wiley never gave her any trouble about teaching the four older girls their lessons after their mid-day meal, but she had to fight him for time with Daniel. Wiley didn't see a future in letters and numbers when strong arms and a strong back got a man everything he needed in this part of the country.

Margaret glanced at her beautiful maturing daughters taking turns braiding each other's hair around the table. In the twelve short years since Daniel's birth, his sisters had changed from little girls into beautiful young women. Before long, her daughters would marry and nothing would be the same. Lately she'd contemplated taking them back to her parent's plantation to find suitable husbands.

This is the best time, Margaret thought. *Everyone home, everyone still mine. My youth's fading, but my daughters are in full bloom. Daniel's growing taller, stronger and more like his father every day.*

Surviving the harsh conditions of frontier life required every member of the household to work hard every day to make food stores enough to get through the harsh winter months year after year. There were crops to plant, water, weed and harvest, livestock to tend and feed, eggs to gather, cows to milk, candles to dip, butter to churn and wool to shear, wash, card, spin and weave. There were fields to clear, fences and barns to build, goods to trade, wood to haul, and clothing to sew. Yet in all her daily commonness Margaret had of late felt a hint of change approaching, an unknown season over the horizon. Though she longed to hold on to the present, Margaret knew she couldn't suspend her family in time.

"Do you think Wiley will ever let me have Danny for his lessons?" Margaret asked as she walked over next to Deborah at the butter churn.

"Not 'til plantin' season done," Deborah answered.

Margaret glanced out the opened door again and saw Wiley and Daniel headed back from the fields, guiding their sweaty horse and mud-covered plow to the barn.

"You's never goin' to get those two apart for long. They be two peas in a pod," Deborah finished.

"Danny's highly intelligent," Margaret answered. "Sometimes I think he understands the Bible better than I; always asking questions about things even I don't have an answer for. He deserves to go to the university some day and become a fine doctor or lawyer. Perhaps follow my brother into the ministry."

"Git more time with Danny if you promise not to bring Brother Gilbert around here any more," Deborah chuckled. "Speak of the devil. Somebody's coming down the road, and they's in a mighty big hurry," Deborah continued as she pointed out the window to the road leading to the house.

Bringing a cloud of dust, a black carriage raced up the dirt lane and stopped on the road near where Wiley and Daniel were walking through the field.

"Speak of the devil . . . it's Brotha Gilbert," Deborah said with an animated voice. "Best be gettin' along."

"Wonder what he wants?" Margaret asked as she stepped quickly toward the door. "Must be important to have him flying up the road like that."

"I don't wanna know," Deborah called through the back door as she stepped outside to make herself scarce as usual.

Margaret raised her tight-waisted, full-skirted day dress topping multiple layers of petticoats and quickly left the house walking briskly toward the newly plowed fields. She could hear her older brother's voice railing from the front porch. As she approached the three standing in the fields, she quickly heard why Gilbert was so agitated.

"My solemn duty to warn you about the evil spreading in our midst," Gilbert said, his black eyes flashing.

"Morning, Brother Gilbert!" Wiley interrupted, ignoring Gilbert's nasty mood.

"Mormons flocking into our county, buying up all the good land," Gilbert continued, hardly stopping for the interruption. Daniel watched Gilbert's bushy eyebrows twitch, all but ignoring what he had to say. Wiley opened his mouth into a wide unimpressed yawn. "First I believed they were only deluded fanatics," Gilbert continued, not noticing everyone's obvious lack of interest. "I was deceived. Band together. Conduct business only amongst themselves."

"Wait a minute," Wiley interrupted with a smile. "What in the blazes are Mormons?"

"Haven't you heard? Maybe you'd benefit by attending my Sunday sermons. Mormons are a band of religious fanatics headed by a man they claim is a prophet named Joseph Smith. Says he had a vision where he talked face to face with God Almighty and Jesus Christ. Claims he translated another holy book like the Bible from gold plates hidden in some hill in New York. Call themselves Saints. Claim power to heal the sick and speak in tongues. Say they alone have the complete truth, the restored gospel of Jesus Christ. Angels and visions? Demons and depravity. Blasphemers, all of them!"

Wiley shook his head and grabbed Gilbert by the arm.

"That's enough," Wiley said. "Frightening the boy. Gilbert, why the blazes do you let yourself get so worked up about a few religious fanatics?"

"They're growing in number, trying to take over. All good men who fear God or love their wives and children should not allow these people to live among us for the cause of public morals. I've read your advertisement for the sale of a parcel of your land. Don't let them trick you into selling your property to them. Prove the ruination of yourself, your family, and this community."

Margaret heard most of the heated conversation as she approached and tried to soften things by softly taking her brother's hand.

"Gilbert," Margaret said, "We've heard all we care to hear about these Mormons. They've been the subject of all of your sermons for quite some time now. Come on to the house now and I'll give you something to eat to quiet your nerves."

"I'm sorry, Margaret, but I must refuse your kind invitation," Gilbert said as he let go of Margaret's hand and shook his head. "Others I must warn. They too have failed to attend my Sunday sermons. And they're preaching to the Indians, convincing them they're remnants of the house of Israel, God's chosen people. We don't need more trouble with the savages around here. And they don't approve of slavery. Mormons are trouble, no-good trouble. Good day, Margaret, Wiley, Daniel. Heed my words." Gilbert smoothed his greasy black hair, licked his thin white lips, then climbed into his buggy and galloped away.

"Mormons, Mormons, that's all my brother can talk about these days. I've yet to even meet one. Surely can't be as numerous or as bad as he says," Margaret said as soon as her brother was out of ear-shot.

Wiley looked over his shoulder with pride at the newly planted fields, then took a deep breath and sighed. He knew spring was the best time; unlimited opportunities always seemed possible during planting season. He wasn't going to let his brother-in-law ruin his mood on this perfect day.

"Pompous old bore," Wiley said as they walked together. "Finding fault with people before he even knows them. Don't believe a word he says. Just worried he might lose his congregation."

"Deborah's beans and pork ribs ready to eat," Margaret said taking Wiley's hand.

Daniel watched his father bring his muscular arms around his mother and draw her near his side. His parents had a way of smiling at each other and holding each other that made Daniel feel safe and warm.

"I'll sell my land to anyone I please," Wiley added as they walked toward the barn. "Who does he think he is? Brother or not, Gilbert's the *real* trouble around these parts. I don't want him coming around here any more."

"Oh, he's harmless," Margaret replied as she walked next her husband.

Wiley had a dark feeling about Gilbert's intentions. He'd heard things from the other settlers living nearby, things that turned his stomach.

"Maggie, don't be so sure about your brother," Wiley answered. "Been hearing ugly stories about Gilbert from other men around the county. He's been holding secret group meetings. Planning to make things hard for the Mormons so they'll leave."

"I don't believe it," Margaret answered obviously unconcerned. "He'd never go that far. My brother *is* a minister after all."

Wiley had always tried to shield Margaret from the harsh realities and lawlessness of frontier life. Now he thought it better to open her eyes. He knew Margaret loved her brother and had a difficult time believing he was capable of any wrongdoing.

"You'd be surprised what drunken men will do after they listen to lies and rumors." Wiley answered wiping his sweaty hands on his dusty pants. "Throw a minister into the mix, especially one who fans the flames of hatred and misinformation, and you've got a powder keg. Men with painted faces riding through the dark looking for trouble have no conscience, Maggie."

Cʃ

Springtime grew into summer, and summer melted into fall. When winter came and the threshing and harvesting were through, Margaret insisted Daniel work on his reading, writing, and numbers. Father and son had been inseparable that previous spring and summer. Even during the months of winter, Wiley and Daniel explored the forest almost every day using the well worn excuse they were hunting game. Sometimes they brought home a plump wild bird or rabbit for supper, but most often they brought home muddy leather boots and two broad smiles.

Lying in bed at night, Daniel related everything Wiley told him about the forest to his four interested older sisters. Wiley taught Daniel which berries and roots were edible, how to find duck eggs along the river and the way wild animals warned each other when a stranger was in the forest. Wiley taught Daniel how to survive in the woods, including how to locate clean water and make temporary shelter.

Daniel and his older sisters slept in the loft above the main floor of the cabin on straw mattresses and goose down pillows. A worn quilt hung over a rope separated Daniel from the girls when they were dressing. Once they were bedded down, the quilt was pulled to one side and Daniel's sisters begged him to begin his forest stories. Daniel often demonstrated bird calls or talked about his hunting trophies. When Daniel was through, Eliza Jane complained nightly about her milking chores, Uncle Gilbert's sermons and the lack of eligible suitors in the area. Angeline read all Margaret's books aloud and was the best story teller. Frances and Susan, an inseparable twosome, always provided an eager audience for their older sisters and younger brother.

During the long winter months, sitting still for lessons proved too much for Daniel. He ached to run outside and explore the woods.

Margaret had to ask him to hold still dozens of times a day. She wondered if Daniel was learning anything and would often give up and let him run outside with his father.

Not long after Christmas, Susan complained of not feeling well. A high fever soon followed. Within a few days all lessons stopped. Margaret spent most of her time comforting Susan. Deborah kept the meals coming and the other children occupied with chores. At first Daniel was happy for all the free time with his father, but soon he sensed the tension and apprehension growing in the house. His mother and father both spent most of their time going back and forth from Susan's bedside and whispering to each other in the corners of the cabin. When the whispering stopped, Daniel noticed both his parents seldom spoke and appeared constantly anxious.

"What's the matter with Susan?" Daniel questioned his father early one morning while they tended the horses in the barn. "Why do you and Mama stay with Susan all the time? Why won't you let the rest of us near her?"

Wiley continued brushing the horse as he answered, "She's ill, Daniel. Getting worse. Hard time breathing. Doctor said tonight should tell. If her fever doesn't break tonight, breathing doesn't improve, she doesn't have a very good chance."

"She's going to get better, I know it," Daniel said trying to reassure himself. "Isn't she?" Wiley didn't respond. "Can't you do something?"

"I don't know son," Wiley finally answered. "Doesn't look good."

Daniel climbed off the post and raced toward the house.

"I want to see Susan!" he shouted. Deborah grabbed his arm as Daniel tried to fling back the quilt his mother used to separate his parent's sleeping quarters from the rest of the household.

"They's tryin' to keep the sickness from spreadin' to the rest of you chil'len," Deborah said gently. "Hafta wait a spell. Come here. Let your old Mammy sing to you."

With worried expressions on their faces, Eliza Jane, Angeline, and Frances sat together next to the fire pretending to read or sew. They all gathered around Deborah and rested their heads against a fold in her long full skirt.

"Gonna be all right now, you hear," Deborah said reassuringly. Then she sang a familiar song the children had heard since they were babies. "I'm just a poor wayfaring stranger, while traveling through this world of woe," Deborah sang in her low mellow alto voice. "But there's no sickness, toil, or danger in that bright land to which I go. I'm going there to meet my father. I'm going there no more to roam. I'm just a-goin' over Jordan. I'm just a goin' over home." Deborah's songs had soothed the children through many sicknesses as they grew up. But today, even Deborah had a hard time getting the words to flow smoothly as her deep alto voice broke. "I know dark clouds will gather 'round me, I know my way is rough and steep; and yet green pastures lie before me where God's redeemed no more shall weep. I'm goin' there to meet my mother. She said she'd meet me when I come. I'm just a-goin' over Jordan. I'm just a-goin' over home. I'm goin' there to see my Savior. To sing His praise forever more; I'm just a-goin' over Jordan, I'm just a-goin' over home."

Suddenly Margaret screamed. Deborah insisted the three girls and Daniel stay put while she found their father in the barn. Wiley bound through the door just as Deborah threw on her shawl and was about to step outside. He ran to the bedside and found Margaret cradling Susan's drooping head in her arms.

"No," Margaret cried. "She's not breathing. Make her breathe Wiley. Please make her breathe. Do something."

Wiley took his limp daughter from Margaret's arms, laid her gently on the bed then frantically tried to revive her. After all attempts failed, Wiley wrapped his aching arms around his lifeless daughter and broke into deep anguished sobs.

"Don't take my children," Wiley cried, "take me."

Margaret's empty arms dropped to her sides as she walked to the opposite side of the bed. Instinctively she and Wiley formed a living cocoon around their dead daughter holding her tightly between their prone bodies. Daniel and his sisters knelt on both sides of the bed reaching up to grasp some small portion of their parents' clothing. Hours later, when tears wouldn't come any more, Deborah roused the family back to living. Walking to the bedside, felt Susan's body grow cold, then whispered to Wiley and Margaret.

"Be strong for your livin' babies. Come on now, Maggy honey," Deborah said pointing to their grief stricken children kneeling around the bed. "We got ta wash your baby now, find her best dress. Make her look like an angel. Wiley, be needin' a coffin and a grave. We all got ta go on living now, hard as it is . . . so's we don't *all* end up buried on that there hill. You takes Danny along to help you. We tend your baby angel."

Wiley and Daniel worked all night on the coffin in the barn. Daniel held the lantern while Wiley sawed and nailed. Deborah, Margaret and the girls worked all night in the house washing and dressing Susan in white burial clothes.

"Oh Momma, looks like she's just sleeping," Frances said. "Do we have to put her in the ground?"

The next day, just as Wiley and Margaret were gently placing their daughter into the coffin, Deborah heard someone riding toward the house. She slipped from the room and out on the porch without being noticed. Once outside, Deborah saw Gilbert stop his buggy in front of the log home and step quickly from his carriage.

"The child?" he asked with a cold compassionless voice. "Doctor said she might not make it. Wiley's never had her properly baptized."

Deborah drew in her breath, squared her shoulders and looked Gilbert straight in the eye without blinking.

"Massa Gilbert, ain't never spoke to you cept'n to say, 'yes sir', or 'no sir', but I gotta speak my peace," Deborah said, shaking her finger in his face. "Child done passed over yesterday. Worked all night gettin' ready to bury that precious child on the hill. Whole house's black today. This lovin' family don't need the likes of you heaping on the grief. They don't need the likes of you around tellin' them they ain't never gonna see their baby saved in the kingdom of God. So pack up your high button britches and fly away, brother, or you'll catch the end of my toe. Get, before they hear you and come out!"

Reverend Marshall wheeled back on the heels of his black boots and gulped. He had never before been spoken to in such a disrespectful manner. Stunned and insulted, he glared at Deborah and inwardly vowed to take his revenge someday. Then in an instant, he turned away and rode out of sight.

Late in the afternoon the Jones family wrapped patchwork quilts and soft tanned hides around themselves before setting out for the knoll of the hill near the forest. Wiley had chosen the spot earlier next to an old oak tree. He and Daniel were still covered with a fine layer of dirt from digging the grave. The whole family helped carry the coffin up the hill. Cold wind blistered their wet, salt-stained faces. After the coffin had been lowered by ropes slowly into the cold hard ground, Wiley and Daniel shoveled the earth and snow on top of the coffin while the women watched. Each dull thud of the earth falling against the coffin made Daniel cringe and the girls weep more loudly.

Deborah sang soft and low in the clear and frozen air, "I know dark clouds will gather 'round me. I know my way is rough and steep and yet green pastures lie before me where God's redeemed no more shall weep. I'm going' there to meet my mother. She said he'd meet me when I come. I'm just a-goin' over Jordan. I'm just a-goin' over home. I'm goin' there to see my Savior. To sing His praise forever more. I'm just a-goin' over Jordan. I'm just a-goin over home."

When Wiley and Daniel finished shoveling, he turned to Deborah and gently whispered, "Take the girls back to the house. I'll be back shortly."

"Come on now, babies," Deborah coaxed as she huddled the sisters together and herded them back toward the cabin.

"I need to stay here a minute," Margaret quietly told Deborah. "I'll join you soon. Just need a minute here by myself."

Daniel ran after his father and caught up with him just as they entered the woods. The trees were black and bare, dark silhouettes piercing the ashen blue sky. Wiley walked with single focus, speed and determination. It was difficult for Daniel to keep up with him. No words were spoken until they were deep in the barren forest. Finally Wiley stopped to rest, his breath billowing like fine smoke into the frigid air from his reddened and chaffed mouth and nose.

"I'm sorry, Daniel," he said. "Must've walked your legs off."

"I'm fine," Daniel answered shivering under the quilt wrapped around his head and shoulders.

As they stood huddled together in the biting wind, Daniel felt salty tears sting his eyes. Wiley lovingly wrapped his arm around his son.

"Look around you, Daniel. What do you see? What do you hear? Listen."

Daniel looked around him. A thick layer of snow and ice blanketed the forest. Bare, lifeless limbs of trees pierced the cold whiteness.

"Everything's dead. It's so cold. I don't hear anything. Let's go home," Daniel answered his teeth chattering in the wind.

"Will that ever change son?" Wiley pleaded as if searching for answers himself.

"Spring's a long way off," Daniel answered.

"How do you know spring will come? What if someone told you it would always be winter?" Wiley asked his son as his breath formed a cloud between them.

Daniel stood still deep in thought.

"I'd tell them everything only looks dead now," Daniel answered. "I'd tell them I know spring will come because I've seen it happen every year."

"Daniel," Wiley whispered, "Susan's spring will come. I know it. Everything in nature tells me this. We have to be patient . . . and trust God."

"Spring's still a long ways off," Daniel said trying to contain his emotions.

"I know son. I know."

When Wiley and Daniel left the woods and headed back toward the cabin, they both noticed Margaret still kneeling at the knoll next to the freshly dug grave, her face drained of all color.

"You go home and help Deborah and your sisters. Your mother needs me," Wiley said, patting Daniel on the back.

Later that evening, no one in the family felt like talking, eating or moving. Getting ready for bed felt like sleep walking in a dream. When Daniel crawled under the quilts that night, he lay awake for a long time staring into the blackness. Just before he drifted into slumber he heard a muffled cry. Daniel threw his quilts off and listened again.

"Frances," Daniel said quietly crawling toward his sister, feeling his way in the darkness with his outstretched hands, "don't cry."

"Danny," Frances said, "I'm so cold. Susan used to keep me warm. Now I'll never see my sister again."

Daniel crawled inside the quilts next to Frances and put his arms around her.

"Susan's not dead. She's sleeping, like the trees in the forest. Her spring will come. We'll see her again. Have to be patient and trust God," Daniel said, recalling the words of his father.

"How can you be so sure?" Frances asked.

"Because our father said so," Daniel answered. "He's never lied to me."

"I'm so cold, Danny. I don't want to be alone tonight. Can't live without Susan for the rest of my life. I want to go with her wherever she is," Frances cried.

"We need you to stay here with us," Daniel answered trying to act strong when he felt like crumbling.

Daniel felt Eliza Jane and Angeline crawl into the quilts on each side. Lacing their arms around each other, Daniel and his sisters held each other in the blackness until the sun rose in the eastern sky.

CHAPTER THREE

The following spring after Susan's death, the Jones family planned a day at the settlement. Both Wiley and Margaret had developed a deep lingering cough after tending to their sick daughter before she died. Neither parent had been able to get their strength back even though they'd tried every home or medical remedy Deborah and the doctor in the settlement had to offer.

Margaret fussed over Wiley's cough as the wagon danced off stones in the roadway into town. Daniel's parents rode on the front-facing buckboard while Deborah rode on the rear facing seat. All the children, along with the items they intended to trade for goods, were piled on top of each other in the crowded bed of the wagon. Margaret insisted Wiley spend more time indoors until his cough cleared up. Wiley shook his head and told Margaret to take it easy herself.

On the way to town, Deborah lectured Daniel and his sisters about proper manners in front of town folk. Daniel heard Deborah speaking, but he wasn't paying much attention to what she was saying. He felt different inside since Susan's death and had a harder time concentrating. As the black carriage sped along toward town, Daniel observed the countryside racing past him. He imagined what heaven might look like if he had the proper eyes to see and tried to feel it so he could be sure his sister was still alive, still with them in another form he couldn't see.

"Daniel Webster!" Deborah huffed. "You ain't listen to a word I done tol' you. Don't you go shaming me now by actin' like a wild child."

"You know what a good boy I am," Daniel answered with a smile.

As they approached the settlement, Wiley slowed the horses, turned to his children and said, "Give you all an hour to use however you'd like.

After an hour, I want you to meet your mother and me back here at the blacksmith's shop."

Wiley stopped the horses at a hitching post and trough, then helped the ladies from the wagon. All the girls ran to the dress shop and Deborah shooed Daniel away as she fiddled with her hair, smoothed her skirt and began a coy conversation with the settlement blacksmith. Daniel felt out of place in town, yet excited to see fresh scrubbed ladies with fancy store bought hats and shoes parade by each other in the square. There were harness and wagon shops next to dry good stores.

Over next to the livery stable, Daniel noticed an old wagon filled with tightly packed furniture and a large family of settlers who looked hot, tired and hungry. A woman sat in the front of the wagon, trying to calm a crying baby as her husband stopped people walking by. He seemed to be asking them all a question. Daniel also noticed a pretty dark-haired girl in the back of the wagon sitting on a trunk. She appeared to be about thirteen-years-old like he was. He couldn't take his eyes off her.

Daniel noticed some of the people who passed ignored the man and some spit chewed tobacco on his shoes. Curious, Daniel walked over near the wagon and listened. The woman in the wagon begged her husband to leave, but the man persisted. While Daniel sat on a hitching post listening, he noticed his own parents approaching. The man from the wagon stopped Wiley and Margaret and introduced himself.

"I'm Philander Colton and this is my wife Polly. We've come a long way. Looking for a place to settle. Would you be having any land you'd be willing to sell for a fair price, sir?"

Wiley stood silent for a time and then noticed Gilbert across the street staring at him. His countenance changed and he smiled brightly.

"As a matter of fact, I have a nice piece I'm willing to sell," Wiley said. "Welcome to it if you can make the payments."

Just as Wiley finished talking, Daniel noticed Uncle Gilbert race up behind his father and mother and rudely interrupt the conversation.

"Wiley, I hope you know these are Mormon settlers! You wouldn't be considering a business arrangement with them would you?"

"No matter of yours, Gilbert," Wiley answered. "Now if you don't mind, Mr. Colton and I have a bit of business to discuss."

Gilbert's bushy eyebrow twitched nervously as he cleared his throat. His face grew red, his eyes threatening.

"You've had fair warning, Wiley. This is a big mistake for you and for them. Don't expect any protection from me from now on."

"Would you like to see the place?" Wiley finished ignoring his brother-in-law.

Gilbert bristled, glared momentarily at Wiley and Margaret, then stomped away mumbling something intimidating under his breath. Wiley jumped onto the buckboard of the wagon with the Colton family and they rode away together.

"How come Father did that?" Daniel said turning to his mother. "Uncle Gilbert says Mormons are trouble. Maybe he shouldn't sell them a piece of our land."

"Oh, Daniel, don't believe everything Uncle Gilbert says," Margaret answered. "He's more a religious fanatic than that poor family. They just want a place to live, son. Just need a roof over their heads like everybody else."

"I've never heard you speak a word against Uncle Gilbert, Mama. Don't you respect him any more?"

"I respect Uncle Gilbert as much as I ever did, Daniel," Margaret answered with a coy grin.

After the hour was over, everyone in the Jones family was waiting at the blacksmith shop except Wiley. He hadn't returned with the Colton family. Daniel's three sisters were chattering on about having Mormons for neighbors and Eliza Jane asked Daniel if the man had any attractive older sons.

"No, but I noticed a pretty young girl about Danny's age in the wagon," Margaret teased as Daniel's face turned instantly crimson.

That night before he went to sleep, Daniel thought about the Mormon girl he'd seen sitting in the wagon. Even though Daniel pretended not to notice, he had. Something about the way she looked made him feel unsettled and excited inside; he couldn't quite sort it out or make sense of it. It was a new feeling and he liked it.

All spring and summer Wiley's cough grew worse and his health steadily declined. Though Wiley's disposition was as mild as ever, he was obviously weakening day by day. At harvest time Wiley was so frail and bedridden Daniel was left to do most of the farm work alone. Though he enlisted help from his sisters, Daniel was able to bring in roughly half the harvest of grain and feed before the first frost hit. Daniel noticed bloody rags in the wash basin every morning before he left for chores. At night in the dark Daniel often heard Wiley coughing in gut-wrenching dry heaves. When Margaret drew the quilt around their bed that autumn and refused to leave Wiley's bedside, a fear took hold of Daniel's heart, instantly bringing him back to the winter Susan died.

Deborah tried to keep the children busy after the first snow fall. With Margaret fussing over her sick husband, there was no time for lessons. On his way to the barn to feed the animals, Daniel often looked out at the wasted and frozen harvest and chided himself for his inability to do the work of a grown man. Even now as he tried to take care of the animals and keep the family in fire wood, too much was left undone. Many evenings Daniel came back inside the cabin in the evenings with his hands bleeding and blistered. Deborah soaked and bandaged his hands, then begged Daniel not to use them for a spell, but Daniel insisted he had to take care of the farm until his father got well.

One night Daniel didn't return home until late in the evening. The house was uncharacteristically dark except for the dying embers in the fire when he entered. Deborah was alone sobbing at the hearth as Daniel walked through the front door.

She spoke softy as Daniel approached her, "Don't need no more grief comin' to this family. Your Mama's bad off. Won't leave his side. Actin' strange. Sick herself. Orders me away. Won't eat. But child, your Papa's dead. Your Mama won't let me touch him. 'Fraid she'll die herself if we don't get somebody to help her."

Daniel lit a candle and went to his mother's bedside. Margaret was sitting on the bed in the dark cradling her husband's head on her lap. By the halo of the candlelight, Daniel watched his mother wipe his father's brow with a damp cloth. Wiley was stretched out on the bed as if sleeping. The distant, empty look in his mother's eyes was more frightening to Daniel than his father's dead body. Daniel placed his candle on the table then sat next to his mother on the bed. At first she didn't notice him, but when Daniel called her name, Margaret lovingly placed her tired hand on Daniel's knee.

"Mamma, he's dead," Daniel said.

"No. It's all right, son. He's only sleeping," Margaret answered.

Daniel didn't know what to say or do, but he couldn't leave his mother alone. He decided to stay with her until morning. When Deborah pulled the quilt aside to take a look an hour later, both mother and son had fallen asleep next to Wiley. She placed a blanket over all three then climbed the ladder to the loft to check on the girls. She couldn't bring herself to wake the girls to tell them of their father's passing. She could barely make it back down the ladder and into her bed before collapsing with exhaustion.

The next day, Uncle Gilbert came to the home and witnessed the helpless state of his sister and the unburied corpse of his brother-in-law. Deborah noticed Gilbert seemed to relish the family's helplessness. He quickly determined they urgently needed someone with a clear head to take over. In Gilbert's estimation, his sister couldn't possibly take care of herself and her herd of unruly children and keep up with the demands of the farm.

"Margaret," Gilbert said shaking his sister awake. "We need to bury Wiley, before he starts to stink."

Gilbert helped his listless sister up from the bed. Margaret nodded, agreeing to her brother's orders in a weak, childlike way.

"Get her something to eat," Gilbert ordered turning to Deborah. "Make it quick."

Wiley's body was buried on the knoll next to Susan's later that day. Gilbert didn't take the time to build a coffin and the rest of the family was too weak with grief to object. Deborah was appreciative of Gilbert's help with the burial, but she knew full well what he was up to. She watched him eyeing the cabin, barn and fields like he was the proud new owner. Deborah silently fumed as Gilbert proceeded to take over the household decisions and the future for his widowed sister and her children.

When the burial was over and the house was back in some sense of order, Gilbert sat Margaret down and lectured, "Margaret, I know what a trying time this must be for you. I want to do everything I can to help you. I've written mother and father. They're expecting you and the girls to come and stay with them until you get stronger. Wiley never should have brought you and the children out here. The girls can find proper husbands, and mother and father can care for you. Daniel should begin his apprenticeship and start some much neglected religious training here with me. Leave him with me until you can get things settled and regain your strength. Then you can send for him."

Margaret nodded approval as if in a trance while Gilbert spoke, but she seemed to come to her senses for a moment when he finished and she had a moment to think. "No. I want the family to stay together. I want Daniel with me," Margaret said weakly.

"Someone will need to take care of this place for you or you'll lose it," Gilbert said. "You're sick. You can't possibly be expected to think clearly at a time like this. Daniel's not old enough to take care of the place alone. He'll need my help. Then we can sell it come spring. This is best for you and the boy."

"I won't ever sell the place. This place was Wiley's dream," Margaret said. "When I'm better, I'll come back."

"Then we won't sell it," Gilbert said. "But you can't possibly expect me to take care of this place and keep up with my ministry. I'll need Daniel to stay on and help."

"I don't need Gilbert's help," Daniel interrupted, breaking into the conversation and pleading with his mother. "Please, Mother, let me take care of our farm by myself."

"You're too young," Margaret said. "You'll need Gilbert's help."

Daniel finally agreed to stay behind with the promise his mother and sisters would return when they were strong again. As Daniel waved good-bye to his mother, sisters, and Deborah later in the week, it was all he could do to keep from running after them. He could remember his mother's words from the night before.

"Danny, it won't be long. When I'm better, I'll all come back. I need someone to look after the place for now. Uncle Gilbert will make sure you get along all right."

Margaret's eyes were blank and tearless that morning as the wagon pulled away. Deborah took the reins, whipped the horses and drove the heavily loaded wagon slowly away from the homestead, wiping her eyes and sobbing like a baby. Still in shock from their sister and father's passing, Eliza Jane, Angeline, and Frances huddled together in the back of the wagon, trembling.

"Let Danny come with us," Frances cried stretching her arms toward her brother.

Daniel's mother turned her head and stared at the road. As they rounded the corner and disappeared from view Daniel turned and saw his uncle's menacing face behind him. Gilbert's countenance changed suddenly from a smile of farewell to an angry threatening glare.

"Things will be different for you from now on," Gilbert said grabbing Daniel by the shoulder. "I'm in charge now. You'll do what I say. Do you understand? Your father was weak. I'm not."

"My father was not weak," Daniel shouted back defiantly.

Gilbert reached to the floor, picked up his walking stick then thrust the cane forcefully across Daniel's head. Stunned, Daniel rolled to the ground in agony. As soon as he recovered, Daniel stood and glared at his uncle.

"Get in the cabin!" Gilbert insisted.

Defiantly, Daniel raced toward the woods, blood trickling between his eyes.

"Come back here, boy," Gilbert wailed. "You'll do what I say, Daniel Webster Jones. Stubborn wild colt! I'll break you yet! Your father neglected your religious training. I shall not!"

A sudden terrifying fear and anger mixed inside Daniel as he tried to run away from the stark reality of his family's total abandonment. He kept running but didn't know where to go. Most of the forest leaves had already fallen, creating a blanket of crunchy leaves on the ground and leaving the woods without the usual canopy. Daniel ran for his father's favorite enclosure but found only tangled bare vines and fallen leaves. There was no place to hide, no place to run. He couldn't think of where to go or what to do. Later, Gilbert found Daniel huddled under a group of leafless vines shivering.

"Don't think you can defy me!" Gilbert yelled. Gilbert struck Daniel several times across his back then dragged him by the shirt collar into a clearing. "Ask God to forgive you, you willful, defiant boy!" Gilbert wailed. "There are no soft women to hide behind now. Get on your feet. Now!"

Daniel stood with great pain and stumbled back toward the cabin. Once inside, Gilbert ordered Daniel to chop wood for the fire, feed the animals, and fix supper while he studied from the Bible. Daniel didn't have the strength or will to resist. When Daniel finally climbed the ladder to the loft that night and crawled under a quilt, he tried to close his eyes and escape into sleep. Gilbert snored loudly below. His uncle had moved his parent's bed in front of the door to prevent Daniel from running again.

When Gilbert woke Daniel the next morning, it was still dark outside. After Daniel pumped water from the well, then washed his face in the basin and dressed, his uncle read from the Bible and insisted Daniel join him in his lengthy pious morning prayers. For Daniel, his uncle's prayers seemed stiff and formal, not like real prayers at all. His father had taught him prayers were more like an ongoing and informal conversation with God.

On Sunday, Daniel attended Gilbert's sermon for the first time. Daniel looked over his shoulder toward the river and woods that had been his church every other Sunday as he rode to church that morning. He desperately wanted to bolt and run, but Gilbert's grasp on his arm was too tight, his threats too real. After they arrived at the church, Gilbert ordered Daniel to sit in the first pew and threatened to beat him again if he tried to escape. Daniel could hear the congregation filing in behind him, but didn't turn to look. Gilbert was sitting by the pulpit in his black suit and stiff white collar with his head bowed as if in prayer when the people from the settlement entered. When the room was full, Gilbert stood and began the Sunday service with prayer. For Daniel, it felt strange to pray inside the cold walls of a church and in front of strangers, not at all what he was used to. Daniel reluctantly listened as his uncle began his sermon.

"Locusts threaten to devour you," Gilbert began. "Swarms of Mormon emigrants from Ohio and New York are pouring into our county. Mass of human corruption. Openly blaspheme the Most High God. Pretend to receive revelations from heaven. Unholy pretenses are derogatory to God an utter subversion of the human race."

Gilbert's voice was cold, stern and threatening. Daniel understood at once why his father had never attended this church. Though he began the sermon with a moderate tone of voice, Gilbert gradually increased the volume and intensity of his sermon until he was bellowing and pounding the pulpit like a mad man.

"*This* is the word of God!" Gilbert yelled as he raised his Bible high above his greasy head. "Jesus said on the cross that His mission was finished. He established His work and church in its fullness. Anything that adds to this is blasphemy! Mormons say they have *new* scripture. I say contemptible gibberish. The Book of Mormon is a ridiculous farce and these so called Saints are low-class, degraded dregs of society."

Daniel heard several people responding behind him saying, "Amen!"

"Mormons say there was an apostasy; God almighty allowed his gospel to be taken from the earth. Blasphemy! Mormons say all the churches on the earth are wrong and they alone have all the truth. Mormons say they have a prophet who has seen the Holy Father and Jesus Christ. Blasphemy! I tell you they are followers of the devil. Do not be fooled. Do not allow this blasphemy to enter your ears. Rid them from our midst!"

To this Daniel heard several in the congregation shout, "Amen!"

"That's not all. These Mormons are opposed to slavery even though it is legal and lawful here. Regard the heathen Indians as a people destined to rise again and assume their rightful heritage in the Promised Land. Mark my words, Mormons will cause a bloody uprising and we'll all be murdered in our beds. Pray with me brothers and sisters. Have the courage to rid our county of this grave menace."

Reverend Gilbert Marshall bowed his head and led the church in prayer, asking the Almighty to bring down retribution on their Mormon enemies. Daniel thought about the land his father had sold to the Mormons and he didn't know whether to feel ashamed of his father or angry at his uncle. He felt confused and scared when he thought about his new life with Gilbert. He knew his mother would never have left him alone with his uncle if she knew how cruel he could be.

In the days and weeks that followed, Gilbert and Daniel spent weekends on the Jones farm and week days at the settlement in Gilbert's rooms attached to the church. Months passed slowly for Daniel. There were mandatory early morning religious lessons and scripture reading before he left for his apprenticeship in the saddle shop. The long hours spent at the shop were relaxing by comparison. The owner of the saddle shop was kind and helped Daniel learn his trade with patience. Yet Daniel's heart wasn't in it.

❀

Spring and summer came and went slowly. Daniel and his uncle gradually spent more and more time at the Jones homestead. Gilbert was little or no help with the farm work. Daniel felt his muscles growing stronger and his appetite heartier with the hard labor now expected of him. The exhaustion he felt at the end of the day was as welcome as the deep sleep it offered. Gilbert refused to allow Daniel any further walks in the woods saying it would bring back all the corrupt ways of his father. He forced Daniel to daily repeat self-reproachful phrases intended to break his spirit.

"I am a sinner," Daniel repeated at Gilbert's insistence each night. "God will never love me unless I repent of my wicked ways. I will burn in hell."

Gilbert ordered Daniel to fix his meals, wash his clothes, shine his shoes, and tend to his animals. He insisted his time was better served studying for his Sunday sermons. On the weekends after supper, men who reeked of body odor, alcohol, urine and tobacco met at the Jones cabin. Daniel hated hearing their vulgar conversations and listening to them curse and spit drool on his mother's hand-tied rag rugs.

After months of following Gilbert's every command, Daniel finally managed to gain his trust and was allowed to stay in the barn while the men were meeting in the cabin. As the group spilled outside on the front porch within earshot of his nephew, Gilbert allowed Daniel to leave the property. His uncle always ordered him away when the men started making specific plans. This was the first opportunity Daniel had to return to the forest since his father's death.

As Daniel approached the woods he heard the wind washing through the trees and noticed large piles of leaves scattered about on the ground making a crunching sound as he walked. As he stepped into the quiet solitude of the trees, Daniel's inner heaviness lifted; yet there remained a lingering feeling of abandonment. It had been months and he'd heard nothing from his mother or sisters. Yet the familiar sights, sounds and smells of the woods soothed Daniel much like Deborah's old melodies. He hadn't allowed himself to grieve since his family left months ago. Daniel refused to give Gilbert the satisfaction of knowing how frightened and broken he felt. Now deep in the seclusion of the forest, Daniel allowed deep feelings of desertion to rise to the surface.

Then, in the distance, Daniel saw a figure silhouetted against the brilliant sunset. He made out the form to be a girl. Her waist-long dark brown hair swayed as she bent over to pick some wild flowers. Daniel stepped behind a tree and stood very quietly as he watched her. She came nearer and nearer without noticing his hiding place. Daniel figured the stranger looked about his age. She had a delicate figure, deep-green eyes and a fair complexion with a small sprinkling of freckles across the bridge of her tiny nose.

Daniel watched as she knelt and held out a crust of bread to lure a nearby squirrel. The animal approached carefully, retreated, then came near again and cautiously nibbled from her hand. Then the girl reached out and gently stroked the squirrel.

Daniel thought her actions were odd. In all his years in the forest, he had hunted squirrels but never fed or petted one. As Daniel stepped forward, a branch broke under his foot startling the girl. She took one frightened look at him, turned and ran.

"No, wait a minute," Daniel called. "I won't hurt you."

The girl stopped, turned and stood nervously staring at Daniel as he stepped toward her. That's when he recognized her face. She was the Mormon girl he'd seen in the wagon that day at the settlement, the one he'd had dreams about ever since.

"I'm sorry I frightened you," he said as he walked to within a few steps of her and stopped. "What's your name?

"Emily Colton. My father bought a piece up the river a while back."

Daniel thought back to the day in town and asked, "Did he buy the land from Wiley Jones?"

"Yes," Emily answered. "Do you know him?"

"He's my father. I thought you looked familiar. I saw you the day my father sold the land. You were sitting in the back of the wagon."

Daniel felt awkward and unpolished as he spoke. He wanted this beautiful girl to like him, but he felt all wrong. Yet something about the soft look in her eyes made Daniel gradually relax and gave him permission to be his unguarded self.

"My father said yours is a good man," Emily said. "We'd been looking for a piece to farm for a long time. Most people around here hate us. Please thank your father. We love it here. Had a great harvest this summer."

"My father's dead," Daniel said, lowering his eyes to the ground.

"Oh, I'm sorry. I didn't know. Wondered why he quit coming around. Mama won't let Papa go to the settlement for fear what the people will do to him, so we don't hear about much of what's going on around here. I'm sorry. Really I am. Your Mama must be pretty lonely."

"She's sick. Went back to live with her parents until she gets better. But she'll be coming back real soon. I have four, I mean three sisters and Deborah."

"I've got three brothers, Robert, Ben, and Amos—and a baby sister, Mary. Mama needs lots of help, but sometimes she lets me go for walks in the woods to get away from my brothers' pestering. I love the forest. Guess I spend every minute here I can."

Daniel smiled then answered, "Kind of like this place myself. I'll bet you don't know even half the secrets the woods have."

"Secrets?" Emily asked. "What do you mean secrets?"

"Well maybe sometime I'll tell you, but I better be getting back before my uncle misses me and gets mad. He gets mad real easy."

"Oh, you live with your uncle now?"

"He's the minister in town."

"Oh," Emily said surprised, lowering her head in disappointment. "He's been by our house a few times. He seems . . . I don't think I'd like to live with him."

Daniel wondered what business Gilbert had with Emily's family. He could imagine the malicious things his uncle might have done or said and blushed.

"I'm sorry he's bothered you. Hope he didn't do anything awful. Hard man. My uncle has lots of people come by the farm on the weekends these days. Always sends me away when they come. I could meet you here sometimes."

Emily looked into Daniel's sad blue eyes. His sandy blond hair fell almost to his shoulders in gentle curls framing his angular yet still boyish face. He was slender but broad shouldered. Emily noticed he had no beard like her father, so she knew he must be close to her age. Fourteen-year-old Emily felt awkward about her new developing figure. She noticed Daniel's muscular arms and callused hands revealing he was no stranger to hard physical labor. Emily liked his shy awkwardness. His inviting smile gave her a sudden urge to take his hand, though she thought it best to hide her feelings.

"I'd like that," Emily said pointing to a group of saplings and vines creating an enclosure near the river. "Mama always lets me take a walk after supper. We could meet over there. Maybe then you could tell me about some of those secrets."

Daniel looked to where Emily pointed and noticed she'd been referring to the place where he used to sit with his father.

"I'd like that," Daniel answered. "Like that a lot." Then he blushed. Emily smiled warmly, her green eyes shining and inviting. Daniel noticed how fragile Emily looked. Her tiny waist and round bodice created pleasing stirrings inside him he'd never felt before. "Better get back now," Daniel finished, breaking the awkward silence.

Daniel was flushed from running when he returned to the cabin. Gilbert was praying at his parent's bedside and called Daniel when he walked through the front door.

"Ask God to forgive you, boy," Gilbert said signaling for Daniel to kneel beside him. "Pray the sins of your father will not be repeated in you. Pray for God to rid you of your pride. Humble yourself."

"You never knew my father," Daniel answered defiantly, even though he was sure those words would bring on another beating. "Don't call him a sinner. He was the kindest man I've ever known. I'm going to tell my mother how you treat me when she comes back."

"Listen to me boy," Gilbert answered. "Your mother left you in my care and you better get used to it. I'm your father now."

"You'll never be my father!" Daniel shouted.

"Prideful, ungrateful colt," Gilbert answered, standing upright then storming over next to Daniel. "She's never coming back for you. She wouldn't have left you with me if she really loved you. Glad to get rid of you. One less mouth to feed. No one loves you, Daniel. No one cares about you. I'm all you've got."

"Yes, she will. She promised me," Daniel answered.

"As soon as you're of age, you can sign this property over to me boy," Gilbert said. "Why do you think I put up with you? Otherwise I'd kick you out to fend for yourself or make sure you ran into some nice little accident. No one would be wiser. No one would miss you. No one would care." Daniel felt the weight of Gilbert's words pressing down on him. During his long nights alone in the loft, he had often wondered if what Gilbert had just said was true. Hearing his worst fears out loud from his uncle was too much. "Get over here boy and pray. Pray for God to forgive you of your ingratitude. Pray, boy, pray!"

"You don't know how to pray," Daniel answered as he squared his jaw and looked his uncle straight in the eye. "You pretend to be righteous in church on Sunday, but you don't fool me. I know what you're doing, the men you meet with."

Gilbert grabbed Daniel by the shoulders then pushed him to his knees. Yanking off his belt, Gilbert flung the leather strap hard across Daniel's back splitting the fabric open on his shirt and cutting into the bare flesh.

"Don't you ever talk back to me again, boy!" Gilbert yelled. "Do you hear me?!" With great force, Gilbert threw his arm back and lunged forward swinging the belt down again . . . and again . . . until Daniel collapsed. "I'll break you yet!" Gilbert screamed. "Don't you ever talk to me like that again. Only reason I let you stay alive is so I can get my name on the deed to this property."

CHAPTER FOUR

The first heavy snow storm forced all the trees in the forest near the Jones homestead to bend low, heavy with the white layered mounds. Gilbert's secret meetings with the men from the settlement were increasing and Daniel was glad of it. Dozens of secret meetings with Emily in the forest had lately become Daniel's reason for living.

One cold evening after several men rode up to the cabin, Gilbert told Daniel to leave. He ran for the woods, hoping he might find Emily there again. After searching without results in their usual place, Daniel noticed Emily off in the distance feeding the woodland birds. She stopped and turned when she heard him coming. Just as Emily smiled at Daniel, a snow packed limb unloaded on her, sending her to the cold forest floor. As Daniel saw her sprawled there in the snow with her petticoats and skirts thrown over her head, he laughed. Embarrassed, Emily quickly stood and smoothed her skirts.

"Guess I don't mind looking silly if it can make you smile. Don't believe I've ever seen you laugh before," Emily said. "If you think I'm so funny, try it yourself."

Emily shook another loaded bough and its contents fell down on Daniel with a whump. Daniel fell backward covered in snow, pulling Emily down with him. Before Emily knew what had happened, they were both rolling around in the snow like bear cubs. The early evening hours cast a blue hue on the snow as the sky darkened and the wind died down. They stopped rolling and Daniel found himself perched on top of Emily with his mouth, ears and nose full of snow. Her green eyes glistened, her red lips opened.

"You're beautiful," Daniel said as if he'd never noticed before.

Embarrassed at his sudden admission, Daniel quickly stood and helped Emily to her feet. They dusted each other off and sat shivering on an old log, wrapping their arms around each other for warmth.

"You're my best friend," Emily said. "Never had a best friend before."

"Me too," Daniel answered. "Used to come here with my father. He told me the forest will tell you all kinds of secrets about life if you're listening. Taught me how to survive out here, how to hunt, fish and find wild berries and roots to eat. I miss him."

Emily took Daniel's face in her hands and kissed him softly on the cheek.

"I'm sorry, Danny," Emily said. "I can tell how much you love him."

Emily's spontaneity and affection instantly melted Daniel. He adored her gentle touch. He'd wanted to kiss her since the first day they met but was afraid she might think him too bold. Her brief kiss was the kindest touch he'd felt in over a year. He placed his hand on his cheek trying to hold the warmth of her affection there.

"Gilbert says my father was a sinner because he never stepped inside a church and didn't have his children baptized. Says I'm a lot like my father and if I don't ask God to forgive me and get baptized, I'll burn in hell. But I don't want my uncle to baptize me. He says my mother doesn't really love me, that she's never coming back. Says he wants me to sign over my father's farm to him when I'm of age. But I won't. This place was my father's dream."

"Awful man," Emily said shaking her head. "Don't believe him, Danny. Awful men say awful things. Doesn't make them true."

Daniel looked into Emily's eyes and asked pleadingly, "Do *you* think my mother will ever come back?"

Emily took Daniel's hand and stroked it as she answered, "She loves you, Daniel. She'll come back. I'm sure of it."

Daniel gazed longingly into Emily's eyes as she spoke. She looked like royalty to him, her hair crowned with glistening lights as tiny snowflakes melted in her hair. Daniel loved the way Emily's dark brown curls softly framed her classic oval face, the pleasant sound of her voice, her regal gentleness, the goodness and love he sensed in her eyes. The chance to be with her was his hidden treasury and all that kept him from running away from his uncle. Their moments in the woods had given him something to plan for, hope for, and live for.

"I love you, Emily," Daniel whispered. "Don't ever die. Don't ever leave me. Everyone I've ever loved dies or leaves."

"I love you, too," Emily whispered. "I promise I'll never leave you."

Daniel knew even though his father had taught him important things about life in this forest, Emily's gentle friendship had awakened in him a part of being alive he'd never known. He longed to be with her all the time, to grow strong and independent, be a man and make a rich life with her at his side. Emily had made him believe again, to look to the future, to know good things were possible. Daniel knew their secret visits had rescued him. Her gentle hands had taught him how to softly stroke a frightened animal or feed a wild bird. Through her eyes he'd learned to notice the changing colors in the night sky and the way the snow sparkled in twilight. Whenever she was near, he felt a wholeness he yearned for when they were apart.

"Come meet my family," Emily said as they both stood. "Then we can dry off before you have to go home."

Daniel hesitated and asked, "They don't want me around do they? I'm not a Mormon. I don't believe like you do."

"Oh, come on," Emily coaxed as she pulled him with her until they were running toward her cabin near the river. "My whole family knows you. I talk about you all the time. They already love you like I do."

Daniel felt his heart pounding in his chest as Emily opened the door to her log home. Her mother was rocking a baby and several boys were romping on the rock hard earthen floor. Daniel found it strange that Emily's father was whistling as he shoveled dirt behind him in the corner of the cabin.

"What's your father doing?" Daniel asked whispering in Emily's ear. "Most people don't dig large holes *inside* their house."

"You ask him," Emily answered, stepping behind a blanket to undress.

"Well this must be Daniel," Emily's father said. He stopped shoveling, set the spade aside and warmly reached out his hand to greet him.

"Yes, sir," Daniel answered feeling embarrassed and awkward, wondering what Emily had told her parents.

"Well, Daniel, this is Emily's mother Polly and I'm her father Philander. These are her brothers Robert, Ben and Amos and her baby sister Mary. It's nice to have a friendly visitor. We don't get many. As a matter of fact, your uncle was here just yesterday. Says he wants us off this land now because we haven't been making our payments. But your father hasn't been around to collect for a long time now. Your uncle says your father died and that he has control of the land now. Is that right?"

"No, but he'd like to," Daniel answered glancing around to look for Emily. He felt strange without her at his side. "My father's dead but my mother still owns the land. She'll be coming back soon and she can straighten things out for you, sir."

"As long as I know I still have a legal right to stay on the land, we won't be moving on account of threats. I'd be happy to make my payments to you from now on."

"That won't be necessary," Daniel answered.

"No, I insist," Emily's father answered.

Daniel noticed a warm and affectionate feeling in the Colton's cabin that reminded him of his own home before Susan and his father died, before his mother went away. He longed to stay yet knew staying would only cause more problems for Emily and her family. Gilbert had determined to run the Colton family off the land and reclaim it for himself. If he knew Daniel had talked to them it would only cause more trouble.

"Let's not talk about Daniel's uncle," Emily interrupted. "He has to live with him. That's enough." Emily suddenly noticed blood oozing through the cloth from under Daniel's shirt in his back. "What's this?" Emily said pointing to Daniel's back. You're bleeding."

Daniel turned his back to the wall embarrassed.

"It's nothing," Daniel answered.

"It's your uncle isn't it?" Emily asked again. "Stay here with us; never go back."

"Just cause more trouble for you and your family. I couldn't do that."

"I'm sorry, son," Emily's father said as he stopped digging the hole. "Do you want my wife to take a look?"

Daniel blushed.

"Step over here," Mrs. Colton commanded directing Daniel to the far corner. "Turn your head, Emily. Don't embarrass the boy." Daniel reluctantly removed his shirt, exposing his sculptured, tanned muscles. Emily dropped her eyes after sneaking a peak. "Who did this to you? There are new and old wounds here." Embarrassed, Daniel didn't answer. "I have something that might help," Mrs. Colton said as she reached inside a large trunk. "Hold still and I'll apply some."

"Why you digging a hole?" Daniel asked trying to redirect the attention.

Philander wiped the sweat off his brow and stopped digging while he answered, "Well son, had some threats lately. Better prepare for the worst. Men on horseback have been here at night, throwing rocks through the windows and running off the livestock. Said if we don't move out, they'd burn us out. Just making sure the family has a safe hiding place case we ever need it," Philander answered.

"Why do you tell me, sir?" Daniel asked. "Aren't you afraid I'll tell my uncle?"

"Course not. Emily's told us all about you," Philander answered. "If we trust you with our daughter, don't you think we'd trust you with this secret?"

Daniel slipped his shirt back on and thanked Emily's mother for the salve.

"Better be getting back before my uncle misses me," Daniel said as he moved quickly toward the door.

"I'll show you out," Emily said as she took Daniel by the hand.

"Why didn't you tell me about what's been happening?" Daniel asked impatiently once they were alone outside the cabin. "I didn't know you were getting threats."

"Why didn't you tell me your uncle was beating you?" Emily answered pointing to Daniel's back. "I'm sorry Danny. Don't be angry. I thought maybe if I told, you wouldn't meet me in the forest any more. I don't want to lose you, not ever."

Daniel stepped closer to Emily's delicate frame, cupped her face in his hands and said, "Should have known me better. I care more about you than anybody in this world. Haven't heard a word from my mother or sisters since they left. Don't even know if they're still alive. You're the only person who loves me. Being with you is the only reason I have for living. I'd never stop seeing you or leave you unless you tell me to go."

Daniel leaned forward and kissed Emily softly on the lips. Emily put her slender arms around Daniel's neck and drew his trembling body toward hers before she quickly turned and walked back into her cabin. Daniel ran back through the forest toward home. After learning what was happening to Emily's family, Daniel decided to stay home and listen to the conversations of the men who came to his cabin almost every night to meet with his Uncle Gilbert.

Throughout the spring and summer, the men from town kept up their random raids on Mormon settlers. Late one summer night after the men arrived and his uncle told him to leave, Daniel walked around to the back of the cabin and waited until the men had all gone inside. Then he walked around to the front of the house and listened at the window. Some of the men sounded drunk and slurred their words.

"Let's do it men. I get the pretty ones," one of the men shouted.

Daniel heard a cane slam on the table as Gilbert shouted.

"Listen to me, all of you," Gilbert said. "Let's make a public example of one of their leaders. They'll all leave then. Take their bishop. Wellington, get the tar and feathers. If the arm of civil law does not afford us a guarantee to rid this county of them, we'll do it ourselves!"

Daniel ran for the rear of the house as the men came pouring out. Hanging back in the shadows, Daniel followed the men on horseback into the settlement and watched the mob drag the Mormon bishop from his house then force him into the public square at gun point. They stripped him from the waist up, screamed profanities at him and spit tobacco drool in his face. When the bishop asked to speak, the mob reluctantly agreed.

"I've done nothing that should offend anyone," the bishop said. "If you abuse me, you abuse an innocent person."

"We've warned you Mormons, but you refuse to leave," a man from the mob cursed. "It's your own fault! Warned you to get out!"

"Say you'll leave and we'll set you free!" another shouted, his face painted black to disguise his identity.

The bishop quietly turned to each man present, looked at each one unflinchingly in the eye then said, "Saints have been persecuted in all the ages. I will suffer for the sake of Christ, but leave my home, I will not!"

The mob burst into angry shouting. Suddenly a man from the crowd poured hot tar on the bishop. Daniel smelled the burning flesh and heard him cry out in pain. Another man dumped feathers on the black smoldering flesh. The bishop stood in trembling silence as the mob finished. Daniel wanted to help but was too afraid to move. Seeing how meekly the bishop took his abuse at the hands of the mob made most of the men in the mob shrink away and leave. After all the other members of the mob left, Gilbert kicked the bishop in the back and sent him to his knees. Then he kicked him again and again until the bishop fell over in the dirt moaning. Daniel burned inside as he saw Gilbert give the bishop a final kick in the face then slink away into the darkness. Bloodied and bruised, the bishop tried to stand but fell back on the ground groaning.

With all the men gone, Daniel felt safe enough to help the bishop back on his feet and return him to his home and family. When they reached the bishop's home, Daniel supported the bishop's weight with one hand while he knocked on his door with the other. Instantly the door flew open and Daniel heard the wild screams of the bishop's wife and his small children as their husband and father collapsed into their open arms. Daniel quickly rode back to the farm and waited for his uncle to return.

When Gilbert walked into the house, Daniel was waiting for him. He stood and pointed an accusing finger, "Told me to read the Bible and repent. Said I'm a sinner. What are you? What you did tonight?"

"Jesus was compelled to cleanse the temple with a whip," Gilbert interrupted.

Daniel turned to climb the loft as he called back, "Cleanse yourself first, uncle!"

Storming up the ladder behind Daniel, Gilbert grabbed his nephew by the arm and hurled him to the floor.

"How dare you speak to me that way? You don't understand why this had to be done!" Gilbert yelled ripping off his belt. "Listen to me boy, if I hadn't taken control, they'd have burned, ravished, and killed the lot of them. You don't understand, too stupid and naive. Tell me again will you, tell me to cleanse myself now!" Gilbert screamed as he brought the belt down across Daniel's frightened upturned face.

Gilbert kicked Daniel across the room into the far wall. Stunned and in pain, Daniel couldn't move. Gilbert stormed over and kicked Daniel in the back and stomach until he vomited and lost consciousness.

For days after the beating, Daniel tried unsuccessfully to regain his former strength by crawling in circles on his hands and knees in the loft. One night when Gilbert believed he was sleeping, Daniel listened to the men at the secret meeting brag about their raids on the Mormons homesteads, burning haystacks, running off livestock and setting fire to cabins. He thought about Emily and wondered if her family might be next. He tried to figure out how he could get to her house and warn her to leave.

One night after another raiding party, Daniel watched his uncle slink into the cabin covered in blood and mud.

"What have you done?" Daniel yelled from the loft trying to sit up in bed.

"It's done," Gilbert answered. "I tried to make the men stop before . . ."

"Before what?" Daniel yelled. "What have you done?"

Gilbert stared up into the loft with a dazed blank expression, "I'm so cold." Daniel painfully and slowly pulled on his boots and coat. "No, come sit by me," Gilbert continued as he watched Daniel descend the loft ladder and walk toward the front door. "Stay with me. I don't want to be alone."

Daniel felt nauseous as he glared at his uncle. His heart raced, contemplating what might have happened to Emily and her family.

"What have you done?" Daniel asked. Gilbert refused to answer. "You make me sick," Daniel said, slamming the door behind him.

Daniel limped from the house and painfully found his way to the woods. He waited at their secret place hoping Emily would eventually come. An hour later as the sun slowly set in the western horizon, Daniel looked up and saw Emily running toward him.

"I'm so glad you're safe," Daniel said as they sat down together under a tree.

"What's happened to you?" Emily winced as she stared at Daniel's bruised and scared face. "Did your uncle do this to you?"

"My uncle and those men who come at night have done something horrible," Daniel said. "Emily, you and your family have to leave now, before it's too late."

"Father won't leave," Emily answered. "Says he won't make decisions based on fear or hate. Says people like your uncle make their own life more miserable than they make his. How can your uncle sleep at night knowing all the terrible things he's done, all the pain he's caused?"

Daniel sat silently listening to Emily and when she was finished he said, "I don't know. We're together now. I just want to forget."

Daniel took Emily's hand and guided her slowly toward the river bank. When they reached the edge of the water, Daniel pulled off his boots, rolled up his pants and took off his shirt. Emily cringed when she saw Daniel's purple bruises and deep scars. She touched him softly on his chest and back.

"What did he do to you? I'm so sorry."

"Feeling better now," Daniel answered. "Just want to forget."

Emily took off her shoes and tied her skirt around her waist as she followed Daniel into the water. Slowly they immersed themselves into the cool river and swam out into the middle where the soft current lulled them gently down stream. They rolled over onto their backs and floated with the current holding tightly to each other's hands. When they separated, Daniel dived in and out around Emily as she floated freely in the cool water. Emily felt Daniel brush against her then quickly swim away. Stars flickered in the night sky and moonlight filtering through the tree tops gave the water an iridescent shimmer. After they pulled themselves onto the shore, wet and shivering, Daniel wrapped his arm around Emily's shoulders.

"If it could always be like this," Daniel whispered. Rainbow prisms glistened off of Emily's wet eyelashes. She trembled. "Emily, you're so beautiful. When I'm with you I can almost forget everything else. Then I remember and I'm afraid again. What's going to happen to us? I don't know what I'd do if I lost you."

"Doesn't have to be like this, Danny. Don't go back tonight," Emily pleaded.

"But I can't go with you. Would just make things worse on your family," Daniel answered with a serious tone of voice.

"If those men get Papa to leave, you'll come with us, won't you?" Emily asked.

"I'd like to do that more than anything. But what would happen if my mother or sisters came back for me?" Daniel asked. "Wouldn't know where to find me."

Emily didn't know how to respond. She softly leaned her head against Daniel's bare shoulder and whispered, "Danny I won't leave you. If we're ever separated, I promise I'll wait for you."

"And I for you," Daniel answered.

When Daniel left the forest that night, he was brutally grabbed from behind by a dark figure. Though he struggled to be set free, the grasp only tightened.

"Let me go!" Daniel shouted as he looked up at the glaring face of his uncle. Something dark, wet, and sticky was drooling from the sides of his mouth and Daniel could see a near empty liquor bottle in his hands.

"You're coming with me boy. Last time you'll leave me alone."

Half dragging and half pushing, Gilbert forced Daniel home. After they entered the cabin, Gilbert spouted a sermon as if he were at the pulpit at church and then suddenly passed out on the floor. Daniel saw several empty liquor bottles lying around on the cabin floor. He dragged his uncle across the room then lifted him up onto his parent's bed. Gilbert suddenly yelled something unintelligible then sat up. After choking and heaving, Gilbert passed out again then fell back on the bed in his own vomit. Daniel turned away in disgust then climbed the loft and tried to sleep.

The next morning Gilbert didn't mention the events of the previous night but ordered Daniel to stay home and become his solitary pupil.

After Gilbert's announcement, Daniel was forced to spend hours reading from the Bible. Gilbert spent most of the day in a chair drinking bottle after bottle. Daniel loathed his uncle but decided to stay with him so he could find out about the next raid in time to warn Emily and her family. In the evenings, when the men from the town met as usual, Gilbert forced Daniel to sit through their meetings. Daniel often wondered what Emily could be thinking as the days went by and he hadn't been able to meet her in the woods. He hoped acting as a spy in the enemy camp was the best way he had to protect her.

Autumn blew into the settlement and set the forest ablaze with color. Soon the weather turned to the first hints of winter and still Daniel had been unable to meet with Emily in the woods near his home. He could feel the tension increasing during his uncle's secret meetings, the threats escalating. One night after a particularly loud and vulgar meeting, Gilbert went down hard on a bottle after the men left. Then Daniel's uncle collapsed on his bed in a drunken stupor. It was late, but Daniel couldn't sleep because Gilbert kept mumbling something unintelligible in his drunken stupor. Daniel climbed down the rungs of the ladder from the loft and tip-toed to his uncle's bedside with a flickering candle to see if Gilbert would reveal any future raiding plan secrets. Daniel listened carefully but Gilbert quit mumbling and began snoring.

As Daniel turned, he noticed a letter that had fallen from Gilbert's Bible. As he bent over to pick it up and return it to the book, Daniel noticed the letter was addressed to him. Already opened, the correspondence had been dated several months ago. The letter was from his oldest sister Eliza Jane.

Daniel set the candle down and eagerly read the first paragraph where his oldest sister made reference to the previous letters the family had written him. Daniel was surprised to learn his family had been writing to him regularly and that his uncle had been keeping the letters from him. Daniel had been led to believe he'd never received letters from his family. When he'd asked his uncle about the matter, Gilbert swore none had arrived. Daniel felt his fists tightening as he continued reading.

His eyes froze with the next line, *Daniel dear, mother's long illness has finally taken her. I'm so sorry you and Uncle Gilbert can't make it here for her funeral. Don't worry about us. We all have suitors and will soon wed. The cabin and all father's land is now yours.*

The letter continued but Daniel couldn't bring himself to read further. The last few years with Gilbert had been bearable only because of his visits with Emily and the hope his family would return. Instantly his reasons for staying on with Gilbert vanished. Daniel threw the letter into the fire then quickly climbed the loft to dress and pack. Unexpectedly several foul smelling men burst through the door. Daniel watched from the loft as the men stormed over to the bed where Gilbert slept and shook him awake.

"Done. Won't be any more trouble with the Colton family!"

"Good work," Gilbert answered slurring his words.

"Warned them," the night raider said boastfully. "Wouldn't leave. Burned the house down around them. Gave 'em a chance. Ashes now."

"The other families on the river?" Gilbert asked.

"Either dead or running like chickens," a man with blood smeared on his coat answered. "I got the pretty one."

"Don't tell anyone," Gilbert said as his eyes darted nervously about the room.

"If there's any trouble, you're in it with us, Gilbert," one of the raiders shouted as they charged from the room leaving the house as abruptly as they entered.

"What have you done?" Daniel shouted after he descended the loft and stormed toward Gilbert. "Tell me!" Daniel grabbed Gilbert and shook him. "Why didn't you tell me my mother died?" Gilbert smiled as he slowly raised one eyebrow. "What have you done to the Colton family?"

"Listen to me boy," Gilbert interrupted. "Doesn't matter now. What's done is done. Don't you see, now we have your father's property back. All Mormon property ripe for picking. We're rich men now with Governor Bogg's blessing."

"I don't want stolen property! I don't want to live with you!" Daniel yelled.

"Then sign your father's deed over to me and leave. I don't care where you go or if you live or die. But you owe me," Gilbert answered.

"I'll never sign. This place is my father's dream. You'll never get your hands on it. What did you do to the Colton family?" Daniel insisted.

"Gave them all the warning they deserved. Stubborn father insisted we let them stay on till spring. We told them we'd burn them out if they didn't leave. Was their own fault, boy. Brought it on themselves."

"You'd turn out women and children in the dead of winter. What kind of a man are you?" Daniel said slowly and deliberately. "If you follow me to the ends of the earth, I'll never let you get your hands on this property. Some day you'll get what you deserve."

Daniel grabbed his coat, pack and boots, then ran from the cabin into the cold evening air. He felt the icy biting wind against his face as he sprinted for the forest.

"Get back here!" Gilbert yelled. "You owe me!"

You'll have to kill me first, Daniel thought. *I'll never give you my father's land, even if you hound me till the day I die.*

Coughing and choking back fear and sobs, Daniel raced through the bare forest trees. When he got to the place where Emily's cabin was built, there was nothing left standing but a lone stone chimney stack. Several animals that fled to the woods during the attack were milling about. Daniel walked slowly toward the smoldering ashes. Remembering the secret room, Daniel kicked through the charred remains of a home as he searched for the trap door to the root cellar. His eyes fell on a small hinged half burned door. Daniel saw a small indentation but no room. He figured the underground room must have never been finished.

"Emily!" Daniel wailed as he fell to his knees in the smoldering ashes and dirt, his voice echoing in the cold air. "Why didn't you hide? Why didn't you run? You promised me you'd never leave me." Daniel's hot tears sizzled on the ashes. "Where do I go? What do I do? Oh, dear God, take me away from this place. Let me die too."

Daniel clenched his fists and bit down on his clenched knuckles until they bled. Then he stood and ran like a madman, deeper and deeper into the dark, cold woods. He ran aimlessly until his body collapsed on the forest floor.

CHAPTER FIVE

Emily wrapped the tattered quilt up around her face as her father drove on. Her mother sat in the rear of the wagon trying to sooth a crying baby while her brothers huddled together, whimpering and coughing from the smoke they'd inhaled. As the night wind howled through the bare limbs of dormant trees, Emily's mind raced back to the events of that awful night.

"Can't we go back and get Daniel?" Emily pleaded with her father as they rode through the woods in the family wagon. "His uncle beats him. I don't think his mother's ever coming back or she would have sent word by now."

Philander quietly and stealthily guided the horses through the forest of bare black trees taking his time to respond.

"No, I'm sorry," Philander answered. "Have to leave while they think we're dead so they won't follow us and give us any more trouble. Daniel will have to believe we're dead too. Can't be helped. Going back to find him now would be suicide for him and for us. Try to understand."

"Why do they hate us so much?" Emily asked as her father slowed the horses. "They don't even know us."

"Don't know," Philander said. "Never should have come out here. We've lost everything *again*." Emily had never seen her father so despondent and it frightened her. Then she noticed her father's face suddenly relax as he took a deep breath and sighed. "What we have left will stand through all of this. What we have left, nobody can take away."

"What's that Papa?" Emily asked.

"Our love for each other and our discipleship of Jesus Christ," her father said.

Emily thought back to earlier in the evening. The whole family had been working together in the yard when her father heard horses thundering toward the house. Philander hurried his family inside the cabin and herded them down into the secret room where he had blankets and food stored. Then he dashed back through the door and quickly led the horses hitched to the wagon into a secluded spot surrounded by trees nearby. Philander had been preparing and drilling his family for this possibility and they were ready.

Emily remembered crouching in the underground room barely able to move or breathe as she huddled next to her brothers, baby sister and mother. The night riders shouted obscene curses when they stopped abruptly in front of their cabin.

"Come out now or we'll burn you alive!" a man shouted followed by a string of profanities.

Emily heard several gun shots ricochet through the cabin. She listened as her father shot back into the mob. Dozens of bullets riveted through the windows and burrowed into the floor in response. Philander raised the trap door and quickly jumped inside with the rest of his family as bullets whizzed all around him. Emily recalled the raw fear on her father's face as he jumped into the room, slammed the trap door over their heads and crouched next to her. She remembered the suffocating smell of black smoke and the sound of crackling timber. Emily heard the men cursing and laughing then the sound of breaking glass. Thundering hoofs circled the cabin. The family listened to loud explosions and the roar of giant flames overheard.

Soon the rumbling sound of galloping horses grew fainter and fainter. Then there was quiet. After Emily's father threw back the trap door, the family quickly climbed out and ran from the almost completely destroyed cabin. Standing outside in the yard, the Colton family watched the remainder of their house turn into ashes in front of them. Emily watched as all of her family's possessions, except the supplies her family had stored in the wagon and secret room, were completely destroyed.

Philander quickly wheeled the wagon into the yard and loaded up his family with the provisions he gathered from their hiding place. Just as they were almost ready to leave, Emily remembered seeing her father walk over to the trap door and look down into the exposed ruins of their secret room. He quickly kicked in dirt, ashes and charred logs enough to conceal the place.

"There won't be anything left now," Philander had said as he jumped into the wagon. "When they come back to gloat over their prize, they'll think they've burnt us alive as they intended. They won't follow us or bother us anymore."

Philander turned the frightened horses into the woods and rode from their home in the dead chill of winter with the smell of smoke still lingering in their nostrils. Shivering in the cold winter air, Emily looked up at her father who was driving the horses as fast as he could with only the moon and stars for light.

"Where will we go now?" Emily asked.

"All I know is we'd better leave the state as soon as we can. The governor's issued an extermination order against the Mormons; said we're to be treated as enemies and driven from the state for the public good. When the governor issues a statement like that, people get it into their heads that it's lawful to do whatever they want. There'll be more looting and killing if we don't move quickly and stay away from the settlements."

Emily was confused. She wanted to understand but nothing her father said made her feel any better.

"Why can a governor tell people in this state that it's lawful to kill us?"

"Only Governor Boggs can answer that," Philander answered as he handed Emily his coat.

All of a sudden Emily smelled the same sickening smoke they'd escaped not long before. Long trails of grey haze rose over the trees in front of them. She motioned to her father, who had already noticed and was hurrying the horses in that direction. As they rounded a corner and came to a clearing near the river, Emily heard a gun shot slice through a tree limb above her head.

"Duck!" her father shouted as he jumped from the wagon to get a closer look.

"Leave me alone!" a woman shouted from the direction of the gun shot. "I'll kill you if you come any closer. I have nothing to lose. Leave me alone or I'll blast your bloody head off!"

"Stop!" Philander shouted in return. "We're friends. Hold your fire. We've come to help you. We're the Colton family from up the river."

The woman stood still pointing the gun directly at Philanders heart. Emily's mother handed the baby to Emily as she climbed from the wagon and slowly walked toward the women holding the gun.

"Don't come any closer!" the woman shouted.

"Don't shoot. It's me, Polly."

The woman looked at Emily's mother, saw someone she recognized, dropped the gun and collapsed. Philander found the woman's husband dead in the dirt at the side of the smoldering house. Emily could see a young girl sitting on a rock near the wagon who rocked back and forth whimpering. A small child was crawling in the dirt, screaming. Emily's brothers in the rear of the wagon woke up and crowded around her and the baby in raw fear. The baby screamed and her younger brothers whimpered as Emily tried unsuccessfully to console them.

Emily watched her father leaning over the dead man's body. He knelt down and put his ear on the man's chest then turned to his wife and shook his head. Polly picked up the screaming baby crawling in the dirt. The young girl on the rock continued rocking back and forth whimpering.

When Philander walked over to help the woman who'd dropped the rifle, she shouted, "Don't touch me!" then ran to the dead man. "He's dead. My husband's dead. They've taken everything, even my daughter's innocence. The woman grabbed the sides of her head and wailed, "God, where are you? We should never have come out here." She turned to Philander. "Leave us alone. Go away. Leave us alone. There's nothing you can do for us now. You're too late."

Polly handed Emily another screaming baby to tend while she tried to calm the desperate woman. She wrapped her arms around the frantic widow who cursed the prophet Joseph Smith and Mormonism. Polly held the woman until the fight seemed to melt from her. Then she suddenly fell limp into Polly's arms.

"They ordered us from our house then set it on fire," the woman cried. "Ran off our animals. Thought we were safe. But three men came back. Grabbed my daughter and dragged her into the woods. My husband tried to stop them. They shot him. While he lay dying, they finished their business. Heard her screaming."

Polly held the woman until she grew silent.

"Your daughter needs you. Go to her," Polly said. "She needs your comfort now."

The woman glanced toward the rock where her daughter was rocking. The young girl's dress was torn, her face streaked with mud and blood. When her mother finally walked over and embraced her, the young girl broke into deep tormented sobs.

Polly walked slowly toward her wagon and took the woman's baby back from Emily. Philander began digging a grave near the house. Then all was quiet except for the lonely howling of the wind and the sound of the shovel hitting the frozen earth. Emily had never seen such a sight. She wanted to scream for her mother to hold her and comfort her, but she had to console her baby sister and younger brothers. It was near dawn before Philander finished the grave.

"Won't you go with us?" Polly pleaded as she stood next to the woman and her daughter after Philander had packed what little they had left into the family's wagon. "You won't be safe here. We all have to leave the state now. Brother Joseph will know what to do."

"How can he?" the woman interrupted bitterly. "He can't even help himself. He's locked up in prison on trumped up charges. I have no more to give. My parents live close by. They'll take me and the children back home if I denounce Mormonism. Warned me something like this would happen. Should've listened. My husband was my strength. He's gone. Can't go on without him. You've done enough. They won't bother us any more now. Took everything they wanted. I just want to go home."

As the Colton family wagon pulled away into the woods, Emily looked back at the destitute family riding in the opposite direction in their wagon. She ached all over. Traveling near the densely wooded river for cover, Emily's father would have to hurry now to get beyond the reach of the night raiders.

❦

When Daniel awoke, he found himself alone on the forest floor shaking with cold. As he stood and looked around, he realized he didn't know where he was or where he was going. The air was frigid, his skin numb. He decided to follow the river through the woods. There was no going back now. Then sun unexpectedly broke through the tree tops, instantly warming his shoulders. To Daniel's mind came the gentle words of his father, "Spring will come. You have to be patient and trust God." Yet Daniel felt only betrayal by his father now.

Where are you? Daniel thought despondently. *Where are you when I need you? I'm alone. I'll always be alone.*

Though he tried not to think about it, vivid pictures of Emily's smoldering house flashed through his mind. He remembered the words in the letter from his sister about his mother's death. He saw his uncle's raging face as he tore off his belt. Daniel willed away the tormenting thoughts whirling through his head. He didn't want to remember, think or feel. He had to get away from everything and everyone he knew, start over somewhere. Daniel was determined not to think about or see anything that reminded him of his past.

Everyone I love either leaves or dies, Daniel thought. *Is it worth loving if loving brings so much pain?*

Daniel walked for hours without stopping to rest, eat or drink. He knew enough to stay near the river so he wouldn't get lost. Exhausted, Daniel failed to notice a low hanging bough and smacked his head on the massive tree limb. Before he came to and opened his eyes, Daniel dreamed of Emily—saw her face and shining green eyes, her arms outstretched toward him. Then Daniel saw Deborah weeping and his sister reaching out for him the day they left the farm.

When he opened his eyes, Daniel realized he'd been unconscious, that his dreams were illusions vanishing like the daylight, leaving only a long dark night ahead. A fine blue mist rose around him, then everything went black. Slowly the moon rose over distant hills casting a faint glow over the forest floor. Daniel stood, stretched then recalled his father's survival lessons in the woods near their home when he was a boy. After locating an old fallen tree, he removed loose sawdust in the center with his hands then crawled inside and stuffed the ends with leaves. Breathing though a knot hole above him, Daniel slept restlessly.

At dawn, Daniel resumed his aimless trek, soon losing track of how many days had passed as he hiked upriver. He ate what few frozen berries were left on bare vines and edible roots dug from the cold forest floor. Days came and went in a blur. He hiked until total exhaustion overwhelmed him and his legs gave way beneath him. Daniel noticed trees whirling in a circle above his head as he fell. Later, when he woke, Daniel found himself in a strange room with warm blankets covering him. He heard someone speaking outside a closed wooden door.

"Why do you bring every lost soul here?" a woman's voice behind the door bellowed. "Then you go to work and expect me to take care of 'em."

"Found him in the forest while I was huntin'. Poor lad, half frozen and delirious. What would you have me do, leave him to die? Have a heart, woman. When he gets better, he can pay for his care by workin' in the shop."

"But who is he? What's he doing in the woods? Most likely in trouble with the law. Should've taken him to the authorities. They could lock him up or send him back where ever he belongs," the woman answered.

"Listen to me. I'll do with him as I see best and don't you be running off to no authorities about him. When he's feeling better, can work in the shop with me, learn my trade if he cares to or he can go on his way. Now calm down and fix some supper."

The door creaked open and a man walked in, stepping quietly over to Daniel's bed. Daniel grabbed the quilts and sat up, his eyes flashing with fear.

"Whoa. Don't mean to frighten you. Name's Nathan. Gave me a pretty good scare for a while, you did. Doctor said you had yourself a bad case of the pneumonia. Nearly froze to death. Wager you been in them woods for quite a spell. It's cold out. Lucky to be alive. How you feeling, lad?"

Daniel immediately surmised the stranger seemed kind enough. He was a large middle-aged man with sweaty muscles bulging beneath his hand-sewn shirt. His hair was messed and his dirty face was round and full.

"Don't have to talk now, lad. Just go back to sleep and I'll be back 'fore you know it with somethin' good to eat."

When the man left the room, Daniel tried to crawl out of bed so he could find his clothes, dress and leave. He was afraid to tell the man about his past for fear he'd contact Gilbert. He collapsed onto the floor, too weak to move.

When the man returned shortly, he helped put Daniel back into bed saying, "What you trying to do lad? Fixing to kill yourself? Still sick. Doc said it'll be awhile 'fore you to get feelin' strong again. Don't have to stay here any longer than you please. Look lad, I've brought you a fine supper. Wife's a good cook. Won't you try it?"

"I'm sorry," Daniel said as he reached for the soup. "Don't want to be a burden. Sounds like your wife's not too happy 'bout having me stay here."

"Sorry you had to hear that. Listen, my Anna's been complaining since the day I met her. If you tried to leave here, she'd be the first one packing your fanny back home. She's a whole kitchen full of stray animals down there. Don't pay her no mind. I don't." Daniel smiled; he liked the man. "Name's Nathan. Yours?"

"Daniel, sir. Daniel Webster Jones."

"Fine name, distinguished. I'll call you Danny, if you don't mind. Eat this soup and get some rest. Be back later, laddy."

After Nathan left the room, Daniel hungrily ate the soup. It was the first time he could remember feeling safe and warm for a long time. He wrapped the soft worn quilts around him, slid down into the bedding, and drifted back into sleep. When he woke, he smelled hot bread baking downstairs and the sound of children's voices. It had been a long time since he'd slept in a soft bed, a long time since he'd heard children's voices or smelled something good to eat.

Nathan creaked open the door and peeked into the room. "See you're awake now," he said as he walked into the room and sat on a chair near Daniel's head. "What's your pleasure today lad?"

Daniel smiled. "Nothing. I'm fine. Thanks."

"Thought maybe you be wantin' to let your folks know you're all right. You just tell me where they live," Nathan continued.

Daniel's face clouded as he answered, "My folks are both dead."

"Oh, I'm sorry, son. But surely there's someone who cares to know if you're dead or alive?"

"There's no one," Daniel answered.

"Sorry," Nathan said. "Wandering half frozen in the woods miles from any town. What is it boy? Does it hurt too much?"

Daniel was silent for a long time before he answered, "There's nothing to go back to. No one to send word to. I'm on my own now."

Daniel heard Anna hollering below, "Come and get it or I'll throw it out!"

Nathan moved toward the door promising to be back with something good to eat.

"Nathan?" Daniel asked before he left. "Where am I?"

"St. Louis," Nathan answered. "Where did you think, the moon?"

CHAPTER SIX

The past few months had been a never ending nightmare for Emily. When the Colton family finally stopped running, it was in a place near Quincy. The people in this small town in western Illinois were willing to offer sanctuary to the Mormons fleeing Governor's Boggs extermination order in Missouri. Emily never forgot the words of the order: "The Mormons must be treated as enemies and must be exterminated or driven from the state if necessary for the public peace."

Maybe now that we're out of Missouri things will finally get better, Emily thought, trying to reassure herself and calm her incessant fears.

Emily's father set up a tent near several dugouts. Saints were streaming in from Missouri every day, each with a more horrific mob crime story than the last. Icy wind off the river made her feet and hands feel numb with cold. Corn meal was all the family had to eat. Emily's father and brothers gathered fire wood and unsuccessfully hunted for wild game. In moments when she was alone with her thoughts, Emily thought about Daniel with great penetrating sadness. Sometimes she had flashbacks about the family they'd found the night they'd fled their home in Missouri. She was glad her parents hadn't lost their courage to move on, but still felt a gnawing sense of dread. She hadn't been able to bathe for so long she could hardly stand her own smell. Her stomach cramped constantly with hunger and dysentery. She shook uncontrollably, never feeling thawed out, even in the warmest part of the day. Nights were sleepless torture.

Before many days had passed, Emily's younger sister and mother were down with cholera. Without warning, this dreaded disease struck with severe vomiting, diarrhea and a high fever. Many victims were dead within hours, so Emily was terrified when her mother and sister lapsed into semi-consciousness. Philander immediately isolated and attended to his wife and daughter in the tent so the other family members wouldn't be infected. He insisted Emily and her younger brothers keep their distance and sleep in the wagon under a canvas cover.

Numerous homeless Saints were camped around the Colton family. Soon each wagon, tent or dugout was filled with the sick and dying. The putrid smell of the camp made it hard to breathe. Emily's mother and sister were groaning and delirious most of the time. Emily wanted to be brave, but she felt terrified she might lose everyone she loved and be left alone. She felt like a haggard old woman one moment and a scared child the next. Emily willed herself not to cry around her father and the boys. Her sick mother and little sister needed her courage, not her tears. But late at night with no one to see or hear, she let the tears come in great rolling waves.

One night she woke from a nightmare in a panic. She wrapped a blanket around her, slipped from the canvas covered wagon and trudged through the snow to a grove of trees just as the moon rose from behind the hills.

"Why?" Emily prayed as she gazed at the canopy of stars overhead in the still darkness. "Why so much suffering and death? For what purpose?"

Then she thought about the Prophet Joseph Smith and the woman who'd cursed him that night in the woods as they fled Missouri saying, "He can't help us now. He can't even help himself." Emily glanced down at her hands. Cracked and bleeding, her bloody knuckles soaked into the cloth of her dress, forming large red circles. Emily knew thousands of the Saints fleeing Missouri had streamed into this make-shift camp trying to stay alive until Joseph was set free and could tell them what to do. The prophet kept ongoing correspondence with members of the Church while he languished in a filthy prison on false charges all winter. When Emily listened to Joseph's words written in letters to the members of the Church, she'd felt a penetrating reverence for this visionary man. She was convinced Joseph Smith was indeed a prophet from her own private prayers and study of the Bible and the Book of Mormon. Yet now on this cold winter night camped near Quincy, Emily felt alone and abandoned by God. She'd memorized many of the Prophet's revelations and knew he taught love and forgiveness while she sometimes secretly harbored thoughts of anger and revenge.

"Help me," Emily whispered shivering in the black solitude of winter's night.

Then Emily unexpectedly remembered the words of Joseph Smith in his most recent correspondence from Liberty Jail. She realized even the prophet struggled to find meaning in suffering when he pleaded, "O God, where art thou? And where is the pavilion that covereth thy hiding place? How long shall thy hand be stayed, and thine eye, yea thy pure eye, behold from the eternal heavens the wrongs of thy people and of thy servants, and thine ear be penetrated with their cries?"

Emily also recalled the words of inspiration in reply to Joseph's desperate pleas, "My son, peace be unto thy soul; thine adversity and thine afflictions shall be but a small moment; and then, if thou endure it well, God shall exalt thee on high; thou shalt triumph over all thy foes . . . How long can rolling waters remain impure? What power shall stay the heavens? As well might man stretch forth his puny arm to stop the Missouri river in its decreed course, or to turn it up stream, as to hinder the Almighty from pouring down knowledge from heaven upon the heads of the Latter-day Saints."

Emily recalled seeing her father weep as he read this moving revelation to the family. She'd memorized much of Joseph's correspondence and it had sustained her, until this night. Now the cruelty of men was the only thing that was real. She wanted to curse the mobbers who had done this to her family, give up and die, but she couldn't. Something deep inside her kept the words of Joseph's revelation flowing into her mind, "Let thy bowels also be full of charity towards all men, and to the household of faith, and let virtue garnish thy thoughts unceasingly; then shall thy confidence wax strong in the presence of God; and the doctrine of the priesthood shall distil upon thy soul as the dews from heaven. The Holy Ghost shall be thy constant companion, and thy scepter an unchanging scepter of righteousness and truth; and thy dominion shall be an everlasting dominion, and without compulsory means it shall flow unto thee forever and ever."

Emily knew that of the twelve thousand Saints scattered along the river near the town of Quincy, many were in much worse shape than her family. Fresh graves were dug every morning. Yet that night in quiet despair and utter loneliness, she wanted personal answers. In the solitude of desperation, Emily prayed to know if God was aware of what was happening to *her*—if Jesus Christ really would comfort her as one who had felt her pain.

She recalled the last words of Joseph's revelation, "If the very jaws of hell shall gape open the mouth wide after thee, know thou, my son, that all these things shall give thee experience, and shall be for thy good. The Son of Man hath descended below them all. Art thou greater than he? . . . Therefore, fear not what man can do, for God shall be with you forever and ever."

"Oh, dear God, stay with me," Emily prayed. "Give me the strength to survive one more night."

All at once, her trembling stopped. She looked up. Catching her breath, she gazed at the vastness of the heavens. She located the unchanging North Star in the moving sea of black shadows. She realized the constant polar star was always there, yet only in darkness was the light revealed. Then she understood. Emily felt a burning bush blazing inside her, firing the soft clay of her soul into a finely glazed vessel of God's design. She knew she was in God's hands. Her people were not alone. She was not alone. Renewed and endowed with pure knowledge and power, she returned to the wagon inwardly changed, ready to accept and endure well whatever life had in store for her. She knew whatever didn't kill her would only make her stronger.

Weeks later when the earliest signs of spring finally appeared and her mother and sister had almost totally recovered, Emily knelt and caressed the first green blade of grass breaking through the cold crusted snow and gently kissed the tender leaves. The eloquent rebirth in nature filled her with renewed hope. She knew she could never again walk sightless in a world of miracles. She was filled with overwhelming awe at God's tender mercies and gentle tutoring.

In April, Emily was surprised to hear that the Prophet Joseph Smith and those with him in Liberty Jail were allowed to escape. The guards let them purchase horses and pretended to be sleeping as Joseph and his companions rode away. Though a beaten, penniless fugitive, Joseph Smith was soon able to rouse the sleeping courage of his destitute people. Even the sickest seemed to revive when news of the prophet's escape and his miraculous healings of many Saints spread through camp. Finally the chill of winter and the cloud of eminent death lifted. Emily felt the hope of a new life ahead.

The Prophet went from tent to dugout, blessing the sick and encouraging and uplifting the Saints with words of comfort and healing. Emily watched Joseph place his loving hands on her mother and sister's head along side her father and witnessed first hand the promised miraculous healings she'd heard from others in camp. Energized warmth filled her from the top of her head to the souls of her feet. She knew, with no room for doubting, that Joseph Smith was indeed a prophet. She would never forget his power to lead, love, heal, and bless.

It wasn't many days before Emily heard Joseph had purchased some swamp land about sixty miles north of Quincy with some promissory notes because neither he nor any other church members had any money. The owners of the bad land were glad to get a note for its purchase for no one else wanted it. Joseph prophesied the Saints they'd make this swamp-land, known as Commerce, into a beautiful city called Nauvoo. The place was covered with thick underbrush and a few scattered trees. The muddy water of the Mississippi surrounded the area on three sides like a horseshoe. Only half a dozen small stone or log homes occupied the deserted place.

Everyone in camp, even the sickest, seemed to get better each day after the Prophet's visionary announcement. Now there was somewhere to go, something to do and something to work for again. Though despised and unwanted everywhere, the Saints had followed their prophet for nine difficult years. They were glad to leave this miserable encampment of dugouts and tents with little shelter but the wide open sky. As Emily helped her father pack the wagon to move on, she heard singing. Everyone in camp had been stripped of almost every earthly possession, yet they had the faith and courage to move on once again.

I wonder if a Zion people were more important to God than a Zion place, Emily thought.

She realized God must be preparing people who were willing to sacrifice everything, even their own lives if necessary, to help His sons and daughters become like Him. Emily knew only those who would remain true to their testimonies of Jesus Christ and the restored gospel would be up to the task that lay ahead.

With springtime in the air and the prophet free, everyone in the destitute camps quickly developed new energy and purpose. Within a few days, Emily's family reached the place Joseph called Nauvoo the beautiful. Emily felt sick when she saw the place. The whole region was infested with mosquitoes. She noticed a few old shacks where earlier settlers had built their homes and later abandoned them because the environment was too harsh. The land was so wet a wagon couldn't be pulled through. It was a struggle even to walk in the region on foot. As they moved into the area, each family was allotted land according to their needs.

The mosquitoes were so thick Emily's eyes soon became swollen shut, making it difficult for her to see. The Saints' new eagerness soon dissolved as malaria spread like wild fire through the thousands of people streaming into this swamp land. Emily, and her fellow Saints, had not expected another trial so soon. Still weak from previous illnesses and living on poor rations, they were left with little resistance to fight the new disease. Within days, Emily's whole family was taken sick. As Emily lay in their wagon, she felt fever race through her body like a flood of fire and ice. One moment she feared she'd be consumed by heat and the next she'd be chilled to the bone. She had no idea whether it was day or night. She heard her family restlessly tossing around her in agony, their groans and cries were no more heeded than her own.

PART II

CHAPTER SEVEN

Days passed quickly in the upper room of Nathan's house. Daniel felt himself gradually gaining new strength. Every morning Anna brought up clean water in a china basin and threatened to wash him. Blushing, Daniel would shoo her from the room and proceed to wash himself. From the upstairs bedroom window, Daniel could look down on the bustling town below.

So this is St. Louis, Daniel thought as he eyed the busy streets lined with ladies in fine dresses and men in black coats and hats.

Nathan had earlier informed Daniel that the city's population numbered around five thousand when he and Anna arrived back in 1822 but had grown to three times that now. This busy riverfront city served as a main port for steamboats traveling on the Mississippi River. Daniel enjoyed watching the town folk pass beneath his bedroom window dressed in fine clothes, accompanied by crisp clean maids donning white hats and aprons, or drivers dressed in shiny black finery.

From his bed, Daniel could hear the brawny bare-chested men down at the docks singing and cursing from sunup to sundown. Wet breezes off the river filled the small bedroom with a humid musty scent. Dozens of stray dogs barked at and chased alley cats while merchants called attention to their cartloads of goods to sell. Daniel listened to the clattering of wheels and hoofs on the cobblestone road. He'd never before seen or heard so many people in one place. Looking out the window at his new world made Daniel feel both excited and frightened. He wasn't accustomed to city life or large crowds.

Each day after work, Nathan came to the bedroom and sat next to the window with Daniel as he slowly recovered his strength. They enjoyed watching the steamboats traveling up and down the Mississippi, then dock and unload their goods. Daniel's favorite building in town was a magnificent cathedral in the square. He's never seen a building on such a grand scale.

Daniel noticed a slave auction held down at the block once a week. He watched as dark skinned men, women and children in heavy leg irons were torn from each other's embraces, then lined up on the block like cattle for inspection. Men with long whips lashed any who showed defiance or resisted attempts at total control. The harsh treatment of the auctioneers made Daniel remember the whippings he'd received by his uncle. He watched in horror as several men and women had their tattered clothing ripped off for further inspection of their naked bodies by interested bidders. He lowered his eyes, mortified and embarrassed by the barbaric treatment.

For the first time in his life, Daniel realized Deborah was probably bought and sold the same way and wondered if she too had been treated in such a humiliating manner. Then he wondered if she'd been separated from her natural family, if she had a husband or children of her own. Daniel had never before imagined Deborah was considered a piece of merchandise offered to the highest bidder. Instead he thought of her as a great aunt or some other member of the family. Now Daniel realized his own grandparents had been bidders at a slave auction, his parents slave holders. Recent beatings by his uncle and mob violence in Missouri had given him a new sensitivity and revulsion for human brutality.

That could be Deborah down there, Daniel thought. *I'll never be part of such cruel treatment of a human being again. Never. Deborah, please forgive me.*

"It's wrong to buy or sell human beings," Daniel blurted one day just as Nathan walked into the bedroom."

Nathan was surprised. Daniel was usually a man of few words.

"Way things are, my boy," Nathan answered shaking his head. "Always been, always will. Tis mighty hard changin'. Hear Mormons feel the same way; their holy book made from gold plates says all men, white, black, bond, free are alike to God. Some folks say Mormons goin' to bring on an uprising . . . tellin' slaves and Indians they'll rise up to their rightful place of glory in the Promised Land."

"Maybe the Mormons are right. Ever thought of that?" Daniel asked.

"No," Nathan answered befuddled by the question. "Thinkin' that way only makes for trouble."

Nathan seemed more worried about the large groups of German and Irish workers pouring into the city than the Indians or slaves. Skilled European emigrants threatened his livelihood. Things were growing and changing too fast in St. Louis, in Nathan's estimation, and it worried him.

"Been living here longer than most," Nathan said. "Life is too hard in the old country. Folks come over here looking for new land, new hope. Whole families get inflicted with the wander lust. Pack up everything they own and sell the rest. Come here or move out West. Don't know where they're going, but they're going to get there first."

"What you suppose they're looking for? Where they all going?" Daniel asked.

"Can't say I do, lad," Nathan answered. "Most likely they're off to a new life, new chance. In this country, if a man's willing to work, he can own land, make a better life for his family than he's had for himself. Not like the old country."

"Feelin' good enough to pay you back for my board and keep," Daniel said.

"You sure lad?"

"Told you I've been ready for a long time, but you've kept me locked up here in this room till I'm plum crazy," Daniel answered.

Nathan looked patiently at Daniel and smiled. He'd never had a son of his own and had enjoyed Daniel's presence immensely.

"Been good to have your company, Danny. Be glad to have your help in my wee shop. You be living with the best saddle maker in town, even if I do say so myself."

"Well, I'm the best apprentice to the best saddle maker in town," Daniel answered.

"All our lasses take their lessons down at the rector's school. Be enjoying a bit of company. 'Spect ye be too old for school, bein' the grand old age of sixteen now."

Daniel nodded. Nathan's saddle shop was attached to the front portion of the house and faced the street. Daniel loved watching the busy town people pass by the shop as he helped Nathan work with the tanned leather. Nathan stopped questioning Daniel about his past and told his family to do the same. When people asked, Nathan said Daniel was his nephew. Nathan was pleased with Daniel's work and often wondered if he had apprenticed in a saddle shop before.

A wealthy man by the name of Mr. Decker often came to the shop to buy things for his rich patrons. He was the owner of the livery stable, among other establishments around town, and often brought his young daughter along on his business errands. Daniel thought it strange his daughter was always dressed so elaborately when her father wore the same gray clothes smelling of sweat and manure day after day. Nathan called Mr. Decker a self-made man, a first generation man of means. Mr. Decker's daughter's name was Catherine and she always looked at Daniel in a condescending yet flirtatious way. She would position herself in a self-conscious alluring pose next to the table where Daniel worked, but she never said anything him. Daniel pretended not to notice.

One morning, after trying for an extra long time to look especially attractive and get Daniel to speak to her, she exasperatedly said, "Well, who do you think you are? You're just an apprentice, you know, and haven't the manners of a stable boy. Suppose you don't know a real lady even when you see one!"

Shocked, Daniel looked up and into Catherine's eyes. He hated to admit it, but she was lovely. Yellow hair curled around her face tucked under a satin bonnet with ribbons and lace. Her flashing cold blue eyes left Daniel at a loss for words.

"I'll know a lady when I see one," Daniel blurted as she turned to leave.

Wheeling her full hoop skirt around and pounding her foot on the floor, Catherine shouted for her father, stormed through the door and fled down the street. Mr. Decker and Nathan were talking and laughing in the rear of the shop.

"Guess I best be getting along, Nathan," Mr. Decker chuckled as he turned to leave. "I don't know why that girl's in such a hurry. Always asking me to take her along when I come here. Never understood Cati or her mother. Like to have a son like that nephew of yours. A son gives a man a legacy."

"What happened with you two?" Nathan asked as he walked toward Daniel after Mr. Decker left the shop.

"Don't know what she was so mad about," Daniel answered. "Never even spoken to her and then she tells me I'm no gentleman and I wouldn't know a lady if I saw one. I simply told her I would know if I ever saw one," Daniel answered.

"That's the trouble, Danny. You haven't spoken to her. Cati considers herself to be quite a beauty, you know. I remember when she was a fat baby bouncin' on her father's knee in the stable with horse droppings and flies in her hair." Nathan laughed then placed his big hands on Daniel's shoulders and continued, "Don't you know she's been trying to catch your eye for weeks now?"

"Funny way of doing it. Looking high and mighty, acting like she's too good for her own father. I don't think she's a lady. Just wants me to speak to her so she can go home and laugh about my awkwardness. She can have her fancy dresses, but that won't make her a lady to me."

Just then Anna called for them to stop their chattering and come for dinner. Daniel relished eating his meals during the workday with Anna and Nathan. Anna's red face was always scrubbed as clean as her kitchen. Yet even surrounded by his new friends, Daniel constantly worried Gilbert would come looking for him, then try to force him to sign the deed over to his father's property. He often pictured his sisters prancing in and out of fine shops with their new husbands and hoped their lives were as easy as Catherine Decker's. He thought about Emily every day and dreamed about her often when he slept.

"Who's Emily?" Anna asked handing Daniel his meal. "Heard you calling out her name last night in your sleep."

"Doesn't matter," Daniel answered. "She's dead."

"I'm sorry, lad," Anna said shaking her head. She worried about Daniel and remained curious about his past. Nathan had made her promise not to pry.

St. Louis was an exhilarating place. Often in the late afternoon when they weren't busy, Daniel and Nathan left the saddle shop and explored the bustling river port city together. Daniel relished watching the steamboats coming around the bend of the Mississippi as he sat on the dock and watched the everyday drama of river life. The coarse language of the dock workers punctuated the damp air as Daniel watched the boats load and unload. It was a different life than he'd known, but he was glad of it.

At home in the evenings, Nathan's girls told him stories about Kit Carson and Col. Copper. Daniel saw Kit Carson himself several times in town. He was always followed by several eager young boys. His hair curled around his ears and his small eyes peered sternly over his bushy mustache. Daniel loved listening to his wild tales of adventure, but stayed in the saddle shop and kept to himself most of the time. He felt at home with Nathan and Anna and their girls, but inwardly restless. Sometimes he'd go for long walks in the evening to get his mind off Emily and his family.

Mr. Decker, the man who owned the livery stable, still came to the shop to visit with Nathan, but his daughter Catherine now stayed outside the shop when she accompanied him. Daniel tried to look busy when she was there, acting as if he didn't notice her presence. Catherine stood outside the shop appearing aloof and only occasionally glanced inside. Mr. Decker offered Daniel the use of any of his horses, but Daniel always refused, afraid he might have to talk to Catherine. One pleasant summer day, Mr. Decker was unusually convincing and Daniel consented to try out one of his best steeds. Daniel could still remember the feeling of freedom he had when he rode his favorite horse before his father died. Daniel still remembered placing his face against the horse's warm neck and giving the animal free reign to gallop at will. He longed for that feeling again, so he accompanied Mr. Decker to the horse barns that afternoon.

Catherine was in the stable brushing one of the riding ponies when they entered, making Daniel wonder if her father had arranged this chance meeting. Catherine wore a form-fitting leather riding jacket, skirt and boots. Her yellow hair was brushed up under a stylish riding hat. She stopped brushing the animal abruptly when Daniel entered and stared at him with her cold blue eyes.

"Daniel," Mr. Decker said, "Got my favorite saddled up and ready to go. There she is, boy. She's all yours. Looks like Catherine might be ready to take a ride too."

"He needn't accompany me, father," Catherine said from the corner of the stable. "I'll be perfectly all right by myself."

Daniel thanked Mr. Decker for the horse, mounted, and gave the horse a nudge in the ribs. He patted the horse on the neck and guided the animal outside the stable. Purposely refusing to look behind him, Daniel heard Catherine getting ready to leave. He gave the horse a sharp kick. Catherine followed. Daniel raced his steed quickly out of town with Catherine close behind him all the way. Finally reaching some trees by the river, Daniel slowed the horse and dismounted. Catherine stopped her horse a short distance behind him and also dismounted. Daniel pretended he hadn't noticed her and took the horse by the reins to a grassy spot in the pasture to let the animal graze. Catherine slowly followed.

"Oh, you're impossible!" Catherine shouted when she approached. "I didn't really mean it. You can ride with me if you want."

"Well, I don't," Daniel answered.

"Why are you so pig-headed?" Catherine huffed. "I know you like me. You're just trying to be smart. I've seen the way your face turns red when you look at me."

Daniel stared at Catherine standing in the pasture still flushed from the ride. She was even more stunning than usual. He could feel his face turning red again.

"You see," Catherine chided, "you're doing it again. Can't help yourself." She placed her hands on her hips. "Do you like my outfit?"

The leather fit tightly to her skin and Daniel liked the way her body filled the tanned leather with soft curves. Catherine walked closer and dropped the reins of the horse. Daniel could feel his heart race.

"Suppose you think you're a fine lady now with all your expensive clothes and fine things," Daniel said nervously. Embarrassed, Daniel removed his eyes from Catherine's body and lowered them to the ground. "Clothes don't make you a lady."

"Did think I could get at least one decent word out of you," Catherine interrupted. "You have your mind all made up about me, don't you? Shouldn't judge me without knowing me. If pride's what you're worried about, I'd suggest a closer look at yourself."

Daniel looked up at Catherine again as she turned to leave. Her eyes seemed softer somehow and sad.

"Didn't mean to be so rude," Daniel said trying to stop her from going. "I do like the way you look. Seems like you're trying to be something you're not."

"Well how do you know if you haven't taken the time to find out what I'm really like?" Catherine asked. "You don't seem so eager to reveal yourself, either. I've noticed you. You're different than the other boys in town. Like your own company. Seem older. Who are you anyway? I know you're not Nathan's nephew."

Daniel didn't know how much of his past he could reveal without leaving himself open to further beatings from his uncle.

"No business of yours," Daniel answered.

"I swear, Daniel Webster, you're the most difficult boy I've ever met. Why do you lock yourself up inside of there?" Catherine asked as she reached over and touched Daniel's chest.

Daniel caught her hand and held it for a moment.

"Why should you care? Who am I to you?" he asked as he quickly removed her fingers from his grip.

"Well I don't know if you mean something to me. You make me curious, I guess. If you don't want to talk, could we at least ride home together?" Daniel nodded in agreement. "I've never had to do the asking before," Catherine said as she walked back toward her horse. "All the boys in town would love to take me anywhere I'd like to go."

Daniel smiled and followed. Before he knew it, Mr. Decker had given him the horse as a gift and he was accompanying Catherine on a daily ride. As the summer turned into fall, Daniel looked forward to their outings. Each time he felt freer to speak and wondered if he might have misjudged her. Even with all her boasting of friends, she still seemed starved for his companionship. Daniel felt proud to be seen with her because she turned the heads of all the other young men in town. It was nearly Christmas time when Catherine invited Daniel to her home for a party after telling him it would do him good.

"You need to get to know the other young people in town," Catherine said. "Keep entirely too much to yourself. This should be a good introduction. Believe I've invited the whole town!"

Daniel felt awkward in large crowds and wouldn't have gone if Anna and Nathan hadn't bought him a new suit and a pair of boots after hearing about the party. Anna made Daniel practice dancing with her so he wouldn't embarrass himself. The suit fit just right but the boots were a bit too small, especially for dancing. Daniel decided he wouldn't venture out on the dance floor.

As Daniel walked through the door to Catherine's house the evening of the party, he could feel himself sweating and blushing. He wanted to turn around and dash back out, but Catherine ran from her chattering friends just as he was about to leave.

"Come right in here, Daniel," she said.

Catherine proceeded to introduce him to almost everyone present. Moments later, she was swept away by two young men with pale white faces. Daniel found a quiet corner and sat down where he thought no one would notice him. His new boots were pinching him so he quickly pulled them off his feet and kicked them under the chair. Several young men at the party sauntered over to Daniel then stood in front of him with condescending looks on their faces.

"Well, saddle boy, don't you look like a gentleman tonight," one of them jeered.

Daniel stood, towering over the three other young men. One of the young men stepped forward and shoved Daniel back into his chair.

"If you want to fight me then step outside," Daniel said calmly standing and squaring his shoulders. "Don't have to ruin Catherine's party."

"Fine," one of the young men said as they all stepped outside into the cold winter air on the terrace.

Two of the young men abruptly grabbed Daniel's arms while the other one slugged him in the face. Then all three young men shoved Daniel to the ground. Before he stood, Daniel tore off his new coat and took a deep cleansing breath. Then he flew into the three young men like a raging bull.

He bloodied one nose, cracked two teeth and sent the third one flying into a railing. Then Daniel calmly picked up his coat, dusted it off and walked back inside to locate his boots. Just as he was about to leave the party, Catherine caught him by the arm and hurried him into a small room by the hallway.

"What happened to you?" she questioned looking at his face and his soiled coat.

"Nothing," Daniel said as he turned to the wall. "I don't feel comfortable here. Rather go home. I'm all wrong in these new clothes and wouldn't have come if Nathan and Anna hadn't taken so much pride in buying them for me. Your friends don't want me here. Don't know how to dance and I can't abide another minute in these boots."

"Well, take them off," Catherine protested. "Come with me. You and I will have our first dancing lesson right now."

After Daniel slipped off his boots, Catherine pushed him from the small room, down the hallway and onto the dance floor. Once in the center of the room, she gently curtsied and Daniel bowed.

"Well, don't you take the cake," Daniel whispered in Catherine's ear as their faces brushed against each other. "Look at you dancing with a barefoot misfit who doesn't know his right foot from his left. Ruin your reputation for sure."

In a few moments, Daniel relaxed his arms around Catherine's waist and listened closely to the music. Most of the other couples were laughing and whispering at them. Three roughed up and bloody young men staggered in from outside on the terrace and left Catherine's house through the front door.

"Well," Catherine said when she noticed them, "you certainly made the three of them look much worse than you. Must've been a pretty good fight. Sorry I missed it."

Daniel and Catherine whirled around the floor until the music stopped and most of the guests had left. Catherine persuaded Daniel to stay for a while. When they were alone, Catherine took a close look at Daniel and laughed.

"Don't you look a sight," Catherine said. "I don't know what I've ever seen in you, Daniel Webster. She threw her arms around him and kissed him softly on the cheek. "Thank you for coming," Catherine finished as she reached for his hand. "It would surely have been the dullest party in the history of St. Louis if you hadn't showed up."

Catherine and Daniel sat down together on a cushioned chair in the hallway. Catherine took the combs from her hair and let her golden curls cascade down her back. Daniel looked uncomfortable and said something about leaving.

"Let's go for a ride," Catherine insisted as she pulled Daniel to his feet.

They both ran to the stable and saddled up two horses. After riding in the moonlight for half an hour, they finally stopped in a secluded place next to the river. The air was cold and they could see their breath like smoke billowing between them as they spoke. Daniel took Catherine's hand and guided her to the river bank.

"You'll never be mine, will you?" Catherine asked sadly as she looked longingly into Daniel's eyes. "Who or what is it that comes between us?"

Daniel was silent for a long time before he answered, "I'm sorry." Catherine's eyes filled with tears. "It was a long time ago, before I met you. I knew a girl. I've tried to forget her, but I can't. I don't think I'll ever feel that way again."

Catherine lowered her face. "Tried my best to make you forget."

"I know," Daniel answered. "But you have your pick of all the young men in town. Don't waste your time on me."

"I can't see you any more," Catherine said unexpectedly as she turned to leave.

Daniel watched silently as Catherine quickly mounted her horse and rode back toward town alone. He wondered if he'd made a mistake. He mounted his horse and rode back to town alone hoping Nathan and Anna wouldn't be waiting up for him.

CHAPTER EIGHT

Emily couldn't hold still with all the excitement and anticipation she felt mixing inside. It was New Year's Eve and she was going to the Mansion House for a dance with Jacob Ford, the most eligible bachelor in Nauvoo.

"How do I look?" Emily asked as she twirled in front of her mother.

"You look beautiful, Emily," Polly answered as she smiled at her daughter, wondering when she had grown into such a beautiful young woman.

Emily's dark brown hair was swept up to the crown of her head with pearled combs. A cascade of ringlet curls fell gracefully down onto her delicate white shoulders. The double tiered blue velvet dress and jeweled slippers she wore were borrowed from Jacob's mother. The pearled combs, dress and slippers were the first party clothing Emily had ever worn. The dome shaped skirt flowed over a chemise, long drawers, corset, flannel under petticoat, and three white starched over petticoats with stiffly starched flounces. The fullness of the skirt at the hips accentuated Emily's small waistline and the velvet dance slippers sparkled on her tiny feet.

In the few short years since the Colton family moved to Nauvoo, Polly watched her oldest child grow into a strikingly beautiful young woman. As she spied Emily primping, Polly recalled seeing her daughter up to her knees in mud, draining the murky water off the swampy pasture. The whole family witnessed a piece of undesirable land transformed into a pleasant and bustling community just as the Prophet had foretold. Hundreds of homes and shops had been built on this gentle bend in the Mississippi, making Nauvoo the largest and most prosperous city in the state.

Polly remembered with tenderness the long, grueling days and sleepless nights when Emily cared for the family while both she and Philander were ill. Emily had seen too much of suffering, loss, and pain to remain a child. Emily, Robert, and Philander had spent months turning the Colton family's private piece of land into a productive farm. While Polly was busy with the younger children, Emily helped in the fields or assisted new emigrant families who'd just arrived from Europe. It saddened Polly to see her small-framed, delicate daughter often called on to do the work of a strong young man. Yet Emily had developed an inner strength and maturity because of those demands. Now as Emily prepared to leave for a dance, it warmed Polly's heart to see her daughter off for a few moments of gaiety and fun at the Mansion House. She wiped a tear from her eye.

"Mama, don't cry," Emily said. "This is the happiest day I can remember for so long. There's only one thing that could make it perfect. Daniel—if he were taking me to the dance."

"You shouldn't think about that boy so much," Polly said. "I don't think your paths will ever cross again."

"He's not a boy anymore. We've both grown up now," Emily answered.

Polly had listened to her daughter speak of Daniel every day for so long that she worried it wasn't healthy. She felt it best Emily give up hope for the boy from Missouri.

"Why doesn't he answer my letters, Mama?" Emily asked. "Sometimes I think it's because his uncle won't allow it. Then I wonder if he doesn't answer because he thinks it will cause us some trouble."

"Emily, forget about Daniel, at least for tonight," her mother chided. "You're going to the dance with Jacob."

"I'm so nervous. I hardly know how to act like a lady."

"Emily, dear, you *are* a lady, a real princess," Polly answered. "Being a princess has more to do with who you are on the inside than what you look like on the outside. Trust me. You're royalty my dear."

"I hope Papa and I've practiced enough so I won't tromp on poor old Jacob's feet too much. Just think, Mama, the Prophet Joseph and his wife Emma will be the hosts. Lots of important people will be there." As

Emily spoke, a knock came at the door. Emily's heart skipped a beat. She ran for the bedroom to grab her cape. "Mama, invite him in and don't let the boys tease him. Tell Papa not to stare. I'll be there in a minute."

Before she left the bedroom to greet Jacob, Emily looked into the mirror at herself one more time. She'd never had her hair swept up to her crown. The new style set off her high cheek bones and long graceful neck. As she turned to the side and followed the satin piping on the dress, Emily noticed the way her body filled out the velvet bodice in smooth graceful lines. She blushed.

Wonder what Daniel would say if he could see me now, Emily thought as she smiled and stepped from the bedroom door to greet her escort.

When she entered the room where Jacob was waiting, Emily's date sat upright in his chair, adjusted his suit coat buttons, and turned cherry red. Emily blushed and nodded.

"Ready?" Emily said with a smile.

Jacob shook his head, staring and speechless. He couldn't take his eyes off her.

"Have a good time," Polly said as she ushered the young couple through the front door. Emily's brothers followed behind the twosome laughing and whispering as Philander and Polly stood in the doorway with their arms around each other.

"You look stunning," Jacob said as Emily took his arm and they walked together down the street toward the Mansion House.

"Thank you, Jacob," Emily said soaking in the magic of the moment.

When they reached the Mansion House, Emily raised her full skirt and walked through the white picket fence surrounding the three-story frame building. It was a beautiful house with twenty-two rooms. The prophet's family lived there, as well as several strangers who were visiting the now famous city. Tonight the whole house was ablaze with light and music. When they walked through the front door, Emily felt as if she were walking into a dream.

Joseph and Emma were standing just inside the door to greet the guests as they entered. Emily loved being in the prophet's presence. He was an athletic man who always seemed full of life and vigor. His eyes flashed with warmth and he commanded interest and attention wherever he went. Emily especially enjoyed Sunday mornings in the grove by the temple site where Joseph preached. Joseph's wife Emma was a beautiful dark haired woman well-known for her compassionate service. Her greeting was soft and polite as she ushered Jacob and Emily into the room with a live string ensemble. There was a long table at the end of the room heaped with food and drink. Emily watched as other happy couples whirled around the room in perfect step to a captivating waltz. Though unsure of her dancing ability, she felt eager to try.

Jacob helped Emily remove her wrap then led her out onto the dance floor. She curtsied and Jacob bowed. String quartet music filled the room with romance and lighted candles brightened every corner as Emily and Thomas glided across the dance floor. Emily felt Jacob's strong arm around her waist and his soft grey eyes constantly upon her. Jacob Ford had joined the church in London with his mother and father and they'd soon sailed across the Atlantic to be with their fellow Saints in Nauvoo. They'd met several months ago when Emily was helping Jacob's family secure a place to live. Later, when the Ford family became ill, Emily stayed with them and nursed them all back to health. Jacob was quiet and often appeared deep in thought. Emily liked his shyness along with his British accent and gentlemanly manners. After they left the dance floor to catch their breath, Jacob and Emily sat together on a bench near the wall for a rest.

"How did you learn to dance so well?" Jacob asked, taking Emily's hand.

"Been practicing with my father," Emily answered. "Tonight's so different from what I'm used to. It feels like a dream. Let's dance some more."

Emily pulled Jacob toward the dance floor. Hours passed in what seemed like moments. When the evening ended, Emily and Jacob were the last couple to leave.

As they walked home in the chilled winter starlight, Jacob turned to Emily and said, "My family and I appreciate everything you've done for us. But that's not why I took you tonight. Ever since I first saw you, I can't get you out of my thoughts."

"Don't . . ." Emily interrupted.

"But I want to," Jacob said. "Please let me go on. I just need to say this. Emily I think you're the most noble, compassionate, beautiful person I've ever known. I want to see you often, if you can abide my company."

Emily smiled softly and answered, "Jacob, I enjoy your company, but I can't promise anything. I don't want to hurt you. Wouldn't have that for the world."

"I'll not request promises, then, but would you see me sometimes?"

"I'd like that Jacob," Emily answered as she walked up the path to her house. "Thank you for a beautiful evening."

As Emily slipped into the house, she found her mother and father waiting up for her in the rocking chairs near the fire. Jacob stood at the door gazing up into the moon for a moment before he left for home.

"I had the most wonderful time!" Emily exclaimed as she danced into the room.

"And Jacob," Philander asked, "was he a gentleman?"

"Of course," Emily answered. "I think he likes me, but it scares me a little. I don't want to hurt him." Polly followed her daughter into her bedroom to undress. "I can't forget Daniel," Emily continued as her mother helped her undo the hook and eyes of her dress. "Even tonight, I was imagining Daniel was there with me instead of Jacob. I think I'll always love him."

"Give yourself time, Emily," Polly said. "Maybe seeing more of Jacob will help."

෴

Both Nathan and Anna sensed Daniel's growing restlessness. Work at the saddle shop was becoming tedious. To avoid a chanced meeting with Catherine, Daniel spent more and more time working, but had been itching to take a trip somewhere.

"Take the day off, Daniel," Anna said one morning at breakfast, "Get!"

"I'll git when I'm good and ready," Daniel answered.

Daniel had noticed reports in the local newspaper about the new

Mormon city called Nauvoo up river from St. Louis. Previously, most of the rumors about Mormons were scandalous, so he never brought up the subject on his own. Now, surprisingly, much of the talk about Nauvoo had become favorable. According to the latest gossip, a mosquito infested swamp had been turned into a prospering city. Daniel wished Emily had lived to enjoy it. Daniel read every bit of written material he could get his hands on about Nauvoo and the untamed West. Every day large groups of emigrants left St. Louis for the unsettled lands beyond the borders of the United States. Those returning always brought back exhilarating stories about Indians and landscapes that ignited Daniel's imagination, stirring his mind to dreams of someday traveling west himself.

"What you reading, lad?" Nathan asked Daniel as he finished his morning meal.

"Wild West tales," Daniel answered. "I think these stories have been retold so often they've turned into tall tales. Still, it's exciting, Nathan. Wouldn't you like to go west some day? Get your own spread?"

"If you need to strike out on your own, lad, you have my blessing. You paid us off long ago for any help we gave you, and you've been more than kind to me and my Anna."

"Trying to make me leave?" Daniel laughed. "Maybe I don't want to."

"Oh, Danny boy, you know I don't mean that. You're my partner now. Can take in half our earnings if you choose to stay. Get your own place, your own wife. Anna and me seen that wanderin' look in your eye. Wish you and Catherine would reconsider. Lovely lass was good for you, not near so gloomy with her pretty face around."

"It was her choosing," Daniel answered.

"Still grieving something in your past, lad?" Nathan asked. "Why don't you be telling me about it."

Daniel turned to Nathan and saw the fatherly look of concern he'd so missed since his father's death.

"My mother and father are dead," Daniel answered. "Guess that makes me an orphan. They were good folks, like you and Anna. Father died when I was young. Then my mother got sick. Had to go away with my sisters and leave me to care for the farm. Then she died. My sisters are

grown and most likely have families of their own by now. I haven't any
family to go back to."

"You've got me and Anna," Nathan said.

"And there was this girl," Daniel continued.

"Aye," Nathan smiled. "Been thinkin' something more is tugging at
your heart."

"She was a Mormon. Missouri mobbers killed her and her family.
Should have figured out a way to warn her or stop the men who did it.
But I didn't. She's dead now and nothing can change that. Cared for her
more than anybody I've ever known. Maybe real love only comes once."

"But if she's dead, you can't spend the rest of your life mourning a
ghost Danny."

"Want to stay, want to go," Daniel answered. "You've been so good
to me. But this is your life. Need to find my own way, far away from here.
I have an uncle. I'm certain he'll come looking for me someday. He wants
my father's land—obsessed with it."

Nathan looked with fatherly pride at Daniel as he spoke. In the years
he'd been living there, Daniel had grown into a strikingly handsome
young man, blond and bronze, tall and lean. Nathan wanted him to stay
but knew Daniel had to decide for himself.

"Be understandin' every man needs to find his own way," Nathan
answered.

That night as he lay in bed looking up at the ceiling, Daniel felt
relieved of a heavy burden. Telling someone about his past was cleansing.
He didn't know what he was going to do or where he was going to go, but
he knew Nathan and Anna would understand. When the occasion arose,
Daniel would know when it was right to leave.

CHAPTER NINE

Stark winter landscapes around Nauvoo soon bowed to vividly colored spring flowers and fields of newly planted grain. The rapid building among the people in the vibrant community had become legend in the area. Partially completed, the gleaming white temple could be seen from almost any location in town. Many of the men in Nauvoo, including Philander Colton and Jacob Ford, willingly donated hundreds of hours to complete this sacred place of worship where they'd someday make eternal covenants with God. Emily often brought her father's midday meal.

"I'll take Papa's lunch to him," Emily volunteered as usual.

Emily's mother winked at her daughter as she handed her a wrapped package then answered, "You mean you'll check the steamers unloading at the docks. "

Emily grinned, knowing her mother understood. On her way to temple hill to bring her father's mid-day meal, Emily always took a detour and stopped by the docks on the Mississippi to watch the steamers. Emily was sure Daniel would be a passenger on one of those boats someday. As she watched the boats dock and unload, her heart raced until the last passenger stepped off the plank. Constantly disappointed, but refusing to give up hope, Emily always inwardly vowed to check again the next day.

After she walked away from the docks and approached the hill, Emily looked up at the partially completed temple and knew she would never be married anywhere else. Only in the temple could a man and wife be sealed together for eternity and no longer subject to death do we part. Emily knew that only after sacred ordinances in that holy place could families be together forever.

"I brought you some food," Emily said after she found her father working on a large white cut stone.

"Jacob's working on the other side. Why don't you go say hello," Philander answered after taking the package of food and finding a place to sit down and eat.

"I came to see you," Emily answered, blushing.

"I know," Philander said, "but I'm sure Jacob wouldn't mind seeing you as well. I'll be fine."

"I love you, Papa," Emily said. "I'll always love you best."

"Maybe for the time being, daughter, but that won't last forever and neither should it. Off with you now," her father answered.

Emily kissed Philander lightly on the cheek, then rounded the corner of the temple foundation where she saw Jacob chiseling the image of a sun on a large piece of stone. His dark hair curled around his forehead as sweat dripped off his face. Emily thought he looked a bit foreign to this hard work and not completely recovered from his family's previous illness. Jacob had become a fine sculptor since arriving in Nauvoo. If he'd remained in England, Jacob would have become a professor at the university like his father. For now he was working with his hands.

"Jacob!" Emily called. Jacob glanced to where Emily was standing, dropped his chisel and walked toward her. "You look tired."

"Bit different work than I'm used to, but I love it," Jacob answered with enthusiasm. Emily was embarrassed with her intrusion but also knew how welcome it would be. She and Jacob had enjoyed spending time together that winter and she'd grown fond of his company. "Thank you for coming to see me. With work on the temple, drills with the legion and my father's farm, I don't see you as often as I'd like."

Emily took a deep breath and looked up to the temple before she said, "It's going to be magnificent when it's completed. So many people have given everything they have to see it finished. Even Joseph tries to work on it whenever he can.

"Share dinner with me?" Jacob asked reaching for his tin of bread and cheese.

Emily nodded then said, "Let's go to the grove."

They hiked together to the grove of trees situated near the temple.

These gentle woods always gave Emily a sense of peace. As they entered the bowery, Emily remembered hearing Joseph Smith preach there in the open air. This peaceful place also reminded Emily of the woods near her home in Missouri. She often thought of Daniel when she was in the grove. As they walked through the trees, Emily could almost see Daniel's face. The moments they'd spent together in the forest in Missouri still lingered in her mind like sweet forbidden treasure. Yet, as more time went by, she seriously doubted if she'd ever see Daniel again.

"What you thinking about? It makes you look so far away," Jacob said as he looked into Emily's eyes.

"Just remembering the woods next to our home in Missouri and how much I loved them," she answered as they both sat on Jacob's coat beneath a tree. "Did you know the woods are full of secrets and if you listen the forest will tell you some of them?" Emily asked.

"Secrets?" Jacob asked. "What do you mean?"

"Never mind. You haven't eaten a thing since we got here. If you don't eat something, how do you expect to have the strength to work?" Emily asked.

"Not hungry. You eat it," Jacob answered smiling and staring at her.

"I'm not hungry either," Emily answered.

"Have you heard about the Fourth of July celebration?" Jacob asked. "Nauvoo legion is already practicing for the parade."

"Bet you look handsome in your uniform," Emily said grinning. "I'm so glad we finally have a way to defend ourselves. Never been able to depend on any one to help us but ourselves. With the legion, the mobs will never be able to drive us from Nauvoo."

"There's going to be a parade, band, speeches and people visiting from all over the state here," Jacob said. "Would you meet me here in the grove after the parade?"

"Love to," Emily said. "But I better get back home. Mother needs my help. We've lots of orders for new dresses with our new sewing business. Goodbye, Jacob."

Jacob watched as Emily ran back down the hill and out of sight. He took a deep breath. Jacob had never known anyone quite like Emily Colton before. He couldn't get enough of her. If it were in his power, he would some day make her his wife.

On her way home, Emily saw a large steamer unloading. She raced to the dock and watched the passengers slowly unload. She carefully searched the faces of all the young men. When all the passengers scattered into the city, Emily sighed, then turned for home.

❦

As Nathan watched Daniel busy working on a saddle, he knew Daniel was destined for a different sort of life. His apprentice was always asking questions, seeking answers, and wrestling with deeper thoughts. He instinctively knew their time together would be short.

"Business never been so good," Nathan said cheerfully. "You made me into a proper business man, Danny. What do you say we take a day off tomorrow? Goin' to be quite a show up north in Nauvoo for the Fourth of July—parades, speeches. Like to see this Nauvoo for myself. Heard lots of stories 'bout those strange Mormons."

"Be a lot friendlier if drunken mobs would stop burning them out of their homes and killing them," Daniel interrupted. "Why can't people just leave them alone?" Nathan drew back and excused himself. "I saw what happened to Mormons in Missouri. That girl I told you about, she was a Mormon. Mobs killed her because of it."

"I'm sorry," Nathan answered apologetically as he walked over to Daniel and placed his hand on his shoulder.

"I just wish she could've lived to see her people safe," Daniel said. "If Missouri settlers had given them half a chance, Emily would be alive today. My own uncle was a major part of the crimes committed against those people. I should've done more to help."

"I still say you be needin' a bit of a holiday," Nathan continued. "Always workin' your fingers to the bone. Be good for the spirits."

"You're right," Daniel answered as he put his leather working tools down on the table. "Like to see what's become of Emily's people."

Early the next morning before the sun was up, Daniel and Nathan left for Nauvoo. The broad rolling river was lazy and slow. Even though Daniel still blamed himself for Emily's death, the festive spirit of the people on the boat turned his thoughts to the celebration. Before they reached Nauvoo, Daniel heard an explosion of cannon fire in the distance. When they rounded the corner, he saw the new city spread out before him and noticed a beautiful white unfinished structure on the crest of a hill. There were thousands of people crowding the docks and a band playing music somewhere in the distance.

"How do you tell which ones are Mormons?" Nathan asked as he stepped off the steamer into the throngs of people hurrying past them.

"Your guess, good as mine," Daniel chuckled. "Looks like everybody's headed up toward that white building on the hill. Might as well follow them," Daniel finished as he and Nathan stepped into the crowd.

Most of the people in the city had gathered at a grove of trees near the temple. As Daniel reached the grove, there was a large brass band playing and a parade of soldiers called the Nauvoo Legion passing by. The Mormon leader, Joseph Smith, was at the head of the procession. The Legion was well trained, impressively clothed and included hundreds of men. Daniel and Nathan were surprised with the spectacle as the parade passed by. Soon several speakers stood before the crowd and began orations the likes of which Daniel and Nathan had never heard before.

"Didn't know Mormons were loyal Americans," Nathan said laughing. "Quite a Fourth of July celebration."

Later as Nathan and Daniel boarded the steamer that evening, they heard the passengers talking among themselves.

"Did you know there were over fifteen thousand people here today?" one passenger said. "Problem was I couldn't tell which ones were the Mormons."

Daniel had to chuckle under his breath.

"Me too," a lady answered. "Came hoping to see me a Mormon, but I couldn't tell 'em apart from regular folk."

Daniel and Nathan turned to each other and smiled as the steamer left port and headed back for St. Louis.

Preparations for the Fourth of July celebration in Nauvoo had been going on for months. Everyone in the city was eager to stage an event to remember.

"Papa, you look mighty handsome," Emily said as she helped her father fasten the shiny buttons on his Nauvoo Legion coat and adjust his sword. "I'll bet all the ladies will be admiring you in the parade today."

Philander grinned. "You'll be admiring someone else today," Emily's father answered. "Bit younger and nicer looking than this old man."

"Oh, Papa," Emily said, "better be going before you're late."

"We can defend ourselves now," Philander said brimming with pride. "I'm tired of running."

Just then, Polly walked into the room and wrapped a gold satin scarf around her husband's neck before she kissed his cheek.

"Don't you look fine," Polly said as she stood back and inspected Philander.

Emily raced into her bedroom as her parents embraced and said goodbye. She brushed her hair back from her face and tied it with a ribbon. Then she smoothed her cotton dress and fluffed the ruffles of her petticoats. After she dusted the dirt off her shoes, she headed for the door.

Before Emily hurried outside, Polly stopped her daughter and asked, "Where do you think you're going, young lady?"

"Promised I'd meet Jacob in the grove after the parade."

"Why do you have to hurry off so fast? Parade hasn't even started."

"Want to see the steamers unload. Heard there'll be three or more today."

"Why do you do that every day?" Polly asked even though she knew the answer.

"It's exciting. All those new people from all over the state. Have such fine clothes and most seem friendly enough."

"Looking for Daniel, you mean," Polly answered as Emily blushed. "Don't waste too much time at the docks. Jacob will be waiting."

Emily raced through the streets until she reached the docks. There were two steamers, one from Quincy and one from Burlington unloading. From the sand bar at the side of the river, Emily carefully watched all the passengers come ashore.

"Will there be any other steamers in today?" Emily asked a woman as the last group of people stepped off the boat and started for town.

"I don't know, dear. I think there's a steamer from St. Louis expected sometime today. By the way, have you seen any of those strange Mormons around? I'd like to get a good look at one of them."

"I don't know where they're hiding, but I'm sure you'll know one when you see one," Emily answered.

As the woman left, Emily looked down the immense rolling river. There were no other boats in sight. Just then she heard the gun salute from the grove marking the beginning of the parade, so she bounded up the hill. As she stood in the place where she'd promised to meet Jacob, the grove became suddenly crowded with people. The brass band played several lively tunes, and a short time later the Legion paraded by. Emily waved and shouted to her father as he passed. When Jacob found Emily's face in the crowd, he waved, tipped his hat, and made a flourish with his sword.

After the parade, Jacob and Emily stole away to the lush rolling pastures surrounding the city. They found a quiet spot in a grain field and lay side by side looking up at the sky.

"I never want to leave this place. Remember what it looked like when we got here?" Jacob asked as he reached for Emily's hand.

"I remember," Emily answered feeling Jacob's fingers tighten around her own. "I hope we'll never have to leave."

Jacob rolled onto his stomach, and then cupped his chin in his hands. He watched Emily's eyes survey the sky.

"Sometimes you seem so far away, even when you're next to me," Jacob said.

"I'm sorry," Emily said. "I'm just a dreamer. You looked real handsome up on your horse in the parade today."

Jacob prized the way Emily's dark brown hair shined in the sun and the slight blush she always held in her cheeks. He longed to put his arms around her. When he moved toward her, Emily suddenly sat up and smoothed her dress. Jacob felt embarrassed. Blushing, he sat up and quickly changed his demeanor.

"Father's been asked to teach at the new school. He wants me to take care of the farm from now on. He said I can keep any profit. Emily, do you think maybe you and me?"

"Jacob, don't say anything," Emily interrupted. "I told you once I can't make any promises right now. I don't want to hurt you, but there's someone else."

"You don't have to make any promises right now," Jacob continued. "Just tell me you'll think about it."

Emily nodded. Later, when she walked home, Emily stopped at the docks. She watched a steamer round the corner and head down river.

"Which steamer just left?" Emily asked a man standing close by.

"I think it was the steamer from St. Louis. Why do you ask?" the man asked, scratching his head.

CHAPTER TEN

On a cold January afternoon, Jacob ran to Emily's home and nervously knocked at the door.

"Jacob," Polly said as she opened the door, "Come in. I'll get Emily for you."

"Thank you," Jacob answered out of breath.

As Polly walked to the rear of the house, Jacob nervously switched his weight back and forth changing feet alternately in the doorway.

"Emily, I need to speak with you. Can you leave?" Jacob quickly asked when Emily came into the room.

Emily nodded, then immediately grabbed her cloak and hat from the closet. After she pulled on her hat, she took Jacob's arm and they left the house together.

"What is it Jacob?" Emily asked. "You look worried. Is your mother getting worse?"

"No," Jacob answered. "About the same. I'm frightened, Emily, for everyone, but mostly for Joseph. Father and I just returned from a meeting where Joseph said it was necessary to increase the police force for the protection of the city. He's appointed Father and me as new officers of the peace. While he was instructing us today, he said some things that frightened me."

The cold air was chilling and Emily shivered as she asked, "What was it Jacob? What did the Prophet say?"

"Said he's exposed to far greater danger from traitors among us than from our enemies without. You know how often and for how many years he's been hounded by civil or state authorities and all those people from Missouri, always on false charges. He said he could escape from the treachery of assassins, could live as Caesar might have lived, were it not for a right-hand Brutus. He said all the cries of the chief priests and elders against the Savior could not bring down the wrath of the Jewish nation upon his head, until Judas. Emily, Judas was one of the twelve apostles. He ate and drank with the Savior. Joseph said we have a Judas in our midst."

"Jacob, who could it be?" Emily asked catching her breath. "Why would anyone close to the prophet want him killed? If we can't trust our fellow brothers and sisters in the church, who can we trust?"

"I don't know," Jacob said as he bowed his head. "I don't know."

Emily wiped her eyes and defiantly said, "No! God wouldn't let it happen. No one who's been with the Prophet and felt his love could ever betray him."

"We can't pretend just because we're baptized into the Church that we'll never be tempted," Jacob said, taking Emily by the shoulders.

"But, if the prophet knows who Judas is, why doesn't he have him removed or at least expose him?" Emily asked.

"I don't know the answers any better than you, Emily. Why didn't the Savior banish Judas?" Jacob asked.

False rumors and salacious news kept the Saints anxious all winter. Even when spring arrived, Jacob brought more tales of treachery and betrayal to Emily almost daily, from those both inside and outside the Church. Then the Prophet's second counselor in the First Presidency was excommunicated along with several others. Soon, one troubling event after another created a downward spiral spinning out of control. When Joseph was incarcerated at Carthage Jail, the Saints were anxious and frightened, but expected his eventual escape like many times before. No one expected his murder.

On a clear mild day in late June, Emily and her family found themselves slowly proceeding toward the Mansion House amidst a throng of mourners. Emily's family walked together with their arms around each other, still in shock about the sudden news of the martyrdom. Before they reached the Mansion House, Emily suddenly turned from the crowd and ran down the street in the opposite direction. Then she heard Jacob's voice calling after her.

"Emily," Jacob shouted as he ran after her.

Jacob had been busy the last few nights trying to guard the city, even though the Nauvoo Legion had their charter removed by the state and their arms taken away. His eyes were blood-shot with dark circles around them.

"I can't," Emily cried. "I can't bear to see the Prophet and his brother, dead. Remember the last time we went there? The whole house was ablaze with light. Now even at midday, there is blackness so deep and dark in this city."

"Then I'll come with you," Jacob said.

Emily reluctantly agreed, took Jacob by the arm and walked back into the throngs of mourners headed for Joseph and Emma Smith's home. As they entered, Emily could hear the Prophet's wife cry coming from a room in the rear of the house.

"Oh, Joseph! Joseph! Oh, my husband! My husband! Have they taken you from me at last?" Emma wailed beyond consoling.

Emily wanted to turn and run but Jacob led her into the room where Joseph and Hyrum were lying dead in their coffins. Emily watched Emma being carried from the room, obviously heavy with child. Suddenly Emily saw the pale and lifeless faces of Joseph and his devoted brother. She felt her head spinning. Jacob grabbed her arm. After they left the house and walked back down the streets filled with hopeless grievers, Emily saw fear in everyone's faces. She seriously doubted if her fellow Saints could move forward without their prophet and leader Joseph Smith. She saw everything they'd all worked toward for years near ruin once again.

"I need to be alone," Emily said as she left Jacob's side and hurried toward the partially built temple on the brow of the hill.

Unfinished, Emily thought, *the temple, Joseph and Hyrum's lives . . . so much left undone. Why?*

Emily walked slowly to the bowery of trees where Joseph often spoke to the Saints. As she entered the canopy of trees, she recalled the times she'd heard Joseph speaking with the voice of a lion from this hallowed place. She remembered the Prophet's exuberance for life and recalled him running in the streets with his children in loud boisterous games. She sealed in her mind Joseph's triumphant rides through the city with the Nauvoo Legion. She remembered his stirring revelation that had sustained her on her darkest night after being expelled from Missouri. She remembered until she couldn't bear to remember anymore.

Lying back in the carpet of ferns and flowers, Emily took a deep breath and looked at the beauty of the woods around her. Then she heard the words. . . "Listen . . . look . . . feel. The woods have secrets to tell you." Emily felt the wind on her face and the sun warming her body as that same voice whispered again . . . "Spring always comes. We have to be patient and trust God."

The words were Daniel's. Even now, Emily knew he was with her, helping her understand. A lone bird pierced the air with song and two squirrels chased each other up the tree next to her. Emily glanced at the tiny tree beside her. She understood life was a continual round in the forest. Even the dying leaves of fall beneath her were now creating rich new earth to nourish the young sapling.

Later, Jacob stepped breathlessly into the small enclosure and found Emily sleeping. Not wanting to wake her, he sat quietly next to her, watching her chest rise and fall in gentle motion, her face glowing in the sunlight. It was almost evening before Emily woke. Jacob was still there. When their eyes met, they didn't speak at first. Then Emily sat up and smiled.

"The woods are important to you, aren't they?" Jacob finally asked.

"Yes," Emily said, trying to rub the sleep from her eyes and smooth her hair away from her face. "This is my school, my home."

"I have to leave for guard duty," Jacob said with a tinge of fear.

Emily gently touched his hand before they parted. Then she walked from the grove toward home.

As Emily walked through the orderly streets of Nauvoo, she felt a sense of pride swell within her. Her clean, starched calico dress and white layered petticoats swayed as she walked with new energy. She'd just washed her hair that morning and it shone with auburn highlights. As she looked above her, she spied the temple glistening on the hill. Only the first story had been completed when Joseph was killed. Now, less than a year after his murder, it was nearly completed.

Emily had worried things would be vastly different after Joseph was killed. He'd been the only prophet and leader the Saints had ever known. As she watched the population of Nauvoo increase and improve their conditions, factories springing up, the temple nearing completion, and many of the men being called on missions, she knew her fellow Saints didn't worship Joseph, but Jesus Christ. Gardens were planted in neat rows and fruit trees were in bloom. Emily relished the scent of cherry blossoms and lilacs as she climbed the hill to the temple with some food for her father. Even though Emily and her mother were busy with their new sewing business, Emily often found time to visit with Jacob. While his father was busy teaching school, Jacob and Emily often helped each other with chores. As Emily neared the temple, she saw Jacob running toward her.

"Emily," he shouted, "I have great news for you." He bounded off the hill and raced toward her smiling. "Father's been called on a mission back home to England. He'll be able to see my grandparents again. Both my grandfather and grandmother said they never wanted to see us again after we joined the church, but I'm sure their hearts will be softened now."

"I hope so," Emily said. "But what will happen to your sick mother? You'll have to take care of her now."

"Father in Heaven will watch out for us while he's gone," Jacob answered.

"You're thinking about your friends and loved ones in England when I'd probably be thinking about myself being left at home with all the work to do," Emily said.

"I can't wait for the day when I can return too," Jacob answered, hardly listening. "Maybe someday we can go there together. England is so lovely in the springtime."

"How can you say that when they've disowned and disinherited you?" Emily asked. "They don't want your love. They don't deserve it."

"I don't believe that," Jacob answered. "Just because they've stopped loving us doesn't mean we have to stop loving them. In time, they'll listen. Mother always says forgiveness is the highest form of love. Better be going now."

After Emily delivered the food to her father, she headed home. She loved to walk the streets of Nauvoo and enjoyed watching the Saints hurrying about their affairs. She savored walking past new brick houses and neat log cabins along with the many shops that lined the streets. Just as she was nearing her home, a large rough hand reached out from behind a corner and grabbed her around her throat then dragged her behind a tree.

"Where is he?" the person holding her throat shouted. "Tell me! Where is he?"

Emily choked trying to regain her voice. Terrified, she turned her head to see who was holding her. There towering above her, breathing heavy with the smell of liquor on his breath, was Daniel's uncle. Emily remembered his angry face from visits to their house in Missouri. She felt a cold chill go down her spine and tried to catch her breath.

"What are you talking about?" Emily gasped. "Who do you want?"

"You know who I'm talking about," Gilbert blurted as he tightened his hold.

Emily grabbed Gilbert's arms and dug her fingernails into his flesh. Swearing, Gilbert released her. Emily straightened herself and dusted off her dress.

"You don't scare me," Emily said defiantly as she turned to leave.

"Where's Daniel?" Gilbert shouted. "If you don't tell me, I'll make it very hard on you and your family. Won't stop until I find him."

"Daniel?" Emily questioned. "Isn't he with you? He's not here. I haven't seen Daniel since we left Missouri. You must have received the letters I sent him."

"I believed those letters for a long time. Now I know they were just a decoy to keep me from coming here and finding him. Where is he?" Gilbert insisted.

"If you try to bother me or my family, I'll have you removed from the city. We have the means of defending ourselves now," Emily answered.

Gilbert swore, then lunged for Emily as he yelled, "You'll be sorry you said that. Protect yourselves? Remember Missouri!"

Emily jumped out of his way and Gilbert sprawled face into the dirt. She raced home. When she rushed through the door of her family home, Polly mother looked at her red face and asked, "What is it? What's happened? Is it your father?"

"No," Emily answered. "Daniel's Uncle Gilbert is here. Grabbed me and tried to force me to tell him where Daniel is. Said he'll cause trouble for us if we don't tell him. I told him we don't know, but he didn't believe me. If *he* doesn't know where Daniel is, where could he be?"

"Maybe he had the good sense to run away. Being so young, though, I wonder if he survived," Polly answered.

"Then he never got any of my letters, Mama. That's why he never wrote back. If I had any idea where he's gone, I'd leave right now to find him."

"Emily," Polly interrupted, "don't think so rashly. He may not even be alive."

"He is," Emily said. "I just know it. I hate to think of him all alone without anybody. Why hasn't he tried to find me?"

"Probably thinks you're dead. What about Jacob? He cares more for you than I think you know," Polly asked.

"Jacob's an angel, Mama. I love everything about him, but Jacob's not Daniel. I can't get him out of my mind. I made promises to him. He's got to be out there somewhere. I think about him every day, every hour. Every time I go into the grove by the temple, I see his face and hear his voice. Until I find him, I have to keep hoping. I promised him I'd never leave him, but I did. I broke my promise. I promised him I'd wait for him if we were ever separated. I can't break that promise as well."

That night just as the Colton family sat down to eat supper, Gilbert stormed into their home unannounced.

"Where is he?" Gilbert spouted as he raced through the house, forcing open the doors to each room. "Should've burned with your house. Where's my nephew?"

Philander rose to his feet in a startling rage yelling, "Leave my home this instant! I have the moral authority to strike you to the earth! We're no longer in Missouri where you hide behind your drunken friends. Leave my home!"

Emily had never seen that hot look in her father's eyes before. Gilbert glared at Philander, belched a filthy oath and turned to leave. As he stormed through the doorway he turned and cursed again,

"Next time, I make certain you're dead even if I have to do it myself. I'll be back!" Gilbert threatened, slamming the wooden door behind him.

"That awful man brings back everything I've tried to forget," Polly said.

"If only the state hadn't repealed our charter, taking away our arms and our right to defend ourselves," Philander said, "Gilbert wouldn't dare set foot in this city. I won't stand by and watch men like him seize power over us again without a fight."

❧

All that spring and summer, Philander was forced to go into hiding. Gilbert relentlessly bribed the lawyers and officers in the area to arrest Philander for the kidnapping of Daniel Webster Jones. Though Gilbert never showed his face again, he kept the officers and lawyers busy on paid errands and lawsuits. Meanwhile, other people in the state were organizing a militia and demanding the removal of the Mormons from their borders. Jacob was savagely beaten while trying to work his father's farm. The Ford barn was burned and their crops destroyed. Emily and her mother were forced to change their sewing business from sewing dresses into sewing tents and wagon covers.

To avoid bloodshed, the Mormon leaders had urged the people of Nauvoo to leave the next spring. Every home became a workshop to prepare the Saints for their departure. Timber was brought into Nauvoo and dried while wagonloads of scrap iron from the surrounding area was converted into rims, axles and other metal parts for wagons and teams. All the horses and oxen that could be purchased were also brought into the city.

On Thanksgiving Day, Emily walked quickly through town to a friend's home where her father was hiding. His seclusion had successfully prevented Gilbert's errand boys from arresting him. Emily brought along some of the holiday dinner her mother had prepared. Emily looked around and behind her to see if anybody was watching. She turned the corner and quickly stepped up to the front door of the house where she knew her father was staying. She knocked and was quickly pulled through. Her father greeted her with a warm embrace.

"We haven't been able to sell any of our land or the house," Emily began as she took off her shawl. "Everyone says it's foolish to pay us for something that will simply fall into their hands when we leave. Papa, I can't bear the thoughts of leaving our home again. Must we?"

Philander took his daughter by the hand and guided her up a flight of stairs to a small table and two chairs in a secret room in the attic. When they were seated, Emily's father leaned across the table and kissed her softly on the cheek.

"Thank you for the food," Philander began. "I've just learned Brigham wants our family to be one of the first to leave Nauvoo. We're one of the few with a father at home and no sickness. We can't stay here. If we do, there'll be bloodshed. If we leave the country, no one will be able to bother us anymore. Joseph talked about a move west before he was murdered. If we go and settle somewhere else, we'll be able to live our religion without constant harassment.

"But we've already left everything and started over so many times," Emily interrupted. "I don't want to leave here, Papa. If Daniel's alive, I have to find him before we go."

"There's not time, Emily. You know it wouldn't be safe for you to leave Nauvoo to find Daniel right now. That's just what Gilbert wants. Don't you see? If we stay together and leave the country together in a large group, he can't stop us or bring charges against me any more."

"Eat your dinner before it gets cold," Emily said despondently.

Philander took the basket Emily was carrying, opened it, then said, "It'll be hard for me to leave here too. Hardest of all to leave the temple. But if I leave, I'll still have my family. If I don't, there's no guarantee. That's what's most important to me, you and your mother and brothers and sister. We no longer have the legal right to defend ourselves like we had before with the Nauvoo Legion. People in this state are just waiting for a chance to take us and our lands by force. Emily, go home; comfort your mother."

"What of Jacob Ford?" Emily asked. "What will he do with a sick mother and a father gone off to missionary work in England and no farm to bring them any food or funds? He'll have to get ready to leave too. But how can he?"

"Hopefully the people so bent on our destruction will allow the sick to stay until they can prepare themselves to leave," Philander answered.

"Why do you always have to be so brave?" Emily whispered. "Know how hard this must be, what you'd really like to do. You don't have to be brave around me. Rather see you curse the mobs than try to soothe me."

"I never could hide myself from you," Philander said looking up into his daughter's eyes. "When I look up on the hill and see our beautiful temple, then think of what will happen when we're forced to leave, I want to fight back with every fiber of my being. All my fine work to the glory of God will be in the hands of drunken fools who've ordered us from our homes at gun point *again* and *again*"

Emily looked at her father with the added insight hardship had taught her. She realized both her parents were willing to give up everything they owned time and time again for their family and their testimonies of Jesus Christ. A renewed respect for their courage swelled inside her as she looked at her father's face filled with deep pain.

"Your mother's faithfully followed me through this whole nightmare," Philander continued. "Can't bear to see her tears again. If it were up to me, I'd dash out the brains of those vile men before I'd let them enter those holy walls, belch out their filthy oaths and smash their whiskey bottles on the temple walls. Die protecting our temple if I were asked to stay. But I've been asked to leave."

"I know Papa," Emily answered.

"In the end," Philander finished, "that would be the easy way. Your mother would be left with a house full of fatherless children. Before I'd leave my family to the mercy of such men as Gilbert Marshall, I'd crawl away in the night on my hands and knees."

A few months later, Philander was called to do what he had predicted. On a bitterly cold night in February, the Colton family turned solemnly down Parley Street with a large group of Saints all leaving Nauvoo for the last time. When they reached the Mississippi with their team and wagon, Polly turned to her husband.

"Look at the temple, Philander," Polly said. "It is stunning in the moonlight."

Philander shook his head. It was too painful to look back. Emily held her small sister's shaking hand as she walked by the side of the ox-pulled wagon. Her younger brothers, wrapped in worn blankets, shivered uncontrollably as they followed behind. Emily watched as numerous wagons drawn by horses and oxen, topped with great canvas covers and loaded with household provisions, drove off the wharf at Nauvoo onto flat boats. After they were ferried across to the Iowa side, they immediately headed west, leaving a muddy trail through the newly fallen snow.

About six or seven miles from the river they made their first temporary camp on the banks of Sugar Creek. Philander helped clear the snow and pitch their tent. Then the temperature dipped below zero. It stormed all night. Wind, rain, sleet and freezing snow blew unceasingly around the Colton wagon and tent until dawn. Hundreds of men, women and children shivered behind the scanty shelter of wagon covers and canvas tents. Emily heard women screaming and babies crying all night. When the sun finally rose the next morning, Emily learned nine babies had been born during the night.

A few weeks later, Brigham Young joined the front group in their first camp. Almost every family reported being without adequate provisions. Families were asked to trade everything they owned that wasn't needed for survival to the local settlers for food. By March, the Colton family, along with five hundred wagons, moved out again. Their next camp was at Garden Grove about one hundred and fifty miles from Nauvoo. Here the men split rails, built houses, dug wells, built bridges, plowed the ground, and planted grain. They knew they wouldn't be around to enjoy the harvest of their labors but hoped to make the way easier for the Saints who followed.

Their next encampment was about two hundred and fifty miles west of Nauvoo. Mount Pisgah was situated on sloping grassy hills framed with great groves of timber next to the Grand River. Though hungry, tired, sick and penniless, the Saints had worked together to build instant cities in both Garden Grove and Mount Pisgah for later Saints traveling west.

In June they reached their next camp at a place called Council Bluffs on the banks of the Missouri river. The plan here was to send one hundred men ahead without their families to select a permanent settlement place in the Rocky Mountains. The federal government changed their plans. Brigham Young was approached and asked for five hundred volunteers to help fight the war with Mexico. To the surprise of many Saints, President Young agreed.

After the soldiers of the Mormon Battalion had moved out, the Saints left behind realized they would be spending the long cold winter on the plains. Some decided to settle at a site across the river that became known as Winter Quarters. They soon built over five hundred log homes and about a hundred sod houses. Winter Quarters sheltered more than six thousand people before the winter was over.

CHAPTER ELEVEN

It had been an unusually prosperous winter, spring, and summer for Daniel and Nathan. They'd sold saddles as fast as they could make them to be shipped to Nauvoo where the Mormons were buying up all they could find. It was autumn before the demand began to decline and Daniel could take a little time off to enjoy himself in town.

After a crisp day in September spent walking and thinking along the banks of the river, Daniel returned to the saddle shop. It was surprisingly empty. Worried, Daniel ran to the rear of the house where he found Nathan and Anna sitting together at the table. When Daniel entered, they looked up at him with red eyes and tight worried looks.

"What is it?" Daniel asked excitedly. "What's the matter?"

Nathan turned to Daniel and said, "Danny, there was a man here today. Said he was looking for his nephew, Daniel Webster Jones who'd run away. Says he's your legal guardian. Said he knows you're here now, that he has the right to take you back with him. Told him the young man working for me was my nephew and he must be mistaken."

"Gilbert? Here?" Daniel asked.

"He accused me of lying," Nathan said. "He said he'd make it hard on me and the wife if I gave him any trouble. Said to tell you he has Emily's father in jail at Nauvoo. If you don't go back with him and sign some papers, he has the power to have him killed. Said he'd be back tomorrow to get you. Now remember, if you choose to stay with us, we'll do anything we can to help you."

"What did he say about Emily?" Daniel asked stunned.

Nathan repeated his story.

"But he couldn't have Emily's father in jail. Emily's whole family was

107

killed in a fire a long time ago. How can he expect me to believe that?"

"Said her family wasn't killed in that fire," Nathan answered. "They've been living in Nauvoo all of this time."

"I won't give him the chance to hurt the Colton family again if they're alive. He has to be lying. I'll leave for Nauvoo and see for myself."

"I'll get your things together, Danny," Anna said, jumping up from her chair. "You'll be needin' some food and money."

"I guess I always knew you'd be leaving sometime," Nathan said, taking Daniel by the shoulders. "You won't be coming back, will you?"

"You've been the closest thing I've had to a father since my own died. If this is true about Emily's family, then I've got to help her. I can't lose her again."

"Don't get to hoping too much," Nathan warned. "Might be a lie, a dirty trick to get you to go back with him."

"I've got to know for myself," Daniel finished.

Anna soon returned with a bag of Daniel's belongings. Nathan slipped some money into Daniel's pocket. When Daniel turned to leave the shop, he felt a knot in his throat. As he walked away, he was certain he'd never return.

"Take care, my boy," Nathan called after Daniel as he walked through the door and headed for the docks. "Goodbye, my sweet Danny boy."

"What'll become of him?" Anna asked as she watched Daniel leave. "There's no Emily in Nauvoo."

Daniel found the next steamer heading up the Mississippi. Anxious to arrive before it was too late, the trip seemed much longer than he remembered. As Daniel neared the bend in the river where Nauvoo came into full view, he felt his heart pounding. At sunset, the city seemed to glisten from the reflected golden glow in the western horizon. Daniel stepped off the steamer alone. It was so quiet he could hear the water lapping on the shoreline and the buzz of flies and mosquitoes around his head.

As Daniel walked into the city, a strange dark feeling enveloped him. He could remember Nauvoo from the Independence Day celebration he'd attended, but something was definitely wrong. Daniel walked alone through the solitary streets lined by new and well cared for brick or log houses surrounded by cool green gardens and fruit orchards. When he looked up toward the domed hill he spied a stately white and gold structure with a high tapering spire. Daniel was amazed that this swamp land had been changed from a mosquito infested wasteland into a thriving city-state in five short years.

There were recent signs of industry and enterprise everywhere—empty wood shops with shavings still scattered on the bench, idle spinning wheels with cards of wool discarded nearby, blacksmith shops with heaps of coal ready for the fire, fresh bark in the tanner's vat, bread still left uneaten in a baker's oven - but there were no people, as if everyone had left for a sudden holiday and would be back soon. The whole city seemed under an evil spell. Daniel could still see the dusty footprints and wagon wheel ruts of the numerous former residents. Walking through the abandoned city felt like walking through a bad dream.

As he reached the eastern suburb of the city, Daniel noticed the whole place showed signs of a recent battle. He saw several gaping holes in the sides of barns. Vacant homes showed the recent destruction of cannon fire with splintered wood, crumbled walls and foundations. Daniel thought about Emily's people and wondered what had become of them. They couldn't just disappear into thin air. As he walked toward temple hill, he turned full circle and looked east and south on the wasted and ruined farms in disbelief.

As he approached the temple, Daniel noticed the white edifice was surrounded by barracks of men and stacks of muskets. On closer inspection, he noticed the temple steeple had recently been struck with lightning. It was obvious to him that the men stationed around the temple had been drinking heavily. After living with his uncle, Daniel knew too well what drinking did to a man's judgment. Daniel was soon stopped by an armed man who pointed a loaded musket in his face.

"Who are you?" the armed stranger asked. "If you're a stinkin' Mormon, blow your head off."

Daniel jumped from the man's reach and shouted.

"Don't shoot. I'm not a Mormon. What's happened to everybody?"

The armed man spit on the dirt and cursed. Daniel smelled liquor on his breath.

"This used to be a well-known place," the man began. "There were more than twenty thousand of 'em living right here. But we finished them, we did. Just a pack of cowards and thieves. Ran like scared rabbits. Got some of 'em. Come with me and I'll show you their holy Mormon temple. Used to do their mystic rites and unhallowed worship in these walls, they did," the man explained as he forcefully pulled Daniel inside the temple.

Daniel saw rotting food and liquor bottles thrown against the temple floor and curses written in blood on the walls. Daniel shuddered as the drunk boasted of his depraved deeds against the fleeing Mormon women and children. He realized this drunken militia camped around him had silenced the hammers, forced people from their homes, and trampled thousands of acres of grain to ruin. These men milling through the temple rooms were the lawless band who'd destroyed a thriving beautiful city and made it into a waste land of unlived lives and fortunes.

"Where's the jail here where you keep the Mormons locked up?" Daniel asked.

The man laughed then spit tobacco on the floor. "What we need a jail for? Don't leave, we shoot them, clean as that. Waging war on dirty Mormons like picking off lice. Don't need no jail. Ain't no more of 'em left. Here, take a drink boy. City's ours now." Daniel refused. "Take a drink boy. Ain't my whiskey good enough for you?"

The drunken man tried to force whisky down Daniel's throat as he grabbed him around the neck. Daniel broke the drunk's grasp and sent him flying across the room then sprinted from the temple, heading back toward the docks of the Mississippi to escape.

"I'll kill you!" the drunk yelled grabbing his gun and firing at Daniel. "You can run but you can't hide from me boy."

Daniel heard the sound of a musket ball slicing through the thick air just above his head. He ran faster hoping to outrun the drunken man. Once Daniel reached the river, sunset soon changed to dusk. He found a small fishing boat, jumped in and rowed to the other ride of the Mississippi to get away from the drunken men occupying the city. Daniel left the boat at the dock then turned inland to find a place to hide.

The temperature dipped suddenly as night fell and everything went black, making it hard for Daniel to see. Just then, he saw a faint light flickering in the distance. Daniel walked toward the dim beam, shockingly stumbling over a group of prone bodies lying on the bare ground with only bulrushes around them for camouflage. Daniel looked around him in horror at bodies in various stages of either sleep or intense suffering. As his eyes gradually adjusted to the moonlight, Daniel was able to see several hundred people cramped with the cold and crippled with disease lying all about him in mass, a groaning human wasteland of sickness and death. He realized these people were Emily's people, the last Nauvoo residents forced from their homes by the lawless men he'd just met on Temple hill.

Daniel gasped as moonlight shone on the face of a young man lying at his feet writhing in agony. He had a gaping bloody wound in his chest. Daniel felt weak in the knees and had to struggle for breath. Then he slowly knelt to see if he could help the stranger. As he sat next to the young man and gently lifted his head onto his lap, the wounded man's jaw gaped open and he moaned. Daniel placed his broad hand on the young man's brow. When he touched him, the young man took a deep breath and relaxed.

"It's all right," Daniel whispered.

All the while Daniel spoke these words he knew there was nothing he could do; it was obvious the young man was too near his end. The dying man's expression instantly brought back stark memories of his own father and sister's deaths. Daniel looked up at the stars feeling his smallness in the universe, then closed his eyes and bowed his head.

"I know dark clouds will gather 'round me," Daniel sang in his low baritone voice, trying to comfort the young man. "I know my way is rough and steep. Yet green pastures lie before me, where God's redeemed no more shall weep. I'm going there to see my Savior, to sing his praises ever more. I'm just going over Jordan. I'm just going over home." Daniel stroked the perspiring brow of the young man's head. "You'll be home soon," he said. "I won't leave you until you get there."

Then the rain began, a few intermittent drops at first, then later a hard, soaking, pelting downpour. As cold rain poured down on the dying young man, Daniel protectively covered him with his own coat. Next to the emaciated stranger was a dead body wrapped in a wet quilt. As the sky overhead filled with rolling thunder and brilliant flashes of lightening, Daniel felt a storm raging inside him as well. Daniel tried desperately to shield the young man from the torrents of rain and blistering wind howling around them. The smell of rotting flesh and excrement was everywhere.

Gilbert was lying, Daniel thought. *Emily was never here. There are no jails. There is no justice. Now her people are dying out here like animals while drunken mobs steal everything they own and defile their temple. Dear God, where are you?"*

"I'm just a poor wayfaring stranger, just traveling through this land of woe," Daniel struggled to continue singing, "but there's no sickness, toil or danger in that bright land to where I go. I'm just a-goin' over Jordan. I'm just a-goin' over home."

All though the long dark night stark troubling images flashed through Daniel's mind—his father on his death bed - his mother's blank stare the morning she left—Emily's house smoldering in the woods and Gilbert's hot face screaming angry threats. Wind and rain chilled Daniel through to the bone. In sheer exhaustion, he fell asleep. He was not aware when the young man's body went limp in his arms.

At dawn a woman touched him on the shoulder awakening him.

"Dead. Can't do nothing for 'im now," she said.

Daniel looked into the face of the deceased young man. His countenance seemed surprisingly peaceful.

"Who is he?" Daniel asked. "What are you doing out here?"

The woman looked down at Daniel and sensing she could speak freely said, "Name's Jacob Ford. His mother over yonder. Got shot defendin' her from the mobs trying to take over their home in Nauvoo. She was too sick to leave. All the other Saints gone. We're the last. Mobs shot Jacob then forced 'em out of town by the butt of a gun. Had no where to go, no help for his wound. His mother died days ago. Father's in England on a mission for the church."

"Where are the others?" Daniel asked.

"The first group left in February," the woman answered. "Mobs said if we started leaving they wouldn't start the killing. They lied."

"Why are you still here?" Daniel asked.

"None of us got money to buy a team and wagon. No one will buy our property in Nauvoo. Why should they? Just take it after they've forced us to leave. Won't let us back into the city to get what's ours."

"Where's your leader? Who's in charge?" Daniel asked. "How can the others leave you behind like this?"

"I'm sure Brother Brigham will send back some of the front wagons for us as soon as he can," the woman answered. "But our people are dying out there on the trail as fast as we're dying here. Don't trouble yourself. Nothing can be done, except survive one more day if we can."

Daniel dipped his hand deep into his pocket and gave the woman all his money.

"Why?" the women asked.

"Knew a Mormon family once. Can't help them now. But I can help you. Take it," Daniel insisted. "Please."

The woman nodded gratefully and took the coins and bills. Daniel dug a shallow grave for the young man and his mother and laid them side by side. After he covered their bodies with earth, he piled stones over the sight and placed a marker at the head. Then Daniel walked back toward the river and waited for the next steamer.

Daniel knew he couldn't go back to St. Louis because his uncle was there. He couldn't go back to his father's farm because Gilbert would return there eventually and find him. He didn't know what to do or where to go. Then Daniel remembered reading about an outfit dressing out volunteers for the war with Mexico. Old Texas Rangers and Missouri planters were signing up. Daniel decided to join. He determined leaving with those men would be his ticket away from his uncle, away from his past, away from everything that haunted him.

℘

Emily kept busy catching drips of muddy water from the leaky roof in their tiny one-room sod house in Winter Quarters while Polly sat next to the fire cooking corn meal. Polly and Emily were both working long hard days to keep the family fed now that Philander and Robert were in the Mormon Battalion and weren't around to help. Emily had recently learned about Jacob Ford's death from a list circulating through camp.

"I know why God took Jacob," Emily said. "He was too good to stay here with the rest of us."

"He was a good man," Polly answered.

"Jacob was so excited his father had the chance to return to England and give his family a second chance to accept the gospel," Emily said. "Those people disowned and disinherited his entire family when his parents were baptized. Jacob always thought everyone deserved a second chance. Sometimes I wonder." Emily was silent for a moment before she finished, "Maybe I should've made the promises Jacob wanted. I didn't even get the chance to say goodbye."

Polly straightened her back as if in pain then rubbed her hand along her rib cage before she answered, "You wouldn't have done poorly with him."

That summer and fall the whole family helped cut and stack thousands of tons of prairie hay with scythes to feed the animals. They also worked with the other Saints to preserve meat and wild game by drying and salting it for the winter. They all helped pick and preserve barrels of wild berries gathered on the river banks. Emily's younger brothers helped tend and feed the sheep and cattle herds. There were thirteen wards in Winter Quarters with a bishop for each. Church meetings were held every Sunday. After snow fell, school was held on week days because there was less work to do outside. Polly was heavy with child. About Christmas time, she expected a new member of the family.

"Mama, I wish you'd rest more. I'm perfectly capable of fixing the cornmeal while you lay down," Emily said.

"I don't mind," Polly answered. "Helps me keep my mind off your father when I stay busy. I miss him. He's been at my side when all you children were born."

"Why didn't you tell Papa about the baby before he left back in July?" Emily questioned. "Maybe he would have stayed with us instead of joining the battalion."

"Didn't know myself," Polly answered. "Just trying to keep us all alive."

Emily grew increasingly irritated as she continued, "I never understood why our men went anyway. We had to flee this country to keep from being killed. Then a few months later here comes some high and mighty American officer asking us for five hundred men to go fight the war in Mexico. Where was the government when *we* needed protection? They take our men and leave us alone on the plains to spend the winter starving and freezing to death. I don't understand why Brother Brigham went along with the idea. Why didn't he refuse?"

Polly interrupted, "Your father sends us his pay. We're better off than we'd be without it."

"I'm going to tell Robert a thing or two next time I see him—running off with Papa when I need him here to help with all the heavy work," Emily said.

"At your brother's age," Polly answered, "marching off to war probably seems a sight more exciting than staying home with the women. Can't say I really blame him. I do wish we had more help, especially for you. Maybe winter won't seem so long if we think about going west to Zion when your father and brother return."

"The boys haven't been well for so long, Mama," Emily said changing the subject. "I think they've got the Blackleg. Almost everybody has it. You don't look well yourself." Emily watched as her mother abruptly and painfully hurried toward the straw bed in the corner of the room. "Are you all right?" Emily asked as she watched her mother's countenance change and her face drain of color.

"Emily," Polly said in a panic, "come here quickly!" Emily hurried to the edge of the bed watching her mother's small palms clench into fists. "Something's wrong. Too early."

"What is it?" Emily asked in a panic. "The baby?" Polly nodded panting. "I'll get the midwives," Emily said hurrying to leave the sod house.

"No," Polly said, quickly undressing between contractions. "Baby's coming, *now*. Need your help." Polly sat with her back to the wall then strained forward, pulling her knees toward her chest. Emily felt her heart race. The pain peaked then subsided. "Baby's coming. Try to remember everything I've taught you. You can do it, Emily. You're all I've got. Get some blankets from the trunk, some string and a knife. Quick!"

Emily raced to the trunk just as her mother groaned again. When the labor pain subsided and Emily returned with the blankets, Polly told her to place several beneath her on the bed and get ready to catch the baby. There was a sudden gush of water and blood. When the next pain peaked Emily positioned herself at the foot of the bed.

"Baby's coming," Polly shouted in a rush. "Help me!" Polly's face turned red as she lunged forward and screamed. Emily reached out and caught the baby's emerging head in her trembling hands. As she supported the neck in her trembling palm, the shoulders turned and the baby slipped into her waiting arms. "Clear the nose and throat," Polly said after Emily quickly cut and tied off the cord, then wrapped the newborn in a soft cloth. "Is the baby alive?"

"Oh, yes, Momma," Emily answered staring down at two baby eyes, a baby nose and a baby mouth. The baby whimpered then howled. "It's a boy. He's beautiful. Sandy blond hair and blue eyes like my Daniel."

"Then that's what we'll name him," Polly whispered exhausted yet relieved to hear the baby crying. "Daniel Webster Colton."

Emily felt relieved and elated. Something about the pressure of the moment and the life force she'd just witnessed gave her new energy. She'd been terrified, but seeing the miracle of her mother's body transform itself before her eyes—the wonder of a new baby pushing into the world, breathing and screaming now held her in reverent awe.

Later when Emily's younger brothers and sister burst through the door from school, they found their mother and older sister sitting together on the bed with a new baby. Both Emily and her mother were wringing wet with perspiration but instantly melted into proud smiles.

"You have a new brother," Polly said, exhausted.

Later, Emily noticed her mother was bleeding heavily and wondered if she might die. She hastily left to fetch a midwife who could asses the situation. When the midwife raced through the door, she quickly handed the newborn to Emily and checked Polly's bleeding. Emily sat in a chair by the fire, gently rocking her new brother. The baby was tiny but breathing well. An overwhelming tenderness washed over Emily as she cradled her infant brother in her arms. She reached out and touched the sleeping baby's tiny hand that instantly curled around her finger.

Why must a mother risk her life to give life? Emily thought. *Why so much pain before so much joy?*

"Early, but he's doing fine," Polly said to the midwife. "A bit blue. but I think he'll make it. Emily took care of everything."

The midwife looked over toward Emily as she whispered, "Brave young woman. God only knows what would have happened if she hadn't been here to help you." Then the midwife asked Emily to come near her mother's beside and showed her how to massage her mother's abdomen to keep the uterus firm. She encouraged Polly to nurse the baby often. "Watch the bleeding. Make sure she stays down," the midwife said as she walked toward the door. "Call on me again if you're concerned about anything. You have courage, child. I'd like to take you with me to help with other births, if that's all right with you." Emily nodded.

In the next few weeks, the baby seemed to be doing well, but Polly was too weak from a continuing loss of blood to stand and walk around without passing out. The care of the house fell on Emily's shoulders. The two younger boys were soon down with the Blackleg and she had to keep Mary home from her lessons to help with the work. Amos seemed to be getting better but Ben kept getting sicker. Emily noticed Ben rarely moved without crying in pain. He was weak, tired, had a poor appetite, and was losing weight. There were blood spots, particularly under his fingernails, around his gums and hair roots. She noticed an unusual row of bumps under the skin on his rib cage. Once when getting up to go to the bathroom, Ben had fallen on the fireplace, cutting a gash on his left leg that never healed.

As the weeks wore on, Emily grew exhausted from lack of sleep. One night, Ben cried out as he tossed in his sleep. No one else was stirring so Emily left her blankets and went to sleep next to her brother to comfort him. The night was long and Ben seemed feverish and in worse pain than usual. Emily fell asleep just before dawn. When she woke, her brother's body was icy cold. Emily wrapped her arms around Ben trying to warm him before she realized he wasn't moving or breathing. She looked into her small brother's face and realized he was dead.

"No!" Emily yelled.

"What is it?" her mother asked.

"Ben's dead," Emily answered. "I'm so sorry."

"It's not your fault. You did everything you could."

Emily's eyes stung and her body trembled as she tenderly wrapped Ben in a blanket and carried him over to her mother's bedside so she could embrace and kiss him for the last time. Later Emily walked outside, still in her night clothes. It was a cold winter morning and the Nebraska prairie was still in early morning slumber, Emily walked through the dirt streets in a daze until Bishop Brown found her wandering aimlessly.

"What is it, child?" he asked looking at the blanket with Ben's body inside.

Emily looked at the bishop with a blank expression and answered, "My brother's dead. Mama's too weak to get out of bed. My Papa and brother are off with the Battalion and the other children are sick too. I don't know what to do. Would you help me please?"

The bishop took the lifeless boy from Emily and took her to his home. Most of his family was down with the same illness. The bishop's wife helped Emily prepare the small body for burial. So far, the bishop had recorded over five hundred deaths that winter from exposure, hunger and poor rations. With over six thousand people to house and feed, the Saints were ill prepared for this cold stormy winter.

Later, when Emily and the bishop walked toward the hill outside the town, Emily could see several other families digging fresh graves. She couldn't bear the thoughts of placing her small brother in the frozen earth when only hours ago she'd been embracing his tiny body to keep him warm.

As they reached the hill, Emily cried, "I can't put him in there alone. He needs someone to stay with him and keep him warm."

"This is only his body," the Bishop answered. "His spirit isn't here. He's gone back home to God. He's not sick any more. He's happy and warm and well. I promise that you'll see him again."

"Not until the day I die," Emily cried.

CHAPTER TWELVE

Daniel couldn't remember how long he'd been on the trail with the Missouri volunteers. He felt adrift in time, one day blending into another as they rode toward Mexico. His shoulders ached under the heavy pack and he never had enough water to satisfy his thirst. Daniel found fighting a war was more tedious than exciting.

Wool cavalry pants made his legs itch and his sweaty shirt clung to his chest, trapping his foul unwashed body odor. Day followed day with roll call at dawn, breakfast, feeding livestock and packing gear. Then the men rode over hills and across valleys from daylight to dusk. At days end it was: halt, make camp, collect buffalo chips, get water, draw rations, cook supper, eat and evening roll call. Then the men would toss and turn all night, trying to sleep on the rough, hard ground.

As his outfit headed south, Daniel often let his mind escape into pleasant memories of Emily in an effort to escape the vulgarity of his companions on their exhausting ride. One late afternoon as his outfit made camp along the Arkansas River, several of the men noticed a few small piles of driftwood across the river. With few trees in this desolate area, their usual fuel was buffalo chips. About thirty men jumped off their horses and ran to the river to retrieve the wood for the camp fire.

As Daniel rode into camp and dismounted, he heard loud screams from the direction of the river. Over twenty mounted Comanche braves charged the men as they gathered the drift wood along the side of the river. Screeching as they rode, the Comanche braves ran several of the men down, speared them through, caught them by the hair, and scalped them without dismounting. Most of Daniel's outfit ran for cover along the river, but those who were caught lay dead in bloody puddles in the sand. Daniel and the other men quickly loaded their rifles then raced toward the river firing. As soon as the Indians saw they were in danger, they retreated. The cavalry quickly mounted their horses and rode after the escaping Indians only to find they were too fast for them.

Daniel was ordered to help with the burials. When he was through, he couldn't get the dead soldier's faces out of his mind. He knew he could easily be one of them and wondered why he was spared. It didn't make sense to Daniel that a man could be breathing one moment then dead the next without some larger meaning or purpose. That night after the cavalry had returned without revenge, the captain of the battalion called all the men together and told them the driftwood was an obvious decoy used by the Indians. He told his men not to leave camp without orders again. All the men agreed and were more alert from that time on.

Why? Daniel thought. *Is this life all there is? There has to be something more.*

As the volunteers broke camp and moved on, Daniel stayed more and more to himself because he declined to drink with the other men. He bristled at the sight of strong drink because he remembered too well the effect liquor had on his uncle. Daniel learned to prefer his own company over the vulgar conversations of the other men. Their stories of prowess with loose women offended his sense of decency.

When they reached Mexico, Daniel was glad he'd seen more of dust and sweat than of blood and fighting. Other than the ambush at the river, the long trip had proved mostly uneventful. Daniel was released from duty after several months but decided to stay in Mexico and learn the Spanish language. He soon preferred the company of the local people over the men in his outfit. On a hot summer day, Daniel sat in the shade with several of his Mexican friends learning Spanish when Daniel noticed one of the men from the Missouri Volunteers staggering down the street cursing at the top of his lungs. Daniel tried to ignore the crude interruption, but the drunken soldier stumbled toward him.

"Who do you think you are?" the drunk spewed in slurred speech as he waved his near empty liquor bottle in Daniel's face. "Too good to drink with us but not to good to keep company with this garbage." Daniel shook his head in disgust. "Drink's on you," the soldier said, turning the bottle upside down and pouring the drink over Daniel's head.

"You're drunk," Daniel said as he grabbed the bottle from the drunk and tossed it down the street smashing it to pieces. "Leave us alone. Don't insult my friends."

"Here's what I think of you and your friends," the drunk blurted as he spit in Daniel's face, kicked dust at his friends, then lunged at Daniel.

Quickly rolling out of the way, Daniel wiped the spit from his face with the sleeve of his shirt then stood to his full stature. The drunk staggered menacingly toward him before tripping and falling face first into the dirt. Daniel helped the intoxicated soldier to his feet and took him to the hotel where they were staying. As Daniel assisted the man into bed, the drunk heaved, then passed out. As Daniel stared at the man laying in his own vomit, he thought of his uncle Gilbert and knew alcohol turned men into animals. He wanted no part of it.

After leaving the drunken soldier in the hotel clerk's care, Daniel walked out of town into the desert. He searched until he found a private area in a sunken gully. With one eye swollen shut, bruised knuckles and a bloody nose, Daniel had a hard time finding a smooth flat rock to sit on.

"My father said I could find you here in nature," Daniel prayed. "Mormons claim to have the restored gospel of Jesus Christ. Gilbert says that's blasphemy. Men here say religion is no good, you don't exist, so they live by the knife or the pistol. What's right? Heavenly Father, are you really there?" Daniel felt his soul yearning for answers, some better way to live than he knew in this remote boorish place, some reason for life and meaning in death. "Be so easy to live like these men. Don't want their chains. Never enough loose women, liquor or gambling to satisfy for long. Soon as they sober up, they get drunk again. Don't want to live or die like that. Tell me where to go, what to do."

As Daniel finished his prayer, the words his father spoke to him as a child in Missouri returned to his mind. "Look around you. What do you see? What do you hear? Listen." Daniel saw desolate and parched sands stretched out for miles around him, an endless desert. Then he noticed a lone towering Saguaro at the brink of a hill just beyond the gully where he prayed. The branches of the giant cactus appeared to him a crucifix curving upward as if in supplication. Daniel had eaten fruit from that cactus with his Mexican friends earlier in the summer. He wondered how the huge plant was able to stay alive and bear fruit under such extreme desert conditions.

Daniel climbed from the gully and walked nearer the Saguaro. He studied the cactus carefully and noticed there were no leaves to produce food for the plant like the trees in Missouri. The bristly upturned stems had taken over the task of making food and storing water for the plant. His friends told him the roots of the Saguaro, though not deep, spread far and wide so they could catch all the water from infrequent rain and sudden floods common to the desert. Daniel remembered again the words of his father, "Spring always comes. We have to be patient and trust God." Daniel knelt then arched his face heavenward in the shadow of the giant cactus.

"Help me," Daniel whispered.

Daniel felt his soul spiraling outward for miles trying to soak up any small drop of direction. Then, the wind picked up as ominous grey storm clouds formed overhead. Great sheets of sand swirled violently around him, stinging his skin. After a frightening moment the wind abruptly stopped and it started to rain, slowly at first, then finally in great torrential sheets, washing over and through him like a cleansing baptism. A lone flash of lightning blazed across the sky followed by a loud clap of thunder.

Daniel's answer came, like the luminous shaft of sunshine piercing through the black clouds overhead—a still and quiet voice. For the first time, his inner thirst was miraculously quenched. Daniel knew at that indescribable moment that God knew him by name, loved him, and would someday lead him from the desert to the Promised Land.

⟶

Emily sighed then plopped down despondently on her mother's straw bed in the corner of their one room sod house. The thought of going to a party when her family had nothing left to eat seemed selfish. Her mother was pretending everything was fine, but Emily knew there was nothing in the house for breakfast the next day.

"I don't want to go tonight. You need my help around here. If anyone should be going, it's you. You haven't been out for months."

"Emily, you've forgotten what it feels like to be young," Polly said. "You act like an old mother hen. Do me more good to see you enjoy yourself."

"Last of the flour got used up today," Emily said. "The chickens all gone. There's nothing to eat and Papa's army pay is all used up. I can't run off to a dance when we don't even know where our next meal is coming from."

"We'll be all right. Have a little faith. Go!" Polly insisted.

"Can't eat faith," Emily said. "You haven't been well since you had the baby. Wish I could give you something more nourishing to eat. I know you'd get better then."

"Will you think about yourself for just one evening? Do this for me."

"All right," Emily answered. "I'll take Amos and Mary. Maybe you could get some rest while we're gone."

"You can take them if you promise not to spend the whole night worrying about them," Polly answered. "Come here. Let me brush your hair." Emily pulled the combs from her hair and let her locks cascade down her back to her waist. "You have such beautiful hair, Emily," Polly said as she brushed the soft waves. "Why don't you wear your hair down tonight?"

With the brushing over, Emily rose and went about getting her younger brother and sister ready for the party. There had been a party nearly every week since the Blackleg had nearly disappeared. The coming of better weather along with a new diet of potatoes and horseradish helped get rid of the illness. Emily had been too busy to go to any of the dances or parties before. The thoughts of getting food for her family constantly worried her. As she pushed her younger brother and sister out the door, she smiled at her mother still sitting in the rocker with her baby brother Daniel.

The party was at the Bishop's house. His house was made of logs, unlike the Colton's sod house, and it seemed brighter and merrier. As Emily and her family walked through the door, the bishop shook her hand and the younger ones ran for the food on the table. There were small cakes and dried fruit for the children to eat.

"How are you Emily?" the bishop asked. He pointed to his table full of food and said, "Eat. Looks like you could use a little something to fill out those bones."

Emily hadn't taken time to notice but the last few months had worn on her young face. She'd lost weight and her usually bright eyes were heavy with concern.

"May I take some home?" Emily asked as the Bishop filled her plate.

"Please take as many as you'd like dear," he answered.

Emily had to hold back the urge to sweep the entire contents of the table of food into her apron. As she glanced around the room, she saw new people she hadn't noticed in their settlement before. She knew most of them were from a group who'd just arrived from Nauvoo. Emily knew these people were the last group to leave and had seen the city completely taken over by the mobs.

"A woman just arrived today," the bishop said pointing to an older lady standing in the corner of the cabin. "Been asking if anyone knows a girl named Emily Colton. Said she was with Jacob Ford when he died. She's been trying to find you and give you something."

Without excusing herself, Emily hurried toward the woman, excitedly took her by the hand and said, "Have you been looking for me? I'm Emily Colton. I was good friends with Jacob Ford."

The woman looked into Emily's eyes, smiled warmly then embraced her before she answered, "So you're Emily. You're even more beautiful than Jacob said. Come sit with me in the corner for a moment. I have a story to tell you."

Emily followed the woman to a quiet area of the cabin before the woman spoke again, "First time I saw Jacob was the night we were forced to leave the city at gunpoint. Couldn't offer much resistance to the mobs. By that time it was only the old and sick, and those kind enough to stay behind and help them who were left. When I first saw Jacob, he was bleeding from a bullet wound and carrying his invalid mother. We all got to work setting up camp with little but bulrushes and sky."

"You were with Jacob and his mother?" Emily asked anxious to hear the rest.

"Yes. I really believe they both would've lived if the mobs hadn't turned us out into the cold with no medical help. Jacob fussed over his mother for a week before she died. His own wound was festering. Suffered terribly." Emily cringed. "Don't say this to give you more grief dear. Before he got bad he told me about a girl named Emily Colton. When he got delirious at the end there after his mother died, he used to call your name." Emily bowed her head unable to stop the deep emotions rising within her. "One cold night, I wrapped Jacob up in a quilt and prayed he'd make it 'til morning. Then I fell asleep. It rained all night, hard. Terrible night. When I woke, I looked over at Jacob and saw a stranger there with him, a young man. I watched him comforting Jacob like they were brothers, protecting him from the rain. Stranger must have come stumbling into our camp that night by accident when I was asleep."

"Did you recognize the other young man?" Emily asked.

"No. Never seen him before," the old woman said. "But that stranger kept watch over Jacob all that night. When I woke the next morning, the stranger was asleep with Jacob lying dead in his arms. Walked over, woke him up and told him Jacob was dead. Then he asked me about him. Told him his Pa was gone to England. Only family he had was his dead mother. Seemed touched. Took all the money he had from his pockets and gave it to me. Didn't feel right 'bout spending all the money. Helped get me this far but I have some left. I think it should go to the person Jacob loved. Please take it."

Emily was overcome as the woman handed her a small purse full of bills and coins. She tried to refuse, but the woman was firm and insisted. That night as she got ready to leave the bishop's house, it seemed a miracle to Emily to have money jingling in her pockets. She gathered up her younger sister and brother and said a hasty good-bye. She couldn't wait to give the badly needed money to her mother so they could buy some food. On the way home, she found herself wondering about the unusual kindness of the stranger who'd given Jacob comfort right before he died and who now had become the answer to her family's desperate prayers.

CHAPTER THIRTEEN

After a few years in Mexico, Daniel heard of a company of sheep herders fitting up at Santa Fe, New Mexico on their way to California by way of the old Spanish trail. The trip would take the herd to the Salt Lake Valley then on the northern route into the upper part of California. Ready for a change, Daniel joined the expedition as a way to earn money and a way to see the untamed west.

During the years he'd been in Mexico, Daniel heard numerous stories about a group of five hundred men called the Mormon Battalion who'd marched through the southwest. Many travelers to Mexico told Daniel stories about the Mormons leaving the United States because of religious persecutions and settling in the Salt Lake Valley. These travelers also told Daniel the Mormons had stopped short of California and other settlements on the west coast so they would be left alone. Daniel wondered why Emily's people had to flee to a God-forsaken desert to find freedom from persecution. Sometimes he felt Mormons foolish for moving from place to place, leaving all their wealth for a certain belief or way of thinking. Other times he admired Mormons for their conviction and courage

Daniel heard several old mountaineers jeering at his group the morning he set out with a company headed for California with eight thousand head of sheep, "You'll never make it with all that meat to tempt those Utes! Better high tail it now while you've got the chance."

The Ute nation possessed the area from settlements in New Mexico to Utah Valley and regularly demanded tribute of any parties passing through. When Daniel heard the jeers, he winced inside, remembering too well the Comanche attack he'd witnessed on his trek to Mexico. He hoped he hadn't made the wrong decision. After leaving the settlement of Abiquin in New Mexico, Daniel watched the trail wind into wild infrequently traveled mountain country few white men had ever seen. The Utes were at peace, but the older men in camp boasted around the fire at night that peace to a Ute meant not scalping you when he killed you.

To Daniel's dismay, the outfit was surrounded and threatened by Indians almost every day. Their guide, a kind man named Thomas, was always able to influence the Indians by talking and trading with them. Daniel realized knowing the language and customs of the local Indians was most helpful while living in or traveling through the west. He determined to ride with their guide everyday and listen to Thomas talk and trade with the Indians every chance he got.

The luck of their trusted guide seemed to run out when the outfit reached a bend in the Dolores River and found themselves surrounded by threatening Indians once again. Daniel's outfit of about fifty men was suddenly surrounded by over five hundred mounted and armed Indian warriors. Daniel took cover and had his rifle ready to fire when a warrior approached the camp with a message from Chief Elk Mountain. He demanded either an American or a Mexican from the outfit be given up for a sacrifice because the Chef's son had died the day before. If the demand wasn't met, he promised his warriors would kill them all. As Thomas translated the demand, Daniel saw his captain grow angry.

"Tell him if he wants any of *my* men, he'll have to fight for them!" the captain said, raising his rifle cursing and spitting.

Thomas seemed uneasy as he relayed the message to the chief. Daniel watched fifty Indian braves cross the river on horseback, ready for battle. Two hundred yards from where Daniel took cover, these Indians stopped. Daniel's finger itched to pull the trigger. Heavily armed and mounted on horses, Daniel then saw other Indians coming toward him in tens and twenties eventually forming a half circle around the camp several men deep.

The chief rode forward and shouted his demands again. Thomas told the chief the men in his camp wanted to pass through the country in peace but were willing to fight for their lives. The chief suddenly dismounted.

Thomas took a deep breath then instructed all the men to quickly bring beads, paints, tobacco so they could make peace. The chief demanded flour. After being told they had none to spare, the chief still demanded flour. Thomas repeated they had none to spare.

"Poor, hungry dog," the chief said as he gave the captain a blanket of meat. "If you have nothing for us, we give you something."

When the chief realized he could only get the gifts offered, he agreed to peace and left. Daniel looked at Thomas with renewed respect that day realizing the part he played in sustaining all their lives was more important than the captain or the chief.

Toward the middle of August, Daniel's camp reached the Green River. The company was about ready to cross when Daniel dismounted while shoving a pistol into his holster. Suddenly the gun went off, the horse bolted and Daniel dropped to the ground. When he saw the ball had hit the button on his waist pants and carved through his flesh exiting at his thigh, Daniel screamed for the men to finish the job. He was writhing in pain when several men reached him and pulled him under a tree.

"Done for. Poor fool. Nothing we can do," one man said.

Daniel's groin and thigh burned, getting hotter and hotter by the minute. He tried but couldn't shout to the men who had given him up for dead. Daniel felt his mind drifting in and out of consciousness. In periods of lucidness, Daniel often saw one or two men above him checking to see if he'd stopped breathing. Daniel felt alternately burning hot and bone chilling cold.

"I'm not dead!" Daniel yelled whenever he was coherent.

The men knew Daniel couldn't last much longer and were glad of it because they didn't know what they'd do with him once they'd finished crossing the river. As he watched the men moving provisions and animals across the river, Daniel felt like living just to spite them. One night after dark, Daniel noticed several men standing above him. Daniel first thought they were going to bury him.

"I'm not dead!" Daniel spouted.

The men told Daniel they were merely going to float him across the river so Daniel stopped struggling. That night he overheard the men talking around the fire.

"At this rate it will take three days to get across the river. Much slower than I planned," the captain said. "Least that'll give Jones a chance to die decent like."

"Daniel would live if he had proper care," Thomas said.

"Now listen," the Captain said, "we don't want to see Jones die, but with a wound like his, probably wouldn't want to."

"I'll get someone to take care of you," Thomas said after walking over next to Daniel. "I know some Indians near here. They'll help you if I tell them you're my son."

Daniel took a deep breath and was finally able to slip into a deep restful sleep. It was nearly dawn when Thomas returned with a group of Indians from Tabby's band. When they saw Daniel, they immediately looked at his wound and tried to help.

"What's going on Thomas?" the captain shouted.

Thomas told the captain the Indians were willing to take Daniel back to their camp and care for him until he was well. Some of the men in the outfit became nervous as a wave of guilt washed over them, realizing they ought to be willing to do the same.

Two of the men approached the Captain and said, "We'll take care of Jones for you, sir. Don't let him be carried away by those savages. What's to become of him?"

The Captain agreed and sent the Indians away.

"I'd rather go with the Indians!" Daniel spouted.

Thomas reassured Daniel and finally persuaded him to stay with the outfit until they reached the Mormon settlements. He told Daniel he'd traveled with the Mormon soldiers from Santa Fe to California in the battalion and they never stole anything from the settlements like the other soldiers. He also told Daniel Mormons didn't drink, chase women, gamble, smoke and curse like the other men in the army.

"Better to leave Jones to the savages than a bunch of Mormons," one of the men said, laughing.

Indignant, Thomas stood and answered, "How can you say that? Have you ever known a Mormon? I've lived with them. They're good people."

The man didn't answer but shook his head and walked away. The two

men who promised to care for Daniel got busy building him a frame so
he could ride atop a stout mule. They noticed he grew paler and thinner
each day waiting for the company to finish crossing the river. When they
were ready to leave, the two men put Daniel on a pole frame placed above
the saddle because his wound wouldn't let him sit upright.

The camp continued to move slowly and several weeks after the
accident, Daniel was still in excruciating pain. Most days Daniel had to
wait for the other men to cut through the brush before he could be moved.
Whenever anyone tried to dress Daniel's wound, he insisted he would
take care of things himself. He was firm about being his own doctor,
so the other men finally gave up trying. Daniel felt if he could reduce
himself to the lowest possible living conditions, his wound wouldn't have
anything to feed on.

After nearly a month, Daniel caught sight of Fort Provo, a Mormon
settlement on a river down in the valley from Spanish Fork Canyon. The
trail down the mountain pass was steep and Daniel was a top-heavy load.
Several of the men set up guy-ropes and tediously lowered Daniel down
the canyon. Eventually the two men with Daniel become separated from
the main group of fifty. When they first sighted the Mormon settlements,
the men with Daniel became frightened and checked their firing arms.
Few in number, they were afraid the Mormons who would ambush them
and take all of their money.

"Knew some Mormons once," Daniel said to quiet their fears. "God
fearing folks. You don't have to worry about them."

"What do you know?" one of the men interrupted, "Heard Mormons
are awful disagreeable to strangers."

The next day, several of the Mormons from a fort near the Provo
River rode into Daniel's camp. There was a general hustling about and
several guns made ready to shoot. When the Mormons expressed a desire
to sell some butter and vegetables, Daniel's companions put their guns
down and cautiously paid the settlers a small sum. One of the Mormons
in the group noticed Daniel lying on the ground. This middle-aged
woman offered to take Daniel home and care for him.

"It's up to him," one of Daniel's companions answered. " He's a bit
partial to you folks."

"Would you like me to take care of you until you're feeling well enough to travel?" the woman asked.

Daniel looked up into the woman's eyes surprised to find genuine compassion before he answered, "Don't know. Hate to leave my friends. On our way to California. Lots of money waiting for us. But thanks."

The woman nodded reluctantly and left with the others in her group.

"Don't look like an evil bunch. Probably just trying to get our confidence so they can rob us in our sleep," one of the men said after the Mormons left. "Good thing you turned 'em down. Imagine being locked up with a bunch of Mormons all winter!"

"Not because that woman's offer wasn't enticing," Daniel interrupted, "but the money in California is a lot better looking."

The men laughed, slapped Daniel on the back and heartily agreed. The next day, Daniel's small party met up with the main group and camped together farther down river. None of the larger group had expected to find Daniel alive. When they saw him riding into camp looking like a skeleton on a horse, they all felt admiration for his tenacity.

For most of the following day, the old Missourians in Daniel's camp swapped stories about Mormons back home and bragged about their raids on their homes. Toward evening one of the men in the group suggested that reading from a Mormon holy book would make great entertainment around the camp fire. The men drew sticks to see who would go to the fort. The man with the short stick had to approach the Mormons settlers under the disguise of friendship. After posing as a potential convert, this man was supposed to get his hands on a Mormon holy book. It was dark before he returned.

"Did it! Got 'em thinking I'm about ready to get dunked. This here's what they call the Doctrine and Covenants," the man said as he waved the book above his head.

Daniel hadn't participated with the previous events and remained separate from the group after the man returned from the fort. Curious, Daniel watched as the man open and read from the book. Every man in camp drew in closer around the camp fire to listen. Daniel crawled nearer until he could easily hear what was being read. Everyone listened while the man read several passages. In this part of the book, God revealed what he wanted the prophet Joseph Smith to accomplish. Daniel had no trouble believing God spoke to other men who prayed for direction or answers for God had spoken to him.

The man reading the book suddenly stopped then belched out a string of profanities and laughed. He made several derogatory comments about Mormons in general and Joseph Smith in specific. From that point on, Daniel was uncomfortable listening. He wanted to grab the book from the man who was reading and order him to stop. Just then, one of the other men in the group snatched the book, flipped through the pages and began reading a part of the book that told about Joseph and Hyrum Smith's martyrdom by two hundred men with painted faces while the Prophet and his brother languished in jail on trumped up charges. The story touched Daniel to the core.

The man reading quoted from the book in a mocking way, "Joseph leaped from the window and was shot dead in the attempt, exclaiming: 'O Lord my God!' He lived great and he died great in the eyes of God and his people." The man quoting from the book clutched his breast as if shot and feigned death. "More like a great fraud," the man finished.

Daniel felt nauseous. He could no longer abide the callous inhumanity. He looked around the circle at the men in his camp and felt soiled for keeping company with them. Filled with an urgent need to distance himself, Daniel made plans to leave as soon as possible. He knew there had to be something better than all the gold in California, and that God might have an easier time helping him find it if he found better companions.

"That's enough," Daniel said, surprising the other men.

Daniel thought about Emily and her family and refused to listen any longer to men ridicule her prophet when he knew the Saints had suffered so much by the hands of evil men. Several others in the group seemed to feel the same way, for the group became deathly silent. The reader, sensing the negative effect his mocking melodrama had on the rest of the men, quickly turned the page and began reading from another section in the book. Then he stopped, cursed and swore that old Joe Smith deserved everything he got. The reading continued but Daniel crawled back to his blanket roll. A feeling of complete repulsion swept over him as he heard several men continue reading, laughing and cursing. Daniel knew he had to leave the group and soon.

When it was first light, a teamster from the fort rode by Daniel's camp.

"Can I have a ride to the fort with you?" Daniel yelled with a booming voice from his blanket roll.

The man was surprised at the request, but agreed. Daniel left his camp with only a moments notice to his captain, who gave him a small sum in payment for services, and a warm embrace with Thomas who'd saved his life. Daniel had to crawl to the stranger's wagon before he could get on. His wound and the long ride had made it so his muscles would no longer straighten out. The sight of a man crawling to his wagon moved the teamster to help, but Daniel refused. The two of them drove off together toward the Mormon settlement with Daniel's horse tied to the rear of the wagon.

"If you stay in Utah long, you'll soon be a Mormon!" the man said, turning to Daniel as they rode.

"About as likely as me becoming a Chinaman," Daniel answered the stranger. The man laughed and drove on. Daniel continued the conversation, "I could never be a Mormon. I believe in the Bible."

"Well, so do we," the driver answered.

"I thought you had your own Bible," Daniel said. "Some holy book written from gold plates."

"We believe in the same Bible you do. Just got us another testament of Jesus Christ called the Book of Mormon." the man answered. "Record of some of the people who lived in the Americas. Tells about the time when Jesus visited those people after his crucifixion and resurrection."

"I'd like to read that book," Daniel said.

"Looks like you'll be a Mormon yet."

Daniel laughed. "Isn't being Mormon something you are or aren't?" Daniel asked.

"Offered to anybody who will repent and be baptized," the driver answered. "It's the same plan of higher living Christ gave to the world when He was here."

Daniel felt puzzled but didn't ask any more questions. After arriving in the settlement, he found the same middle aged woman who'd offered to help him when he was back in camp and proceeded to make an agreement with her on reasonable terms. Daniel was surprised to find he enjoyed staying at the Higbee home, a modest cabin run by a hard-working, stout woman in her middle years, surrounded by countless noisy children. The Mormon settlement was surrounded by several Indian camps. Daniel felt surprised to be living among both the Mormons and the Indians. He'd been taught to hate and fear them, yet on this trip, he'd been offered kindness by both groups. Daniel eventually came to feel at home in the Higbee house.

As time went on, Daniel got so that he could hobble around a little with the help of a crutch he'd made for himself while he was laid up. Though often invited, Daniel declined joining the family when they prayed or when the other families came over to the Higbee house to eat, sing, play games, have worship services or talk doctrine.

One autumn day Daniel set out for the trees hugging the banks of the Provo River so he could be alone with his thoughts. Daniel had never spoken of Emily to the Higbee family or any other Mormon he knew. He was afraid they'd believe he had part in the Missouri persecutions. The night before, Daniel heard the men at the Higbee house discussing Missourians and how it would be hard for them to find salvation because of their cruelty to the Saints. Daniel felt ashamed and worried his salvation might be in jeopardy since he had failed to defend or protect even his best friend.

Emily, is this what it felt like to be in Missouri when everybody hated you because you were a Mormon? Daniel thought as he walked along the river bank. *Strange how I ended up among your people without you. If I could be in two places at the one time, I'd be with you.*

Daniel spent the night sleeping on the soft sand next to the river and listened to water lap against the rocks, trying to decide where to go and what to do. That same restless spirit moved him to look for work the next morning. A man at the fort in Provo hired him for a job in Sanpete Valley when he learned Daniel knew how to sell and barter with Indians. The next day Daniel thanked the Higbee family, then traveled south to

Sanpete Valley, a known trading center with the Ute Indians. Daniel hoped he could remember the trading skills Thomas had taught him on their long trip from Mexico.

CHAPTER FOURTEEN

Daniel worked for the men who hired him to trade with the Indians in Manti all that winter. Trading sessions with the Ute tribe were sporadic, so there were long unfilled hours to think and ponder. Daniel often wondered about the ideas and theology he'd heard discussed at the bishop's house that previous winter in Provo. He was also intrigued with the Ute culture. Ever since the day when Indians near the Green River had offered to care for him after his accidental shooting, Daniel felt an eagerness to learn about their customs and language. He spent a great deal of time visiting his Indian neighbors in their cone-shaped framed shelters made from brush, bark, reeds and clay.

After acquiring a rudimentary form of their language, Daniel was able to ask questions and learn about additional Indian traditions. He learned Ute bands assigned hunting grounds to family groups and were excellent hunters. Each year several members of the tribe would travel to New Mexico to trade. They'd developed an advanced economy that involved trading meat and hides for cloth, guns, liquor and metal tools. Daniel noticed the Ute diet consisted mainly of meat combined with some berries, nuts, roots, seeds and wild plants. Much of their meat was roasted over a fire, smoked or dried in the sun. Dry manure was used for fuel as well as wood and brush. Daniel observed that polygamy was common. He watched Indian women make earthen ovens by lining holes in the ground with hot stones.

Daniel enjoyed watching the Indians fashion clothing sewn together with sharp bone tools and long narrow strips of hide or animal internals. He especially admired their clothing made from tanned deer or buffalo hides, rabbit pelts and brightly colored bird feathers. Daniel eventually traded some of his personal belongings for a buckskin long shirt decorated with quillwork, leggings and long breechcloth along with high-topped moccasins and a heavy buffalo robe to keep him warm on cold nights. Daniel tried his hand at most of the common domestic activities, including cooking, weaving plant fibers into sandals and fashioning pottery from clay found on the river bank, along with making his own fur hat and leather gloves.

After acquiring a basic knowledge of Spanish from his stay in Mexico and several Indian languages from his stay in Sanpete Valley, Daniel noticed he had a great advantage over all the other traders in the area. He was able to understand the tribal leader's specific desires and learned to appreciate and accommodate to their trading customs and unique bargaining styles.

Not far from where Daniel was staying was a Mormon family by the name of Morley who befriended Daniel. He found a good friend in Isaac, the father. Daniel didn't bring up the subject of religion with him, but watched Isaac closely and respected his way of life. After a long day of trading, Daniel decided to visit Isaac rather than return to his empty quarters alone. Isaac's wife asked Daniel to stay for dinner. While the family was sitting around the table, Daniel brought up the subject of his Indian companions.

"Lots of Indians are more Christ-like than us so-called Christians," Daniel said turning to Isaac. "I think most have been forced into violent actions contrary to their basic natures. If given the same opportunities for learning, they'd do better than we've done. Felt the same way about the native people in Mexico when I lived there."

Isaac's eyes brightened. He sat silently and let Daniel speak freely.

"Have you read the Book of Mormon?" Isaac asked when Daniel was through.

"No," Daniel answered. "Why?"

"The Book of Mormon is the story of some of the ancestors of those people native to the Americas," Isaac said as he stepped over to a shelf and brought back a badly worn copy of a small bound book. "You're right; they have a rich heritage. Their history's been lost until this record was translated by Joseph Smith with divine help." Daniel was surprised and curious about the book. He took the book in his hands and turned it over, observing the well-used leather cover. "When the Savior said He had other sheep to feed who were not of this fold, He was referring, at least in part, to the people in the Americas. Some of those people kept a record for future generations like the prophets in the Old World did for the Bible. Go ahead. Take it. It's yours if you promise to read it."

Daniel thanked Isaac and felt eager to begin reading the history. It made perfect sense to him that Jesus would visit other people in different parts of the world after His crucifixion and resurrection in the Old World. It was reassuring to contemplate that God could still have prophets on the earth to translate such records.

During that long cold winter, several emigrants on their way to California stopped over in Utah to spend the winter. One group, headed by a man named Loomas, stopped in the Sanpete Valley and stayed close to where Daniel was lodging. Daniel noticed that within a few weeks this group asked for baptism. They were a rough bunch and he felt Isaac foolish to take them into the church so quickly. When he told his friend not to baptize them, Isaac told Daniel he wouldn't refuse that right to anyone who expressed a desire to change their ways and become disciples of Jesus Christ. Daniel had eavesdropped and heard Loomas and his men laughing at the gullibility of the Mormons and their naive eagerness to find new members. Loomas and his men routinely begged Isaac for handouts of food and supplies while they spent most of the winter loafing around Daniel's place joking about their Mormon slaves who were doing all the hard work. During one of their vulgar bragging sessions, Daniel walked toward the group set on putting them in their place.

"Hypocrites!" Daniel said sternly. At this, the group only laughed louder. "Believe by fooling a kind man into thinking you want to become members of his church, you've done quite a trick," Daniel continued. "Baptism means you're willing to become disciples of Christ. Do you even know who Jesus is?"

Loomas laughed and belched a long list of profanities. "Do a sight better with these fine looking Mormon women yourself if you'd have yourself dunked in that river. You can't tell me you ain't been looking at 'em and wanting 'em, can you, Jones?"

"No good Mormon girl would have anything to do with you whether you're baptized or not," Daniel replied.

"Just watch," Loomas said as he spit on the ground and turned to leave. "Won't be any good girls left in these parts when I leave. You'll be getting baptized soon as you take a fancy to one of 'em and you know it."

Several days later, two men from that same group came to Daniel's cabin and asked him to accompany them back to their camp. Daniel agreed only because he wanted to see what they were up to. As he approached their camp, Daniel saw Loomas sitting by a roaring fire with a large group of his men seated all around him. They were talking and whispering, their bright faces reflecting the flames. Daniel approached cautiously.

"Jones, get over here," Loomas said when he saw Daniel. "Heard tell you'd be the best guide in these parts, and seen most of the country south of here. Got a proposition you can't refuse. You got guts and brains. I like that." Daniel sat down next to Loomas and listened attentively. "When things thaw out come spring, we're raidin' all the settlements from Draperville through the valley up yonder and get our hands on all the horses around these parts. That's where you come in. You needn't bother with the horse stealing. But if you like the looks of the money those horses will bring, you're in. Give you a quarter profit if you'll meet us at the head of the Spanish Fork Canyon and take us through to New Mexico. Fine offer. What do you say?"

Daniel sat in awkward silence. He knew if he reprimanded or cursed these men for their plans, they'd have to kill him to keep him quiet. Yet he also knew he could never betray Emily's people and those who had shown him kindness. He tried to think up a quick excuse. He put his hand on his old wound and winced.

"Sounds like a smart plan. Mormons surely won't be suspicious now you're baptized. Told Isaac he was a fool to dunk the lot of you. Figured you had some plan brewing. Well, I wish I could cash in on this one, but my old wound's still giving me fits. Can't take a long trip just yet. Close as I can figure you'll probably get away with it. Already fooled 'em once."

"You'll be missing out," Loomas said adding a string of vulgar words

for emphasis. "You got guts. I like a man speaks his mind. I'll get someone
else, but if you tell anybody about our plans, I'll finish you off. So keep
your mouth shut."

Daniel nodded and left the camp for his cabin. In bed that night
his mind raced, thinking about all the people who would be wronged if
Loomas carried out his plans. When early morning light seeped through
the door, he decided to ride to the fort at Provo the first chance he got.
Daniel knew if he informed Bishop Higbee about the horse thieves, his
life would be in danger. He decided to warn the Mormons then finish
out the last few temperate weeks of winter camping and hunting alone
in Spanish Fork canyon. He'd heard the area was full of game. Within
a week, Daniel left Sanpete Valley and rode to the fort in Provo. After
locating Bishop Higbee, he told him about the horse stealing plans. The
Bishop listened carefully then thanked Daniel profusely when he rose to
leave.

"Now you've warned us, better stay here or your life will be in
danger," the bishop said.

"If I stay with you, *your* life will be in danger," Daniel answered. "I'll
finish out the winter in the canyons south of here. When they've gone,
send someone to tell me."

"Thank you, Daniel," the bishop said. "I'll warn the other settlers
and have them on their guard from now on."

Daniel gave the bishop detailed directions to where he planned to
camp then quickly left. He looked forward to this period of solitude as a
time to study the Book of Mormon and practice the hunting and domestic
skills his Indian friends had taught him. Several times during the next
few weeks while camping alone in the canyon, Daniel entertained several
riders from the fort in Provo. They brought him supplies and informed
him of the well-publicized promise Loomas made to shoot Daniel on the
spot when he found him. He felt glad to be so well-hidden.

Daniel thought a lot about his new Mormon friends during those
weeks in the canyon. After constructing a crude shelter, he read the
Book of Mormon that Isaac Morley had given him. He felt convinced
immediately that it was a true historical and spiritual account of real
groups of people native to the Americas. Daniel's favorite section was

the description of Christ's visit after His crucifixion and resurrection along with His teachings. As he read about generation after generation of continual wars and bloodshed, he realized the events in ancient American history closely paralleled those of the present.

After he finished reading the book, Daniel decided he needed to know for himself if Joseph Smith was in fact a prophet, if he'd really seen God the Father and His son Jesus Christ in a grove of trees as a boy of fourteen. If God had appeared, the world would *never* be the same. If he didn't, the world would *always* be the same. Daniel knew the only one who could permanently convince him was God. He prepared himself to ask by going without food for a day, following the example he'd seen in the Higbee home. As the sun set, Daniel knelt next to his fire and offered a simple prayer. He remained on his knees in deep supplication as light faded, his fire went out and numberless stars filled the vast black canopy of sky overhead.

All at once a sensation resembling fluid power flowed through Daniel's body from the ends of his toes and out the top of his head. He felt light and energy all around and through him. Suspended in time and space, Daniel was filled with an indescribable love and joy he'd never experienced before. He could almost touch and see unseen beings all around him. Catching his breath, Daniel opened his eyes. Like the shooting star he spied on the horizon, God's presence blazed through his soul like lightning illuminating the darkness and endowing him with light. He had found the promised land.

Daniel instantly realized his life could never be the same again; the world would never be the same. He was too excited to sleep. The next day, Daniel reread the Book of Mormon from dawn to dusk like a starving man at a lavish banquet. He found dozens of insights he'd missed the first time through and answers to long sought questions. For days on end, Daniel talked with God like one man would talk to another. With each question and answer, Daniel felt his vision expanding, his mind quickened. He felt at peace and at the same time energized, connected to all the forces of nature around him, radiant, immortal and full of love. Everything had changed, as if his life had transformed from darkness to full and living color.

Daniel interrupted his spiritual tutoring only long enough to hunt for game. Yet even hunting took on a new purpose. Daniel experienced a new awareness and appreciation for the animal's sacrifice so he could live. He longed to remain in this wrinkle in time, suspended between yesterday and tomorrow. Daniel knew this miraculous teaching season would be fleeting, that what he was experiencing would leave long before he was ready to return to his usual life in the valley.

Several weeks later after a day spent in the hills hunting, Daniel's horse pulled the carcass of a dead deer down the steep incline toward his hideout. As he neared his camp, Daniel saw a lone figure with his back turned sitting on a log next to his extinguished camp fire. He hadn't heard Daniel coming and sat perfectly still waiting for him to return. The man waiting at his camp looked like Loomas and Daniel felt a cold shiver run through his entire body. He grabbed his gun and got ready to defend himself. Daniel knew if the situation were reversed, Loomas would shoot him on sight.

Daniel cocked his gun then shouted, "Loomas!"

In a split second Daniel realized it wasn't his enemy.

The stranger turned around and yelled, "Don't shoot!" The man put his hands up in the air. "I'm not Loomas."

Daniel put his gun down, dismounted, and walked over to the man.

"The bishop sent me to tell you Loomas and his gang have left the valley. They're headed for California without any of our horses, thanks to you. I thought I was a dead man. Good thing you shout before you shoot!"

The man rode off in a big hurry to Daniel's disappointment. With Loomas gone, Daniel realized he was free to go back down in the valley, but wasn't sure he was ready to leave. He debated whether he should stay in Utah Valley or go on to California. He could make a lot of money in California in the gold mines and then return. He didn't want his new friends to think he was a "winter Mormon" like Loomas, who had joined for hand-outs, convenience or trickery.

Daniel worried about his Mormon friend's distrust and hatred of Missourians. Though Daniel knew he'd tried to warn Emily and her family, he still felt guilty he hadn't done more to prevent their deaths. So far, he hadn't dared speak about the events he'd witnessed back in Missouri for fear his new Mormon friends would see him in an accusing light or reject him altogether. Yet Daniel now felt a new burning desire to be baptized that eventually propelled him to action.

When he left his camp in Spanish Fork canyon, Daniel remembered Isaac Morley and knew he'd be the right person to talk to. He was a good listener and a good friend. He turned south. When Daniel got back to the Sanpete Valley, he found Isaac with an ax headed toward the hills to cut fuel for his family. Daniel asked if he could accompany him. As the two walked toward the hills, Daniel stammered searching for the right words.

"Isaac, I'm a Missourian," Daniel finally gushed. "My father hated mobs. Rightly accused of being a Mormon lover, but my uncle led an effort to drive Mormons in our county from the state. I was too young at the time to stop it. I only knew one Mormon family. Had a girl my age." Isaac acted surprised but remained silent. He allowed Daniel to continue his confession uninterrupted. "That Mormon girl was my best friend. She didn't talk much about her beliefs, but I saw how her family lived. I knew the horrible things people said about Mormons were lies, and I tried to get her family to leave before something bad happened to them, but they wouldn't go. They were burned alive in their house by men with black faces led by my uncle. Even though he didn't carry the torch, I knew he gave the order. He was a minister who pretended to be a man of God. When I found out what he'd done to the Colton family, I left. Haven't been back since."

Isaac looked at Daniel with a new fatherly concern. He realized Daniel's past had been gnawing at him and keeping him at a distance for some time. Being from Missouri in Utah was like being a Mormon in Missouri.

"Wasn't your fault," Isaac said. "Can't keep packing around another man's sins. Nothing you could have done."

Daniel heaved a huge sigh of relief, grateful to feel understood.

"At the time I didn't know what Mormons believed," Daniel answered. "Just knew one, and loved her. Now there's something burning inside me telling me she was and you are sincere, that what you teach is the truth, the better way of life I've been searching for all my life. I've read and studied the Book of Mormon. I've asked God to know if all this is true. Now I know for myself. It is."

"That's how I gained my testimony," Isaac said smiling. "Read that book and prayed about it. Never deny my answer."

"I know how you feel about Missourians," Daniel added. "I don't blame you. If I go to California and come back with some money before I ask for baptism, will you know I'm sincere and not another winter Mormon?"

Isaac placed his arm around Daniel's shoulder. "You don't have to go to California to prove your sincerity; it's all over your face. If you're ready for baptism, so am I. Been expecting this for quite some time. Here's my ax to cut the ice. Let me get two men to stand as witnesses. I'll be right back."

Daniel was surprised because he'd never spoken to Isaac about the penetrating feelings he'd been having. He'd expected reluctance, not eagerness at his baptism request. As he waited for Isaac to return with the other men, Daniel knelt, bowed his head and prayed.

Dear Father, Daniel thought. *Please take my sins away. I want a new life. I give you all myself.*

When Isaac returned with two friends, the four men walked together to the lake near the Morley home. It was still frozen over with a thin layer of ice. When they got there, Isaac pulled his ax out from under his arm, swung the blade over his head and immediately cracked a hole in the ice big enough to form a small opening. Isaac wrapped his arm around Daniel's shoulder and side by side, they both stepped into the freezing water. Daniel felt the numbing cold waters lapping against his skin and trembled. Yet moments later when Isaac laid him back into the icy water, Daniel felt as if liquid love flowed over him and through him filling his whole body with warmth and light. He had been dead and was about to be reborn.

"Having been commissioned of Jesus Christ, I baptize you in the name of the Father and of the Son and of the Holy Ghost. Amen," Isaac said, completely immersing Daniel in the lake. Then Isaac quickly brought Daniel out of the water and embraced him like an adoring father. As they climbed from the freezing water and up onto shore, they were both weeping and shaking.

"Clean as a newborn, fresh as new snow . . . all your sins forgiven," Isaac said. "Now your life is not your own."

Daniel nodded silently, unable to speak and blinking back tears. Isaac threw his dry coat around Daniel to keep him warm.

"Thank you," Daniel said.

The two men who stood as witnesses surrounded Daniel and Isaac blocking the wind from their trembling bodies as they slipped their boots back on. As he stood and received the embraces of his new brothers, Daniel felt as if he had come home. When the circle broke and the four men started back to the Morley place, each man wrapped his arms securely around each other forming a living chain. Daniel gazed up at the trees in the distant hills with the sun glowing behind them and heard the words of his father. "We have to be patient and trust God. Spring always comes."

It's spring, Daniel thought feeling God's love enter every cell of his body with warmth, joy and light. Daniel knew that his life was now forever changed. He had given his will over to God. When he glanced down at the ground, he felt suddenly as if he should take off his boots once more because he was walking on sacred ground. The whole world had become holy. Daniel noticed the crusted snow intermingled with small patches of new grass and felt instantly the promise of new life ahead.

CHAPTER FIFTEEN

Emily looked at her mother working so anxiously her hands trembled. It was the first time in several years she'd seen her mother that full of excitement. Emily realized her mother had been hiding her true feelings during her father's long separation.

"Papa's never seen the baby," Emily said as she helped her mother pour the melted tallow into the candle molds.

"But he'll be home soon," Polly answered, her dark eyes flashing. "Feel like a foolish girl waiting for a gentleman caller. Want to wear my best. Have all you children clean and shining. Don't want Philander to think we've been suffering. Your father's built a house for us to live in when we get to the Salt Lake Valley."

"Do you suppose Robert looks like Papa now?" Emily asked. "I can't picture him as anything but the scared boy who ran away and left me here to do all the work."

Polly didn't seem to hear Emily as she walked dreamily over to the straw bed in the corner of the room. She re-read a letter from Philander telling of his return.

"Your father and brother marched over two thousand miles with the Battalion," Polly said. "Marched through places few white men have ever seen before. Then they wintered in California. Both your own father and brother were there at Sutter's Mill when gold was found. Imagine leaving all that gold behind to come back to us."

Emily smiled faintly not matching her mother's enthusiasm. "Why are you happy about that? Don't you want to be rich?"

"My family makes me rich," Polly answered. "Philander never once told me about the hard things that happened on the march and I'm sure

146

there were plenty. I know it must have been a terrible ordeal. At least they didn't get into any fighting. Been thinking all this time maybe the next letter I received would be telling me your father or brother was dead. My friend Lois Coon said her husband died on the march. Dragged by a mule." Polly picked up the last correspondence she'd received and held it over her heart. "Now this letter! He's coming here and taking us to Zion. I've probably never told you how much I love your father."

"You don't have to tell me, Momma," Emily said as she walked toward her mother. "But remember you thought Missouri was Zion, then Nauvoo. What's so special about where we're going? What if Zion isn't somewhere else?"

"You're right," Polly answered smiling. "Zion is anywhere on earth where people love God and each other. Zion starts right here, inside us."

"Papa will be proud to see how well we managed with the money he sent us from his army wages," Emily added.

Just as they finished talking, Mary and the boys ran into the house upsetting everything in their path and yelling, "There's men riding in! Maybe Papa's with them!"

"Don't get your hopes up. Your father isn't supposed to arrive for a few more weeks," Polly answered.

Even as she was speaking, Polly heard a faint knock at the door of their sod house. She caught her breath as the door slowly creaked open. Polly turned. There in the doorway, covered with a heavy layer of mud and sweat, stood Philander with Robert smiling at his side. Emily screamed and upset several candles as the rest of the children squealed. Philander dropped his duffle bag as he quickly searched the room. When their eyes met, Polly gasped. Philander instantly raced toward her and gathered Polly in his arms. Lifting her into the air, Philander whirled his wife around the room, then set her back down and kissed her face a dozen times. Polly burst into tears. Mary and the boys gathered around their parents and pulled at their father's coat. The baby, suddenly finding himself alone, wailed in response to all the commotion.

Philander turned his head. There, with spring berries smeared around his mouth, sat his youngest son staring up at him in fear. He'd never seen Danny before and he was almost two years old. He walked softly over to the crying toddler and took him into his arms. Then he placed the child's tiny head gently against his shoulder and soothed him.

"It's all right," Philander whispered. "Your father's here now."

Philanders eyes filled with tears as the rest of his children surrounded him and pulled him to the floor, clinging to his coat and laughing. Emily glanced at the doorway and saw her younger brother standing there awkwardly. Robert had changed dramatically. His arms were much too long for his home spun shirt and his thread-bare trousers hit him at mid-calf. Robert's face seemed older with large cheek and jaw bones protruding from his sunburned face. His broad shoulders over-filled his opened shirt. All the resentment Emily had felt for months because of his unnecessary abandonment suddenly evaporated as she ran to her younger brother.

"You've gone and grown into a man without me seeing it," Emily cried as she looked Robert over from head to foot before she hugged him.

"And you," Robert said, "a regular lady now."

Polly walked over to her two oldest children and embraced them both.

"Did we surprise you?" Robert asked. "Been ridin' like madmen for the last few days hopin' to get here a little sooner than expected."

"Yes, you surprised me," Polly answered. "Had so much I wanted to get done before you got here. Look at me, not fit for a proper homecoming. Wanted to look so fine when you got here, have everything ready for you."

"Papa said if we were late, you'd work yourself sick tryin' to get ready for us, but if we were early, we'd save you all the fuss. Guess he was right," Robert answered.

"You've never looked more beautiful to me in your life, Polly," Philander said as he walked awkwardly back toward his wife with several children hanging around his belt.

When Polly sat next to her husband and began talking, Emily took Robert into the corner of the house and said, "Sometime tell me what it was *really* like, not what Papa wrote in his letters. Then I'll tell you what it was *really* like here, not what Mama wrote in her letters."

Robert nodded as he answered, "I shouldn't have left you here to do all the hard work without my help. Sorry for that. I just *had* to go with Pa. I think if I'd known what the march would be like, I'd been glad to stay. Served me right. By the time they found me, the battalion had marched too far to send me back."

"I don't want to hear any apologizing. Just tell me what it's like in the Salt Lake Valley. Some say it's terrible. I don't believe it can be that bad. What's it really like?"

Robert looked at Emily and shook his head, "Not so bad, but it's different. No trees and forests like you love, except in the canyons up in the mountains. Lots of insects and hardly any rain. When I first saw it, I thought it was the most God-forsaken place I'd ever seen. But it grows on you after you stay a spell. Has its own beauty."

Emily seemed stunned, "Why would President Young want to settle there of all places? I heard California is beautiful, with a moderate climate—and they've found gold."

"Yes, California is beautiful and we did find gold," Robert said. "I guess the prophet figures no one but Mormons would want that desert land. Maybe folks will leave us alone for a while. Brother Brigham says we can make it blossom like a rose. I wonder."

As the family gathered around the table that night, Philander led the family in prayer, "Father in Heaven, though this table is adorned with meager rations, seems the greatest feast 'cause we're together. Bless this food and bless this family on our journey west. With Thy help, we'll never be separated again, not in this life or in the eternities."

Philander and Robert spent most of the next day packing up the family's goods and getting ready to return to the valley. The sooner they could get a company of fellow Saints together, the better. They'd need to arrive in the valley in time to plant crops, if possible, and before the winter snows. Emily and Polly had been preparing for this trip across the plains for months now. They'd knitted socks and shawls, stitched quilts from worn clothing, sewn canvas into wagon covers and tents, prepared containers of dried fruit and meat, and had a wagon with a pair of oxen for the long trip. They'd woven willows from the river into baskets and ground wheat into flour. They also had seeds, sapling trees and farming tools ready for the journey west. The extra money they'd received from the stranger who'd been with Jacob Ford after the siege at Nauvoo had proved to be a life saver for the family.

When the day finally arrived for their wagon company to leave for the Salt Lake Valley, the Colton family was more than eager to start. Emily had mixed feelings about leaving. She and Robert sat together talking in the house after the busy preparations were completed.

"If I leave here now, I'll probably never see Daniel again," Emily said. "If he's still alive, my only hope to find him would be to stay here. Every step I take west feels like one step further away from him. Mom thinks I should try to forget. But I can't. I promised Daniel I'd wait for him if we were ever separated. Do you think I'm foolish?"

"I think we need to leave this country, put all this hate and violence behind us, and start out fresh," Robert said as he wrapped his arm around Emily's shoulder. "If we brood about what we're leaving behind, we'd never go. I think Daniel would want you to forget about him and go on with your life."

Emily had enjoyed her brother's company since he'd come home. She knew he was trying to be encouraging, but it felt as if no one understood her.

"It hurts to leave Ben here too. Seems like we're leaving him here all alone," Emily said.

Robert didn't answer for a moment. He'd seen Emily go to Ben's grave every day since they'd returned.

"Papa says he's going to give baby Danny a belated infant's blessing and dedicate Ben's grave before we leave today," Robert said. "Maybe that will help you let go."

"I'm an elder in the priesthood now," Robert said as he took Emily by the hand and led her from the empty sod house. "I can assist when Papa blesses Daniel."

Emily and Robert found their parents and younger brothers and sister outside waiting. They all walked together to the hill where Ben had been buried. The prairie was ablaze with wild flowers. Emily eagerly gathered a bouquet. After they arrived at the brow of the hill, the Colton family formed a circle around Ben's small grave.

"Father in Heaven," Philander said as he stood at the grave marker, "we dedicate this spot as the final resting place of our dear son and brother, Benjamin Colton. We recognize his spirit is with Thee and only his body remains in the grave. Please keep this hallowed spot free from any harm. We have to leave today. Please protect this place and keep it safe until the second coming of our Lord and Savior Jesus Christ, amen."

As Philander finished, Robert walked around to the grave marker and knelt next to his father. Polly brought her youngest son forward, whispering in his ear concerning what was going to happen to reassure and prepare him. Young Daniel sat at the head of Ben's grave on the grassy knoll and Philander and Robert knelt next to him. They both placed their hands on his tiny head as Philander began his father's blessing.

"Father in Heaven, we present this child before you to give him a name and a blessing. The name we have chosen is Daniel Webster Colton. We give thanks to thee for giving us this child to love and nurture. We give thanks that Thou hast seen fit to bring this family back together again. Now, I bless you, Daniel, that you may grow up in a place where you're free from the threat of death and violence, where you're allowed to live your religion and worship according to the dictates of your own conscience. We bless you to grow in faith and in stature and with the desire to be baptized and receive the gift of the Holy Ghost when you're eight years of age. We bless you with curiosity and a desire to know the truth; that you will seek for added light and knowledge out of the great books of life and schools of learning. We bless you that you will be worthy to serve a mission and share the blessings of the restored gospel of Jesus Christ with the world. We bless you that you will be worthy to be sealed in the temple for time and all eternity to your chosen mate. We bless you that you will be true and faithful to the covenants you make that day. We bless you with a posterity that will rise up and call your name blessed. We pronounce these blessings on you by the power of the holy Melchizedek Priesthood and in the name of our Lord and Savior, Jesus Christ, amen."

Emily laid the bouquet of prairie flowers on Ben's grave. No one stood or moved for a few minutes feeling the reverence of the moment until young Daniel reached over and patted the heap of earth at his feet.

"Goodbye, Ben," Danny whispered, cupping his small palm on the dirt covering his brother's grave. Then the family broke circle and headed back toward their wagon.

❧

Emily felt dirt grinding in her teeth and saw clouds of dust billowing from her full skirt as she walked. Her sunbonnet helped keep the sun off but trapped her body heat and sweaty hair around her face. Her high button shoes and long stockings were both worn through and Emily could feel every rock on the trail.

"When I get to the valley," Emily said as she walked next to her brother Robert, "I'm going to plant me a whole forest if I have to. A person shouldn't live without trees, it seems to me."

Emily stopped by the side of the footpath and stuffed an old piece of cloth from her torn skirt into her shoe in an effort to cushion her blisters and patch the holes. As she licked her lips, she could taste the salty sweat and dirt on her face. The tender skin on her nose, forehead and chin was raw and blistering. When she finished stuffing her shoe, she looked up and saw her family pulling ahead of her. The grass near the trail was curled and limp in the noon day sun and the sky was blue and clear without a trace of clouds. Emily coughed as she brushed off her skirt creating a cloud of dust, then hurried to catch up with the family. When she reached them, Philander was singing at the top of his lungs while he urged the oxen forward.

"Come, come ye Saints, no toil nor labor fear," Philander sang, "but with joy wend your way . . ." The song he was singing had become a favorite with the pioneers since those words penned by William Clayton were combined with the music of an old English folk song. Emily and her family had learned all the verses to new hymn by heart from listening to Philander and were often annoyed by his cheerful renditions.

Each teamster in their company, including Emily's father, was required to ride with a loaded rifle at his side. The wagons in the Colton's company drove three or four abreast during the day and circled in the evening for added protection from sudden Indian attacks. Camp life had become a monotonous routine for Emily—up at dawn, prayers, breakfast, feed the animals and move on—step after step, mile after mile, day after day. Emily looked at her mother breathing heavily as she walked over the sharp stones.

"Why don't you ride in the wagon?" Emily asked. "It's too hot for you out here."

Polly smiled and answered, "I want to see it all and feel it all going past me. Besides, those poor oxen are pulling all they can without my weight to tire them, I'm all right. It won't be long before we stop for the night."

Baby Daniel cried from the wagon and Robert reached in for him. He gave him a piece of dried fruit and propped him up on his shoulders.

"Not quite as exciting as when we first started, is it?" Robert said.

"How long has it been, Robert?" Emily asked.

"Well according to my calculations, we've been gone two months now and we're about halfway there. We have to walk over a thousand miles one step at a time."

As Robert spoke, Emily noticed a large herd of buffalo in the distance. They were a common sight on the trail now and Emily enjoyed watching the beasts graze together or run as swiftly as horses through the grasslands. Her family had been following the northern banks of the Platte River for a long time, avoiding the southern banks that were known as the Oregon Trail. Saints who had gone before them had set up settlements along the way and planted crops for the ones who'd follow them. This would have been impossible if the Mormons had followed the easier and more frequently traveled Oregon Trail. That trail was frequented by many Missourians and avoiding it helped unnecessary confrontations between Mormons and their hostile Missouri neighbors.

The next day, their company reached the area just opposite Fort Laramie, marking the halfway point to the valley. The fort was situated next to a river. After a mile and a half, this river joined with the Platte. The fort was made of clay and belonged to fur companies that housed several of the men and their families. From here, the company had to ferry across the Platte River. It was impassible on the northern side. It took several days before the entire company had been ferried across.

From Fort Laramie, the company took the more frequently traveled

Oregon Trail until they got to Fort Bridger. It wasn't unusual for Emily to see other wagon trains going in the same direction. They were headed for Oregon or California, unlike her company. Soon the group crossed the Green River on a ferry and from there, Fort Bridger was only a few days away.

After leaving Fort Bridger, the travel seemed almost unbearable to Emily. The valley felt so close and yet it seemed this part of the trail was the most difficult. Her whole body ached after days of climbing through rough hills and valleys. Yet no matter how exhausted everyone was, Philander always insisted everyone in the family pitch in and help make camp as quickly as possible so that they could dance and sing with the other members of the company at night. Most of the time, Emily was too exhausted to move after a day on the trail. Yet she found that when she did what her father requested, she felt refreshed and ready for sleep.

Emily often took the dirty clothes down to a nearby stream after they'd stopped for the day. First she looked for a large, smooth stone and then placed a filthy shirt or dress across it. Then she rubbed the clothing with a large chunk of lye soap her mother had made from ashes and animal fat. Next she'd run water over the clothes until they were full of suds. Then Emily would take a stick and pound the lingering suds and dirt out on the rock before a final rinse. Papa would start a fire and Mama would get some beans and flour on for supper.

Soon the incline of the trail became steeper and harder to climb. Every night when they stopped, Philander took something out of the wagon and left it by the side of the trail to lighten the load. Almost everything they'd started the journey with had been gradually abandoned. Only food, clothing and bedding had a secure place in the wagon. Sometimes as Emily watched Philander pull out another piece of the family's furniture or some other unnecessary belonging, she'd gather up the dirty clothes and hurry to the river. One of these times when Emily hurried off especially fast, Polly noticed tears in her eyes and followed.

As Emily threw the clothes over the rock, her mother came up behind her and asked, "What is it, Emily?"

Emily turned her eyes from her mother and wiped them before she answered.

"Hurts to see all of our nice things left on the trail to rot when we have so little anyway. Seems like such a waste. I know the team won't be able to climb through these mountains if we don't leave everything but necessities behind. But Mama, what will we do when we get to the valley if we don't have anything with us?"

Polly hesitated before she answered. She wanted Emily to know she understood her concerns but had a different vision of what was important.

"Emily, there was a time when your father and I felt the same way about possessions you do. Then the Mormon elders came. Before the missionaries taught us, I believed there was a certain beauty and security in fine possessions. But with each new possession, I found I wasn't satisfied. I was always thinking about something more I wanted." Emily was surprised. Her mother had never spoken of their early years of affluence. "Your father and I didn't start out wealthy. But as the years went by and your father's business went well, we were able to get a lovely home and all the furnishings I'd always dreamed of. I had everything I wanted, but I still felt something was missing."

"I never knew any of this," Emily interrupted.

"After the elders came and told us about the gospel of Jesus Christ being restored through Joseph Smith and the publication of the Book of Mormon, something came alive inside me. Even as a child I'd always searched for the meaning of life. Missionaries told me where I lived before I was born, why I was here on earth and where I was going after death. Their teachings filled a void in me that nothing else could. Now we've moved from Ohio, to Missouri, to Illinois, to Winter Quarters and now to the Salt Lake Valley. Every time we've left our home and most of our possessions. But there's something inside me nobody can take away. Do you understand?" Polly asked.

"I'm not sure," Emily said quietly trying to understand what her mother was trying to say.

"Don't need a lot around us if we have a lot inside us," Polly continued. "The gospel of Jesus Christ has taught me how to live and how to love. Now I don't ask myself *what* I want to have but *who* I want to be. I could lose everything, even Philander and all you children in death and still be at peace 'cause I know you've all been sealed to me forever. Being a member of the restored gospel of Jesus Christ has given me that privilege."

Emily contemplated the difference in having and being. She thought about her parent's sealing ordinance of eternal marriage in the Nauvoo Temple before they left. She knew her mother spoke the truth and it made her complaints seem small and petty.

"I feel so selfish," Emily said. "But don't you *ever* regret losing so much?"

"I get real tired when I think about all we've lost. Not so different than anybody else. We spent our lives building new homes and farms, just to leave it all behind. But I can go on because I know all these experiences are for a reason. God is teaching me, loves me, and knows my sacrifices."

The days seemed to blur together as the Colton family neared the valley. It had been nearly four grueling months since they'd started west, four months of painstakingly slow step-by-step travel. Even though Emily knew they were near the end of their journey, it still surprised her one morning when, after a steep climb, she suddenly glimpsed before her a broad expansive of land stretching into the horizon.

Standing at the mouth of Emigration Canyon, Emily saw the Salt Lake Valley for the first time. She quickly climbed a small hill where she could get a better view. There before her spread the open valley. In the distance, sunlight danced off a large saltwater lake. It had been an endless trail to get here through the flats of the Platte River, steps of the Black Hills, and on to the Rocky Mountains. There had been burning sands, eternal sage brush, rocky canyons and rock upon stone. Now there lay Zion surrounded with the everlasting hills.

Emily grabbed her long skirt and flung it into the air, then let out a yell that could be heard for miles. She twirled herself in a circle until she fell to the ground in a heap. Soon Emily's whole family climbed the hill and circled around her. Philander wrapped his arms around his wife then looked beneath them toward their new home in the distance. Robert helped Emily to her feet, laughing. Baby Danny raced around in circles screaming, "What's the matter?"

Philander took his baby boy into his arms and boosted him up to his shoulder as he said, "That's our new home Daniel. You can't see it from here, but I promise you, tonight we'll be together in our new home in the Promised Land. You'll grow up here without fear. We'll work hard, so you'll have trees to climb, rivers to fish from and fine homes to gather in. We'll build another temple to our God, finer than the one we left in Nauvoo. You'll be proud to be a member of The Church of Jesus Christ of Latter-day Saints. I swear I'll work the rest of my days so you can hold up your head high and kneel to your Maker without fear."

The trip down the canyon into the valley was slow going. When they reached the valley floor Emily was surprised to see mostly adobe and log structures surrounded by large fields of grain and pasture.

Not exactly a gleaming city on a hill, but it'll do, Emily thought.

After passing the major settlement in Salt Lake, the family neared their homestead on the banks of the Jordan River. Philander and Robert had built an adobe home there while they wintered in the Salt Lake Valley before returning to Winter Quarters. After being in California when gold was discovered, Philander and Robert wondered why Brigham Young had chosen this location.

God must have a different way of seeing, Philander thought. *Only He could see this place as the promised land.*

Their home was several miles from any other Mormon dwelling in the valley yet near an Indian camp. The Jordan River flowed from Utah Lake in the south to the Great Salt Lake much like the Sea of Galilee and Dead Sea layout in the Holy Land. Philander knew only the Almighty could make this valley into their promised land like he did for the Israelites after their long exodus from Egypt.

"There it is!" Philander shouted after he stopped the team of oxen.

In the distance, Emily saw a small adobe house next to the river. There was one small struggling tree leaning next to the house.

"Papa," Emily said, "you've settled here next to that lonely scrubby tree for me, haven't you?" Philander nodded.

The trip through the valley had sent the wagon bumping through mile after mile of sage brush, and Emily was elated to see a tree, even if it was only a scrubby one. When they got to their modest adobe house,

Philander lifted Polly into his arms and carried her through the doorway. Once inside, Polly knelt on the dirt floor and kissed it. The children slowly filled the house after their parents. Polly led the family in prayer.

"Dear God, thank you for our lives, each other, and our home. Bless this house with peace and love. Amen."

The Dutch oven was soon sitting on a ledge in a stone wall in the corner. Philander went for fuel to start a fire for supper. Emily took Mary and Danny down to the river to wash as Robert brought in their last barrel of flour for his mother to use for supper. Polly made some round, flat wheat cakes and baked them in the oven as Emily scrubbed the rough wooden table in the corner and put out the dishes. Their first supper in the valley was a simple meal, but to the Colton family it was a feast fit for royalty. That night the summer sun was warm and everyone stretched out on the floor on blankets and slept, too exhausted to move.

PART III

CHAPTER SIXTEEN

Spring was more than welcome in the Colton household. Long winter months of short daylight had recently transformed into longer hours of sunshine and new opportunities to improve their living conditions. The only thing Emily wanted to keep from their first winter in the Salt Lake Valley was her new friend. Her parents didn't approve. Though the Colton family had an adobe house near the river made with willows and clay, they also had a room at the fort in town if the local Indian tribes started any trouble. The fort had a solid wall on the outside that was arranged with small openings to shoot through if necessary for protection.

"Emily," Polly said as she sewed pieces of their newly dyed wagon tarp into useable clothing for her family. "I don't know if it's wise for you to see so much of that young Indian brave who comes around here. No way to know what he's thinking."

"You're afraid of him because you don't know him," Emily answered. "Wants me to teach him how to speak English. He's so eager to learn."

Polly realized how naïve Emily was. She didn't know how to tell her daughter to be leery of strangers without sounding judgmental.

"You don't know anything about his customs," Polly added. "I wish you'd at least stay around the house when you're with him and not go wandering off with him alone."

"I teach him a few new words every day," Emily said. "When we're through, he takes me for rides on his pony or we go to his camp and talk with his mother. She wants to learn English too. Then he tells me the Indian names for everything. I can't act like I don't trust him."

"Why not?" Polly asked. "Trust is earned. You barely know him."

"You should see the way his family has to live," Emily answered.

"They hardly have anything to eat. Last year Chief Walker's warriors attacked his camp. Took some of his brothers and sisters to sell to the Mexicans. They had to eat most of their horses last winter."

"What's his name?" Polly asked.

"His name means 'free wind' in English," Emily answered. "So that's what I call him. Sometimes he rubs oil over his skin that smells so good. It makes his skin shine."

"That's what I'm talking about, Emily," Polly said, here eyes widening. "You're a girl and he's a boy. It's not hard to figure out what comes next."

"Don't worry," Emily said. "We're not courting, just teaching each other our different languages. When he gets so he speaks English well enough to understand and I learn his language, I'm going to tell him about the Book of Mormon. Then he'll know for himself about the people he's descended from."

"Just promise me you'll be wise," Polly said. "Remember, he is a young man and you are a very beautiful young woman. His customs are different from yours. He's a pagan. You don't know what he believes."

"If Free Wind is pagan, it's because he's never been given the chance to learn a different way. I can give him that chance."

As they were speaking, Free Wind rode up to the Colton home, raced up to the door and pounded loudly until Emily responded.

"I'll teach him to knock properly today," Emily said as she swept her long skirt out the door. "Don't worry about me. I'll be fine."

Polly watched through the doorway as Free Wind lifted Emily onto his pony and rode away. She couldn't help feeling worried. Most of the settlers were afraid of the Indians, with good reason, and Polly had heard many troubling stories. The Indians who lived around their homestead seemed peaceful enough, but Polly still worried. She decided to have Philander talk to Emily when he wasn't so busy working in the fields, trading his labor for live stock, or building houses.

Philander and Robert had worked hard to stock the house with fuel and food for the winter after their arrival in the valley too late in the season to plant their own crops. They traded day labor for food supplies by helping with the wheat and barley harvest of the other farmers and hauling wood from the canyons. The settlers had no threshing machines so they cut the grain with a sickle or scythe.

If the farmer hiring their labor had horses, ground was leveled and a canvas thrown down. A post ten or twelve feet high was set in the ground with a sweep on top to which the horses were fastened to take them around in a circle. As the cut wheat was tramped out, it would be thrown around the pole and the straw to the outside. Then the wheat would be cleaned. If the farmer didn't have horses, the wheat head was cut off with a knife then thrown in baskets and later thrashed with two sticks tied together loosely. Philander and Robert also worked for other settlers who made molasses from corn that didn't have time to mature.

Polly, Emily and the younger children followed behind the threshers working long hours gleaning in the wheat fields. Day after day they bent low, searching the stubble for a chance head of grain. Their bodies ached; their fingers and feet bruised and bled. Brigham had put up a mill and they were able to grind their small stores of gleaned wheat and corn before winter set in.

Indians tribes camped nearby their home had come asking for handouts all winter, keeping food scarce for the Colton family. They finally resorted to rationing their remaining food stores. Now that it was spring, Philander and Robert had already started an irrigation system, planted their own grain fields and a large vegetable garden, along with a few small saplings for fruit and shade. An expert mason, plasterer and bricklayer, Philander also found plenty of work in town. Emily was more than eager to help her father with the farm work around their home. She preferred outside labor to domestic work. It had been a long winter with little to eat but sego lily roots, corn meal, smutty wheat flour, wild onions, thistle roots and pigweed greens. She hoped for better food to eat next winter.

Philander had recently been able to trade his masonry labor for a flock of chickens and geese, along with a milk cow and a few sheep. Emily and her younger brothers and sister worked with their mother to spin the sheered wool into usable fibers for making clothing and blankets. First they washed the sheered wool, then picked it over carefully before carding and making it into rolls. Then they spun the wool into long fibers and finally wove it into cloth. They also milked the cow, gathered eggs, washed clothes, fed livestock, fixed meals, churned butter, made soap and dipped candles.

When her chores where done, Emily felt free to enjoy several hours a day with Free Wind, teaching each other their respective languages. Emily had seen several Indian tribes on the trail across the plains who were friendly to her wagon company. They often traded beads, grain and fish hooks for meat. Emily had never seen any fighting or violence so she felt completely safe when she saw the Indians camped around her family's new home. There were no neighbors for miles and Emily enjoyed her companionship with the young Indian brave.

Free Wind's pony was black and white with a flowing mane. Emily enjoyed watching her new friend brush the horse with corn cobs and talk softly in the animal's ear. He lifted Emily onto the unsaddled pony then leaped in front and nudged the pony to a full gallop. Free Wind wrapped his arms around the pony's neck and told Emily to hold tight to his waist. Emily loved the wind on her face as they rode through the sage brush. The fast rides gave her an exciting feeling of power and freedom.

Emily and Free Wind stopped by the side of the river and let the pony eat the tender green grass growing around the banks, then sat across from each other exchanging new words. With each lesson, they watched the land gradually come back to life around them. Though the Salt Lake Valley was a desert, Emily had learned from Free Wind how to see her new home's beauty in a different way. He'd given her a deeper appreciation for the varied forms of life giving resources around her. The scent of grey sage had become as intoxicating as the smell of damp ferns on the forest floor in Missouri.

Tired of their language lesson, Emily lay back on the grass and sighed.

"What a perfect day," Emily said. Free Wind looked puzzled. Emily looked at him and laughed softly. "I wish you could understand everything I want to say. For the first time in my life, I don't feel afraid. It feels so good. In springtime, anything seems possible." Free Wind tilted his head as if trying to understand. "My family wants me to be afraid of you, but I won't go back to being afraid," Emily continued. "People in Missouri used to be afraid of us. I won't do the same thing to you. Being with you makes me feel free like the wind, just like your name."

"You free. Me free," Free Wind said. "My sisters, brothers no free."

"I'm sorry about what happened to your family," Emily answered. "I know Walker's men attacked your tribe last year. Took the children to sell to the Mexicans."

"Find brothers, sisters. Make free," Free Wind continued. "You help?"

"How can we help them now?" Emily asked. "They're probably in California or New Mexico."

"You teach me white man's ways. I find them."

Emily took Free Wind's hand and looked into his restless dark brown eyes.

"I can't tell you to forget your little brothers and sisters. Never forget people you love. Never give up hope. But right now I don't know what we can do."

Free Wind shook his head, "Find them!"

"I'm sure you will some day Free Wind. Never forget them. Never give up."

Free Wind reached out and stroked Emily's long hair. When she looked up, she saw herself reflected in the deep pools of Free Wind's dark eyes.

"I better get home," Emily said, standing quickly, but wishing she could stay.

❧

With the coming of spring, Daniel decided to visit Salt Lake City, the center of activity for the territory. He felt grateful his gunshot wound had entirely healed without any lingering effects, and he hoped to find a place of employment. The day after he arrived in Salt Lake City, he met Alex Wood, an old friend from the fort in Provo. As they began a conversation, a man walked briskly up to Alex and interrupted him. He asked if he knew anyone who could help him with his planting. Alex introduced Daniel to the man.

"Daniel, this is President Young's son-in-law, Edmund Ellsworth. If you're looking for work, here it is."

"Let's be going. There's work to be done!" Mr. Ellsworth said as he took Daniel by the arm and walked away with him.

Within the hour, Daniel had changed into his buckskins and was riding to the field with Edmund. The next few weeks, Daniel worked side by side with Mr. Ellsworth helping him till, furrow and plant the fields. They often talked about the rapid growth of Salt Lake City and their dreams for the future. When the work was finished, Daniel felt he had found a good friend.

"Let's go see Brother Brigham. He lives near my house in town," Edmund said to Daniel on their ride home after the last day of work.

"Better change my clothes first and get cleaned up before I talk to a prophet," Daniel said as he looked down at his dirty buckskins, manure smeared on his boots and sweat streaked arms.

"Brigham doesn't judge a man by his clothes," Edmund said resolutely. Daniel looked worried as Edmund chuckled, "Don't worry about Brother Brigham."

When they reached town, Daniel walked with Edmund toward President Young's house. Daniel could feel a lump rising in his throat when they walked through the door. Then he noticed a large man coming toward them with his hand outstretched. Daniel's heart skipped a beat as Edmund took the prophet's hand.

"Brother Brigham, this is Daniel Webster Jones, the man I've told you about."

"So, you're the one my son-in-law speaks so highly of. A pleasure to meet you, Brother Jones," Brigham said.

Daniel noticed President Young was a large barrel-chested man like himself. His hair curled under at his broad level shoulders. As Daniel looked into his eyes, he felt as if they were penetrating his soul. He took Daniel and Edmund by the arms and led them from the front parlor into his study. As they entered the room, Brigham directed Daniel to sit in a chair next to him.

"Brother Jones," Brigham began, "Edmund tells me you were baptized only a few months ago. What do you think of your new religion?"

"Well sir, that's a question that deserves more than a moment's thought for an answer," Daniel said at a sudden loss for words.

Brigham smiled and continued, "Edmund tells me you've spent the winter trading with Indians down in Sanpete Valley. He says you speak their language and also speak Spanish. Why are you so interested in conversing with these people?"

"Well, sir," Daniel began, "figure we can learn from each other." Brigham nodded in agreement. "Lots of things need changin' for the better. Mexicans have a slave trade with the Indians as lucrative as any on the high seas. Indians sell their children to the Mexicans for horses they have to turn around and eat to stay alive. That's the major reasons Indians fight each other. One tribe attacks another for the children, then sells them to these traders. Surely be kinder to each other if no such market existed. If these natives were given a way to better their conditions, they wouldn't have to sell their children just to stay alive on horse meat. Excuse me. I shouldn't get started on that subject."

"On the contrary, Brother Jones," Brigham said leaning forward in his chair. "This has been a grave concern of mine for some time now. I want to know everything. Have you had any dealings with these slave traders?"

"Yes sir," Daniel answered. "Seen them while I've been in Sanpete Valley and at the fort in Provo. Most from New Mexico. They have a few goods to start with. Trade goods along the way for horses. Then they take these horses and trade with the poorer Indians for their children. They take these children to lower California where they trade them to the Mexican-Californians for horses, goods or money. As they make the return trip, they buy more children and take them back to New Mexico where they sell them. I've heard them say girls bring $150 to $200. The boys bring about $100. Girls are in demand because the owners bring them up for house servants. It needs to stop."

"What are your plans now that you and Edmund are finished with planting?" Brigham asked.

"I'll return to Provo," Daniel said. "I know some people there."

"I want you to do something for me Brother Jones. It pleases me very much to see your kind feeling toward the Indian tribes. I'm the governor of this territory now. I want you to inform me as soon as you see any more of these traders in the area. We'll see if we can't put a stop to this awful business."

Elated, Daniel jumped from his seat and blurted, "Thank you, sir! Be a pleasure."

"That's not all I want to talk to you about, Brother Jones," Brigham interrupted. "Sit down and make yourself comfortable. Because you have a kindly feeling toward these people and have learned their language, you'd be a good missionary to them. I want you to preach the restored gospel of Jesus Christ whenever you go."

Daniel settled back in a chair and listened as Brigham continued for another hour. He felt himself growing more and more at ease as they discussed the Book of Mormon at length. President Young also asked Daniel to assist him with interpreting in the future. Daniel told him his conversion story and how he worried people in the church would doubt his sincerity.

"I don't doubt it," Brigham said. "I'm an excellent judge of character. Daniel, as you know, priesthood authority has been restored to the earth. Are you ready? Are you worthy?" Daniel nodded. "Priesthood gives a man the authority to act in God's name."

When Edmund and Daniel left the house that day, Brigham handed Daniel a note addressed to Mr. Joseph Young, directing him to ordain Daniel to the priesthood. Daniel knew then that President Young didn't doubt his sincerity.

Within a few weeks after Daniel's return to the fort at Provo, he noticed several Mexicans traders in town. These traders camped near the fort and let everyone know they were in the business of buying Indian children to sell for slaves. Daniel sent word to President Young as soon as possible. When President Young arrived in Provo, he met with the leader of the slave traders and asked Daniel to act as interpreter.

"Brother Jones," Brigham began at the meeting, "read this to them first. It's the law that prohibits the slave business." Daniel proceeded to read the law as the traders listened. "Tell them they're under the laws of the United State now and not Mexico," Brigham continued. "The treaty of Guadalupe de Hidalgo has changed the conditions. They are under the control of the United States from this time on. Tell them I am the governor of Utah and have oversight. It's my duty to see that this unlawful trade ceases to exist." The traders grew increasingly nervous as Daniel continued to translate for Brigham. "I understand this is an old custom and I don't condemn your practice in the past. I do hold you responsible for it now. It must discontinue. It is no man's right to hold another under bondage, least of all children. Aren't your hearts touched when you see young children torn from their parents?"

As Daniel interpreted for Brigham, the faces of the traders softened. When Brigham finished, the traders told Daniel they agreed the practice had to stop. They promised to discontinue the slave trade. Daniel interpreted as each man came before President Young and pledged his word. Daniel was surprised to realize most of the traders seemed truly sorry for this cruel practice. Even though they were getting rich from it, most were willing to put a stop to it when asked to do so. They'd looked at the business as a manner of earning food for their families and had never seriously considered how cruel the practice was. But there was one group led by a man named Pedro Lion that didn't seem sincere. They quickly pledged their consent but their dark countenances gave away their true intensions to Daniel's sensitive eye. Daniel felt he ought to warn Brigham about this group before be left to go back to Salt Lake City.

"Thank you for helping me, Daniel," Brigham said as he mounted his horse.

"Thank you, sir," Daniel replied, "but I'm concerned about a few of the traders here today. Pedro Lion's group seems insincere to me."

"Well, we can only wait and see," President Young said as he rode away. "We teach correct principles then hope people will govern themselves. Joseph Smith taught me that a long time ago."

It was late and the night air was cooling the small house as Emily sat next to her bed brushing her hair in the candlelight. Suddenly she heard the sound of several horses stopping outside their home. The door to the house flew open and in burst several Indians. Free Wind was with them. He ran over to Emily, swept her up into his arms and started carrying her from the house. Philander shot up from his bed and instantly reached for his gun. He pointed the gun at Free Wind's head. The older Indians with Free Wind pointed their fingers outside the house to several fine horses and then back to Emily.

"Put her down or I'll shoot!" Philander shouted at Free Wind.

"Wait, Papa!" Emily interrupted trembling. "Let me talk to him."

"Talk fast," Philander shouted. "I'll blow his head off if he takes one more step."

Emily listened as the elder Indians pointed to the horses and then said, "They say the ponies are yours. They are payment for me. Free Wind wants me for his wife."

"No deal," Philander said. "Tell Free Wind to put you down now or I'll shoot!"

"Just a minute, Papa," Emily said as she slid to the floor in her bare feet with her nightgown billowing around her ankles. "Let me talk to him. Please!"

"What do you think got you into this mess?" Philander shouted. "Come over here next to me right now young lady."

Emily stamped her foot defiantly and said, "Papa, they wouldn't hurt me. I'm their friend. This is their custom. It's a great honor. They want me to be part of their tribe. I won't do what you say unless you let me talk to Free Wind alone. Put your gun down. You're scaring them."

"I'm scaring them?" Philander shouted. "They barged in here!"

"Put the gun down. Please trust me," Emily pleaded.

"Philander, let her talk to him," Polly insisted.

Philander reluctantly lowered the muzzle of the gun but refused to let go. Baby Daniel screamed from his bed and Mary shouted for her Mama as Emily stepped out onto the porch with Free Wind. The tribal elders stayed inside with Philander and Polly. Emily noticed the stars overheard as the wind blew her gauze nightgown tightly against her bare body. Her hair fell gently around her shoulders in soft curls. She noticed Free Wind looked frightened and angry.

"I come for you. Fine horses, big price. Why gun?"

"My family doesn't understand," Emily said as she took his smooth brown hands into hers. "My Papa thought you were stealing me. Why didn't you tell me about this?"

Free Wind bowed his head and quietly said, "No tell. You know."

Emily continued, "You want me to be your wife and part of your tribe. Thank you. You've honored me. I don't want to shame you." Free Wind dropped his hands. "I care for you very much. You've taught me much more than I have taught you. You are my friend. How can I say it? I love you like a brother. I can't be your wife."

Free Wind took Emily's hand. "Want you. Come with me."

Emily drew back. Her heart pounding searching for the right words to say.

Philander burst through the front door shouting, "Enough time! Come back in this house, young lady! And you! Leave my house and never come back!"

Free Wind ran to his horse, mounted and galloped away before Emily could interfere. The Indians in the house quietly left with the wedding ponies following behind.

"If you had listened to us in the first place, this never would have happened," Philander shouted as Emily ran to her bed.

"Philander," Polly interrupted, "let me talk to her."

Emily was lying face down on her bed when Polly approached. She put her hand gently on her daughter's back and sat silently until the candles were put out and the house was quiet.

"Emily, your father is right," Polly said. "You shouldn't see him any more. You see how he feels about you. Please listen to us. He lives in a different world. Let him go."

"Mama, I can't let everybody go," Emily cried.

"You'll find someone, Emily. Please let him go."

Two weeks later, Emily found a moment to slip away from her home unnoticed. She rode her father's horse to Free Wind's camp hoping to find him. She'd been to Free Wind's camp many times and knew his mother well. As she rode into camp, no one looked up. Always before the friends and family of Free Wind had greeted her warmly and made her feel welcome. Today she felt as if she were an uninvited stranger. She noticed Free Wind's mother hurrying away. She jumped off the horse and shouted her name. The old woman stopped and turned toward Emily with a frown.

"You shame my son. He leaves. Why you come now? You make heart heavy."

"I'm so sorry," Emily said. "My family doesn't understand your customs. Please tell me where he's gone."

"Go with Pedro Lion. Bad man. My son die."

Emily knew Pedro Lion was an Indian slave trader. She knew Brigham Young had warned all the traders to discontinue the trade and Pedro had promised to return to his southern home. Emily had heard about many of the cruel things Pedro's gang had done and knew he was not a man of his word. She felt responsible for Free Wind's decision to leave, yet helpless to prevent what would happen next.

"I'm sorry," Emily said as she reached out to the old woman. She drew away. "What can I do now?"

"All my children gone," the woman said. "You go now. Never come back."

Emily mounted her horse and slowly rode from camp. Then she brought the horse to a gallop and rode as fast as she could until she reached the bank of the river. It was hours until she tired and returned home. After nightfall Emily rode up to her house and dismounted. Philander dashed from the cabin and grabbed Emily by the shoulders.

"Where've you been? I've told you not to leave this place unless I go with you. Why did you defy me? Have you been with him?" Emily refused to speak and ran into the house. "Emily, I've never known you to defy me. Why now?" Her father continued following her into the house. "Why do you go to him when I forbid it?"

Emily sat rigid on her bed and quietly said, "I didn't see him, Papa. I'll never see him again. He's gone with Pedro Lion because of me. They probably made him promises about finding his brothers and sisters. He'll probably die before they reach New Mexico."

Philander walked over to Emily's bed. "It's all for the best," he said. "You're from two different worlds."

"How do you know what's best for me?" Emily asked. "You've never taken the time to get to know him. He's fine, good and strong. I never intended to marry him. But he's a good friend. You've never even asked me how I felt about him. You just fear him and his tribe because they're not like us. How are you any different than those mobs in Missouri or Illinois if you hate a group of people before you even know them?"

"Emily, you don't understand," Philander said. "You're too young to know the problems involved. I'm your father. I deserve your respect."

"Too young!" Emily said as she wiped her face. "How old do you have to be before you learn to hate and fear people because they're different? I'm old enough to know how to love. If you'd just have let me talk to him, without bringing out your gun and shaming him before his elders. Now it's too late. He's gone."

CHAPTER SEVENTEEN

Several weeks had passed since Emily learned of Free Wind's departure. She'd alienated herself from her family by taking long walks and speaking only when spoken to. She missed her friend and companion more than she ever imagined she would.

"Emily, I can't bear to see you like this. Won't you share it with me?" Polly said as she and Emily sat side by side tying rags into rugs.

"It's not your fault," Emily finally answered, looking toward her mother. "I have to work this out on my own."

"I know how you must feel about Free Wind," Polly said. "I feel responsible for him leaving. There's more to this than you can understand. It's not just that Free Wind is Indian. He's not of our faith."

"I never said I was going to marry him. But I care about him . . . and his tribe."

"Emily, I'm going to tell you something," Polly said quietly. "Your father told me not to tell you this, but I feel you have a right to know. When Philander and I went into Salt Lake City the other day, we found out Pedro Lion and his gang has been thrown in jail there. They're awaiting trial for breaking the slave trade law. Free Wind is with them. Pedro's gang has accused him of murder. His trial will follow the others."

Emily's heart sank. "Surely no one will believe Pedro!" Emily said. "He's a known liar. Free Wind would never harm anyone."

"The court will have to decide that now," Polly answered. "Trial's tomorrow. Your father would be very angry with me if he knew I'd told you. He feels telling you would only cause more trouble. He believes his opinion of Free Wind has proven out. I'll send you into Salt Lake City tomorrow for some supplies. Go to the trial if you feel you should."

"Free Wind's mother told me her son was as good as dead," Emily said. "She was right. I feel responsible. I should do something."

Polly took Emily's hand. "They said Free Wind won't talk. He offers no defense. Maybe he'll tell you what happened. One of Pedro's gang was hauled in dead. Someone killed him. Maybe Free Wind will tell you who did."

"They're taking advantage of him. He probably doesn't even understand what's happening to him or he's too scared to speak."

Emily spent the rest of that day getting ready for her trip to Salt Lake City. The next morning before the sun rose, Polly prepared Emily's food and packed a bag for her horse. Emily was ready to leave before anyone else in the house stirred. Polly thought it best for her to leave before Philander woke. Emily mounted the horse, took a deep breath then leaned down and kissed her mother's cheek before galloping away. The air was chilly and damp with no sun to warm her. She shivered as the brisk wind hit her face. When Emily had ridden nearly out of sight, Philander emerged from the house fully dressed. He stood next to Polly and put his arm around her.

"Do you think she'll be all right?" he whispered softly.

Stunned, Polly glanced up into her husband's eyes, "But Philander, I thought . . ."

"I know what I said," Philander interrupted. "I've seen her face. I knew you'd tell her about the trial. I thought a lot about what Emily said to me. She's grown now, and I can't force her or make her decisions any more. I've watched her grieving the last few weeks. I love her and only want the best for her."

"I know," Polly said as she took his hand and they walked back into the house.

Emily rode quickly into Salt Lake City and located the place where the trial was already in progress. As Emily walked through the door, a man ushered her toward the stairs saying, "There's no more room on the ground floor. You'll have to sit in the balcony."

Emily quietly climbed the stairs, listening to the voices from the main floor. She found a place to sit on a hard wooden bench and gazed down on the court below her. Near the front of the room was a long table where

Judge Snow sat presiding over the trial. To one side of the room, a group of Mexicans sat with George A. Smith speaking for them. Emily could see Free Wind sitting with the other prisoners. Emily couldn't make out what George Smith was saying as she took off her wrap and bonnet.

A man on the main floor stood and in a loud voice announced, "Your honor, I feel it's about time we get to the official business of this trial. The defense has of yet been unable to prove that a trial is not necessary. Let's begin."

Emily knew the man speaking was Colonel Blair. He had been in the Texan war. She also noticed two large men seated in the front of the room with their backs toward her. She recognized one of the men as Brigham Young when he turned around and looked at the crowd. The people observing the hearing were applauding Colonel Blair. Brigham Young silenced them with his upturned hand. The balcony was packed with people from town and the stuffiness of the air around her made Emily feel light headed.

"Wish they'd forget the bother of a trial. They're guilty as sin and everybody knows it," a woman next to her said.

Judge Snow answered Colonel Blair, "Well, sir, you may begin. We are now officially starting this trial. Silence."

"I call as my first witness, Pedro Lion," the Colonel said.

Pedro stood and walked to a seat in the front of the room next to the judge. He cleared his throat and spit before he stretched his legs out in front of him.

"Pedro," the judge began, "you know we expect you to tell the truth. There are serious consequences if you don't."

Pedro interrupted the judge and said something in Spanish. Judge Snow called for the man seated next to Brigham Young to come forward and interpret for the man.

Taking off his hat as he came to the front of the room, the interpreter began, "I'd rather not translate what he said, sir."

Crinkling his brow, the judge looked at Pedro and continued, "Colonel Blair, continue please and tell your man to be more careful with his responses."

"It is known," Blair continued, "that you were caught in the southern part of this territory with many Indian children in your possession. You cannot deny that. There are people in this room who witnessed you selling these children. What can you say in your defense when you have been advised of the law in this land?"

The interpreter, beckoned by the judge, translated the question and Pedro's reply.

"He admits he was found with Indian children," the interpreter said, "says he had a good reason for it."

"Well, ask him to tell us about it," the judge said shifting in his seat.

Pedro listened as the interpreter asked him the question. He spoke quickly in response, using his arms to demonstrate his side of the story as he spoke.

The interpreter then turned back to the judge and said, "He says his group had many horses stolen from them. They followed the thieves and overtook them. He says when they came into camp, they found the thieves were filthy Indians. They killed the horses and ate them. The Indians offered to give them some children in payment for the horses. He says he didn't mean to break his promise to President Young, but he had no other choice."

As the interpreter was speaking, Emily stared at his back. Something quickened inside her. Emily knew she'd heard that voice before. Until he turned around, she couldn't be sure. The interpreter was large of stature and his sandy blond hair fell to his shoulders. Emily listened again and felt her heart racing. She rubbed her sweaty palms together as she leaned forward on the bench, straining to hear the interpreter's voice more clearly. She sat on the edge of the bench and listened as Colonel Blair spoke again.

"Thank the man. That will be enough," the Colonel said.

As the interpreter returned to his seat next to Brigham, Emily saw his features clearly. The young man's face was more angular and whiskered, unlike she remembered, yet the sad blue eyes were the same. Emily wanted to jump up and shout but restrained herself. She was suddenly transported to a quiet forest in Missouri and the boy she'd never been able to forget.

Daniel, Emily thought. *Could it really be you?*

Emily's mind whirled. She turned to the woman whispering beside her and asked, "The man who's interpreting . . . who is he?"

The woman looked surprised at Emily's question and replied, "I don't know, but I'll ask my husband." Emily waited as the lady turned and whispered to her husband. "My husband says his name is Jones. Says he interprets for President Young."

"Thank you," Emily said as she turned and watched Daniel walk over to Free Wind and speak to him. Free Wind turned his head and refused to answer.

"Sir, that Indian seated over there was with this group," Colonel Blair said as he approached the judge. "He surely saw what happened but refuses to speak. Pedro has accused him of murdering one of his men. He refuses to speak against these men or for himself. It's our only recourse to try him."

Judge Snow sat back in his chair and yawned, "One trial at a time Colonel. First, we have to decide whether these men are guilty of taking part in the illegal slave trade."

Several witnesses were called to the front of the room and all spoke of witnessing Pedro's gang selling the Indian's children. The day wore into the afternoon and at the conclusion of one witness's testimony, the judge interrupted the proceedings.

"I think we've heard enough of this business. These men have been involved in this business for many years and old habits, especially profitable ones, are hard to break. They were given the warning and they chose to disobey it. If I say it is all right to sell human beings for any reason, then this law is a farce. More incidents will surely infest these courts. But to be unduly hard would also be unjust. These men are guilty of dealing in the slave trade at their own admission. Fine each of them and be done with it. But they will be watched from now on. They've been delayed in this trip and will have to return to their homes now without any gold or horses. Maybe that is fine enough. Send them home. If they choose to put this young brave on trial for murder, let them make it known now."

Daniel turned to Pedro and asked him his wishes and told him the decision of the judge. Pedro seemed pleased but pointed to Free Wind and shouted in Spanish.

"He wants the young man tried, sir," Daniel told the judge.

"Did you tell him he'd have to remain here for the trial?" the judge asked.

"Yes, sir," Daniel answered. "Says he wants to see the Indian hang."

"Tell him that decision will be made by me, not him. We'll start a new trial tomorrow. Court is adjourned for today."

Emily saw the judge stand and leave before the crowd was dispersed. Several men ushered the prisoners from the building as Emily raced down the stairs. The balcony was full of people trying to find their way outside and she was pushed back as she tried to hurry below. Emily elbowed her way toward the entrance.

"Glad to see those Mexicans finally brought to trial," one woman said. "Imagine one of them was an Indian, selling his own kind!"

"You have no way of knowing if the Indian did anything of the kind," Emily said as she turned and ran down the stairs.

When she reached the bottom, the people in the lower part of the building had already left. She hurriedly searched the crowd but couldn't see Daniel anywhere. Then she noticed President Young climbing into a carriage.

"Where's the man who was interpreting for the court, sir?" she quickly asked leaning into President Young's carriage.

"Happy to meet you," Brigham answered smiling. "May I introduce myself? I'm Brigham Young. Who have I the pleasure of meeting?"

Emily looked embarrassed and answered, "I'm sorry, sir. I know who you are and I don't want to bother you. But, the young man interpreting for you . . . is his name Daniel Jones?"

"The young man I was seated next to," Brigham answered, "is called by that name. Says he has no family in these parts. Do you know of him? He is a man of few words." Emily nodded. "Fine man. Don't know where he's gone. I have seen him head up the canyon. I'm told he spends hours there. Maybe that's where you'll find him. Come with me. I'll send someone after him."

"No, thank you," Emily answered as she rushed away, forgetting to say goodbye.

Emily quickly found her horse, then rode toward City Creek Canyon. It was autumn and the leaves on the trees in the canyons were amber and gold. Emily breathed in the brisk mountain air as she rode at full speed toward the woods. When she reached the river, she realized her effort to find Daniel was too immense.

Emily dismounted and quietly led her horse through the soft leaf canopy. The lonely wind whispering through the leaves calmed her and made her feel at home. Pulsating sounds of crickets hummed in her ears as the sun sent shafts of gold filtering through the trees. Then from the corner of her eye, Emily noticed a man kneeling at the side of the river. She dropped the reins of her horse and walked slowly toward the dark figure silhouetted against the trees, approaching him from behind.

"Did you know these woods are full of all kinds of secrets if you'll just listen?" Emily said softly as she approached.

The man's back stiffened for a moment. Then Daniel turned and glanced in the direction of Emily's voice. He quickly stood. Dropping his hands to his sides, Daniel saw the face of a beautiful young woman coming toward him in the glow of the setting sun. Her face had matured and become even more beautiful, yet Daniel knew instantly who was standing before him.

"Emily!" Daniel said breathlessly.

"Daniel!" Emily replied.

He ran toward her and wrapped his broad arms around her waist, lifting her feet off the forest floor then swinging her in a broad circle. Emily felt the warmth and trembling of Daniel's body as he wrapped himself tightly around her.

"I thought you were dead," Daniel said, his voice breaking with emotion.

"How did you get here?" Emily asked.

A lone leaf fell from a tree above them, landing on Emily's upturned face. Daniel brushed it from her nose and kissed her. The sun lazily slipped behind the western horizon and slowly, one by one, stars began to glisten through the silhouette of darkened trees. Daniel and Emily sat huddled together on the forest floor as the hushed sounds of nightfall and evening winds swept over them and echoed down the canyon walls.

Hours passed in what seemed only moments as they recalled their long years of separation and all the events that had brought them both to Salt Lake City. Emily told Daniel about her years in Nauvoo, Winter Quarters and her long trek to Utah. Daniel told Emily about his years in St. Louis and Mexico, and his long trek to California that left him recovering from a gunshot wound in Utah.

"A wound?" Emily asked. "Where?"

"Completely healed," Daniel said blushing with embarrassment. "Don't worry. Everything still works. I'm completely recovered."

Emily melted into Daniel's shoulder as he wrapped his arm around her even tighter. Then he reached over and touched Emily's soft cheek turning her face upward toward his.

"I've been baptized," Daniel said looking deep into Emily green eyes. "I know for myself that the gospel of Jesus Christ has been restored."

"Daniel," Emily said surprised and obviously pleased. "How? Where? Tell me."

Daniel related details about his accidental shooting, the Higbee home in Provo, trading with the Utes in Sanpete and his conversion after reading and praying about the Book of Mormon in Spanish Fork Canyon while hiding from Loomas.

"Maybe there's some grand design to all this madness after all," Emily said.

"I've missed you more than you'll ever know," Daniel said, his emotions rising. He took her hands and kissed them softly. "I still can't believe you're alive."

"I missed you too," Emily answered. "Never thought I'd see you again."

"You're the love of my life," Daniel said.

"And you mine," Emily answered.

Later, when they discussed the ongoing trial, Emily offered to help by talking with Free Wind.

"Do you know him?" Daniel asked.

"Yes," Emily answered. "We're good friends. Would you see if I can talk to him before the trial starts tomorrow? I feel responsible for his trouble."

Daniel felt confused but didn't pry. He nodded. Afterward, they both mounted their horses and rode back to town. It was late and Daniel had a hard time finding a place for Emily to stay the night. Finally he found her a room at a boarding house. When he left that night, he promised to return early in the morning for her.

When Emily walked into the strange room at the boarding house, she felt suddenly very much alone. She quickly undressed and sandwiched herself between the quilts of the bed. The room was dark and quiet, yet the excitement of finding Daniel lingered, making it difficult to sleep. She stayed awake thinking about everything he'd told her that night and recalled the warmth of his embrace. Yet images of Free Wind and thoughts of his imminent hanging made sleep impossible. She turned over onto her stomach and mashed her face into the feather pillow. Her thoughts drifted back and forth between the past and the present. Emily didn't know what tomorrow would bring, but she knew she had to help Free Wind. Turning over, moonlight from the window illuminated her face.

"Thank you for giving Daniel back to me," Emily whispered.

Slowly the light from the moon faded and morning sun brought a brilliant dawn. Emily washed, dressed and was waiting when Daniel came for her.

"If you want to talk to the brave, we'll have to hurry," Daniel said as he placed his arms around Emily and hurried her toward the stone jail where Free Wind was being held. As they entered the building, Emily felt the cold chill and dampness of the rock walls around her. She looked slowly around the room and spied Free Wind hunched over against the wall on the far side, restrained with ropes. Emily quickly reached for a knife from the guard's desk and dashed over where Free Wind was held. He was half asleep when Emily took his arms and cut the ropes from his wrists. He stiffened and jerked abruptly back against the wall.

When he saw it was Emily, Free Wind relaxed and asked, "Why?"

"Where's some food for this man?' Emily shouted.

The guard, already surprised at Emily's behavior, defiantly said, "He won't eat anything we give him. What do you think you're doing?"

Daniel took the guard by the arm and began a sudden conversation with him, guiding him out the door. Emily looked back at Free Wind.

"You need to speak to the man who came with me. He wants to help you."

Emily gently touched the rough, bloody cuts on his wrists.

"I kill man. They kill me now," Free Wind said as he looked into Emily's eyes.

"What happened?"

"No matter. I die."

"No, you won't die. I won't let them kill you. Tell me what happened."

"Why now?" Free Wind asked as he looked down at the floor.

"I care about you. You're my friend. You know that," Emily answered.

Free Wind looked up. "Pedro promise, take me to brothers and sisters in land south. Say I talk with Indians on trail. Pedro say Indians steal horses. He lies. Indians find stray horses and eat. Pedro steal Indian children. When he sleep, I take Indian children back to parents. Pedro come. We fight. One man die. Pedro say he kill me. Other men come. Pedro says I die for white man I kill. I die for Indian children."

Emily looked imploringly into Free Wind's eyes and asked, "Why don't you tell the other white men what happened? They won't hang you for trying to save the children. Free Wind, these people are trying to help you. Don't let Pedro have you killed."

"I kill man. They kill me. White man's law."

"No, Free Wind. That is not the law. Please tell them what happened when you stand before the judge. He'll understand, it was self defense."

Free Wind looked at Emily as she pleaded and reached for her hands. He gently pulled her head toward his shoulder just as Daniel and the guard walked back into the room. Daniel watched as Emily and Free Wind embraced in the corner and quickly diverted his eyes as he turned to leave the room embarrassed.

"He wants to tell the judge what happened now," Emily said after she found Daniel standing outside the jail waiting.

Within a few moments, several men came for Free Wind. Daniel and Emily followed them to the place where the trial was being held. The judge was already seated when they reached the court, the room buzzing with conversation. Daniel took Emily by the arm and guided her over to a seat next to President Young.

When Brigham saw Emily for the second time, he held out his hand in greeting and said, "See you found Daniel. Sorry, you never told me your name."

"Emily Colton. And yes, thank you, I found him."

Daniel looked flushed and sat down quickly.

"What do you think of the trial, Emily?" Brigham asked.

"I know the man being accused. He shouldn't be on trial for self defense."

"How do you know what happened?" Brigham asked. "Brave's never spoken."

"He's my friend and he told me what happened this morning. He was trying to save the Indian children and it was Pedro who attacked him and caused the fight. I'm sorry sir, but I feel responsible for all of this," Emily said apologetically.

"Responsible?" Brigham asked surprised. "How could you be responsible?"

"Free Wind came to my home one night and wanted me to go with him and marry him," Emily answered as Daniel listened. "He brought several fine horses as a gift for my parents. My father took out a gun, insisted he leave and shamed him before his elders. He left soon after that to find his younger brothers and sisters who were sold into slavery with Pedro. Free Wind wouldn't have gone if I hadn't rejected his marriage proposal."

As Daniel listened to Emily he realized she had a new life separate from his and he'd been intruding into circumstances where he had no right to interfere. He felt embarrassed he'd assumed Emily would still love him as much as he loved her. But she obviously cared for Free Wind very much. As Emily spoke, Judge Snow hushed the people in the room and called for the trial to begin. Pedro was called first to give his story. Translating for Pedro, Daniel came forward and listened as he spoke.

Daniel turned to the judge when Pedro was through and said, "He says this Indian thief tried to steal the Indian children from him. He says this Indian killed one of his men when they tried to stop him."

Daniel continued with Pedro's story and later also translated the stories of several of his gang. They all stayed with the same story about Free Wind when they testified. When Pedro's gang was through, Free Wind was called to the stand.

"Pedro lies," Free Wind said after he was seated on the stand and asked to relate his side of the story. "Pedro say Indian steal horses. Indians find stray horses. Eat for food." Free Wind stood up and pointed at Pedro. "Pedro steal Indian children. Cry all night. Pedro sleep. I take children away. Pedro chase. I fight for children."

Free Wind opened his shirt and exposed a bloody wound no one knew he had. Emily, Daniel and Brigham gasped.

"Pedro take Free Wind and children back to camp. Rip off clothes. Tie me to tree. Make Indian children spit at Free Wind. Pedro promise to kill Free Wind. Then other white men come. Pedro set Free Wind loose before white men see ropes. Pedro say white men kill me. White man's law. Free Wind ready to die. I die for Indian children."

The people in the building were silent as Free Wind spoke. There was a hush and a respectful pause before Judge Snow interrupted, "Young man, you can sit down now. If what you say is true, you should not be on trial but these men should be."

The judge looked at Pedro who was nervously shifting back and forth in his chair, obviously surprised to learn Free Wind knew how to speak English. His eyes darted around the room looking for a quick escape route.

The judge turned to Daniel and asked him to translate again, "Tell Pedro if he wants to pursue this case, there will have to be another trial held. This Indian brings new light on everything."

Pedro listened as Daniel translated and quickly replied. Daniel listened, turned to the judge and said, "He says he'll drop his charge if you will promise to let him go free."

Asking Daniel to translate, the judge turned to Pedro and said, "I will let you go, but we will be watching you. If you ever harm this young brave again, I will personally see that you are brought back here to stand trial and pay for your crimes."

Free Wind sat straight in his chair as the judge adjourned the session and Pedro and his men left the building. Emily ran to Free Wind and wrapped her arms around him.

"See, I told you if you told the truth everything would be all right!" Emily said.

Daniel awkwardly watched Free Wind and Emily embrace then quickly left the building through the back door. Emily took Free Wind by the arm and guided him to where President Young was seated.

"This is my friend Free Wind," Emily said to President Young.

President Young took Free Wind's hand and said, "You speak English very well. Who taught you?"

Free Wind turned to Emily and smiled. Brigham paused before he turned to Emily and said, "Will you do something for me?" Brigham asked. "Will you two stay here in town and start a school for others who want to learn English? Your friend here can be your first official assistant. I'll get you all the students you can handle." Brigham turned to Free Wind and smiled as he extended his arm for a firm handshake. "When you've finished learning English," Brigham said, "we'll teach you the gospel and give you a Book of Mormon and let you read it for yourself. You ought to know what noble people you came from." Brigham turned back to Emily. "Will you do this?"

"I'll have to ask my parents first," Emily slowly answered. "I think they'll agree."

"Who is your father?" Brigham asked.

"Philander Colton. We live near the Jordan River."

"I know your father well," Brigham said. "He served in the Mormon Battalion. In fact, he was my first volunteer. I think he'll be pleased to hear his daughter will be the first teacher in this important work. I'll speak to him myself. You two come with me now and I'll show you a place for your first classroom."

Emily glanced around before leaving and noticed for the first time that Daniel had left. She was disappointed and wondered where he went as both she and Free Wind followed Brigham. Within an hour, Emily had a classroom, a list of pupils, and a place to live and eat. President Young also located a family for Free Wind to board with several blocks away.

Emily searched for Daniel for the rest of the afternoon. She wanted to tell him the good news. She finally found him in a saddle shop working on a piece of leather.

"I've got wonderful news," Emily said as she bustled into the saddle shop. "Why did you leave so quickly from the trial?"

"I have things to do," Daniel said as he went back to work.

"Well, listen to this. President Young has asked me to stay in town and start a school for the Indians. He wants me to teach them to speak English. Free Wind will be my first assistant. Isn't that wonderful? I'll be able to see you every day now."

Daniel turned away and was silent for a moment before he answered, "I wish you well. Always thought well of Indians myself."

"But I was hoping you'd help me. President Young said you know Spanish and also have a good knowledge of some Indian languages."

"Told you I have work to do," Daniel said curtly as Emily finished, pretending to be busy.

"What is it?" Emily asked. "What the matter?"

"Nothing," Daniel answered. "Nothing."

Emily was surprised to find teaching came as naturally to her as loving the children in her classroom. Free Wind watched in amazement as the normally unruly children from his tribe worked hard to learn the new language. He realized Emily respected each child and they in turn respected her. Though foreign to him, Free Wind tried to mimic her tender and patient handling of the children.

"You should see all the beautiful children in my school," Emily gushed as she ran into the saddle shop where Daniel was working several weeks later. "They're doing so well. Free Wind is invaluable. He speaks English better every day. He's very intelligent. Brigham is paying us both with room and board. But even without that, I think I'd continue."

She paused, but when Daniel didn't respond, she added, "When I see the children's eager faces, I want to give them everything they deserve. Every day their shining eyes look up at me and beg for more. Some of the older boys are a bit cocky, but Free Wind can handle them. Daniel,

I wish you would come down to the school, even if just for an hour, and see what we're doing."

Daniel continued working, appearing only half-interested.

"Emily, why do you come here every day and tell me about Free Wind?"

"I'm sorry, Daniel," Emily said apologetically. "I thought you'd be as excited as I am about the school."

"School's a good idea. But why do you have to talk about Free Wind?"

"Well, let's not talk about the school or Free Wind then. Let's go for a walk in the woods," Emily said as she grabbed Daniel's arm and pulled him from the shop.

Acting reluctant, Daniel followed her. When they reached the hitching post, he lifted Emily up onto his horse then mounted himself. Emily put her arms securely around his chest as Daniel quickly trotted the horse out of town headed for the canyons. Emily took a deep breath as Daniel slowly guided the horse over the sharp rocks and stones. Emily rested her cheek against Daniel's back as he led the horse through the low maple brush covering the foothills. They rode farther and farther into the canyon until large evergreens, maples and aspens canopied the sky.

"Stop right here," Emily begged. "It's beautiful."

Emily slid from the horse and walked through the crisp fallen leaves. Twirling, Emily spun in a circle until she was dizzy then fell into a heap of leaves against a tree. Daniel imitated her, accidentally falling on top of her. He turned and saw Emily's face inches from his own then laughed warmly at her new appearance—leaves sticking out from her hair and falling from every fold in her dress. Rolling over and lying back in the leaves, Daniel stretched his arms above his head and sighed.

"Why do you put up with me?" he asked. "All of the other young men in town would love to be in my place."

Daniel gazed up at Emily who was now kneeling at his side smiling down at him. She gently placed her small hand on Daniel's moist brow and stroked his sandy hair back from his forehead.

"But everybody else isn't you," Emily answered. "Don't you understand how I feel about you? Even after all the time we've spent together lately, don't you know?" Daniel shook his head. "When my family left Missouri, I wanted to go back for you. It seemed everything was tearing me away from you. Had no control. Then I wrote letter after letter to make sure you knew I was alive and where to find me. At first I thought your uncle wouldn't let you answer, and then I wondered if you didn't care any more."

"I never saw any letters," Daniel answered. "Except one from my oldest sister and that was by accident. I don't know how many letters my uncle kept from me. I was sure you died in the fire."

"While we were in Nauvoo," Emily continued, "I watched the docks every day for a steamer bringing you back to me. Every time we were forced to move again, I dreaded the thought of leaving you farther and farther behind. I missed you every single day. Every time we had to leave, it felt as if part of me was left behind."

Emily kissed Daniel on the forehead.

"It's been a long time," Daniel said taking her hand. "Nothing stays the same. You have new friends now. I want you to be free to make decisions without me getting in your way. Won't bind you to any past promises."

"It was a promise I chose to make. I *never* want to lose you again," Emily answered, confused by Daniel's words. "You're not binding me to the past. I'm free to choose and I've chosen."

Daniel sat up and wrapped his arm around Emily's shoulders. He pressed her head softly against his shoulder and stroked her long dark hair.

"I can step back for a while," Daniel said. "I'll give you some more time to think."

"I don't want that," Emily said frustrated. "I thought I'd lost you forever."

Daniel continued, "But if you hadn't seen me when you did, things might be different with you and Free Wind."

"He's my friend," Emily said, "and nothing more."

"I've seen the look in his eyes and yours. I've seen the fulfillment you have with him at the school. You shouldn't feel bound to old promises. I want you to be happy."

"If you want me to be happy," Emily said, "then be quiet and hold me. Don't talk this way anymore."

Daniel was silent. He wanted to hold Emily and never let go more than he wanted to breathe.

On Monday when Emily walked into the saddle shop to talk to Daniel, she found it empty except for the owner. She quickly searched through the room for Daniel.

"He's gone," the owner said.

"Where?" Emily asked. "Where is he?"

"President Young asked for volunteers at conference to go to the aid of some of our people stranded on the plains with handcarts. Daniel left early this morning to help."

"Did he leave any messages?" Emily asked.

"This letter for you."

Emily took the letter and slowly walked back through the entrance to the saddle shop. She couldn't bear the thought of Daniel leaving. She ran to the school and collapsed in an empty chair. Just then, Free Wind came into the room. He walked to where she was sitting and noticed the tears streaming down her face.

"What is it?" he asked as he sat down next to her. "Why are you crying?"

Emily held the unopened letter in her trembling hands.

"Daniel's gone," she said. "I don't know if I'll ever see him again."

Free Wind looked into Emily's eyes.

"This is the man you love?"

"Yes," Emily answered. "President Young needed volunteers, but I think it's more than that. Daniel thinks I love you, that I need time to make my decision without him around. But I've already made my decision. I can't live without him."

"If he leaves now, he might lose you," Free Wind answered as he brushed away the tears on Emily's cheek." Emily shook her head. Free Wind squared his shoulders and changed his countenance. "I have good news. I'll be baptized tomorrow afternoon. Will you come to my baptism? President Young will be there."

"Of course I'll be there," Emily answered. "I'm so happy for you."

"Thank you," Free Wind said, taking Emily's hand and kissing her palm. "I'll always love you for giving me a new life."

Later that night Emily opened the letter from Daniel in the privacy of her boarding room.

Dearest Emily, I truly want your happiness. Do not feel I've deserted you. You should be free to take your time before you make your choice. If God is willing, we will meet again. I love you. I will always love you.

Daniel

CHAPTER EIGHTEEN

Daniel spent the day traveling to the Big and Little Mountains with several men to rendezvous with other volunteers. Once they reached the place, he silently watched the other men drive in with their teams and wagons full of provisions. However, his mind was not on the events of the camp. He watched George Grant named as captain, but let his mind wander just before the men named Daniel as the chief cook.

"You'll be the most popular man in camp on this trip," one volunteer yelled.

'What's that?" Daniel asked.

"You're chief cook!" the man said as he walked away, laughing.

Camp moved out the next morning and traveled as quickly as their animals would allow. They hoped to reach the first stranded emigrant company soon. The men rode tirelessly to the point of total exhaustion, not stopping for supper until dark. After they camped, the heavens opened and snow fell. The whirling, blinding flurry made it difficult to move or see. Daniel thought of the stranded Saints and knew a blizzard could prove fatal if the handcart groups were ill-prepared for the wind and cold.

Later the next day when Daniel's group of volunteers reached the Green River, they were surprised and disappointed to find no one there. No one in the rescue party voiced their concerns but all silently wondered if they were too late and feared they'd find no one alive. When the rescue party camped again, those in charge decided it would be best to send a few men ahead to locate the handcart companies. This small group was instructed to give hope to the marooned Saints by informing them that more help was coming. Daniel was selected to go with that group.

At South Pass the most severe snow storm hit. Daniel's small front group could barely press on through the blinding blizzard or ride through the huge snow drifts blocking their way. Even though they knew they had enough provisions and fuel to camp and wait out the storm, they also understood stopping meant lost time and lost lives. Contemplating the emigrant's critical condition made Daniel's small group press on against indescribable obstacles.

After crossing the divide, Daniel's group turned down into a sheltered place on the Sweetwater. They set up camp and all offered fervent prayers that night. Later, Daniel tried to rest but some gnawing anxiousness kept him awake. He felt impressed to leave camp and walk toward a grove of trees nearby just before nightfall. Once inside the cluster of trees Daniel was surprised to see two men on horses riding toward him.

"Who are you?" Daniel shouted with his hands cupped around his mouth so he could be heard above the howl of the raging wind whipping about him.

The men dismounted and trudged toward Daniel before they answered, "I'm Brother Willie and this is J. B. Elder. We're Mormon emigrants from England. We need help. Are you alone?"

Daniel slipped from his horse, leaped into the air and yelled. He ran to the men and embraced them heartily saying, "We've come to help you. Where's your company? Are they all dead but you two?"

"No, but they're dying quickly," Brother Willie pleaded.

Daniel directed these two men back to his camp and shouted for the others. Brother Willie quickly informed them about the condition of his company. Daniel and the other men immediately packed up and left camp following Brother Willie and Brother Elder. As night fell, Daniel urged his horse forward using only the moon for light. They rode all through the night.

When morning dawned, snow was still falling. As they rode into Brother Willie's camp, Daniel's heart sank. After surveying their conditions, he saw there were no provisions to be seen anywhere. He could hear the sounds of children crying and women weeping. As they walked from tent to tent, Daniel saw whole families huddled together with no fire to warm them. The dead lay unburied. No one was strong enough to dig a grave. One of the men in Daniel's group went for fire wood while another passed out their meager food provisions to the starving people.

Daniel found a spade and immediately commenced digging a large grave. He pushed and kicked away the snow, then plunged the shovel into the hard earth with all his strength. When he finished, he looked back dismayed to see the newly dug hole filling up with new snow. Then Daniel slowly walked from tent to tent asking for the dead. Most of the families were huddled in frozen silence. Daniel was forced to enter the tents and carry away the frozen bodies himself.

At one of the tents, Daniel found a family huddled in a circle while a young woman sat alone in the corner cradling an infant in her arms. She was singing a lullaby as she rocked the child. When Daniel asked for the dead, a young man in the circle rose and told Daniel the baby the woman was holding was dead. Daniel walked over to the woman and asked for her child.

"You can't have my baby," she said. "He's only sleeping. I have to keep him warm. So cold. He needs to stay close to me or he'll perish."

Daniel remembered his mother's reaction after his father death and knew this young mother needed someone to help her let go. He looked in desperation to the young man he figured was the husband.

"Eliza," the man said, imploringly. "Baby's dead. Been dead for days. Let the man take our child and bury him. Eliza, please let the man bury our son."

The young woman continued rocking the baby in her arms and sang her lullaby louder as her husband continued pleading. Daniel looked closely at the young woman's face. It was blue with cold. She had a blanket wrapped around the baby but not herself. He walked over to her and put his own coat around her shoulders.

"What's your baby's name?" Daniel asked softly. The woman continued singing. "I can tell you love your baby very much."

The young woman turned, looked at Daniel and tried to smile.

"His name's Caleb. Isn't he beautiful? He's my only son. Been married for ten years and couldn't have any children. God blessed us with this miracle. Want to raise him in Zion with the Saints. He's so tiny. I would show him to you, but it's too cold to unwrap him."

As the woman continued rocking her child, Daniel placed his gloved hand gently on her shoulder then parted the baby's blanket so he could see the child's face. Though he had seen death many times before, nothing prepared him for what he saw. The tiny child looked like a sleeping angel sculpted in ice. The baby's eyes were closed with frost still lingering on the lashes.

"He's beautiful," Daniel said. "He's lucky to have you for his mother."

"He'll grow fine and strong and live in the valley of the mountains with the Saints. Doctor said I can't have any more babies. He'll be my only child."

"May I hold him for a while?" Daniel asked. "I'll be very gentle."

The woman looked at Daniel and hesitantly answered, "Only for a moment. You must promise to be very careful. Don't let the wraps fall."

Daniel took the blanket covered babe into his arms and gently rocked the small child as his mother watched. Daniel hummed the haunting melody he'd learned as a child then quietly sang, "I'm goin' there to see my mother. She said she'd meet me when I come. I'm just a-goin' over Jordan. I'm just a-goin' over home." Bowing his head, Daniel gently kissed the baby and said, "Mother in Heaven will hold you now. She'll keep you warm."

Suddenly the woman burst into deep anguished sobs. The young father ran toward his wife and grasped her tightly as her empty arms fell limply to her sides.

"Oh Eliza, will you let me comfort you now?" the young man said.

"I can't bear it. I didn't think God gave you things you can't bear," the woman wailed as her stiffness melted and she suddenly collapsed in her husband's embrace.

Daniel walked silently from the tent and back into a bitter blast of cold air holding tightly to the young child. This was the last of the tents. He lovingly carried the small bundle in his arms toward the open grave he'd finished before. He slowly climbed down into the hole and gently placed the tiny babe in the arms of a deceased woman. Daniel looked about him on the dozens of bodies and reverently counted each one. As he knelt and gently brushed the newly fallen snow from their frozen faces he wondered who they were and why they were willing to risk everything to come to Zion. He thought of his own conversion and baptism and understood. Whether in life or death, they had each willingly placed their lives in God's hands. Snow flurries continued to blanket the frozen bodies as he slowly climbed from the grave.

Daniel picked up the spade and hesitantly shoveled heavy frozen earth and snow over the bodies lying side by side, covered in worn blankets and tattered shawls. It felt cruel to throw dirt over their angelic faces, yet he knew it had to be done. He'd seen what wolves could do with a dead body. When he was through, he could stand erect no longer. He sank to his knees and wept.

Hours later, after helping the stranded handcart company as much as they could, Daniel's small front group told the emigrants about additional help ahead on the trail and encouraged them to move on as quickly as possible. Then Daniel's group set out to find the other companies who remained scattered across the frozen prairie. No one in Daniel's group expected to go any farther than Devil's Gate. When they reached that place, none of the other emigrant parties were in sight. Despondently, Daniel's group stopped and camped for the night. As they sat around the fire, Daniel heard the men talking to each other. Several of the men with Daniel felt responsible for the companies now stranded and dying. In their eagerness to get their friends and family to Zion, they'd encouraged them to start to the valley even though it was late in the season. They had no idea snow would come so soon, so cold, so deep.

One of the men turned to Daniel and said, "My dearest friends are with these companies. I encouraged them to come. This'll haunt me forever. I should have told them to wait for spring. I had no idea we'd have an early winter."

Daniel sympathetically listened before he answered, "You couldn't know what would happen, how the early snows would trap them out here. Don't blame yourself."

"Why did you come?" the man asked. "You have no family in these groups and you were well settled in Salt Lake City. My conscience was stinging when Brigham asked for volunteers, but surely your conscience was not. Why? Why risk your life?"

"When President Young asked for volunteers," Daniel answered, "I wanted to help, but it was also a convenient time to leave. Maybe God doesn't need heroes, just men like you and me with complicated reasons. Maybe we're all God has."

"Heck of a situation to get ourselves into, Jones," the man continued. "We're all fools. Probably freeze out here with the rest of 'em."

Daniel nodded and settled in for the long cold night. In the morning, the group got together and decided to send a few of their men on ahead to find the rest of the emigrants. Daniel, Joe Young, and Abe Garr were selected. They looked at each other, grasped forearms, and promised not to return until they'd found the last of the emigrants. Then the three men rode their horses slowly out into the white bleakness and the cutting wind of the snow-swept Wyoming high plains. Every yard seemed a mile, every mile seemed ten. Daniel and his companions rode on and on with no end in sight. There were no signs of life anywhere. They all silently wondered if the marooned Saints were all buried somewhere under a huge blanket of white and wouldn't be found until spring.

When the men camped that night, they still had not found any trace of the other stranded parties. They hated to imagine what would happen if they didn't find the companies soon. Daniel's mind wrestled between thoughts of Emily and fear of the life and death situation he was in. Now that his chances of survival appeared remote, he regretted leaving Emily without saying goodbye in person. He hoped she'd understand, but now seriously wondered if he'd ever see her again.

Daniel's group headed out the next morning freezing, hungry and discouraged. Mile after freezing mile passed and still they spied no signs of life any where. Daniel bowed his head to avoid the cutting wind's blast and watched the snow pass beneath him as they continued on through the white wasteland. Suddenly Daniel noticed a human footprint in the snow and followed the trail of indentations in the snow with his eyes.

"Here they are!" he shouted as he spied the emigrant camp far off in the distance.

The three men rode quickly into camp. They were at Red Bluff and much father from the valley than any of the original group of volunteers believed they'd need to travel to find these groups. Edward Martin was the leader the handcart company they found and Ben Hodgett led the wagon company. They soon learned another company was down near the Platte crossing. As they rode into camp, the stone cold bodies came to life. They rushed at the men, desperately grabbing at their heels and pulling at their hands.

"Angels from God sent to rescue us from death!" several of the people cried as they reached up frantically to grab Daniel's hand.

Daniel's companions seemed to relish the admiration, but Daniel realized what had to happen quickly to save this group of people so ill equipped to handle the condition they were in. He quickly pushed the people off, dismounted and shouted.

"We're not angels! We're men much more suited to this occasion. We've come from the Salt Lake Valley to help you. Our company and wagons are loaded with provisions and they're not far from here. Listen to me. You'll need to keep moving or you'll die."

When Daniel finished, a general quieting settled over the camp. Daniel and the two other men surveyed the people and found they were nearly as bad off as the first group they'd found.

"Your only salvation will be to travel a little each day," Daniel said as he gathered the people together. "Please listen. Get your things together. Leave right now. You will meet with our rescue party before long and they will help you. We have to leave you here now and search for others."

Daniel watched the people slowly packing their goods as the three left the camp. He heard many of them praising God vocally. The trail was much the same after leaving this second camp. Snow covered everything and the air was deathly cold. About fifteen miles father down the trail, they came to John Hunt's camp. As they rode through the company, no one seemed to notice the three men had arrived. The people in this group seemed in better shape than the others they'd seen. Daniel saw wood was plentiful and the people seemed pretty well off.

"It appears we're not needed here," Joe said.

Daniel and Abe agreed and followed Joe down to the bottoms where they set up camp. While they were warming themselves by the fire, a man from the emigrant company walked into their camp. Recognizing Joe, he rushed back and told the people about the three men camped nearby.

Suddenly all the people in the emigrant company ran toward Daniel's group. They picked up the three men and carried them back on their shoulders shouting and singing all the way. When they reached camp, they pitched a special tent for Daniel's group and tried to make amends for their lack of appreciation.

The next morning, Joe left and told Daniel and Abe to get the camp moving. Joe went ahead with some other men to the next company at Platte Bridge. Unlike the companies Daniel had seen before, this group seemed apathetic about leaving. When they were advised to move on, they began arguing about who should go and who should stay. As they watched the fighting, Daniel and Abe looked at each other in utter disbelief. They shouted for the people to stop fighting and immediately form a circle around them.

"You people don't know what's ahead of you or what's in store for you if you stay," Daniel said as Abe silenced the people.

The emigrants were quiet for a moment then immediately began arguing again. Daniel and Abe saddled up and made ready to leave, feeling disgusted. Just before they rode out, the sky filled with dark threatening clouds. Snow fell; first large downy flakes floated in the air about them but soon the entire heavens were a blanket of dark storm clouds. Daniel looked up and noticed one small opening in the ominous threatening sky. This hole in the storm cloud took the shape of an arrow pointing toward the valley. Sun shone through the opening illuminating the space as if it were on fire.

"Do you see that?" Daniel shouted as he mounted his mule and pointed to the sky. "See that shining arrow in the sky? Better get out of here before it closes up. It's pointing the way to the valley. We're going. If that arrow closes up before you leave, you're all lost. It's up to you. Don't delay or you'll die!"

Daniel and Joe left the camp and began the long ride back to the other companies. When they reached the place where the Martin Company had been camped, they found this group of emigrants had already left. The Hodgett wagon company was just beginning to leave. As the three rode on, they found the Martin Company trying to push their way over a steep and rocky ridge. Daniel's face cringed when he saw the company strung out for three or four miles over the barren expanse and difficult climb. The emigrants were all pulling and pushing their heavy carts filled with their meager belongings and family members through the thick mud under terrible conditions.

Daniel watched tired, grey-haired men pulling and pushing their carts filled with sick and dying wives and children. He saw women pulling and pushing their carts filled with sick and dying husbands while children clung to their long skirts. Daniel saw a trail of blood left in the snow from the emigrants bloody feet wrapped in rags after shoes had long worn away. Small children carried crying babies on their shoulders and fell repeatedly under the heavy load. With each step the hill became steeper and rockier until their strength was completely exhausted.

Daniel and Abe rushed toward a handcart where a young girl was the only member of her family well enough to push or pull. They hooked their mules to her cart and helped pull her up the hill. One by one, Daniel and Abe hooked their animals to the emigrant carts as more and more people tried to ascend the rocky ridge. But there were too many carts to adequately assist. They could not possibly do all that needed to be done to help these desperate Saints.

The entire company reached the top of the hill by night fall. Bitter cold air sent a freezing death threat through camp. Daniel saw children huddled with their parents, mud frozen on their faces, feet and clothes shivering with only a canvas tent between them and the north wind and snow. Only a little sage brush in the area was suitable for fuel. Daniel dug another large grave that night and filled it.

The next morning, Joe came into camp and the three headed back to their original rescue party at Devil's Gate. When the three arrived, the original volunteers thought all the Saints had perished. They shouted and clapped heartily when Daniel told them of the stranded companies, one of which was close behind them. Within an hour, the whole rescue group fitted up and left at full speed to assist the struggling emigrants.

All that day, the rescuers helped the exhausted emigrants back to the fort. Some of the groups were in hand carts and some in wagons with teams. By the time the last of the companies reached the fort, Daniel counted twelve hundred people. Soon the raging winter storm increased in its severity. Conditions at the trader's fort just above Devil's Gate grew intolerable. The provisions Daniel's group brought did not last long with all the people who were in such desperate need. Daniel's rescue party waited for days at the fort for additional help to reach them from the valley. Days passed and still no help arrived. Each morning, dozens of fresh graves were dug.

A few days later, one handcart company asked to move over into a cove near the mountains, believing the location would provide more shelter, a wind break, and fuel for warmth. The group with wagons stayed at the fort because it was impossible to move the heavily loaded wagons in the snowy conditions. The emigrants who remained at the fort crowded into the store rooms and began tearing down walls for fuel. Days passed and still no help arrived. Soon the leaders of Daniel's group decided they'd have to do something quickly or they'd all die. They called a meeting for all the men in the original rescue party. Daniel had been thinking about the situation for several days, so when suggestions were sought, Daniel was ready with an idea.

"Do any of you have a plan?" Captain Grant asked as the men were all seated. The men stared at each other and were silent.

"Sir," Daniel said stepping forward, "we have to get moving. We can't stay here waiting for more help from the valley. May never come. We could unload all the freight wagons and fill them with the sickest Saints and small children. The rest will have to go on foot. If the emigrants leave all their unnecessary goods here at the fort for a few of us to watch, we'll all have a better chance to make it back to the valley alive. Allow each person only a change of clothes, bedding and a few cooking supplies along with the remaining food. If we all stay here with the goods, we'll all die."

"Thank you," Captain Grant said. "I've thought of that myself but dismissed the idea because it would be too much to ask of any man to stay. We wouldn't be able to leave provisions. Those who stay would probably freeze to death or die of starvation."

Daniel rose again and said, "Every man here would do it if you asked."

"I know. Thank you," Captain Grant answered.

"Lots of folks are destitute. They trusted these shipping companies with everything they own," Daniel continued. "Teamsters are under contract to deliver these loads to the valley. Be hard on many families if their possessions are lost or left here unguarded."

After Daniel sat down, Captain Grant called for a raise of hands. Everyone agreed to Daniel's plan. The next day was spent filling the storerooms of the fort with the contents of two hundred wagons. It took three days with every well person helping to finish the task.

"Daniel, I want you to stay at the fort, be in charge here," Captain Grant said on the third day when the unloading was finished. "I've asked Aaron to stay on as well. Told Hunt and Hodgett to leave behind a dozen or more of their best teamsters to help. You'll have no provisions but what the teamsters keep. Eat the worn out cattle we leave. After that, I don't know what you'll do. It's a lot to ask. Daniel, will you do this?"

Daniel looked solemnly into the captain's face and answered without hesitation, "You know I will."

The next day when all the hands were pulling out, Daniel and all the men who were asked to stay at the fort gathered together. Daniel told them what to expect.

"If there is a man in this group who will not be willing to eat the last poor animal, his hides and all, suffer everything God has in store, then go now with the emigrants before it's too late," Daniel finished preparing his men for what would surely follow.

None of the men moved and all agreed to stick together. Daniel looked with admiration at his new comrades and put them to work finding out what provisions were left. He knew the rest of the winter lay ahead with very little to eat. They soon found food of any kind was almost non-existent except a few sick and dying cattle. Daniel assigned several men to fix up the fort and several others to see about the remaining cattle.

After several hours, Daniel rode out after the departing emigrants to see if they were making progress. After he'd ridden for several miles, he noticed someone sitting in the road ahead of him. He gave the horse a nudge and galloped to where he saw a lone figure in the snow. As he neared the person, he saw it was a fine healthy woman in her middle years wearing a very elegant velvet dress. She was sitting on a rock at the side of the road where the other emigrants had passed by earlier.

"What is it?" Daniel said as he approached her, "You hurt?"

"Leave me alone!" the woman shouted as she looked up at Daniel. "There's nothing wrong with me. Leave me alone! I want to die."

Daniel dismounted and walked over to the women, "You don't want to die. You're healthy as an ox."

"That's the problem. If I were sick, they wouldn't treat me this way," the woman sobbed, "I can't take this any more. It's all too much for me. I'm not used to such treatment. My husband and I are wealthy. We have a fine team and wagon with ample goods for ourselves if everyone would just leave us alone. We could have driven me into the valley in our wagon in fine comfort. But no! They unloaded all our goods and filled our wagon with the sick women and children. Then they told me to walk! Me! When I refused, even my husband told them to leave me here."

Daniel had to smile inside, but he was able to hide his emotions from the woman who obviously found no humor in her self-important drama.

"They had no right," the woman continued. "That was my wagon and team. Those were all my fine things they unloaded at the fort. What right do they have to tell me to move my fat posterior off of my own wagon? I will not walk through mud and snow all the way to the valley. My own husband walked on ahead without me. I'm humiliated. I swear I'll sit here until I die!"

Daniel knew the other emigrants were probably several miles ahead and this self-important woman would never catch up with them on her own. His first thought was to leave the lady to her own self-appointed death, but soon thought better and decided to reason with her on her own terms.

"What sense does it make to sit here and die?" Daniel said. "Do you want these people to regret what they've done to you? Then walk to the valley and live. If you stay here, you'll be forgotten and die. Think how you can flaunt your wealth when you get there," Daniel said with a smile.

The woman thought for a moment. "Well maybe you're right. I'll ride ahead with you."

Daniel smiled broadly as he lifted the stout woman with great effort onto his horse and rode ahead to find the company pushing forward toward the valley. When Daniel brought the woman into the camp that evening he saw Captain Grant.

"See you've found our dear Sister Linforth!" Captain Grant said as he shook Daniel's hand smiling and winking. Captain Grant reached out to help the woman off Daniel's horse but she refused help. She slid off the horse and huffed off to find her husband. "Thank you, Daniel. We needed her wagon for the sick and young children. How are things with the men at the fort?"

"Fine. Good men. Must admit I hate to see you go on without me. We'll be all right if we can catch some game. You've done everything you can for us. Get the rest of these people to the valley as fast as you can," Daniel said.

"God go with you!" the captain said warmly.

"And with you," Daniel answered.

Daniel spent the night at the emigrant camp, then saddled up and prepared to return to the fort the next morning. Before he left, Mrs. Linforth talked to him privately about her trailside incident and vowed him to secrecy.

"Your secret is good with me," Daniel answered.

As the emigrant camp moved out the next morning, Daniel nudged his horse forward in the opposite direction. As he headed back to the fort, he had an empty gnawing feeling in the pit of his stomach. He glanced over his shoulder and watched the companies roll slowly out of sight. Daniel desperately longed to return to the valley with the rescue party and the emigrants so he could be with Emily. But there was no choice. He turned his horse toward the fort and the men who were waiting for him to return.

After a loud clap of thunder, clouds overhead opened. Heavy pelting rain drenched Daniel's coat through to the skin. Over three hundred snow covered miles lay between him and Emily. What he previously determined would be a two or three week separation was now a six month long uncertainty. He'd never felt so alone. He bowed his head in prayer.

"Please help those people make it back to the valley," Daniel prayed.

"Help me keep the good men at the fort alive. Help Emily remember I love her."

As Daniel rode to the fort alone, grey skies and cold rain turned to freezing snow. When he finally spied the fort off in the distance, it looked like an ominous prison. The cold endless winter stretched before him like a vast empty void.

༄

After Daniel left the valley with the rescue party, even Emily's Indian students noticed a drastic change in her countenance. In late November when the Willie and Martin Company arrived in the Salt Lake City and Daniel wasn't with them, Emily was crushed. She later learned nearly two hundred Saints died near where Daniel was staying and that his chances of survival were slim. Free Wind noticed the drastic transformation in Emily's normally cheerful personality and tried to help.

"Light gone from your eyes," Free Wind said as he watched Emily put her things away and glance thoughtfully out the window.

"I'm sorry," Emily said apologetically.

"Wish it was me who put light in your eyes," Free Wind said.

"I don't want to hurt you," Emily said as they exited the building into the cold winter air. "But I love Daniel. I miss him. Now I don't know if he's ever coming back. The captain of the rescue party said they didn't have any provisions to spare for the men who stayed at the fort. He'll probably starve or freeze to death. Why did Daniel have to stay?"

"Daniel is a good man," Free Wind answered.

"I know," Emily said.

As they walked together down the street, Emily and Free Wind noticed President Young coming toward them. He looked worried as he approached.

"What is it President Young?" Emily asked.

"Trouble with the Indians in Walker's band," Brigham answered folding his large arms across his barrel chest. "They're angry we've stopped the slave trade. They've been to every family outside the city trying to sell small children. Say we ought to buy the children because we stopped the Mexican trade. There have been some awful, cruel reports. Emily, tell your parents I'm asking every family living outside the city to move into the fort so we can defend ourselves if there is an uprising. Washington has a man here representing the federal government to help with Indian affairs by the name of Timothy Lee. You might be a good person to work with him with your language skills."

Just then Emily heard a thunder of horses galloping swiftly toward them. In a matter of seconds, the steeds and their riders stopped directly in front of them in a huge billowing cloud of dust.

"These men are from Walkers band," Free Wind said turning to Brigham.

Emily noticed the group of Indians on horseback had several small almost naked children with them. She saw the frightened children shivering in the cold, wincing at the harsh treatment of their captors. Emily longed to reach out and grab the children from the angry men. Just then the brave in charge of the group shouted something Free Wind understood. Seeing that Brigham didn't understand, Free Wind translated.

"You stop slave trade. You buy children now!" The brave yelled, pushing one of the children toward President Young. "You take this one."

Brigham shook his head in the negative. Enraged, the brave jumped from his horse dangling the small child by his feet and angrily smashed the child's head on a rock. Emily screamed.

"You have no heart or you would have bought this child to save his life!" the brave shouted as Free Wind translated.

The brave let the child fall lifeless from his grasp to the ground. Then he mounted his horse and rode off as quickly as he'd come. Emily felt sick as she ran toward the small child's body lying dead on the muddy road. Trembling, Emily gently took the little girl into her arms, but there was no hint of breathing and the child's damaged head bled profusely.

She held the tiny lifeless body close to her breast, glared up at Free Wind and wailed, "Why?" Free Wind dropped his head and looked as though he might be sick. "Why?" Emily wailed again as she looked up into Brigham's face. "This beautiful child had a whole lifetime ahead of her."

"I know her," Free Wind interrupted. "Let me take her back to her parents."

Emily shook her head and continued to cradle the little girl. When she stood up, both Free Wind and President Young supported her by grabbing her elbows when Emily's knees gave way.

"Let me wash and dress her first," Emily insisted as she walked with support toward her small boarding room with Free Wind at her side. Brigham left the scene, angrily repeating aloud what he promised to do about the whole dreadful business.

When Free Wind and Emily reached her room, Emily laid the dead child's body on her bed and walked to her closet. She found her best white chemise and laid it out on the bed for later. Then she took the child over to the wash basin and gently washed the tiny girl's small body while Free Wind silently watched from the corner of the room.

"I washed my brother's body once," Emily said. "He was about the same age as this beautiful little girl. This child deserves no less. Why? This is so senseless."

Free Wind didn't answer for a moment. He stood silently in the corner of the room watching and shook his head.

"There are bad men in every tribe," Free Wind finally answered, "even yours."

An hour passed as she washed the child's matted insect infested hair and gently combed the strands into neat black curls. Emily then secured a dressing over the child's head wound. She clothed the body in a clean white chemise and replaced the dressing over the wound several more times. Then she wrapped the body in her only decent shawl.

When she was finished, she and Free Wind knelt next to the child as Free Wind prayed, "God in Heaven, take this daughter home. Saw no beauty or kindness here. Help me teach my people better ways. You have taught me a better ways through this woman. Help me return to my people Emily's love. Help me teach my people who they are."

Emily turned toward her friend as he finished praying. As she looked at Free Wind kneeling beside her with tears streaming down his face, she knew he would keep his promise to God.

"Amen," Emily whispered as she leaned over and kissed Free Wind's wet cheek. "I'll always be your friend. God go with you."

"I'll always love you," Free Wind answered looking deep into Emily's eyes.

Free Wind took the small lifeless body into his arms, stood and turned to leave. He slowly walked through the door and outside to his horse with Emily following closely behind. Emily held the tiny bundle as he mounted his horse, then returned the child to Free Wind's arms just before he rode away. Free Wind looked down at Emily one last time, then nudged the pony forward and rode slowly out of town. Emily wondered if she'd ever see him again.

Emily walked back inside her small boarding room and scrubbed the blood stains left behind. She realized both Free Wind and Daniel were gone and the winter stretched before her like some unanswered prayer. She had never felt so alone.

The next day after sunrise, Emily rode out to her family's home. She wanted to warn them of the problems with the Indians in Walker's band. When she got there, she saw the whole household already packing a wagon ready to leave for the fort in town. Emily jumped off her horse and ran inside her family's cabin. After seeing Emily in the doorway, Polly and Philander turned their heads in surprise and called her name. Emily ran into their open arms.

"Mama and Papa," she said as she tried to embrace them both at the same time, "I've missed you both so much."

"Brigham's asked us to move into town and live at the fort," Philander said.

Emily helped with the last of the household goods and then jumped into the wagon with the rest of the family. Later when they reached Salt Lake City, Emily helped her family move into a room at the fort.

"Emily, what's happened to Free Wind?" Polly questioned as they worked.

"He's gone back to his people. He wants to share the gospel of Jesus Christ with his tribe and help them learn better ways to live."

"Since you've been living at the boarding house, we haven't had the time to talk the way we used to. I've missed that," Polly said. "You haven't told me much about the new school and your feelings for Daniel."

"I've missed talking to you too," Emily said. "Do you think Daniel will come back?"

"Do you doubt it?" Polly answered.

"They have no provisions. Hundreds of Saints died up there," Emily answered.

"He's strong. He'll find a way to survive," Polly said.

"I love him," Emily said. "Part of the reason he left is because he thinks he's pushing me into a decision. He thinks I'm choosing between him and Free Wind."

"Are you?"

"No. Free Wind is my friend, nothing more," Emily answered.

"Brigham asked for every able-bodied man to help rescue the stranded emigrants at conference. No good man could refuse. Maybe you just need to be patient," Polly said.

"Patient?" Emily replied insolently. "I'm tired of being patient! The rest of the rescue party is back now. Daniel stayed up there at the fort. Why?"

"He was asked to stay," Polly said. "He's a good man. How could he refuse?"

CHAPTER NINETEEN

When Daniel returned to the fort at Devil's Gate, he had his men take stock of all their provisions. They found twenty days rations with over five or six months of winter ahead. No flour or salt remained. With the exception of a few crackers, they had only a few dying cattle to eat.

Winter set in, hard. Wind blew incessantly, drifting snow into huge mounds high against the fort walls. For nearly a mile on both sides of the fort, over a hundred dead cattle were strung out all along the trail. Wolves from miles around ventured from the mountains to devour the carcasses at night. Daniel asked several of the men to corral all the living cattle for protection. They each took turns keeping watch over the small herd day and night. Every evening after night fall Daniel and his men heard wolves feasting on dead carcasses. When the dead animals had all been devoured, the wolves began approaching the fort and attacking the living cattle at night. The men on guard watched as flashing green eyes circled them and wondered what the wolves would feast on when the sick cattle where all gone.

A week later, twenty-five head of corralled cattle had been devoured by the wolves. Daniel had no choice but to kill the remaining forty or fifty cattle before the wolves beat them to it. Luckily, one of the men at the fort was a butcher and expertly prepared the carcasses, leaving the worst of the meat for wolf bait to use in their traps. To keep the men busy, Daniel had his men roof the cabins at the fort, fix a stable for the saddle horses and make an inventory of the emigrant's goods. With the meat from the cattle to eat, the men grew stronger for a time. Before long the good meat ran out and wolf bait had to be eaten.

Daniel watched as the men under his command became lean, pale and weak. Their eyes grew hollow and the death-like expressions on their faces haunted him. Daniel sent out a hunting party whenever the weather permitted, but nearly every effort was a failure. The men returned from hunting weaker and hungrier than when they'd left. Daniel knew all the men at the fort were in constant danger. He seldom slept well at night. He tried to keep the men busy with jobs repairing the fort and rearranging the goods during the day, along with cleaning their guns, ammunition and cooking utensils. The wolves in the hills became increasingly more fearless in their strikes, some attacking the men on their hunting expeditions. When the meat meant for wolf bait was completely eaten, Daniel's men sunk back into ghost-like living.

Daniel decided to head up the next hunting party and promised himself he wouldn't come back empty-handed. He couldn't bear to look at his men and feel helpless in any efforts to help them. One man by the name of Aaron, a valley boy, had been particularly helpful during their stay at the fort. Daniel and Aaron became good friends, so Daniel decided to take him on the hunt. On the morning Aaron and Daniel left, all the men at the fort were sitting around one room in total silence. There'd been nothing to eat for a long time. They'd found a bit of sugar, but eating it only seemed to make their hunger pains more severe. As Aaron and Daniel rode through the gate of the fort, Daniel thought he heard a voice. He listened again.

"God go with you," one of the men said faintly.

Daniel felt his own strength weakening as he and Aaron trudged through deep crusted snow into the woods near the fort. Aaron hummed a song and Daniel listened, hoping to get his mind off the hunger pains shooting through his body.

"Daniel," Aaron said, "we're going to find something. I know it. I spent most of last night praying and this morning as we left, I felt something hopeful inside me. We're on God's business, and he won't let us starve."

Daniel listened but didn't offer a response.

"Quiet," Daniel said softly. "I think I hear something."

Aaron stopped the horse and held perfectly still. Daniel heard the wind howling through the trees as a rumbling roar of frozen snow cracking in the distance grew in intensity. Suddenly over the brow of the hill, Daniel and Aaron spied a small herd of buffalo racing toward them. Daniel quickly pushed Aaron out of the way of the animals and stood firmly aiming his gun. He cocked his gun then stared into the face of the leader of the herd coming straight for him.

"Move!" Aaron shouted as he tried to get up from the snow where Daniel had pushed him. "Move, or they'll trample you!"

Daniel waited for a few seconds until the bull was within shooting range, and then took one shot. The ball hit the bull right between the eyes. Stunned, the animal fell to his knees. The rest of the herd rumbled past Daniel on both sides, galloping down the hill. Aaron got a shot off but missed the quick moving animals. Daniel ran to the bull lying in the snow breathing heavily. He quickly shot the animal again and soon the buffalo stopped breathing. The heat from the animal's body made the snow evaporate around him in a fine mist. The animal was so huge it astounded Daniel for he'd seen many herds but never a buffalo this size.

"Missed the rest of them!" Aaron shouted as he came running up to Daniel. "Look at the size of that animal!"

"It's big, all right," Daniel smiled. "Maybe too big. How are we ever going to get this animal back to the fort?"

"Just have to ask the men at the fort to come and help us," Aaron answered.

"But they're too weak to come way out here," Daniel said.

"Even starving men move for food. Just wait and see."

As Daniel and Aaron rode back toward the fort, Aaron asked, "Why did you save my life and risk your own?"

"I'm no hero," Daniel answered. "Any starving man would risk his life to get some food in his belly."

"It's more than that. I've been with you all this time at the fort and I've been watching you. You're different. It seems like you're here by choice, not just because you got the short end of the stick like the rest of us. You don't have to take risks like that for us. All in this together, you know."

"I know that," Daniel answered.

"You seem so quiet, and you never talk about your family in the valley. Who do you have to go back to when all this is over? You never speak of anyone."

Daniel slowed his horse before he answered, "I don't have any family waiting for me, if that's what you mean."

"Not anyone?"

"There is someone. But I don't know if she's still waiting for me."

"She . . . oh, I see. Well, do you love her?" Aaron asked.

"Yes," Daniel answered.

"What is it then? Doesn't she feel the same way?" Aaron asked.

"Says she does . . . but there's another man. I've seen the way she looks at him. We were separated for years, thought she was dead. When we found each other, I was free but she was involved with someone else. Thought I'd give her some time to choose between us," Daniel answered.

"Jealous, huh?" Aaron said. "That's what it sounds like to me. If you really loved her, you wouldn't give up so easily. You'd stay and fight for her."

"What do you mean?" Daniel asked annoyed. "It's none of your business."

"Might tell yourself you're doing something noble. You're just jealous. Want her to suffer, want her to wonder if you really love her. What you afraid of anyway?"

Daniel was silent.

"Do you love her?" Aaron asked.

"Yes," Daniel answered. "Never been able to get her completely out of my mind since the first day I met her."

"Ever told her that? Ever told her about how you feel?" Aaron asked.

"Yes."

"And has she told you the same?"

"Yes."

"Well," Aaron said, "Like you say, it's none of my business but I think you did a stupid thing. Leaving with another wolf on the prowl is just plain stupid."

Daniel didn't answer for a while.

"Maybe you're right," Daniel answered. "I hope it's not too late."

"It takes more courage to face the loss of love than the loss of life," Aaron answered.

"I've lost everyone I've ever loved," Daniel answered, his voice breaking.

Aaron looked at his leader with surprise and increased understanding.

"You don't have to stop loving her Daniel, even if she doesn't wait for you—even if she doesn't choose you. You can always love her. That's your choice. Whether she loves you back—that's her choice."

Daniel nodded, rubbing his forehead as if in pain.

"You're right."

"Choose love," Aaron finished. "Love's everything worth living for. Stay alive, Daniel."

Daniel was quiet and subdued for the rest of the ride back to the fort. Later when they told the men about the buffalo, the starving men jumped up and hurriedly rode back with Aaron and Daniel to the place where the animal fell. All the men took their knives and several brought firewood. They immediately commenced cutting the bull into manageable pieces and roasted a portion for a feast right there. Only part of the animal could be moved that day. It took several men constantly guarding the carcass from wolves and two more hauling days to bring the entire animal back to the fort.

Even with the huge bull to eat, the meat soon gave out again and the camp remained in the same state of near starvation. The hides of the dead animals were all that was left. Several more days went by. In desperation, the men decided to eat the hides. They gathered several of the hides together, cooked and ate them. As soon as the hides were eaten, the men ran from the pot vomiting, holding their stomachs.

Daniel soon felt his own stomach rumbling. He broke out in a cold sweat and felt faint, then his whole body lunged forward, spilling the unwanted contents on the ground. The men in camp lay about him like injured soldiers after a battle. With great effort, Daniel stood up and walked away from the fort. He stumbled toward the woods near the fort then found a circle of protective trees.

"God, what do I do now?" Daniel said after kneeling in the snow. "We're starving. Only thing we have left in camp, even our own starving bodies reject. Tell me what to do." Wind whipped against his face making his eyes water. "I dare not ask you to change those rotten hides into something more fit to eat, but could you help our stomachs accept the poor stuff. Tell me how to cook the hides so we can survive."

Just then a sudden knowledge poured into Daniel's mind. He knew instantly what he needed to do. After he left the woods and returned to the fort, he found his men moaning on the ground. Daniel quickly walked over to the uneaten hides, took one and placed it in the boiling water just long enough to scorch. Then he removed the hide and scraped the hair off. Some of the men grew interested in what he was doing and watched. Others were confused by his actions and wondered why he was quietly and confidently tending to the hides that had just made them all so sick.

"Leave the hides alone!" one man shouted. "Leave 'em to the wolves."

Daniel ignored the man as he placed the scraped hides into the water again and let them boil for an hour. Later, some of the men gathered around Daniel as he proceeded to pour off the water. Next, Daniel took clean cold water and washed the boiled hides, then boiled it to a jelly and let it cool. By this time, most of the men in the camp had recuperated enough to join the others watching curiously as their leader continued engaging in their time consuming supper preparation. Then Daniel found some sugar and sprinkled it on the cooled hides. After serving each man a portion for his supper, Daniel took his meal and put it reluctantly in his lap. The men waited. Daniel took off his hat and bowed his head. Each man at the fort did the same.

"Did what you told me to do. Now it's your turn," Daniel prayed.

All of the men watched Daniel take the first bite. They waited to see if he was going to vomit. When he didn't, each man reluctantly followed Daniel. With each bite, the tired worried faces softened and soon a festive mood returned. Daniel smiled and continued with his meal as everyone joined him. No one got sick and they were filled. Six weeks later, the men had not only eaten all of the hides, but the wrapping from the wagon tongues, old moccasin soles, and pieces of a buffalo hide they'd been using for a foot mat for two months. Then starvation stalked the camp once again.

Then the day of the month arrived when a twenty-four hour fast was universally observed by the Saints. Daniel gathered his men around him and announced they'd begin their fast with the morning meal. He promised his men if they joined in fasting and prayer, God would provide them with their supper that night. Several of the men laughed at Daniel's suggestion.

"We've been fasting all winter! What makes today special?" one man jeered. "We're already starving."

Daniel turned to the man speaking, looked him squarely in the eye and sternly answered, "We'll observe the fast today not because necessity demands it, but because we want to offer ourselves to God with clean hands and hearts."

Though he didn't say anything to the men, Daniel knew something ugly was coming in upon them. Someone at the fort had begun cutting meat off unclean carcasses of long dead cattle and frozen wolves stacked in the yard. Daniel knew what unclean meat could do to his men and feared most what the starving men might consider next. He knew they were on the God's business and felt they would be provided with clean food if they purified their hearts. The men soon quieted and left the group to wash themselves and clean the fort. When this was done, several of the men came to Daniel.

"Jones, there's nearly a hundred wolf carcasses around the fort. Gettin' to look like fine mutton. Maybe they're the supper you promised us."

Daniel turned to the men and answered, "I don't figure God wants us eating unclean meat. If we fast, prepare our hearts and the fort, we can expect better. I've never known God not to keep his end of any agreement we've made."

With some reluctance, the men finally agreed. During the day they all helped haul cattle internals and frozen wolf carcasses to the Sweetwater, cut a hole in the ice, and dumped them in. At the end of the day, after the sun set and the men made everything ready, Daniel gathered everyone in one room at the fort. Then he led the men in prayer. Gradually darkness fell and hours passed. Still there was no supper as promised. Many of the men grew restless as they waited. They watched Daniel closely.

"Well, Daniel, it's almost supper time," Aaron cheerfully said. All of the men laughed. Just then, they heard a noise. "There's our supper!" Aaron shouted as he leaped to his feet. "Just like Daniel promised."

Aaron raced from the room and ran through the fort. Some of the men followed. When Aaron returned, he seemed frightened.

"Daniel, there's something strange going on down the road. Hear voices but I can't understand what they're saying," Aaron said quickly.

All the men went for their guns and followed Daniel from the fort. Not far from the gate, they found a coach party. The strange voices came from the French Canadian drivers swearing at their mules. When the men at the fort saw the party meant no harm, they put their arms aside and ran to the aid of stranded party. By the dim moonlight all the men at the fort helped the coach party move inside the fort. They all found shelter in the largest room then rebuilt the fires. The warmth felt most welcome to the new comers and they thanked Daniel and his men. The leader of the group was named Jesse.

"I was afraid we'd never make it," Jesse said. "People down at the Butte said we'd likely find dead men in this fort. Said you have no provisions."

"We haven't had a bite to eat for quite some time," Daniel answered. "We've been waiting for you to bring our supper tonight."

"Well sir, you'll have that supper, even if it takes everything!" Jesse answered.

Jesse instructed his cook to give Daniel's cook all of their provisions. It was late that night when all the men sat down to a feast. Daniel's men had not seen that much food since leaving their homes. Later, after eating, Daniel and Jesse talked about the difficult journey Jesse's party had been through on their way to the fort.

"Been lucky," Jesse said. "Got through all right. All my men are stout and strong. We passed people in worse shape. Only a few miles from here there's a group of people camped for the winter in a cove against the mountain. Half the people are dead already and those still living haven't the strength to leave."

"Close to this fort?" Daniel questioned.

"Yes," Jesse answered. "One fellow had the devil in him. He raved at us, called us filthy Mormons and told us to leave him alone. The cold seems to suck the good sense out of folks. They think they're better off stoppin' and waitin' for the snow to melt. Anybody with half a brain knows you have to keep movin', find better shelter, or die."

Daniel thought back to the stranded emigrant companies he'd found earlier that winter and remembered how many were content to stay put and wait for the snow to disappear. Daniel expressed his agreement.

In a few days, Jesse's party left, leaving behind all their spare provisions. After they left, Daniel's thoughts turned to the group Jesse talked about. When he spoke with his men, most agreed it wasn't their business to interfere because staying alive at the fort was hard enough. Only Aaron agreed to go with Daniel to see if they could find the stranded group.

CHAPTER TWENTY

The day was bitter cold when Daniel and Aaron set out to find the stranded party. They rode their horses with great difficulty through the arching drifts near the fort then traveled near the mountains most of the day. In late afternoon Daniel noticed smoke rising through a small grouping of trees. Daniel and Aaron hurried their horses to the partially hidden cove. As they approached, they saw or heard no signs of life.

"Hello," Daniel called, his voice echoing. "Is anyone still alive?"

"Here," a quiet voice replied, "I'm here."

Daniel and Aaron followed the sound of the voice to a tent entrance. When Daniel threw the entrance of the tent open, he saw a sight that sickened him. In the corner of the tent sat an old man almost frozen to the ground. He was covered with a layer of frost and his skin appeared deathly grey.

"Here," the man faintly whispered. The voice seemed familiar. As Daniel walked to the rear of the tent, he realized the old man was his uncle Gilbert. "Help me. I'm so cold," Gilbert said faintly.

Daniel's mind instantly exploded with images of the numerous beatings he'd received from Gilbert. He saw his uncle's screaming face, the arching belt, heavy walking stick and stiff boot flashing before him. Daniel's first impulse was to walk away and never look back. Just then Aaron threw back the blanket covering the old man and gasped. Gilbert's legs were frozen stiff to the cold ground. Sickened, Aaron turned away. Daniel slowly knelt next to his uncle.

"I'll take care of you," Daniel said quietly.

"I'm so cold," Gilbert mumbled before he lost consciousness.

"It will be all right, Gilbert," Daniel said reassuringly.

"Do you know the man?" Aaron questioned as he helped Daniel lift his uncle from the tent and onto Daniel's horse.

"Long time ago," Daniel answered as they both mounted their horses.

As they rode toward the fort, Daniel kept one arm tightly around Gilbert to keep him from falling off the horse. He kept his eyes on the snow covered road ahead and hoped they'd make it back before nightfall.

"Should have spent the night in the old man's tent," Aaron said shaking his head as the sun set and a blinding blizzard and blackness soon enveloped the riders.

"This man won't survive another night out here. He'll die if we don't get him back to the fort," Daniel said as he urged his horse forward.

"Old man will die anyway," Aaron said as the wind whipped around him. "Surely you know that. Isn't even conscious."

"He's not dead yet," Daniel answered making little headway in the strong wind. "Feel him breathing. Have to keep moving for his sake."

"Then we'll all die!" Aaron shouted. "No one has to know we found someone alive. Man's half dead. We'll all freeze to death if we don't back to his tent and build a fire!" Aaron turned his horse around. "I won't go farther. I'm going back."

Daniel stopped his horse and listened to Aaron's voice trailing off with the wind.

"Won't last that long," Daniel yelled. "Turn your horse around! We have to stay together!" Aaron ignored Daniel. "You'll die out there Aaron. Come back!"

Daniel slipped off his horse, ran toward Aaron and threw himself at his legs, dragging him off his horse to the ground. Then Daniel punched Aaron in the face with a closed fist. The force of the blow sent Aaron falling backward into a drift.

"You're coming with me," Daniel. "I will not leave you out here to die."

Daniel quickly picked up Aaron like a bag of potatoes and threw him over his own horse. Gilbert had fallen off Daniel's horse in his absence so he threw his uncle's body next to Aaron then lashed them both to Aaron's saddle. After mounting his horse, Daniel took the reins of both frightened animals and urged them toward the fort.

Daniel's hands were numb and breathing was difficult in the frigid air. The merciless wind and snow swirled about the frozen riders with no end to the cold and blackness. Daniel didn't know which way to go, losing all sense of direction in the storm. He knew the horse's instincts would be their only chance to find their way back to the fort in this white-out. He tied both horses' reins together, laid his head on the neck of the animal and prayed.

First the freezing cold made his body tremble, then he felt numb and gradually Daniel noticed he felt warm and sleepy. He knew death was next for all of them. He tried to move but couldn't. Then suddenly when Daniel was about to give up, he felt the horse beneath him stop abruptly. With great difficulty, Daniel dismounted and blindly walked ahead. Placing his hands out in front of him to feel his way, he suddenly felt something hard and knew the horse had located the fort. He stumbled along the rough wall until he found the gate then went back for his companions. Daniel took the reins wrapped around the horn and pulled both horses toward the fort entrance. He grabbed the latch and pulled with all his might to open the gate wide enough to let the two horses through. Following the path to a lighted room, Daniel tied the horses to a post. First he untied Aaron and carried him to the door. Knocking hard, he heard his men's loud voices inside.

When the men in the room opened the door and saw Daniel standing there holding Aaron in his arms, they quickly moved to help. Several men tried to drag Daniel inside. He fought them off and went back for Gilbert. After untying his uncle, Daniel carried him through the opened door. By that time Aaron had regained consciousness.

"Get me some water!" Daniel shouted as he laid Gilbert on a blanket in the room.

Daniel unwrapped the stiff body and tried to remove some of Gilbert's clothing. He rubbed Gilbert's arms and chest. One of the men tried rubbing Gilbert's legs. Daniel heard a sickening moan as one man touched Gilbert's lower leg and the frozen blackened skin fell off to his touch. Daniel shouted for the man to leave.

"We can't do anything for his lower legs now," Daniel said quietly.

"They'll have to be removed. We better do it now, before he comes to."

A sharp knife was held above the flame of the fire for a long time and then handed to Daniel. Softly touching the skin on Gilbert's legs, Daniel found the place where he had to cut. He took the blade and sliced through the flesh and bone. Even unconscious, Gilbert's body jerked and trembled. He finished the gruesome task then dressed the wounds the best he could. Daniel stayed awake with Gilbert the rest of the night warming him slowly and trying to keep the bleeding to a minimum. Several times in the night, Gilbert cried out in pain. Daniel comforted him the best he could and finally in desperation asked Aaron to help him give Gilbert a priesthood blessing.

After placing his hands on Gilbert's head Daniel heard himself say, "By the authority of the holy Melchizedek Priesthood, I bless you, Gilbert Marshall, to overcome these grave injuries and live."

The men in the room watched silently from their beds. When the sun rose over the eastern mountains and filled the room with light, Gilbert was still alive. Daniel had never been so glad to see the dawn.

"Daniel, you've got to eat something and get those wet clothes off," Aaron said. "Let me take over for a while. Least I can do." Daniel refused to leave Gilbert's side. "Sorry about last night," Aaron continued. "Lost my head. Never been like that before. Hope you'll forgive me. Why'd you risk your life for this stranger?"

Daniel turned abruptly and answered, "He deserved a chance."

Aaron walked away and left Daniel to his vigil. Several days went by as Daniel kept constant watch over his uncle. Gilbert continued to rage in an unconscious stupor. Several days later Gilbert opened his eyes and looked around the room unable to focus.

"Where's my glasses," Gilbert yelled. "I can't see without my glasses."

"Must have fallen off in the storm," Daniel answered. "You'll have to get along without them for a while. Here's something to eat."

Gilbert felt a strange sensation when he had tried to sit up. "My legs! What has happened to my legs?" he shouted.

Daniel tried to get him to lie still. "They were frozen . . . black. I had to cut them off to save your life," Daniel shouted back.

"No! Why didn't you let me die with the others?" Gilbert yelled, lunging forward to scratch Daniel's eyes.

Just then Aaron came into the room and called several others in after him. He held Gilbert's arms and told Daniel to leave the room. Then several other men at the fort entered the room to help subdue Gilbert. Daniel walked from the room and took a few steps outside before he collapsed on the ground completely exhausted.

"What do you think you're doing?" Aaron said. "That man saved your life. Almost died saving you. Ought to thank him. If it wasn't for him, you'd be dead."

❦

As he walked around the perimeter of the fort with Aaron, Daniel noticed signs of approaching spring everywhere. He hoped the warmer temperatures would soon open the pass, allowing help to reach them.

"None of the men can abide the man," Aaron said as he walked with Daniel toward the room where Gilbert was staying at the fort. "Can't help feeling sorry for him. Nearly blind. Can't walk any more. But you'd think he'd try to be a little kinder to the people who saved his life."

"Proud man," Daniel answered as they neared the door. "Being forced to accept charity from people you hate, hard for any man. Know how hard it would be for me if the situation was reversed. He won't die. He's too mean to die."

"Why have you asked the men not to use your name in front of him?" Aaron asked, "Why don't you want him to know who you are?"

"Rather not talk about it," Daniel answered. "Better he doesn't know."

Just then, the two men reached the door to Gilbert's room. When Daniel pushed the door open, he noticed Gilbert was hunched against a wall.

"Get out of here and leave me alone!" Gilbert cursed.

"Here's your supper." Daniel said as he walked toward his uncle.

Gilbert grabbed the bowl and threw it back into Daniel's face. Slowly wiping off his face with the sleeve of his shirt, Daniel knelt on the floor and placed the meat back in the bowl. Then he set the soiled meal on the floor near the door before he left the room.

"He gave you his own supper," Aaron said sternly to Gilbert from the doorway after Daniel left. "He's starving just so you can eat and you throw it in his face. No one else in this group is willing to give you even a small portion of our meager rations let alone the whole. We'd all rather see you starve."

"Get out!" Gilbert bellowed again. "I don't need you. I don't need anybody."

Aaron shook his head in disgust then left the room in search of his friend.

"Why?" Aaron asked after he located Daniel. "He's not worth it."

"Brother Brigham will send someone out with supplies for us soon," Daniel answered. "I'm sure of it."

"You've been saying that all winter," Aaron answered shaking his head.

Daniel surveyed the horizon for any sign of an Indian camp nearby. He noticed a trail of smoke coming from a group of trees not far from the fort. After he pointed the smoke out to Aaron, they walked back into the fort and talked with the men.

"Rations low again," Daniel said. "Spotted smoke. Likely coming from an Indian camp we haven't seen before. Going to need a few of you to go with me and pack some things to trade. Go through your possessions one more time and see what you have left."

The men grumbled as they scattered to find what few possessions they had left.

"Why do *we* have to trade away all of our goods, when the fort is full of goods?" one of the men asked angrily. "We deserve to be paid. We're risking our lives out here."

"If we use the settlers' goods to get our food," Daniel answered, "we'll surely be called for stealing when we get home. Shouldn't be much longer 'til people from the valley reach us with supplies."

After several minutes, some of the men brought the last of their possessions forward. Daniel selected five men to go with him to the Indian camp. Aaron was left in charge of the fort. When Daniel's small group entered the Indian camp they'd located earlier, they found the people more impoverished than any of the other tribes they'd traded with that winter.

"No surplus here," Daniel said as he turned to the man at his side. "Better turn back." Just as he finished, he noticed a young brave walking toward him. "Trade for food," Daniel shouted in an Indian language he hoped the brave would understand.

"I speak English," the brave said as he approached. Suddenly Daniel and Free Wind recognized each other. "Daniel?" Free Wind asked. Daniel nodded. "Never thought I'd be happy to see you!"

"Never thought I'd be glad to see you either!" Daniel laughed as Free Wind invited him and his men to enter his winter home.

Daniel welcomed the warmth and hospitality of his host. When the men were seated, Free Wind motioned for a woman to get something for Daniel and his men to eat.

"I'd like to trade for game," Daniel said, nodding at Free Wind.

The woman brought Daniel and his men each a piece of meat and a strong drink of herbs. Daniel noticed the woman who was serving them was graceful and beautiful; her dark eyes greeted each guest warmly as she spoke a soft greeting in English.

"My wife," Free Wind said with a smile.

Each of the men with Daniel nodded and went back to their meal. Surprised, Daniel turned and stared at Free Wind. Later, Daniel's men finished eating and gratefully thanked Free Wind. Daniel instructed them to go outside and trade with the other members of the tribe while he finished trading with Free Wind. As the men left, Daniel stared at Free Wind again who was smiling at him from the corner of the shelter.

"Surprised?" Free Wind asked as he sat down near Daniel.

"Yes," Daniel answered. "Thought you were in love with Emily."

"I love Emily," Free Wind continued. "Always love her and what she did for me and my people. But her love is not the same. My place is with my people. Her place is with hers. Why did you leave?"

"Handcart companies stranded," Daniel answered. Free Wind tilted his head as if to disagree. "People dying." Daniel was silent for a moment. "Told myself I was leaving because I wanted Emily free to choose between us. Didn't want to force her hand. Truth is, I was afraid she didn't love me as much as I loved her."

"Emily loves you," Free Wind said. "You cared for your heart more than hers."

"I think about her all the time," Daniel answered, "but I've given my promise to care for the goods at the fort. I'd go back today if I could."

"Maybe it's too late now."

"I hope not," Daniel said as he stood.

"My place is here," Free Wind said. He reached out and grabbed Daniel's shoulder before he left. "Love her, Daniel," Free Wind said. "There is no fear in love."

Daniel stopped, looked Free Wind in the eye and nodded. Then he thanked him for the meat, turned and slowly walked away. After he gathered his men together, they gratefully left for the fort with enough meat to last a few more days.

The meat Daniel traded for in Free Wind's camp didn't last long and soon the men were down to only a day's rations again. Daniel kept someone on the lookout for help from the valley. He knew the road was passable now and had been expecting a relief company from the valley for weeks. Aaron was the man on watch when a rescue party was spotted.

"They're here and their wagons are loaded!" Aaron shouted as he jumped off the wall and raced through the fort to find Daniel.

Daniel and Aaron both raced toward the gate with the rest of the men following behind. When Daniel swung the gate wide, all of the men ran from the fort yelling. They reached the relief company not far from the gate with wild cheers. The men from the valley jumped off their wagons and eagerly embraced the men at the fort then quickly opened the boxes of food supplies.

Fires flared in record time and food was prepared, cooked and consumed in minutes. The relief company and Daniel's men talked loudly and quickly about the winter and what had transpired during the past months. The men in the relief company seemed appalled to learn the men at the fort had suffered so much. When they were full, all the men were in the mood for fun. While the men were busy with a stick-pulling contest, Daniel and the leader of the relief company talked privately.

"Wish I had better news for you," the leader began. "Afraid our purpose in coming here was not only to bring you supplies. We were sent to strengthen your post."

"Strengthen our post?" Daniel questioned.

"Afraid so," the leader continued. "There's a large company of apostates on the road this minute led by Tom Williams. Before they left the valley, they made threats concerning you and your men here at the fort."

"What could possibly be their reason for threatening us?" Daniel asked surprised.

"The goods you're guarding belong to last season's emigrants. Drivers are under contract to deliver the goods to their owners in Salt Lake City. Some of the owners of these goods here at the fort are dissatisfied with Mormonism and left the valley on a trip back to the states. As you know, their goods have not yet been delivered. These people haven't settled their freight bills with the proper company. They say if their goods aren't handed over to them when they arrive here, they'll take the fort by force. There are fifty men in the group, which puts my men along with yours about even with them"

"Does the apostate group know you've come to help us?" Daniel asked.

"No, we slipped out of the valley without their knowledge. I know you have arms here at the fort, so we can give 'em a good fight if needs be. Brigham says you shouldn't deliver up any goods to anyone unless they present you with a true order from the freighting company. None of these men have one."

Several days later, the men on guard at the gate met a single man approaching the fort on foot. The guards stopped him and brought him to Daniel. The man seemed frightened as he handed Daniel a slip of paper he claimed was an order from a freight company. Daniel could tell at a glance it was not a genuine order. Daniel refused the man and sent him away empty handed. Within twenty minutes, Williams and his entire force of men rode up near the fort and demanded to speak with Daniel.

"If you don't give up our goods to us, we'll tear down the fort around you," Williams said when presented to Daniel.

Daniel listened as the man went on with his threats.

"I've been given my instructions from Brigham Young and I mean to follow them," Daniel answered.

"Brigham Young is a liar and a thief. Has no right to keep our goods from us. I'll give you an hour, Jones. If you don't let us have our goods, we'll kill every last one of you."

Williams left the fort and rode back to join his men. Daniel returned to the inside of the fort and called all of his men together. Some were given instructions to make port holes in front of the fort. Others were stationed around the fort to observe any intruders from the back and sides. Then the best shots of the group were positioned in the front of the fort and made ready.

All the men were stationed and ready when Williams and his followers returned on horse back. As Daniel spied Williams approaching, he turned to some of the men positioned at the front gate and told them what they should do if any shooting began. As Williams and his group galloped toward the fort and shouted for Jones, Daniel stepped outside the fort alone to meet them. Daniel had known Williams in the valley and thought him a bully and a coward. With this on his mind, he stepped boldly before the man with a pistol in his hand.

"Halt! You'll go no father!" Daniel shouted. Williams' men swore and oath and spit on the ground. "We're the custodians of these goods," Daniel continued with authority. "We don't know who they belong to. We haven't spent a winter starving to let them fall into hands like yours. I'm here under the orders of Brigham Young and won't recognize your orders for I know them to be forged."

"Well, let's take a vote," Williams interrupted. "Should we leave these goods here and go on without them?"

"No!" all the men yelled in unison.

Williams continued, "Should we take them?"

"Yes!" the men around him shouted again.

Williams cocked his gun.

"Now just hold on here one minute!" Daniel said. "Told you we've been here at the fort guarding these goods all winter eating poor beef and rawhide. Been little fun, and we'd surely welcome some. In fact brothers, we'd relish a little row. I think you can take this fort from us, try it. There is not one of you that can take me and the first man who tries is a dead man. Now I dare you to go past me and into the fort!"

Williams seemed a bit taken back. He knew Daniel from the valley and had seen him take many a man in a fight. He knew him to be a man of his word.

"You're a fool, Jones, just fool enough to die before you'd give up those goods. You've got guts. This time I'll spare you," Williams said.

After that statement, Williams turned his horse around. All the others in the group followed behind and rode out of sight. When Daniel walked back through the gate in the fort, he was met with handshakes and slaps on the back. When he walked away from the happy, congratulatory men, Aaron followed.

"Why didn't you just show him all your armed men?" Aaron asked.

"Know the man," Daniel said. "Conceited bully. Felt like taking him down a notch."

After Williams' group was safely out of sight and on their way back to the states, the men at the fort spent most of their time loading goods into the wagons for the return trip to the valley. Daniel often wondered about transporting Gilbert. Almost blind and without the use of his legs, his uncle couldn't ride in a saddle. Daniel decided to construct a wooden bed to drag from the rear of his horse.

As Daniel's men worked loading the goods, more and more wagons from the valley arrived and these also were loaded. After a week's time, over two hundred wagons were loaded. Daniel knew how impatient many of the owners were back in the valley and supervised the loading of goods with as much haste as possible. Daniel organized the drivers of the wagons into companies. Before he sent them to the valley, he double-checked to see if the goods matched the shipping orders. He kept careful detailed records to hand over to Brigham Young.

When everything was ready, Daniel gave the word and the long train of loaded wagons headed toward Salt Lake City. When the fort was empty and all the men and wagons had left, Daniel walked to the room where Gilbert stayed. His uncle was asleep on the floor when he entered the room. Daniel quietly bent over to pick him up, then carried Gilbert to the waiting bed outside attached to his horse. He placed his uncle on the bed of blankets over the wood slats and ropes then tied him to it so he wouldn't fall off. Before long, Gilbert was awake, complaining and cursing. Daniel paid him no heed, mounted his horse and left for the valley.

CHAPTER TWENTY-ONE

When Emily opened the three lined boxes on her bed, she found a pair of silk gloves, a feathered bonnet and an emerald green satin gown.

"Nothing's too good for you," Emily remembered Timothy saying when he presented her with the large boxes earlier that evening. "You're stunning, Emily, more beautiful than any woman I've ever known. Quick, try them on, now. I want to see how you look."

"Not now, Timothy. I can't undress here," Emily answered. "I'll wear them on Saturday when we go to the dance."

Emily had accepted a pearl necklace the week before and a tiny bottle of French perfume the week before that. Now as she sat staring at the lavish gifts, she wondered if she should have ever accepted anything.

He'll expect something in return, Emily thought, *something I'm not willing to give.*

Timothy Lee, Emily's gift bearer and new suitor was the buzz of Salt Lake City. Every single girl swooned when he walked past—every girl but Emily.

Why me? Emily asked herself. He *could have his pick.*

Her French lessons at Mrs. Linforth's house, paid for by Timothy, were going well. Yet Emily was beginning to wonder why she let Timothy talk her into learning French or spending so much time with him. He had a smooth way of persuasion that was difficult to refuse. Timothy often told her she deserved more than her present circumstances and he was willing and able to give it to her.

Why am I so nervous about all this? Emily thought. *I should be flattered. I should be happy.*

Emily had lately tried to imagine herself stepping into another life vastly different from the one she'd always known. Timothy Lee was wealthy, well-educated and world-traveled. He was pursuing her with an obsession and attentiveness she'd never experienced before. Emily knew Timothy was the wrong man at the right time. He'd taken advantage of her self doubts about Daniel's true feelings for her when he didn't return with the rescue party. Whenever Emily listened to people talking about the men left up at the fort, the news she heard went from bad to worse. She knew Daniel and his men were left with little to eat and the long winter months had proved unusually bitter cold. Emily was left constantly wondering if he was still alive.

"Jones and his men will never make it out," Emily had heard a dozen people say. "Never should have agreed to stay up there. They'll all starve. What was the captain thinking?"

When Emily first saw Timothy Lee standing in the doorway of her school room proudly introducing himself, she remembered President Young had asked her to work with him. He was a government official sent from Washington to assist with the Indian affairs. He needed her Indian language translation skills.

Emily could tell immediately that Timothy Lee was the most arrogant and haughty man she'd ever seen. His eyes drifted over her body like he was slowly undressing her. Embarrassed and uncomfortable, Emily immediately asked him to leave and tried to ignore him for days after their first introduction. Mister Lee was not a man accustomed to rejection. He proved to be unusually persistent.

Emily had never met a man like Timothy. His clothing was clean, crisp and tailor-made, his diction perfect, his manners impeccable. At first Emily refused to give him the time of day, but ignoring Timothy Lee just seemed to make him more interested and determined. Occasionally President Young asked Emily for updates about their work together, so she felt obligated to help. Before long Emily found herself being caught up in an uncharted course she was ill-equipped to navigate.

Eventually Timothy had worn Emily down. His determined attempts to win her attention with lavish gifts made Emily's rebukes feel ungrateful and snobbish. Eventually relenting, Emily began accepting small gifts and subtle suggestions for more refinement in her life. Emily was embarrassed to admit she liked the way she looked in the new clothes Timothy bought. Yet a nagging feeling of doubt and suspicion kept her wondering if Timothy was not everything he pretended to be.

When Timothy began reciting poetry, Emily felt the first chink in her armor. She loved the way he strung long memorized lines of words together like a fine connoisseur of words. Eventually Emily discovered even she couldn't ignore him forever. She was lonely. She hadn't heard a word from Daniel in months and didn't even know if he were still alive.

Now as Emily eyed her latest boxes of gifts, she felt confused.

If Daniel's dead, I don't want to be alone for the rest of my life, Emily thought. *It would be so easy to just let go and let myself really care about Timothy.*

CHAPTER TWENTY-TWO

Daniel breathed in the cool crisp mountain air as he rode toward the Salt Lake Valley. Much of the mountain snow pack had melted transforming small mountain streams into roaring rivers tumbling over rocks and cliffs near the trail. Gilbert slept most of the way on a make-shift traveling bed hitched to Daniel's horse. Daniel was grateful for the peace and quiet his uncle's silence offered.

As he rode through the high mountain meadows, Daniel wondered what would become of Gilbert when they reached the valley. His uncle was too lame and blind to be much use to anyone. Daniel knew Gilbert was alone and, without his help, didn't have much hope of a decent old age. He'd been wrestling all winter with stark memories of his boyhood in Gilbert's care. He still bore the scars of his uncle's frequent beatings. He remembered all too well the mob violence Gilbert ignited against the Mormons in Missouri. Before his conversion and baptism, Daniel had spent years devising elaborate plans for his return trip to Missouri to reclaim his father's farm and make Gilbert pay for what he'd done. Now that desire was gone.

Seeing the wreck of a man Gilbert had become renewed Daniel's desire to live a different sort of life than his uncle, to find a way of living beyond what greed and power offered him. Daniel knew his ordination to the priesthood had given the privilege to act in God's name in order to bless lives, not destroy them. He knew God loved all his children completely and equally. Daniel felt only pity for the cursing wreck of a man in the bed behind him who'd squandered his life.

During the long days and nights as he rode toward the valley, Daniel often wondered if Emily was waiting for him or if she had moved on with her life. He remembered the first time he'd passed through these hills five months earlier. The same mountain passes that earlier held death and starvation now seemed freely offering life and warmth. Now as they rode along, Daniel described the pristine beauty of the mountains to his uncle. He knew Gilbert was almost blind and would only be able to see the breath-taking surroundings through Daniel's eyes.

"Nothing like the Rockies," Daniel said after a vivid description of a mountain pass. Gilbert grunted and buried his face into the blanket. "Lots of people froze here last winter. Doesn't seem possible now," Daniel finished. Gilbert pretended not to listen.

Daniel knew Gilbert was a proud man and his new dependency was difficult for someone without family or friends. He had struggled to erase from his memory the dozens of beatings he'd received as a boy and the mob violence Gilbert ignited in Missouri. Yet now as he rode toward home he realized he might never be able to forget Gilbert's abuse, but the sting was gone, the desire for revenge vanished.

Daniel recalled with absolute clarity his conversion in the Spanish Fork Canyon after reading the Book of Mormon and his subsequent baptism in the frozen lake near Isaac Morley's home. Like the warm mountain sunshine on his shoulders, Daniel realized all the pieces of his life were coming together like a puzzle and it warmed him. He found it healing that God would put Gilbert back in his life after so many years of hatred and bitterness had passed between them. He knew forgiving and serving his uncle had given him a sweet and separate peace he'd never felt before.

"I'm nervous about going back to the valley," Daniel said. "There's a girl down there waiting for me. At least I hope she is. If she still wants me, I'll never be foolish enough to leave her again, that's for sure. Anybody you'll be looking for?"

"No business of yours," Gilbert said gruffly. "You think I'm a lame, blind old man. You're wrong. I'm an important minister from Missouri. People respect me back there. I had money, lot's of it. I won't stay in Mormon country any longer than I have to. I have business to take care of here, some papers I want signed, then I'm going back."

"Who's your business with?" Daniel asked.

"My nephew," Gilbert answered. "Ever heard tale of Daniel Webster Jones? Heard he's living in these parts."

"Never heard of him," Daniel replied. "Must have received bad information about his whereabouts. If I were you, I wouldn't tell anybody you're from Missouri. Mormons in the Salt Lake Valley don't take kindly to old mobbers."

"Who asked for your opinion?" Gilbert said defiantly. "Why didn't you let me die? Who gave you the right to play God?"

Daniel became more serious and thoughtfully answered, "Wasn't thinking about rights. Knew you'd die if I didn't do something. Decided *not* to play God."

"I heard the men at the fort talking. They'd have let me die and you know it. So what makes you such a saint?"

"I'm no saint. Said so yourself. I'd have done the same thing for my worst enemy. Every man deserves a second chance."

"Don't want your charity," Gilbert grunted.

"I'll find you a room and doctor when we get to the valley," Daniel replied. Then Daniel noticed a break through the canyon walls below them. As he rode toward the opening, Daniel saw the scenic valley spread before him like a green and brown patchwork quilt. A chill ran up his spine. "Look!" Daniel shouted turning to Gilbert. "We're home."

Gilbert turned but saw only a blurred landscape.

"What does it look like?" Gilbert asked.

"Beautiful," Daniel answered.

"That's a lie," Gilbert said. "Salt Lake Valley is an old desert nobody else wants. Proves you're all crazy. Anybody who'd settle in this God forsaken place has to be mad."

"But it's my home!" Daniel answered. "There were times this past winter I doubted I'd ever live to see it again."

Daniel threw the reins in the air and yelled as he gave the horse a sharp kick. The horse started in full gallop for the valley.

"Stop!" Gilbert shouted as he held on tightly to the bed.

The bed flew over several large rocks protruding from the ground in the trail and came down with a hard thump.

"Excuse me," Daniel laughed as he turned and saw the terrified expression on Gilbert's face. "I've got some unfinished business down there and I'm more than excited to see someone."

"Been in these hills all winter. Few more minutes won't make any difference," Gilbert answered.

Daniel chuckled as he slowed the horse and carefully rode down into the valley trying not to jolt his passenger any more than necessary. When they got into the city, Daniel quickly asked around, then found a place for Gilbert to stay. The owner of the boarding house agreed to find a doctor after Daniel gave him a promissory note. Then Daniel ran for Brigham's house.

A kind woman greeted him when he reached the door to the prophet's home and took him into a small room to wait for President Young. Daniel looked into a framed mirror hanging on the wall. He was shocked by his own appearance. He hadn't shaved all winter and his buckskin clothing was worn and dirty. He knew he should take a bath, put on a fresh set of clothes and shave before he found Emily, but wasn't sure he could wait that long. Daniel sat down in the chair next to the wall nervously waiting for President Young. He heard some heavy footsteps in the hallway and looked up into the doorway just as Brigham entered with a broad smile and outstretched arms.

"Daniel," Brigham said in a deep voice as he walked over to where he was sitting. "Welcome home."

Daniel stood and shook Brigham's hand vigorously.

"Is it you or your ghost?" Brigham laughed. "Heard reports of late. If I'd known how much you were suffering at the fort, I'd have ridden my own team up there with supplies. I'm sorry. Reports came too late."

"We did all right with some good help," Daniel answered pointing heavenward.

Daniel handed Brigham the ledger where he'd kept a detailed record of the stored goods at the fort. Brigham took the book and looked through it quickly.

"Looks like the records are complete. Good work my friend. You deserve a hero's welcome." Daniel took Brigham's outstretched hand and shook it again.

"What can I do for you?" Brigham asked as Daniel turned to leave.

"Wagon drivers are waiting for word from you to tell them where to unload the goods until they can be dispersed," Daniel answered.

"Anything else?" Brigham added.

"Well, maybe you could tell me about that new school for the Indian children," Daniel answered.

"You mean, where's Emily, don't you?" Brigham asked.

Daniel felt the skin on his face grow hot. "Yes, sir," Daniel answered. "I sure want to see her."

"The school's doing fine. Emily's wonderful with children. Although lately Emily's been spending quite a lot of time with a government official sent out here by Washington. I've seen them both coming and going from Mrs. Linforth's house. I believe she's one of the emigrants you saved up at the fort."

"Mrs. Linforth," Daniel smiled broadly. "I remember well the day I met her on the road, quite literally. Maybe I shouldn't have talked her out of being left behind the way she intended."

"Needless to say," Brigham continued, "I'm glad you're back. You two were made for each other. Do you know anything about Free Wind?"

"I saw him camped near the fort with his new wife. Good man. But if you don't mind, I'll be going," Daniel said anxiously as he turned to leave again.

"I understand," Brigham answered. "Good luck. Don't give her up too easily."

Daniel left the house and walked down the streets of Salt Lake City. Wagons on each side of him sloshed through the mud, flipping the brown ooze up on his face. Daniel knew he should worry about his dirty appearance before he found Emily but he couldn't restrain himself. He turned into the old saddle shop where he'd been working before he left to rescue the stranded emigrants. When he saw his former employer at a table in the back of the room, he rushed toward him and called out his name.

"Need any help around here?" Daniel asked.

"Daniel!" the shop owner said surprised. "So good to see you again. You've got a job here whenever you want one. I'm mighty glad to see you. Just arrive?"

"Made my report to President Young just two minutes ago."

"And Emily?"

"Haven't seen her yet."

"Then get. See you tomorrow."

Daniel bounded for the door and only paused for a moment to ask, "Know where I might find her?"

"Colton family moved in during the Indian scare. Room at the fort. Emily's been spending time with a government official by the name of Timothy Lee up at Mrs. Linforth's. Can't miss the Linforth place. Biggest house in town. South two blocks."

Daniel thanked his former employer and hurried out the door. He ran down the street and stopped just short of the big house. He walked up the impressive walkway and stood on the steps ready to knock. Feeling his heart pounding in his chest, Daniel reached for the door and gave it a good hard knock. An older woman came and asked Daniel what he wanted.

"Is Miss Emily Colton here?" Daniel asked excitedly.

"Yes," the woman said, "but she can't be disturbed right now."

"Why not?" Daniel asked, noticeably disappointed.

"She's entertaining someone, an important government official. But I'll ask my mistress if you can call later."

The woman left Daniel standing on the doorstep as she went back into the house. When she returned, Mrs. Linforth came with her. She took one look at Daniel and told him to step inside.

"Come with me, young man," Mrs. Linforth said as she strode down the long hall in the entrance of her large home. "Step right in here."

She led Daniel into an empty room.

"Where's Emily? I came to see Emily," Daniel said.

"You'll speak to me first, young man," Mrs. Linforth said abruptly. "Suppose you recognize me. Caught me at a delicate moment when you found me on the road last winter. I'd prefer you didn't pass that incident around. It would be quite an embarrassment to me."

"That's the least of my worries. I've come to see Emily Colton. Would you tell her Daniel is here? I'm sure she'll want to see me."

"Don't be so sure, young man," Mr. Linforth replied. "It so happens

Miss Emily is entertaining a very important person just now. She won't be able to see you today."

"Entertaining?" Daniel asked. "What's that supposed to mean?"

"She has another young man with her and if you had the sense you were born with, you'd leave here right now."

"I want to see her and if you don't tell me where she is, I'll break into every room in this house and look for her myself," Daniel said as he turned and walked away.

"You'll not order me about in my own home," Mrs. Linforth called after him.

"If you won't escort me, I'll show myself around," Daniel said.

Daniel walked from the room into the hallway. He nosily opened doors as he continued toward the entry. When he threw the third door open, it startled Emily and a handsome well dressed young man seated together on a couch.

"Daniel!" Emily said surprised. "What are you doing here?"

"I want to see you," Daniel said as he walked toward her.

Emily turned to Timothy then turned back to Daniel and said, "I'm sorry. I'm busy. I'll see you later."

Daniel was stunned. Just then Mrs. Linforth walked into the room.

"Well, I *said* she was busy. That should have been enough for you," Mrs. Linforth said, flipping her nose in the air.

Daniel looked searchingly into Emily's eyes and found only a nervous silent response. He reluctantly turned, walked quietly from the room and left the house in a daze. Emily moved to the edge of the couch shaking as Daniel left the room, wishing she hadn't said those words, wanting desperately to stop him from leaving.

"I hope you two weren't disturbed too much by that awful filthy man," Mrs. Linforth said as she breezed through the room pulling the curtain aside to watch Daniel walk slowly down the street alone.

"He's gone now. So, how are you two getting along? It's such a lovely day. You ought to go on a picnic and enjoy it."

Emily hadn't moved or spoken since Daniel left.

Timothy Lee took Emily's trembling hand and asked, "What is it? Has that man disturbed you so much?"

Timothy was dressed in a double breasted frockcoat, duster and silk vest. He always looked impeccable, a stark contrast to the other men in the Salt Lake Valley. Emily was accustomed to the dirty trousers or overalls her father and brothers wore with homemade drop sleeve cotton shirts. Timothy always kept his red hair combed away from his face with oil and his waxed handlebar mustache expertly trimmed.

Emily pulled away from Timothy as she answered, "What? I'm sorry. What did you say?"

"Did that filthy man disturb you?"

Emily paused before she answered, "No. He simply caught me off guard. I wasn't expecting to see him. Feels like I've just seen a ghost."

"He certainly has his nerve, doesn't he?" Mrs. Linforth interrupted. "I mean the way he marched in here like he owned you. I told him you had company. He insisted you'd want to see him anyway. Certainly takes a lot for granted. And the way he smelled. Probably hasn't bathed in a year. Hope we don't see him around here any more." As Emily listened, she felt an urge to defend Daniel but slid back in the couch and let Mrs. Linforth go on. "Why don't you two take my carriage and go for a little drive?"

"Thank you," Timothy replied, "but it's up to Miss Colton. If she'd like to get a bit of fresh air, then I'll agree."

Mrs. Linforth and Timothy looked over at Emily and waited for an answer.

"I'd like that," Emily said as she stood, took a deep breath and walked toward the door. "Haven't been out for ages. Could we go to City Creek Canyon?"

"Why certainly, Emily," Timothy said as he took her arm and guided her out the door. "You know I'd be glad to escort you anywhere or give you anything I thought would please you."

Emily reached for her wrap as they turned to leave. Mrs. Linforth's maid handed Mr. Lee his hat. Timothy went for the carriage as Emily waited on the porch. Her cheeks felt hot and flushed as Timothy came around the corner. She forced a smile. Timothy quickly jumped off the carriage and ran around to help her. After placing his two hands around her small waist, Timothy lifted Emily being careful to retrieve her dress ruffle so it wouldn't get dusty. Emily forced another smile as Timothy took her hand and kissed it before he bounded back around the carriage and jumped into the seat beside her.

Timothy gave the horse a limp whip as if unaccustomed to driving his own wagon. Then they trotted out of town toward the canyons. Emily turned her head and watched the valley pass by. It was spring now and signs of new life were everywhere. Timothy stared as she brushed a tear from her eye.

"He's really upset you, hasn't he?" Timothy asked. "Who is he anyway?"

"Just an old friend. Didn't expect to see him again. Surprised me."

"He certainly is a smelly, rude and brass fellow. I'm not sure he appreciates having an acquaintance with such a fine lady as you. I don't want you to see him any more. He seems only to upset you. Interrupted something very important I wanted to ask you. But I guess it will be all right if I continue with our conversation here in this primitive area. Where would you like to stop, Emily?"

Emily asked Timothy to drive a bit farther before she instructed him to turn into the trees at a certain spot. Timothy helped her from the carriage with the same gentleness he'd offered her since they'd met earlier that winter. Emily walked over toward the river. She could remember finding Daniel in a spot not far from this place. She felt guilty for having Timothy bring her there.

"Emily, won't you come and sit with me for a while?" Timothy asked. "I have something very important I want to talk to you about."

Emily walked back to where Timothy was sitting in the long weed grass, picked up her skirts and sat across from him. She looked around her and breathed the fresh mountain air.

"It's beautiful, isn't it?" Emily said as she took a deep breath and closed her eyes. She could hear the wild birds and feel the soft wind blowing all around her as she finished, "I feel at home here, Timothy. This is where I feel like the real me. I don't know if you understand that. Do you?"

"Perhaps it has a certain primitive beauty," Timothy answered. "But it's so dirty." Mr. Lee took a white handkerchief from his pocket then wiped the dust from his perfectly pressed trousers. "Emily, ever since I was sent out here, I've seen you almost every day. I do a lot of traveling with this job of mine. When they assigned me to come out to Mormon country, I almost refused. Must admit the things I'd heard about your people weren't too flattering. Now I feel it was the best trip I've ever taken. From the first day when I saw you at your school, I knew you were different. First it was the way you ignored me that intrigued me. After that, it wasn't so much the challenge, but you. Emily, you are different than any woman I've ever met. I thought Mormon women were all plain, dressed in black clothes and hid away in great polygamy houses having endless snot-nosed brats. I wasn't expecting you. I'm leaving to go on another assignment in a few weeks. My next assignment will be in Europe. I want you to go with me."

"Timothy," Emily replied surprised, "I don't know what to say. Thank you for everything you've done for me, the French lessons and gifts; you were there when I needed someone. It's been like a different world for me since you came. I don't know what to say."

"No need to thank me. Your beauty far surpasses most, and I've know many women. All I want to hear is that you'll go away with me. I must admit I've never waited this long for any one. Emily, say yes." Timothy put his arms around Emily's waist and brought her toward him forcefully. "You didn't ask me out here where we could be alone just so we could talk."

"Timothy, don't," Emily said as she pulled away. "You'll have to give me time to think about it. I feel confused right now. My whole life until I met you was my family and my faith. To marry someone who didn't feel the same about it would be like saying my whole life was a lie. In my church we marry in the temple forever. I won't settle for anything less."

"If you'll go away with me, I'm sure in time I'll feel the same way you do and then we can be married your way," Timothy answered.

"You have everything a man could ever want. Why me?" Emily asked.

"Emily, I've thought this all out. I want you, and I'll have you," Timothy answered as he took Emily hands and kissed them. "I always get what I want, always."

"What if it's simply the fact I'm unavailable that makes you want me?" Emily asked. "If I say yes, you'll tire of me soon enough."

Timothy's countenance darkened. "Don't play hard to get with me, Emily," Timothy said in a voice that frightened her. "I've always respected your wishes, kept my hands off you."

Timothy grabbed Emily around the waist again and kissed her hard.

"No," Emily pleaded as she struggled to be free of his grasp.

Emily broke and ran for the river. Timothy, stunned only for a moment, followed. Emily raced over the rocks on the river bank then suddenly tripped and fell. Timothy ran up next to her, straddled the ground where she lay in pain then took her arms and held them tight against the ground above her head.

"No!" Emily screamed.

Just as Timothy reached up to cover Emily's mouth, someone grabbed him from behind, throwing him back several yards into the bushes. Emily quickly sat up then spied Daniel in the river grass wrestling with Timothy. She watched as Daniel's fists slammed into Timothy's frightened face. Stunned and wincing in pain, Timothy offered little resistance. Emily noticed Timothy's nose bleeding red down his starched white shirt as she ran for the carriage and gave the pony a whip.

Emily quickly sped from the canyons and headed back toward the valley. Her head aching, Emily's mind whirled and her heart raced. She galloped the horse back into town and stopped the carriage abruptly in front of Mrs. Linforth's house. Then she ran on foot to her parent's residence a few blocks away. When Emily burst through the door of the room where her family was staying, Polly took one look at her daughter and screamed. Emily's hair was messed, her face dirty and streaked with tears. Her dress was torn and a large growing circle of blood soaked the back of her dress.

"Emily!" Polly shouted. "What's happened?"

Emily fell into her mother's arms, "Why am I so stupid? Timothy's a cad. I should have known and stayed away from him. Showed his true colors today."

"Did he hurt you?" Polly asked.

"No, but he was going to. If Daniel hadn't been there I don't know what would've happened. Why did I have to move in with Mrs. Linforth and see so much of him? I don't know what to do now."

Polly sat Emily down on the bed and poured some water from the pitcher next to the bed on a cloth.

"Don't talk just now. Let me see to your head."

"It'll be all right," Emily interrupted. "I fell. Hit my head on a rock. Daniel and Timothy are fighting in the canyons right now."

"Won't last long. Bit of difference in the size of those two," Polly said washing Emily's head and trying to calm her daughter.

"I feel so guilty about Timothy. Let him buy me presents and pay for French lessons. Let him take me everywhere. Flattered such a sophisticated man would see something in me. He's rich, handsome and I was lonely. Wasn't sure how Daniel felt about me or if he was coming back. He's back now."

"I'm so glad," Polly answered with a sigh. "Daniel loves you for all the right reasons."

"Daniel barged through the door of Mrs. Linforth's hallway and demanded to see me while I was entertaining Timothy. I told him I was busy. You should have seen the look on his face."

"That was cruel," Polly said as she kept tending to the gash on her daughter's head. "What were you thinking?"

"I don't know what I was thinking. For just a second I was glad he found me with Timothy. Daniel left me without even saying goodbye. Timothy's leaving for Europe and he's asked me to come. That's why he had me take French lessons. I feel like such a fool."

"I tried to warn you," Polly said.

"I know. I'm so sorry. Now I've messed up a lot of lives, including my own. I don't think Daniel will ever forgive me."

"We all make mistakes," Polly said reassuringly.

"Don't be so understanding. Why don't you just tell me how stupid and vain I am?"

Polly took the blood soaked cloth from Emily's head, applied another, then wrapped a piece of torn bedding around Emily's forehead to keep it in place.

"If that's what you want then that's what you'll get," Polly answered. "I saw this coming. You're a grown woman now. I can't force you to see things my way. I knew Timothy Lee was a man of the world, and I told you a dozen times. You wouldn't listen."

"I never want to see him again," Emily answered. "Showed his true intentions."

"Just be honest with Daniel, Emily. Don't play games. He deserves better," Polly said hugging her daughter.

"Look where honesty got me. Told Daniel I loved him. He left. Thought he was doing me a favor. I just don't know. If I followed my heart, I'd have run right into Daniel's arms when I saw him standing there in the doorway with that foolish whiskered grin on his face at Mrs. Linforth's house. Really wanted to, but I was so stupid; thought I had to show him he didn't make the sun rise and set for me. *But he does.*" Polly nodded and smiled. "Timothy scared me today," Emily continued. "He frightens me. I'll never deny my testimony of Jesus Christ or the people who are most precious to me. I realize now Daniel just hurt my pride when he left. I didn't think he could live without me again. But he can and I can. Just not very well. I'll always love him."

"Emily," Polly said, "when you really love someone, you stop worrying about who has the upper hand. Be honest with yourself and him. Can't protect you or Daniel from the hurt or the happiness life brings, but you can face it together."

Hours later after her head quit bleeding and she'd changed her dress, Emily heard a knock at the door. She hurried into the bedroom, afraid it might be Timothy.

"It's Daniel," Polly whispered after she opened the front door then walked back to the bedroom. "He wants to talk to you."

Emily looked up at her mother nervously and asked, "Why am I so afraid to go out there? Maybe he hates me now. You'd better tell him to come back later."

"Are you crazy? If he hated you, he wouldn't be here. If you want him to go away, you'll have to tell him yourself," Polly said shaking her head.

"Look at me. I look awful."

"Do you think he cares about that? Don't you make him wait one minute longer, Harriet Emily Colton. Now get out there," Polly said as she pushed Emily toward the bedroom door.

Emily took a deep breath and walked from the bedroom into the main room where Daniel stood nervously with his back to the outside door. His appearance had drastically changed. He'd cut his long hair, bathed, shaved and changed his buckskins for clean trousers and a shirt. He held a hat in his hands, gripping and turning the brim with sweaty palms. Emily was speechless as she walked slowly toward him. She stopped several feet away and stood perfectly still as she looked deep into his piercing blue eyes. Daniel politely nodded with a shaky head.

"You all right?" Daniel asked nervously.

Emily nodded. Daniel returned Emily's steady gaze. She looked radiant to him. Nervously, he dropped his hat and reached out to her. Emily leaped into his outstretched arms and wrapped herself around him as she felt her feet slip off the floor.

"You're here," Emily gushed. "I didn't know if you'd ever come back. This has been the worst winter of my life."

"Me too," Daniel answered.

As Daniel felt his cheeks grow hot, he stroked Emily's hair and kissed the top of her head.

"Did he hurt you?" Daniel asked quietly.

"I'm fine. Never want to see him again. You're thin," Emily said, poking Daniel in the ribs. "Did you have a hard time of it?"

"Guess you could say that. But winter's over. Don't want to think about it any more. All I want to do for the rest of my life is hold you."

"Why did you leave without seeing me?" Emily asked "You broke my heart."

"I told myself I was giving you the freedom to decide between me and Free Wind. Jealous pride. I'll never leave you again unless you tell me go."

"I'll never tell you to go," Emily answered.

"I love you, Emily. You mean everything to me," Daniel said, his voice breaking with emotion.

"I love you too," Emily whispered.

Emily glanced up at Daniel towering a foot above her and felt instantly at home. Then Emily's brothers and sister burst into the room and asked him a hundred questions about his winter at the fort. Later, after he'd visited with the Colton family, Daniel took Emily outside. He lifted her onto his horse then mounted. Emily gathered her long dark hair into her hands and let it fall down her back in a long cascade. Then she brought her arms around Daniel's chest, breathed in his freshly washed skin, and laid her cheek against his back. He gave the horse a kick and they rode away. On their way out of town, Emily noticed Timothy in tattered, bloody clothes walking down the street.

"Emily!" Timothy shouted when he saw them.

"Do you want to talk to him?" Daniel asked.

"No, I never want to speak to him again."

Daniel gave the horse a hard kick as they galloped toward City Creek together. Emily brought her arms tighter around his chest. She could feel the heat radiating from his body. Rocks flew and dust billowed behind them as they headed into the canyon. Gray sagebrush covered hillsides burst with springtime grass and wildflowers. Chipmunks scampered on the road and the sound of meadowlarks filled the air as they headed further up City Creek Canyon.

As they climbed higher, the air cooled. Several of the cottonwood trees sent small tufts of white floating through the air like bits of cotton. Deep green pines mingled with quaking aspens and scrub oak softened the sounds of the city until they disappeared altogether and the quiet pulsating sound of crickets filled the air. They rode deeper and deeper into the trees.

City Creek transformed every season. In spring, the runoff from the upper mountains made the creek swell and dash against the rocks as it tumbled down the canyon floor. In autumn, City Creek changed into a small meandering brook, trickling softly over a few rocks in the nearly dry riverbed. Spring always came later in the mountains than it did in the valley. Most of the settlers had already planted their gardens and the open fields were a study in long green furrowed rows. Fruit trees blossomed in profusion, each one taking their turn filling the air with the hope of future harvest.

Emily relished this time, this moment . . . riding with Daniel in the forest they both loved. He slowed the horse to a trot as they entered the whispering trees. Once enclosed in the forest, he slipped from the animal, took the reigns and walked the horse toward the river. After Daniel helped Emily from the horse, he threw his coat down on the new grass near the bank. Emily fluffed her skirt around her as she sat cross-legged directly in front of Daniel.

"I'm sorry. I was a fool to leave," Daniel said.

"Stranded Saints needed your help," Emily answered. "You're a good man."

"When I saw you with that other man today, felt like I did when I saw you with Free Wind. Jealous. That's the truth of it. Rode out here to get rid of those dark feelings. Being jealous isn't part of love. If you really love someone you want their happiness before your own. Decided I want you to be happy even if it didn't include me. Then I heard someone scream."

"Hate to think what might have happened if you hadn't been here," Emily said. "I'm sorry too. Afraid you didn't love me or that you wouldn't come back. Timothy was there at a very lonely time for me."

"Tired of worrying about me, about getting hurt," Daniel said. "Faced death too many times this winter to waste even one more day. Have to tell you how I feel. I love you, Emily. I'll always love you. Will you marry me?" Emily looked lovingly at Daniel as he stumbled over his words with a soft imploring look in his eyes. "I can't promise you anything in the way of worldly goods like your fancy friend, but I can promise I will cherish and love you forever."

"I've waited so long to hear you say those words to me," Emily said. "Almost decided you never would." She wrapped her arms around Daniel's neck as he leaned forward and kissed her. "I love you," Emily whispered touching his ear with her lips. "Of course I'll marry you."

Daniel smiled long and deep. Then Emily quickly jumped up and pulled him toward the river. She quickly slipped off her shoes and tied the skirt of her dress up around her waist as Daniel rolled up his pants and slipped off his boots. Taking each other by the hand, they both waded into the cool stream, icy water splashing against their thighs. Daniel picked Emily up and set her down on a large flat rock in the river.

As the cold water flowed over her naked feet, Emily felt herself trembling. Watching Daniel wade through the water gave Emily the most peaceful feeling she'd ever known.

Later Emily carefully stepped off the rock, back through the water, and sat down on the tender new grass growing on the river bank. Daniel remained in the river skipping small flat stones off the water that created circles spiraling outward until they reached the shore. Emily shook her hair out in the sun and stretched her white legs out to dry. She watched Daniel silhouetted against the trees, his large muscular body moving musically as he pushed the wet hair away from his face. A sudden gust of wind and shimmer of sunlight sent chills up both their spines. Their eyes met and for one brief shining moment they were permitted to catch a glimpse of another luminous shore, a higher kingdom, a chance for reality and eternity to meet in their love. Long years of unanswered hope had instantly transformed into a future of joy.

This is real, Emily thought. *If I could only make this moment last forever.*

Yet life had taught her that treasured moments like these soon vanish like a leaf in the wind, here one moment, and then gone on the next breeze. She knew there would be other black nights followed by brilliant sunrises, cold winters followed by temperate springs, darkness always followed by light. Emily sighed.

Love is the only thing that matters, she thought. *It is the only thing that lasts.*

Later, toward evening, Daniel and Emily road back into Salt Lake City with damp wrinkled clothes and radiant smiles. They'd already set a date and made plans for their upcoming wedding. On their way to tell Emily's parents, they both noticed Brigham Young walking down the street. When he saw Daniel and Emily approaching, he seemed concerned and called out for them to stop. Brigham nodded at Emily and said hello as Daniel dismounted.

"I hate to tell you this bad news," Brigham began. "Hate to even bring it up, but my hand's been forced. Some of the emigrants have come to me with complaints against you. Say they haven't had all of their goods returned. Accused you of stealing them. Simply dismissed the complaints until now. But today Timothy Lee, the government official from Washington, came to my home and demanded a hearing. He wants to prosecute you. I just wanted you to know I will personally be acting in your defense. Do you have anyone beside the men in your group who could testify for you?"

"No. There isn't anyone," Daniel said surprised. "Only one other man stayed with us for any length of time. He hates the Mormons. He'll probably testify for the other side."

"Don't understand how these accusations started but we've got to answer for them now," Brigham said as he placed his hand on Daniel's shoulder. "Hearing is set for next week. Mr. Lee has seen to that. After all you men went through to protect those goods, I'll never understand. Like to curse some of those people. Who is this other man you speak of?"

"Name's Gilbert Marshall. Probably be leaving before the hearing is held. Wants to get out of Mormon country as soon as possible."

"Well, speak with him and see what he thinks," Brigham continued. "Get back with you later and we'll prepare your case. If you could get that man to speak for you, we wouldn't even need to have this hearing." Brigham took Daniel's hand, shook it and left.

"Gilbert?" Emily said apprehensively. "Is Gilbert here in Salt Lake?"

"I found him on the trail near the fort this winter. You wouldn't know the man. He's old now and nearly blind. Had to remove part of his legs or he'd have died. He's as bitter as he ever was. Rest of his party all died."

"Surely he'll speak for you, Daniel. He's your uncle. He couldn't turn against his own blood like that," Emily said.

"He doesn't know who I am and I won't tell him now that I need his help," Daniel answered. "He never recognized me. Just think its best he doesn't know."

Emily was silent. She took Daniel by the hand and they headed toward her parent's room.

"Let's tell Momma and Papa about us," Emily said, trying to put a smile on Daniel's face.

Daniel answered, "But with this hearing, it will probably be quite a while now before we can get married. If Timothy has his way, I'll be thrown in jail. If I can't prove I'm innocent, that's where I'll end up."

"Just tell Gilbert who you are and I'm sure he'll speak for you. Then we won't have to worry about a hearing. Timothy will be leaving in a few weeks and everything will be all right then."

"Emily, promise me that you won't go to Gilbert and tell him who I am."

"But he's your only help right now."

"I'll answer my accusers and Timothy Lee by myself. I don't need Gilbert's help," Daniel answered.

CHAPTER TWENTY-THREE

Early the next day, Emily put on her shawl and walked to Timothy Lee's residence. When he came into the doorway, he smiled as though he'd won the match then grabbed Emily by the arm and pulled her inside.

"Well, Emily, it's good of you to come. I'm glad to see you've come to your senses."

Emily forced Timothy's hand off her arm and said defiantly, "This isn't a social call, Timothy, and you know it."

"Come right in here," Timothy continued as he guided Emily to a sitting room in the house. "We can talk privately in here."

Emily followed him into the richly decorated room and sat down on the chair farthest from the one he was going to sit on.

"How could you do it, Timothy? Emily blurted, her cheeks fiery red. "I thought better of you."

"I've never seen you angry before. It looks well on you," Timothy said, eyeing her from head to toe. He sauntered triumphantly across the room to where Emily was sitting. "I'll be leaving for Europe soon. Are you sure you won't reconsider?"

"Do you really think you can manipulate me so easily?" Emily answered.

"Manipulate you!" Timothy said with an irritated voice. "What games were you playing with me? You were always more than happy to see me before this Jones character came into town. Now you act like I have the plague. I won't have it! If you'll promise to go away with me, I'll drop the charges. If you don't, I'll make sure you won't have the chance to be with him."

Emily looked into Timothy's threatening eyes as he spoke, realizing how deceived she'd been for the past few months. Timothy Lee was not what he appeared to be. He'd stop at nothing to get what he wanted and he wanted her. She also knew full well he'd soon tire of her and move on to someone else. Emily wished she'd never met him.

"I'm sorry, Timothy, but it would never work out with us. I know that and I think you know it too. You just want me because you can't have me. My family and my testimony of Jesus Christ is my life. And I love someone else—always have, always will. You don't really love me, you don't even know me. You can't force me to leave with you."

"Who do you think you are to refuse me, Emily Colton?" Timothy said with an arrogant turn of his head. "You're a nobody, a penniless girl joined to a queer sect out here in the middle of nowhere. I could rescue you from all this if you'd go away with me. You'd have beautiful things, go places. I could make you a princess. Money is freedom, Emily. Trust me. Your life here will be drudgery, endless snot-nosed brats, hard labor in the fields, slim school teacher earnings, house cleaning, and fixing meals. You'll be an old woman before you know it; all your beauty faded away. And for nothing, for some uneducated foul-smelling man in buckskin. If you continue to refuse me, you leave me no other choice."

Emily realized Timothy had his mind made up. She looked at him in his perfectly starched shirt and silk tie, his pasty white face and soft hands, then wondered what she'd ever seen in him. As she looked down at her plain faded cotton dress and callused sun-burned hands she felt a sense of unexpected self-respect swelling inside her.

"I'm already a princess," Emily answered with her head held high. Timothy was at a loss for words. "What makes you so sure you can convict Daniel when you know those accusations are false? It's vindictive and you know it. Those emigrants wouldn't dare make their complaints formal unless you had something to do with it."

Timothy gazed at Emily like forbidden fruit. Never in his life had he waited to have any woman he desired. His money and charm had a way of clouding the resistance of dozens of women in his past. He vowed to himself that Emily Colton would not be his first defeat.

"I don't just have the emigrant's complaints. I have an eyewitness as well," Timothy answered running his fingers through his auburn hair.

"There's an old man who stayed at the fort who's willing to testify he saw Daniel take some of the goods himself."

"Gilbert!" Emily said with fire in her eyes. "He's an old Missouri mob leader. He'd say anything to hurt any Mormon. He hates us. He burned my family out of our home in Missouri and thought he'd killed us all. How could you use him?"

"Does it matter? Do you want Daniel to go to jail just for your arrogant pride?" Timothy answered sure his schemes would change her mind.

"My pride or yours?" Emily answered slowly and deliberately. "I appreciate everything you've given me. I'm sorry your investment didn't pay off. What good will it do to ruin my life and Daniel's, just to get back at me? Charge *me* with something. Leave Daniel alone. Timothy, I love him. When I started seeing you, I thought I'd never see him again. We've known each other since we were children. We have a bond so deep; *nothing* can come between us, not even you. Please reconsider if you care for me as you claim."

"I won't give you up," Timothy said. "If I can't have you, neither will Jones."

Emily realized there was no changing Timothy's mind. She felt foolish for coming to see him. She turned and started to leave. Timothy reached out and caught her by the arm.

"Don't go," he said.

Emily shook her arm free and turned again to leave the room. Timothy backed her against a wall. Blocking her forward movement with his arms, he leaned forward and tried to kiss her. Emily turned her face and pushed him forcefully away.

"I never should have come," Emily said. "Never want to see you again."

Emily dashed from the room, down the hallway and out the door. She took her hand and wiped off the place where Timothy touched her feeling suddenly sullied. Her mind raced, wondering what was left for her to do in order to help Daniel. So far all of her attempts had failed.

Emily walked directly to where she knew her father was working on a new temple in the heart of Salt Lake City. Almost immediately after

Emily's family had moved into town, Philander was the first to volunteer his construction skills. Emily remembered how difficult it had been for her father to leave the temple in Nauvoo and marveled at his faith to work on a new one. When Philander looked down the street and saw Emily walking toward the temple with tears in her eyes, he stopped his work immediately.

"Papa," Emily cried as she reached her father. "Timothy won't back down. He's sworn to put Daniel in jail. It's my fault. He's got Gilbert Marshall ready to testify he saw Daniel stealing while he was staying at the fort. Gilbert doesn't even know the man he's sending to jail is his nephew. He's never been told. No one but us even knows they're related. Daniel made me promise I won't tell Gilbert who he is. I can't believe those ungrateful emigrants would actually accuse him after all he went through for them."

"I'm sorry," Philander said trying to comfort his daughter. "Daniel surely doesn't deserve this. Sometimes the people you sacrifice the most for appreciate it the least. But Daniel's efforts are known to God. I'm sure Brigham will defend him. Daniel won't go to jail for something he didn't do. Go home and pray. We'll just have to leave the matter in God's hands."

Emily looked despondent as she left and quietly walked home. Philander waited until Emily was out of sight before he set his tools down and left the temple sight. He walked resolutely toward the boarding house where he knew Gilbert was staying.

Daniel made you promise not to talk to Gilbert, but he didn't make me, Philander thought as he was walking. *Sometimes God needs a helping hand.*

Gilbert was staying in a boarding house with his own private room. As Philander walked into the house, he tucked in his shirt, took a deep breath and squared his shoulders.

"Sorry, but Mr. Marshall insists I allow no unannounced strangers entrance to his room," a woman said as Philander approached the door.

"We're not strangers. I'm an old friend from Missouri. Sure he'll be glad to see me again," Philander said as he knocked on the door to Gilbert's room.

"He's nearly blind, you know. You'll have to tell him who you are," the woman said.

"I intend to do just that," Philander said with a sly smile.

"Go away. I don't want any supper," Gilbert said gruffly when Philander opened the door.

"This isn't supper," Philander answered. "It's an old friend from Missouri."

"Old friend?" Gilbert questioned. "Who are you? Better tell me quick or I'll have you thrown out."

"Good to see you again," Philander began as he walked across the room and sat down on a chair near Gilbert. "Colton's the name. Philander Colton. Remember me? I lived near your sister's farm in Missouri."

"Get out!" Gilbert answered nervously. "Leave me alone!"

"Just listen to me for a few minutes. You owe me that much, Reverend Marshall."

"I owe you nothing," Gilbert said fidgeting nervously obviously contemplating what might happen next. "Get out and leave me alone. Not here because I want to be. One of you Mormons dragged me here to this stinking hole."

"Your story is a little different and you know it. A young man saved your life. If he hadn't been a Mormon, you'd feel deeply indebted to him."

"What do you want with me?" Gilbert asked again apprehensively.

Philander now looked with pity on the broken man before him. With most of his hair missing, his lower legs gone and eyesight dimmed, Gilbert Marshal didn't seem half the menacing character Philander remembered back in Missouri. His appearance was ill kept and he had an offensive odor about him

"I heard you're going to testify against the young man who saved your life," Philander said. "You say he stole from the emigrants."

"It won't be me who puts him away. It's your own kind," Gilbert said defensively. "Mormon emigrants, not me. Some government official promised me quick money and an escort out this Mormon infested rat's nest if I testify. He means nothing to me. My testimony wouldn't make any difference one way or the other."

"Believe me, your testimony will make a great deal of difference," Philander answered. Then he paused. "Do you remember a long time ago when you came to Nauvoo and threatened me and my family if we didn't tell you where Daniel was?"

"I remember," Gilbert said. "What of it? Are you going to put me on trial too?"

"No," Philander answered. "You deserve it, but I won't. You wanted us to tell you where you could find Daniel and we said we didn't know. That was the truth then. But maybe now I can help you."

"Daniel!" Gilbert said surprised. "Do you know where he is?"

"Friday when you go to the trial," Philander said as he stood to leave, "Daniel will be there. It's his trial."

"Daniel?" Gilbert asked slinking back into his chair. "Liar! Leave me alone. I don't believe you!"

Philander turned and walked quietly from the room. He closed the door behind him, shook his head then returned to his work site at the temple.

❦

Twenty people crowded into President Young's office for the hearing on charges brought against Daniel Webster Jones. The air felt suffocating as Daniel walked through the doorway to face his accusers. As he looked around the room, Daniel realized most of the people there were strangers to him. He recognized only a few.

President Young welcomed Daniel warmly when he entered his office and invited him to find a seat. Daniel found an empty chair then looked to the right, then left at his accusers. Seated closest to him were several of the emigrants he vividly remembered rescuing just months before. All winter he'd faced starvation to protect their goods and now it seemed a nightmare that these same people were accusing him, not thanking him.

"Sister Linforth," Daniel said to the woman seated at his right. "So good to see you. How's the family?"

Sister Linforth turned her head and refused to reply. Daniel glanced around the room at the other accusers. Several had been to his boarding room during the previous few days insisting they had the right to search for stolen goods on his premises. Though hurt and disappointed, Daniel had complied with every demand knowing he had nothing to hide. Timothy Lee was seated at the side of Brigham Young at the front of the room. Gilbert sat in a dark corner with his collar pulled up around his face.

"Let's get on with this!" Timothy said as he stood and walked into the center of the room.

The judge, seated on the other side of Brigham, told Timothy to be quiet and sit down before he brought a mallet down on the desk in front of him and said, "The hearing will begin now. You may call your first witness, President Young."

Brigham stood, walked slowly around the room and glared into the faces of all the people who were present.

"I have only one witness, sir," he said. "I call Daniel Webster Jones."

"Daniel Webster Jones," the judge said, "stand and be heard."

Daniel walked to the center of the room as the onlookers became deathly silent.

"Daniel, tell these people what it was like last winter while you were taking care of their goods," Brigham began.

"Well, sir," Daniel began, "I spent five or six months of winter up there. Emigrants weren't able to leave us any provisions. Starving themselves. Lived pretty well on poor cattle that died around the fort at first. When the meat ran out we scraped the hides of the animals and ate them too. Got some buffalo now and then. Traded with Indians for game. Ate thistles, garlic and prickly pear leaves too. Most the time there was nothing to eat. We used our own goods when we traded with the Indians."

Daniel heard whispering. The judge ordered quiet.

"We kept the goods locked up and didn't bother them," Daniel said. "We were too worried about starving, too weak to think about stealing. I'm accountable for the actions of all of my men. None of us took anything that didn't belong to us. I kept a record of everything stored there and what we used. It's all in a book I gave to President Young."

Brigham held up the ledger and threw it into the lap of one of the accusers.

"Daniel's been modest in his description of those winter months at up the fort. Go ahead, read it for yourself," Brigham said angrily.

The man with the book in his lap shouted, "Well, if not Daniel, then maybe it was one of his men!"

Brigham interrupted, "Mr. Jones just said he stands accountable for all of his men. If you have any complaints against any of them, it will be decided today."

"Well then, if Daniel and his men didn't take anything, then why is it that I have so much missing?" the man asked.

"That, my good man," Brigham said, "is because you lie. When you first came to me you complained about missing goods even while Daniel and his men were back at the fort eating hides to protect them. I've since learned the very things you complained were stolen have come back into your hands. It's your pride that should be on trial today. Can't you admit you made a mistake?"

Brigham swung around and looked into each accuser's face directly and asked them if they did not believe Daniel had told the truth. Each man and woman in turn agreed they did.

"How does all this look to you now? After accusing this man of stealing from you when he spent the whole winter staring death in the face just to protect your goods, you come here to accuse him and not to thank him. You should be ashamed."

One of the accusers stood and said, "Mr. Lee said he had a witness who'd testify he saw Daniel stealing. Said we could be sure our suspicions were right if we came and listened to that witness today."

The man sat down as Brigham turned to Timothy seated in the front of the room and said, "Mr. Lee, now you may begin with your eyewitness, if you have him."

Brigham sat down as Timothy stood. The judge told Daniel to go back to his seat.

"It's a mockery to the judicial system to witness what has gone on today," Timothy said. "President Young has intimidated these people into saying what he wants to hear. But you will eat your words shortly. I call Gilbert Marshall to the stand."

The people in the room glanced around looking for the stranger no one knew. Daniel saw his uncle in the rear of the room. Several men went to the back and carried Gilbert's chair to the center of the room.

Gilbert cleared his throat after the men set him down and returned to their seats.

"You have to answer truthfully about what you saw, Mr. Marshall," the judge began. "We're all very anxious to hear what you have to say."

"Guess it's my turn to speak my peace," Gilbert began. "I want you to know I don't think very highly of Mormons. Witnessed their schemes in Missouri."

"Just a minute," Timothy interrupted, "I haven't asked you anything yet."

"Everybody knows what you want me to say," Gilbert interrupted. "So I'll just get on with this. Came west with a group from Missouri. Caught in an early season storm. All the people in my group refused to keep going. Told them they'd all die but they didn't believe me. Wasn't going to let their stupidity kill me. Paced back and forth in front of my tent until I couldn't feel the cold. Always kept my fire burning. After a while I couldn't feel anything in my legs. Sat down in my tent and waited because I knew it wouldn't be long. That's when two men rode into my camp."

Daniel looked at Gilbert with surprise. He expected a much different attitude from his uncle and was interested to listen to hear his side of the story.

"One man forced me to go with him," Gilbert continued. "Wouldn't let me die. Don't remember anything from the time they found me until I woke up in the fort with the same man who rescued me. Soon found out he'd cut off both of my lower legs to save my life. Hated him for it. Wanted to kill him. He forced me to live."

"Mr. Marshall," Timothy interrupted, "I fail to see how any of . . ."

"Go ahead," the judge said. "Sit down, Mr. Lee."

"That same man dragged me to this valley on a make-shift bed behind his horse. None of the other men up at the fort would help me. He got me a room, a doctor. Even though I'm an old man, I don't want to die any more. That man gave me a second chance. Hate Mormons! But that man saved my life . . . and maybe my soul."

"Mr. Marshall, I'm sure everybody enjoyed your grand little speech, but I want to know what you saw at the fort," Timothy interrupted.

"You really want to know what I saw?" Gilbert answered.

"Please," Mr. Lee answered.

"Saw this man give me his last meal," Gilbert said. "Saw this man risk his life for a bunch of stupid emigrants like me and the rest of the people in this room who started west too late in the season. I never saw him or any of his men take anything they didn't need to stay alive. You sir, have tried to get me to say something different. This is the truth, I swear to God."

"But you said . . ." Timothy said angrily.

"I know what I said," Gilbert answered. "You paid me to lie, but I changed my mind. A man can change, even me. Perhaps even you."

"That will be all, Mr. Marshall," Timothy said as he pointed his finger accusingly.

"Mr. Lee, you have accused this court of being a mockery to justice," Brigham bellowed as he rose to his feet. "I say you'd better define your meaning of the word." Brigham turned to Daniel's accusers, pointed at them individually and continued, "All of you have accused Mr. Jones of stealing from you. Started complaining even while Daniel and his men were still at the fort living off rawhides. With the help of this government official, who for personal reasons wants to send Daniel to jail, you've came here hoping to get something for nothing. I tell you your ingratitude will curse you for the rest of your life. This man was tied to your goods all winter, risking his life for the whole lot of you. Certainly he could have expected your gratitude. Now I want you to know if this good man had set fire to the whole lot of your goods *and* the fort, then run away by the light of the burning mess, I would *not* have found fault with him!"

Brigham sat down. Each of the people in the room nervously cleared their throats and appeared anxious to leave.

"Case dismissed," the judge said before he stood and left the room.

As the onlookers quickly left, Brigham motioned to Timothy so he could speak with him privately.

"If I ever see you again, Mr. Lee, I will personally see that you stand trial yourself for what you attempted to do today," Brigham said.

Timothy listened nervously to President Young then left the room in a hurry. Daniel walked up to Gilbert as Timothy slammed the door shut behind him.

"Thank you," Daniel said placing his hand on his uncle's shoulder.

"Well, don't just stand there. Get me out of here!" Gilbert blurted.

"Some things never change," Daniel laughed, shaking his head.

"Looks like your friend the government official has forgotten all about you," Brigham chided. "So much for paid friendship."

"May I do the honors?" Daniel asked lifting Gilbert from his chair. "I'd be proud to take you home, uncle."

Daniel felt Gilbert's body tremble then noticed tears streaming down his wrinkled whiskered face.

"Don't deserve it," Gilbert said, his voice breaking as they reached the street.

Daniel took a deep breath of the fresh air outside the court room door. He spied Emily across the street smiling and waving and hurried toward her. Just as he reached her side, Daniel noticed snowflakes floating all about them. He looked up. Falling from a sunlit cloudless sky, they were suddenly enclosed in a gentle iridescent shower of crystal white—as if numberless angels had each dropped one small white feather earthward on their last journey home.

CHAPTER TWENTY-FOUR

The wind in the trees near City Creek Canyon was caressingly warm as Daniel and Emily made their way toward their favorite secluded place in the woods. Deep green pines, quaking aspens and abundant maple and oak trees were rapidly reawakening from the harsh winter. This canyon, near their log house in Salt Lake City had become their second home. Daniel and Emily searched for the same secluded enclosure where Daniel proposed marriage a year earlier, before they'd been sealed forever as husband and wife in the endowment house. Heavy snowfall from a long winter in the Rockies had melted quickly that spring, filling the rocky creek beds to overflowing. This morning was the first day warm enough to bring their newborn son outside for an outing.

Daniel and Emily both knew from the day their son was born, without saying a word to each other, where they'd take newborn Wiley for his first journey into the world. Daniel silently led the way, pulling back the limbs of trees as they hiked deep into the woods. The pulsating hum of winged insects filled the forested air, ebbing and flowing in intensity as they moved. Trees unfolding with spring's first tender leaves sheltered new nests of returning meadowlarks and robins.

"There it is," Daniel said pointing to a small natural enclosure near the water. Daniel and Emily bowed low, then stepped inside. The overhanging boughs completely encased the new family in a warm womb. Emily gently placed Wiley in his father's waiting arms. Then Daniel and Emily knelt down side by side, ready to offer a prayer. Supporting his son's small neck and back with his broad open palms, Daniel brought his newborn son forward so they could both get a good look at him. Something about holding his infant son made Daniel feel younger and stronger, that his real life was just beginning.

"Hello there," Daniel said softly as his infant son began to stir, opening his tiny eyes to the light. "We're so glad you've come."

Emily smiled at her husband and new son with a depth of love and sense of clarity and wholeness she'd never experienced before. Everything she and Daniel had lived through waiting for this moment now seemed worth the price. All their past years of love and loss combined to create a deeper fullness of joy. The long journey from Missouri to Utah had woven their new lives together in an infinitely more meaningful design.

"It was all worth it," Emily said turning to her husband.

Daniel smiled and nodded. As they knelt together as husband and wife, mother and father, Emily recalled with tenderness the first time she saw Daniel's lonely blue eyes in the woods of Missouri. Daniel remembered with breathless clarity their first swim in the river by moonlight. Spring had grown into summer and autumn faded to winter, year passing into year, dark fading to light and loss to gain.

"*I'm just a poor wayfaring stranger,*" Daniel sang softly to his newborn son in his low bass voice, "*while traveling through . . .*"

"I never heard you sing that before," Emily whispered. "Who taught you?"

"Someone I loved and lost a long time ago," Daniel answered. "I've been remembering her love songs and feeling my mother and father near me all morning."

Unexpectedly the clear piercing song of a meadowlark filled the air. Emily remembered her own mother imitating the bird's melody with her voice, inserting the name of every place they'd lived.

"Salt Lake City is a pretty little town," Emily sang, imitating the meadowlark's song, continuing her mother's legacy.

Daniel smiled. "Sometimes I think this is all a dream. I'll wake up and you'll be gone again," Daniel admitted.

"Me too," Emily answered.

Emily watched as her new husband and tiny son touched noses in the soft rays of sunlight filtering through the overhanging boughs, creating dappled patches of sunshine and shadow. Both Daniel and Emily bowed their heads and closed their eyes.

"Dear God," Daniel whispered, "thank you for our lives, our love and our son."

"Amen," Emily added.

The meadowlark echoed his familiar piercing song once again.

Spring at last, Daniel thought slowly exhaling and relaxing.

"Can you feel it, Emily?" Daniel asked.

"What Daniel? The wind?"

"Heaven," Daniel answered. "It's all around us."

Though he understood moments of darkness and loss would inevitably return, Daniel also knew as he wrapped his broad arm around his wife and child, enclosing his new family, that their circle of life and love would never be permanently broken by time or place again. It came to him that winter's promise was the certainty of spring. Like the seasons passing over his fields—like the rising of the sun after a long lonely night—cold empty blackness was always dispersed unexpectedly and completely, illuminating another radiant, unlived day.

Wayfarin' Stranger

American Folk Hym

I am a poor wayfarin' stranger
While trav'lin' through this world of woe,
But there's no sickness, toil nor danger
In that bright land to which I go.

I'm goin' there to see my father.
I'm goin' there no more to roam;
I'm just a-goin' over Jordan,
I'm just a-goin' over home.

I know dark clouds will gather 'round me,
I know my way is rough and steep;
And yet green pastures lie before me
Where God's redeemed no more shall weep.

I'm goin' there to see my mother.
She said she'd meet me when I come;
I'm just a-goin' over Jordan,
I'm just a-goin' over home.

I'm goin' there to see my Savior.
To sing His praise forever more;
I'm just a-goin' over Jordan,
I'm just a-goin' over home.

The origins of this melody were first chronicled in early American music compilations in the mid-1800s. The song has since become a beloved American folk hymn.

ABOUT THE AUTHOR

Janene Wolsey Baadsgaard was born in Provo, Utah, and graduated from Brigham Young University in Communications. She has taught English and literature courses for Utah Valley State College. She has written about families with warmth and humor for many years and is the author of eleven books and hundreds of newspaper columns, features and magazine articles.

Janene and her husband Ross are the parents of ten children and live on two acres in the countryside between Spanish Fork and Mapleton, Utah. First written when Janene was twenty-three-years-old, *Winter's Promise* was her first book-length work. After reading and being inspired by her great-great-grandfather's memoirs, *Forty Years Among the Indians*, she wrote this novel in tribute to all her Mormon pioneer ancestors for their legacy of courage, faith and love.

Some of her other book titles include: *Is There Life After Birth?*, *A Sense of Wonder*, *Why Does My Mother's Day Potted Plant Always Die?*, *On the Roller Coaster Called Motherhood*, *Families Who Laugh . . . Last*, *Family Finances for the Flabbergasted*, *Grin and Share It . . . Raising a Family with a Sense of Humor*, *Sister Bishop's Christmas Miracle*, *Expecting Joy*, and *The LDS Mother's Almanac*.